LESLEY CREWE

RELATIVE HAPPINESS

Vagrant Press is an imprint of
Nimbus Publishing Limited
PO Box 9166
Halifax, NS   B3K 5M8
(902) 455-4286

Printed and bound in Canada
NB1161
Design: Margaret Issenman, mgdc
Author photo: John Ratchford

Library and Archives Canada Cataloguing in Publication

       Crewe, Lesley, 1955-, author
       Relative happiness / Lesley Crewe.

       First published: Halifax, NS : Vagrant Press, c2005.
       Issued in print and electronic formats.

ISBN 978-1-77108-209-9 (pbk.).— ISBN 978-1-77108-117-7 (mobi).
— ISBN 978-1-55109-835-7 (html)

I. Title.
PS8605.R48R44 2014   C813'.6   C2014-903205-6
                               C2014-903206-4

Canada Council Conseil des arts
for the Arts   du Canada

FILM & CREATIVE INDUSTRIES
NOVA SCOTIA

Nimbus Publishing acknowledges the financial support for its publishing activities from the Government of Canada through the Canada Book Fund (CBF) and the Canada Council for the Arts, and from the Province of Nova Scotia through Film & Creative Industries Nova Scotia. We are pleased to work in partnership with Film & Creative Industries Nova Scotia to develop and promote our creative industries for the benefit of all Nova Scotians.

ANCIENT FOREST
FRIENDLY™

Nimbus Publishing/Vagrant Press is committed to protecting our natural environment. As part of our efforts, this book is printed on 100% recycled content, Ancient-Forest Friendly paper.

For Joshua

In this world of my own making, you will forever live.

Chapter One

"I'VE NEVER LOVED you. Not for a single second, you horrible man."

Lexie threw herself across the room and fumbled with the doorknob in her haste to escape. She couldn't get the door open.

"Let me out. Let me out!" She rattled it again and again but the door wouldn't budge.

Her husband stormed over and grabbed her arm. "You're a liar!" Then he looked away and muttered, "Will you knock it off with the doorknob, already? It's the only one we have."

Lexie rattled some more. "Take your hands off me!" She whispered, "Actually, we have two knobs — because you're here."

He shouted, "You'll always love me!"

"I hate you." Lexie pulled her arm out of his grasp and turned to the front of the stage. "I hate this guy."

"Okay, stop. Stop. Jesus, Lexie. Those aren't the lines."

Lexie jerked her thumb at her fellow thespian. "No, I mean, I really hate this guy."

The husband sneered. "And you're such a prize."

"God, Todd. I have to rattle the doorknob. I'm supposed to be in a frenzy. It's called acting."

"You couldn't act your way out of a paper bag. A very large paper bag."

The director threw his hands on his head. "Lord, why me? Okay, everyone. Take a break."

"Moron," Lexie grumbled as she huffed off the stage. Todd gave her the finger. She hurried down the side steps and stomped up the aisle of the theatre until she saw Susan, who sat in one of the top rows chowing down on a bag of Cheetos.

"Wow, you were really convincing," she said with her mouth full. "I could feel your hate from here."

Lexie plunked into the seat beside her. She reached into Susan's bag and grabbed a handful of orange junk.

"Why do I come here, year after year? I need this like a hole in the head." She stuffed her face and sighed at the same time, which caused her to choke.

Susan passed her a bottle of root beer. Lexie chugged it down and passed the empty bottle back.

"Thanks. Now I have none."

"Quit bitching."

"And ruin the only entertainment I have? Not on your life."

They smiled at each other. Because it was true. Lexie and Susan were two frumpy old maids. If they didn't have each other, they'd be total losers.

Susie licked her fingers. "So. What's on the agenda for this weekend? Shall we colour our grey or lose fifty pounds?"

"I say we shag the first guy we see," Lexie proposed. "And Todd doesn't count. Actually, what am I saying? No one in this stupid theatre qualifies. No one in this whole stupid town does either."

Susan tried to get a drop of root beer to drip on her tongue. It didn't work, so she stuck her tongue in the bottle. Lexie made a face.

"You'll get your tongue stuck if you keep that up."

Susan suddenly froze, the bottle hanging from her mouth. Her eyes bugged out of her head. She whacked Lexie on the shoulder about five times.

"God, Susan. Can you breathe? Are you dying?"

Susan continued to whack and waggle the bottle back and forth. Lexie started to panic. "It's all right, just let me grab it." She took the end of the bottle and yanked for all she was worth. A huge pop caused everyone in the place to swing around and gawk.

"Are you okay?"

"No."

"What's wrong, for heaven's sake?"

"Holy shit, look behind you," Susan hissed out of the side of her mouth. "Am I dreaming?"

Lexie swivelled in her seat and saw a young man standing at the top of the aisle. He wore a pair of old jeans, a sweater that was too big for him with holes in the sleeves, and a long scarf wrapped around his neck about four times. He had on a pair of knitted gloves with the fingertips cut off, and carried an old army knapsack that had seen a lot of action.

It seemed impossible, but it was as if he'd been plucked from the streets of Paris and dropped out of the sky into the middle of this dreary, dirty coal town. Nothing this exciting had happened in years.

He smiled at them and Lexie had a hard time catching her breath. As she drank him in, it registered that he was tall and lean, with a mass of shoulder-length brown hair falling in his eyes. His teeth were a beautiful white and his eyes were very blue. It looked as if he hadn't shaved in a couple of days. He wasn't classically handsome — his face was too angular for that — but Lexie knew she'd never forget him for as long as she lived.

"Anyone looking for an off-Broadway actor?"

Lexie stood, or at least tried to. Susan was directly behind her, holding the hem of Lexie's blouse in a tight grip. "Oh my God…what are you doing?"

Lexie had no idea, but she kept moving until Susan let go. She stretched out her hand and said, "Hi. I'm Lexie."

"Hello Lexie." He took her hand and gave it a warm shake. "What a beautiful name."

If she didn't love him before, she sure as shootin' loved him now.

Lexie Ivy hated her name. Who wouldn't? Just try and get your fingers wrapped around an "x," a "v" and a "y" when you're five and learning the alphabet. Her younger sisters, Beth, Gabby, and Kate, had an easier time of it. Of course they had an easier time of everything, being gorgeous and slim, slim, slim while she was fat, fat, fat. Why she even talked to her sisters was a mystery. The three of them personified perfection. Growing up, Lexie fantasized about locking her sisters in a tower, but even in her own daydreams princes pushed past her. They were the fair maidens, after all.

Unfortunately, not much had changed over the years. Lexie's mother still made it quite clear that at the ripe old age of thirty, her oldest daughter was still a work in progress.

All of this ran through her head as she stared at this man. He said something because his lips moved.

"Excuse me?"

He laughed. "I said, I'm Adrian Davenport."

"That's wonderful."

He laughed again. "Is it?"

Get a grip, Lex. You're acting like an idiot. She finally let go of his hand and was instantly left out in the cold.

"Somehow I can't quite believe you're a Broadway actor. Don't you know you're in the middle of nowhere? You must be lost."

He hesitated for only half a second, but it was long enough for her to know. He *was* lost. His eyes betrayed him.

He threw his hands in the air and shrugged his shoulders. "I knew I should have turned left at the border."

They grinned at each other.

"Well, since you're here, why don't I ask you a few questions. I happen to be the producer of this particular play, and the starring lead." She leaned closer to him. "There are so few of us, we all have to take turns. I'm the stagehand next time round. Or is it director? I forget."

He gave her a little bow. "I'm at your service."

Holy moley, I sure hope so. What should she do now? She had a brainstorm. "Why don't I take you across the street to Tim Horton's and we'll get a coffee. My treat."

"That would be lovely."

This couldn't be happening. She turned around and screamed back to earth. Susan sat there with her mouth agape, as if her jaw was unhinged.

"Oh, gee. Adrian, this is my friend, Susie."

"How do you do?" He reached out and held his hand in the air.

Susie was frozen. And she stayed frozen.

Adrian dropped his arm.

"Susie!"

"Wha…?"

"This is Adrian."

"Yea…"

"We're going for a cup of coffee."

"Wha…?"

"Good grief, woman. I'm taking Adrian for a cup of coffee. Tell Todd the nob I'll be back in half an hour."

She didn't wait for Susie to reply because there was no point. Her eyes were still glazed over.

Lexie ushered Adrian out of the theatre, but not before she saw Susan suddenly spring to life and hightail it down to the stage, her hands flapping. No doubt her gums were flapping too, but Lexie would worry about that later. She picked up her coat at the door. It was a huge woven shawl she had made herself. She felt good in it because it covered a multitude of sins.

Adrian walked beside her and that's when she knew she was in a dream. Stuff like this didn't happen to her. Where, oh where, were her sisters at this particular moment? She was dying for someone to notice her as she walked down the sidewalk with the most gorgeously romantic man she'd ever laid eyes on.

It was too windy to talk, so they smiled at each other and she gestured to the door of the coffee shop. He opened it for her. The warmth inside was a pleasant change from the blustery cold gusts they'd walked against.

The pimply teenager behind the counter looked like she'd swallowed her gum. Lexie preened, as if she were responsible.

"I'll have a large coffee. Black." She needed to shed a few pounds. She looked at Adrian. "What can I get you?"

"You will get me nothing. I insist on paying. I'll have a large double double," he announced proudly. "Can I talk you into one too, Lexie?"

"Oh, go on then."

"Make that two," he smiled at the lovestruck high schooler. He turned to Lexie. "Ever since I arrived in Canada, I've wanted to say that. 'Double double.'"

"Well, if you insist on being a Canadian, you better get us two maple donuts, too."

"Sounds great."

Lexie wandered over to the far corner by the window and found a table. She sat and watched as he charmed everyone behind the counter. She had only one thought in her head. She knew it was ridiculous, even for her, but she wanted to take care of him. She made up her mind he could join the theatre company.

He returned with their coffee and donuts on a tray. He placed her order in front of her. "Thank you," she said. "I knew by your accent you weren't from this country, but I can't quite place it."

"No one can." He shrugged off his knapsack and took his seat. "It's a combination of seventeen different lingoes. Dad's a diplomat. My mother eventually went mad packing our belongings for the twenty-fifth time. Poor Mum."

"Wow. I can tell right off the bat your life story will be

a hundred times more fascinating than mine. Where were you born?"

"South Africa. Johannesburg, to be specific."

"You're kidding!"

"Everyone has to be born somewhere," he smiled, "and from what I've seen of this glorious island, I'd give my eye teeth to have been born here."

"You've been over the Trail, then?"

"Mmm." He held up his fingers and started to count. "I've been to Mabou, Meat Cove, Bay St. Lawrence, Chéticamp, and Ingonish, just to name a few stops."

"Did you drive?"

"Lord no, I don't know how to drive. I biked. North Mountain proved a little challenging."

"You *biked* up North Mountain? Are you insane?"

He took a sip of his coffee. "Actually I biked down. It took me thirty seconds. I attained a speed of two hundred miles an hour, involuntarily of course. I eventually closed my eyes since I figured I was dead anyway."

Lexie laughed and couldn't stop. The image of him hanging on for dear life to a rickety bike was more than she could stand.

Adrian grinned at her.

Lexie took a sip of her coffee before she nodded, "Yes, you are definitely round the twist. It's November, for heaven's sake, which means it's freezing outside, or haven't you noticed? How can you bike in this weather?"

"I must confess, I get where I'm going rather quickly. No dilly-dallying for me."

"I shouldn't wonder. They said on the radio this morning that we may have flurries tonight."

"I'll face that when I come to it."

"Obviously you live by the seat of your pants," she smirked.

Adrian took a bite of his donut before he answered her. "You're quite right. Trouble is, after biking for months on end, I have no seat on any of my pants anymore. It can be a tad embarrassing."

"You'll be run out of town before nightfall."

"It's a risk I'll have to take."

They finished their coffee and Lexie decided it was time to introduce him to the others. She couldn't wait, because she was certain none of them had ever met a character like Adrian, a man who could waltz into a theatre and ask people if they needed his services. Who has that kind of confidence?

Everyone was taken with him. Their dramatic ensemble had hung around with each other for so long, a new personality was like a breath of fresh air. Lexie always played the dowdy girl, Susie was the older mother/crone, and their nemesis, Donalda, the raving lunatic. It wasn't much of a stretch for any of them.

The same two men acted every male role in all their plays and didn't inspire much passion in the bosoms of the paying public. And the fact they were both called Todd made rehearsals a nightmare. But they put up with it — there weren't many coal miners, steelworkers, and fishermen clamouring to be part of the theatre group.

Now in walked the hero-who-saved-the-day type and everyone felt renewed. How lucky was that?

Adrian attracted attention without doing anything. Every one of them stared at him out of the corner of their eye. His magnetism was undeniable. He was born for the theatre, but as animated as he was, Lexie saw something else, something she couldn't put her finger on.

Susan finally thawed and flitted around Adrian all afternoon. But not to be outdone was the dratted Donalda. She was another old maid, but even more pathetic than Lexie or Sue. She reminded Lexie of a small mouse with her furtive, scampering ways. Her buck teeth and sniffy nose didn't help. She'd pop up behind Lexie and scare the life out of her. For someone who was only five feet tall, that was quite an accomplishment.

Susan and Donalda asked Adrian about Broadway. It turned out it was so off-Broadway, there were only five people in the audience. But they were impressed anyway and so was everyone else. None of them had ever been to New York so everyone had a million questions. Adrian indulged his captive audience with plenty of juicy stories and although Lexie wanted to hear every word, she really had to use the washroom, a direct result of too much coffee. The minute she dashed out to the foyer and into the loo, Susan and Donalda zoomed in behind her.

Susan could hardly contain herself. "I can't believe you went for coffee with him! How did you get so brave?"

Donalda sniffed. "What's brave about that? I think it's brave he went with her."

"Oh shut up, Donalda." Susie continued, "So? Lex? Who is this yummy creature?"

Lexie answered from her stall. "He says he's from Johannesburg. Can you believe it?"

"How in the name of God did he find himself in Glace Bay of all places? Who in their right mind would want to come here?"

Lexie flushed, opened the door, and went to the sink to wash her hands. "Look, Sue, I don't know another thing about him. I could hardly interrogate him."

"Well, I don't see why not. How often does a creature like him sashay into town? If you don't want him, I'd sure like a crack at him." She fluffed her thin, stringy hair in the mirror.

Lexie frowned. "Get real. As if he'd look at either one of us." She glanced in the mirror to confirm her suspicions. All she saw was a mop of long, dark curly hair, while her plump body was hidden under a flowing ankle-length skirt and peasant blouse. Wrap a scarf around her head and she'd look like a fortune teller.

Susan stopped fluffing and her shoulders slumped. "You're right. Drat and darn."

Donalda rubbed her hands together. "Truer words were never spoken. The boy is mine."

Lexie and Sue rolled their eyes and chanted their mantra. "Shut up, Donalda."

Eventually it was time to go, and everyone started to drift away. Adrian lingered behind and fiddled with his knapsack. Lexie walked over to him. She hauled her huge cloth purse over her shoulder. "Where are you staying?"

"I'm not certain. There must be a bed and breakfast some-where. I may be here a while. Biking in the snow doesn't sound too appealing." He smiled at her. "Don't worry. I'll find a phone book."

She looked at his slender frame and wanted to feed him. She considered they'd only just met, and you never invite a stranger home, but there was something about Adrian. She knew him. She'd known him forever.

"Why don't you come home with me for a good hot meal? You can look through my phone book. I'm sure we'll get you settled somewhere before the night is over."

He seemed surprised. That's when Donalda pounced on him. She batted her eyelashes. "Adrian, if you're not doing anything, I make a mean corn beef hash."

"Thank you. That's a lovely offer, but Lexie's already invited me."

"Oh, right." Donalda gave her a withering look and stalked off.

"I've done it now. She'll forget her lines at our next rehearsal just to bug me."

He looked worried. "Sorry, I didn't mean to start a mutiny."

"Listen, she wouldn't be happy unless she griped about something at least once a day."

They walked out of the building and into the parking lot. Lexie pointed to her old rusty Volkswagen bus, Betsy. He pointed to his old rusty bike. It had no name. They loaded the bike into the back. After moving a pile of books from the passenger seat Lexie slid behind the wheel.

"Do you read?"

He nodded. "I like non-fiction. Mostly history and

travelogues. I've lived everywhere, so reading about the places I've been is enjoyable. I can picture them in my head."

"Well, since I've been exactly nowhere, my brain has turned to mush. Which is why I confess to reading romance novels in my spare time. Gosh, I can't believe I said that out loud."

"I won't squeal."

"Good."

"Now tell me about this place."

"I will, as soon as I can get this rattle trap of a bus going."

They lurched out of the theatre parking lot and drove down Commercial Street.

"These old storefronts are pretty run down, as you can see, but plans are in the works to spruce the place up, because this is the main drag in town, the place where kids drive up and down and eyeball each other. It's sort of an ancient ritual here. And that cement fence in front of the church on your right is where teenagers hang out on warm summer nights."

Adrian smiled. "Like small towns everywhere."

"Glace Bay was once a prosperous and thriving community, but it's suffered since they closed the mines. Hence the rather shabby appearance. People don't have a lot of money here, but what they don't have in money, they make up for in spirit."

She drove past the wharf and pointed out where the lobster boats were beached for the winter, then drove to the end of South Street to see the water. On this day, the ocean was the colour of steel and looked angry as it pounded the shoreline. The wind whipped up whitecaps. Adrian wanted to get out of the car and have a closer look.

"It's not a great day to be near the shore," she said as he opened the door. It ripped out of his hand, and he struggled trying to shut it again.

"I told you," Lexie laughed. "It's always amazed me that the senior citizen's home was built here because anyone frail would blow right out to sea."

"You're absolutely right."

She looked in the rear-view mirror. "I guess that leaves me out."

Lexie gave him a sideways glance and continued on her way, driving past the school where her mother had once taught, and pointed out her father's medical practice. She drove past the house where she grew up as a child, even though it was out of her way. She'd always been proud of her family home.

It was a gorgeous old place, back off the road in a grove of birch and maple trees. It had a wraparound porch and Lexie called Adrian's attention to the ivy vines that crawled up the side near the chimney. Ivy for the Ivy house, she laughed. It was painted white, and black shutters framed all the gabled windows. It looked like a house in a picture book, he told her.

She nodded happily. "My own house comes straight out of a fairy tale book too. The old woman who lived in a shoe."

"I can't wait."

She drove up a potholed street, grinding the gears to slow down in front of a dear little cottage. It was old and worn in, its shingles a bleached grey from years of wind and saltwater that blew off the nearby cliff. She was surrounded on three sides by water.

"Another windy spot, I see."

She cut the engine. "You're darn tootin.'"

The house was encircled by rose bushes, which looked pretty scraggly without their rosy finery. A small crooked white fence surrounded the place. A wicker rocking chair sat on the front porch. It was quaint and cosy and yes, as if to complement the fence, sort of crooked.

"Home sweet home."

They got out of the van and trooped up the front steps. Lexie rooted through her purse for the keys.

"I really must get a smaller bag."

"Or a bigger key."

She finally found it and opened the door. She went in ahead of him and tossed her head to the left. "You can put your things on this chair."

"On this chair? The one with a mile-high stack of books?"

She looked down. "Oh dear. Just throw everything on the floor and I'll clear it off in a minute. In the meantime, make yourself at home."

As she hurried into the kitchen, she heard him say, "This is the most fabulous house. It's so full of stuff."

Lexie grinned and hollered over her shoulder. "You mean it's a pigsty."

"No. That's not what I mean at all. It's just so snug. Although how you haven't managed to burn it down is beyond me."

"If you're referring to my candle collection, it's an art."

The living room looked like a student's dorm, filled as it was with flags and posters. An easel held a large colourful canvas, while paintbrushes sat in murky jars of water on the table beside it. There were coffee cups and wine glasses and empty wine bottles with even more candles stuffed inside them, beautiful hooked rugs and walls of books. Books were piled up here and there, and magazines were strewn on the floor. A quilting frame in the corner by the window held a quilt half done.

The focal point in the room was the fireplace, its mantel crammed with candles, pictures and beach wood, seashells and sand dollars. Pillows were strewn in front of it, just waiting for someone to get comfortable.

Lexie opened the fridge to see what she could rustle up for supper and that's when she heard him yell, "Oh my God!"

She ran down the hall and poked her head in the living room. "What is it?"

He pointed to a chair in the darkest corner. "I was about to ask you the same thing."

"Hey, don't insult Sophie. She's my only child." She hurried over to reassure her thirty-pound baby.

"Is it a dog?"

"You, sir, will be thrown out on your ear if you keep insulting my cat."

"A *cat*? Are you sure of that? I've seen smaller ponies."

She carried the enormous angora fur-bag into the kitchen, murmuring as she went. "Mama's going to give her precious her supper. Yes she is."

Adrian followed her. "I don't think that creature needs to be fed until this time next year."

Lexie pouted. "Who asked you?"

During their first supper together, Lexie realized two

things: Adrian was starved for food and starved for company. She doled out leftover beef stew with dumplings and served it with cornbread. His eyes lit up.

Then she passed him apple strudel and old cheese for dessert. He polished his plate. Unsure if he was still hungry, she produced a tin of homemade chocolate chip cookies, just to be on the safe side. He wolfed half of them down with his tea.

He certainly talked. He talked endlessly about everything and while he was very entertaining, it wasn't until an hour into their meal that she realized he'd said nothing about himself.

"So," she finally asked, "how did you happen to wander into the Savoy Theatre?"

"I'd heard of it in my travels around the island. I wanted to see it for myself. And now that I have I can tell you everyone was right. It's a beautiful venue. A credit to your town."

"But why come to Cape Breton in the first place?"

"A friend once mentioned you had a beautiful coastline and I wanted to see it." He looked down at his plate. "I don't think I want to leave here."

She watched his face. "Well, someone would miss you if you stayed, surely?"

He didn't answer right away. "My life is my own. I come and go. I always have."

She risked being nosy. "Where is home for you now?"

"My parents are in New York City at the moment. I was with them for a while when I came back from Tanzania. But I couldn't breathe there. It's too big, too busy."

Lexie was aware that his speech slowed down with every question, as if the answers were heavy.

"What was your job, in Tanzania, if you don't mind me asking?"

"I took languages in university, since I had a smattering of everything growing up. I was a translator."

"Very cool. Who did you translate for?"

"UNESCO, humanitarian groups, places like that."

"Wow. That must be rewarding work. Why did they need you?"

He looked away. "Refugees."

He said no more.

She knew when to stop. She poured more tea into their cups and began to fill the silence.

"I haven't done a thing. I've led a very shallow and uncharitable life, compared to yours."

"I'm sure that's not true."

Lexie stirred milk into her mug. "As it happens, it is. I grew up here with three sisters. I'm the biggest. Oldest, I mean, and the most boring. Beth is hard to describe. A law unto herself. She's married with kids. Gabby's a flight attendant. Her claim to fame is her stunning beauty…more's the pity…and baby Kate has the brains in the family. She's a professor in Halifax."

Looking at the ceiling, she tried to think of something else to tell him. "I went to university to get a library science degree because I love books."

She leaned towards him. "Remember when you were a kid and you went to the library and they had that pencil with the little rubber stamp clipped to the top, to press into an ink pad?"

He nodded.

"All I ever wanted to do was to use that pencil."

He gave her a grin.

She laughed. "But guess what? Now you swipe a card on the computer. We hardly use it at all."

"What a horrible shame."

She could tell he was trying to keep a straight face. "Hey you. Stop it. I came home after I graduated and moved in here." She gestured around the kitchen with her free hand. "I work at — you guessed it — the library. Not a great place to meet guys, unless you happen to like ten-year-olds. I go to drama a few nights a week and do arts and crafts to keep from going insane during long winter evenings. There. Does that sound pathetic enough for you? Are you asleep yet?"

He crossed his arms and leaned on the tabletop. "Of course not. You've managed something I haven't. You have a home and a steady job and you take care of yourself." He looked toward the dark window above the sink. "I roam. Endlessly, according to my father. I'm not sure what I want, or where I should go."

"I imagine working with refugees is exhausting. How long were you there?"

He looked back and sighed, "Two years."

"Oh, Adrian. You're just burnt out. That's understandable."

He slumped in his chair. He looked done in. She suddenly noticed the dark shadows under his eyes, and the almost gaunt hollows below his cheekbones.

"Why don't you stay here?" It came right out of the blue. She didn't even know she was going to say it.

He shook his head and gave her a small smile. "Oh, no thanks, Lexie. You've been so kind already. I don't want to wear out my welcome."

"Look, I have an extra bedroom upstairs. It's not much to look at, but it's clean, or will be, once I drag a couple of garbage bags of art supplies out of there. And quite frankly I could use the rent. I'm always gasping for money. Stay for a week, stay for a month, however long it takes to sort yourself out. At least until the snow melts."

She looked into his beautiful sad eyes, and thought she saw tears well up for a moment.

Then he said quietly, "You're brilliant. Thank you."

Chapter Two

THEY CERTAINLY MADE an odd couple — Lexie as round as an apple, Adrian a long drink of water. No one knew what to make of it. Lexie's mother was flabbergasted. Lexie stopped in to see if she had a couple of extra pillows she could borrow for Adrian. Her mother, in a pair of linen slacks and a cashmere top, was housecleaning. The only concession she made to domesticity was a silk scarf wrapped around her newly done hair.

She threw her sponge mop into a bucket of hot, soapy water. "You invited a man to live with you four hours after you met? How positively horrifying."

Lexie rolled her eyes.

"Is he single?"

"Obviously."

"Please tell me he's not over forty, because if he is, he's a mama's boy and you'll have a hard time getting rid of him. Unmarried men are very needy at that age."

"Where do you come up with this stuff?"

"It's a proven fact."

Lexie sighed. "Well, he's twenty-six if you must know."

Her mother peeled off her rubber gloves. "Oh. Well, don't get your hopes up dearest. He's much too young for you. I don't understand why you don't join a dating service. They screen potential nutcases and God knows what else. It's safer."

Lexie kept her mouth shut and waited because she knew the lecture wasn't over.

Her mom picked up a mister and started to spray her plants. "Lord knows, I want you to get married, but not to the first vagabond who roams into town." She shook her head and pumped away. Lexie followed her around because she wouldn't stay still.

"I didn't say I'd marry him. He's a boarder."

"I want you to get one of those emergency button do-hickeys. You know the type. You press the thing if he gets fresh." She sprayed mist in Lexie's face.

"First of all, Mother, no one gets fresh these days, and secondly, no one would want to if I wore a huge alarm buzzer around my neck."

She took the pillows and left. Lexie knew her mom would tell her dad the minute he got home. He wouldn't say anything because he trusted her. Her mother forgot she wasn't a teenager anymore. But her sisters weren't enthusiastic either.

"Oh my God, Lex," Kate worried over the phone from Halifax. "Do you know what you're doing? You don't know him very well. Is it possible to do a background check on him?"

"What is it with you university professors?" Lexie laughed. "Everything's an essay."

Kate and Lexie talked every week. She didn't mind Kate's comments. Her youngest sister was a worrywart, but she was kind about it.

Beth, on the other hand, had her own take on things.

"Are you fucking nuts?"

Lexie bumped into her in the small appliance aisle at Wal-Mart the day after she'd told Mom.

The Ivy family had a system for familial dirt and gossip. Lexie called it the "underground thumping." Someone heard something juicy and, like a throbbing beat, other members of the tribe picked up the signal and weighed in with their two cents.

Beth had a tendency to curse when she was at the end of her rope or when she got excited. So did Lexie, but never in front of children. She felt morally superior about this position.

She covered her niece's ears with her gloved hands. This delighted Maddie. "I wish you wouldn't talk like that in front of Madison."

Beth blew air up into her bangs. "Oh for the love of Pete, she's only nine months old."

"Do you really want her first word to be f-u-c-k?"

"Lexie, have your own baby and then tell me what to do. Until then, keep it zipped."

That hurt. Lexie had always wanted children. Beth had four girls, all a year apart. That's why she was a grouch so much of the time — exhaustion. The fact that Beth had four daughters was a source of great delight to their parents. Imagine having four girls and one of your four girls having four girls. Ha Ha. Worse, her blonde perky sister looked about eighteen years old, with a teensy body to match. And her stomach was still as flat as a board.

Lexie stuck up for herself. "Unlike you, I live by myself and I get lonely if you must know. He's a great guy and I like him. Not to mention, it'll help financially since I make peanuts. We're not all married to a big shot accountant."

Beth had the good grace to look chastened.

"Sorry. You're a big girl. You can take care of yourself."

There it was again. That word. Big.

Did she do it on purpose?

Lexie felt like a rebel for keeping Adrian as a house guest. After only days, they were like an old married couple, settled into a comfortable routine. She'd go to work and he'd have supper on when she got home. They shared the household duties; in fact, the house never looked better.

The first time she took him back to the theatre, everyone was glad to see him, especially Donalda.

"Did you find a place to kip, Adrian?" Donalda always tried to impress people with her *Coronation Street* dialect.

"Yes, I'm staying with Lexie."

Oh, the look she gave. Lexie loved it — nothing made her day more than irritating Donalda. And Donalda was determined to get her back, she could tell. Sometimes Lexie wanted to shake her, because she was talented and fun when she wanted to be, but she sabotaged everyone who came near her. It wore Lexie out.

Donalda had obviously decided to make Lexie's day as miserable as possible. As they sat in a circle and discussed the third act, Donalda spoke up.

"I think we should change the ending."

Lexie hit her knee with a rolled up script. "What are you talking about? How can we change the ending if the ending has to end the way it ends? It's called *Murder by Mother*. It ends with a murder. By a mother."

"How come I always play the one who gets killed?"

Lexie shrugged.

"Come to think of it, every time I get killed in a play, you happen to be the murderer. You've choked me, dropped me down a well, electrocuted me in a bathtub, and beaten me with a rolling pin."

"Coincidence, I'm sure." Lexie glanced at Susan, who refused to look back.

"Well, next time we do a play, I better have the lead role."

"Fine. But just to warn you, we're doing *Frankenstein*."

Lexie thought that would be the end of it, but it wasn't. Both Todds couldn't make rehearsal so Donalda asked Adrian if he'd read through the scene with her. It was the love scene, Lexie realized too late.

Adrian said he didn't mind. They walked on stage and went through their lines. Donalda was so melodramatic Adrian looked a little worried. He read his part with growing apprehension. Donalda continued her advance across the stage and suddenly threw herself on him. She grabbed his neck, pulled him down, and kissed him with as much passion as she could muster.

She hung off him. His arms were out to the sides in an attempt to balance them both so they wouldn't crash to the floor. She stayed attached to his lips. When she finally came up for air, Adrian managed to get some leverage and shake her off.

"Was it good for you?" she asked.

"I've never experienced anything like it."

Donalda threw Lexie a look. Adrian threw her one too. His said "get me out of here."

❧

THE SUN WAS barely up and Lexie was still in her pyjamas when she hung up the phone and fell into her old, beat-up chair by the fire. It was her personal life preserver, a comfortable nest on days like this.

Adrian thumped down the stairs and smiled at her as he walked past the open doors of the living room. She heard the fridge open.

"Adrian?"

"Mmm?"

"Remind me to kill myself on Thursday."

She heard the fridge door close. A moment later he returned with a glass of milk.

"Have some consideration, Lexie. I just got here. You wouldn't leave me already, would you?"

"It's all about you, isn't it?" Lexie gave him a smirk. "You haven't been here long enough to know what a soap opera my life is. That was my mother. When you meet her, it will become abundantly clear why I must jump off the nearest cliff ASAP."

"I haven't met anyone. Am I a secret?"

"I'm doing you a favour. You'll meet them all in good time. And when you do, don't come crying to me about it."

He sat on the floor pillow by the fireplace, next to Sophie, patting her thick coat. "What did your mom want?"

She sank deeper into her chair. "It's half price to join Weight Watchers this week. She calls me at 7:00 A.M. to tell me this." She glanced at him. "Is your mother a lunatic?"

He shook his head. "No. Sorry."

She twisted her hair around her finger. "Wonderful. You

could lie to me. I wouldn't know the difference."

Adrian put his glass on the nearest book. "I'd like to meet your mother."

"They do know you're here. I did tell them about you."

"What did they say?"

The phone rang and saved her from answering.

"Get that and say I'm not here. Please."

"You shouldn't be afraid of your mother. She's your mother." Adrian reached for the phone. "She can't drag you to this weight-loss thing if you don't want to go."

"That's for sure, I'd give her a hernia."

"Hello? Yes, this is Adrian. Well, thank you. I hope we do too. No, I'm sorry, Lexie isn't in. She just ran out to get more cat food for Sophie. You're right, she is gigantic."

Lexie threw a pillow at him.

"I'll be sure to tell her you called. Yes. That would be great. Thanks. Goodbye."

Adrian hung up the phone. "That was your mom, obviously, and she sounded awfully nice — and perfectly ordinary."

Lexie pouted. "She is nice. When she's not being a pain in the…"

A pillow hit her.

❧

EVERY MORNING WHEN Lexie went to work, Adrian told her what he had planned for the day. He still wanted to sightsee, thought he might volunteer at the food bank. He'd pick up her groceries and do any odd jobs that needed doing. If it snowed, he'd shovel the driveway, or he'd chop wood for the fire.

At first the odd jobs were done promptly, but after a while he forgot. She didn't like to mention it because it wasn't important. It was just curious.

Then she noticed something. She started to look for it and sure enough it was true. Adrian was always on the beach, which was madness at this time of year. He wandered close to the shore, a lonely spectacle.

She started to knit Adrian a sweater. The wind had to chill his bones on his solitary sojourns, and she wanted him to be warm.

One night, as she sat in her chair knitting, Adrian lay in front of the fire with a book. She glanced at him and realized he was just staring into the fire.

He suddenly looked around. "Lex?"

"Yeah?"

"What's it like to grow up in the same place your whole life?"

She counted the stitches on her needle before she answered him. "Boring."

"No really, I want to know."

She put down her wool. "It was fun. I played with my sisters and cousins. I have lots of them."

"What did you do?"

She looked into the fire and smiled. "God. What didn't we do? Went to the cottage in the summer and lived in our bathing suits. Built forts, played baseball, got into fights."

"Fights?"

She laughed, "Mostly with my cousin Jimmy. Now there was a brat. He and my sister Beth were constantly at each others' throats. We'd play cards on rainy days and Beth would accuse him of cheating and he'd say prove it and she'd jump across the table every time, scattering cards and glasses of pop. She'd grab him and the two of them would fall backwards out of the chair. I can see her yet, fifty pounds soaking wet and pigtails flying. But she was always right. No, you never told Beth to prove something. Because she would."

Adrian grinned and looked back into the fire. So did Lexie. Memories swirled around as she gazed into the flames. Whenever she thought of her childhood, she always remembered the night she was let in on the family secret and was shown the moon through the coat sleeve.

The summer she turned twelve, she was considered old enough to know. The night it happened, she was beside herself. She wasn't sure why this was so exciting. She wasn't old enough to guess.

The adults escorted Lexie into the backyard. Her older cousins were allowed to come too. The younger ones were warned to stay indoors and away from windows.

Her father told her to lie down on the grass. As she did, she shivered, even in the warm evening air. The grass felt damp and unfamiliar. He put a coat sleeve over her face and told her to look up and see if she could see the moon.

Nothing happened at first. She thought she could see a star, but it might have been her imagination. It was dark and hot. She was suffocating. She strained to see something.

That's when it hit her. It was a big shock.

Her father poured a small glass of water down the sleeve.

She didn't know what it was at first. She grabbed the coat and threw it away. She coughed and spit. She was mad.

"What did you do that for?"

Everyone laughed and patted her on the back. Oh, no. The big secret donned on her. That's all it was. She couldn't believe she'd been hoodwinked her whole life. Once she got over the humiliation, the fun started. Her sisters begged to know the secret, but she wouldn't tell. Oh, the power it gave her.

When she sat on the porch swing that night and looked at the moon, her father came out and sat beside her. He told her she was a good sport and that he'd let her in on a little secret: When it happened to her cousin Jimmy, he cried like a baby and sulked in the garage for twenty minutes. She snuggled up against her dad. He always knew just what to say.

She was about to tell Adrian about it, when he said, "I wish I had one home I could point to and say, that's where I grew up."

He seemed sad.

"Listen, Adrian. Living in the same town all your life has its advantages. People know who you are, but it's not always so wonderful."

"What do you mean?"

"If you have a secret, it's hard to keep. If you're labelled a kook, a kook you'll remain until your dying day. You can't reinvent yourself. You'll always be the girl who wasn't popular in high school."

She looked away. She hadn't meant to say so much.

"Were you that girl?"

She shrugged. "I had three beautiful sisters in the same school."

"You think you're not beautiful?"

Her mouth went dry. "Well, hardly."

"What's your idea of beauty then?"

"Can we please stop this stupid conversation?"

"No. I want to know. What is beautiful to you?"

She rolled her eyes. "I don't know. Being thinner?"

"Beauty is warmth, Lexie." He watched her as he spoke. "It's comfort and peace. It's safety and caring. It's everything you are."

She felt tears behind her eyes. She didn't want him to see. She couldn't go there so she picked up her knitting. "Well, thank you kind sir." She turned the tables on him. "What's it like to grow up everywhere?"

He didn't answer her at first. She could tell he was annoyed. "Have you ever noticed when I try to compliment you, you either shut up or shut down?"

"Which is it? You can't have it both ways."

He sighed and put his arms behind his head. "You're impossible."

"Answer the question."

"It was difficult," he admitted. "I hated being the new kid. To say goodbye to my friends and start over. My brother thrived on new adventures, and my little sister spent so much of her life in ballet school, she wasn't affected." He stroked Sophie's fur. "The only reason I didn't go crazy was my mother. She was always there for me. She's beautiful."

"Adrian, if you want to call her, please do."

"Thanks, that's okay. I write to her. Don't worry, I do call her occasionally, mostly to find out where they'll be next."

Lexie continued to knit. "I can't imagine my mother not phoning me."

"She loves you."

"Of course she loves me, I just wish she wouldn't suffocate me. That's another thing about life in a small town. Your relatives are always in your face." She knit another row. "She wants me to get married. What is it with mothers? Does yours bug you about that?"

"Not really. She thinks I'll always wander, but that's not true. I haven't found home yet, that's all. This island is as close as I've come."

What did he mean? She didn't look at him. It was too hard. She kept knitting, then the phone rang and for once she was glad of the distraction.

ADRIAN BROUGHT HOME an answering machine. Why hadn't she thought of that?

"Hi there. Sophie refuses to answer the phone and I can't right now, so you're out of luck. *Beep.*"

"Lexie darling, it's your mother. Call me back please, and for heaven's sake change that message."

Again.

"Lexie, it's Mom. Are you there? Call me as soon as you get in."

Again.

"Lexie, pick up this phone. I know you're there."

Again.

"Lexie, I have cancer."

LEXIE CALLED HER back.

"Hi Mom."

"Dearest, why do I have to resort to some awful disease to get you to call me?

"Sorry."

"I'll forgive you."

"I knew you would."

"I'm having a little dinner party."

Her mother threw wonderful parties. "Didn't you just have one?" Lexie filled in the word for eagle's nest in her crossword puzzle but the pencil made a hole through the newspaper, so she biffed it. She picked up a book of poetry by Leonard Cohen instead.

"This is just family. Gabby called me the other day, and from what I can gather, Richard's about to pop the question. I think a celebration's in order."

She thumbed through her book. "Gabby's had questions popped at her a hundred times. She must be pooped from all that popping."

"You should be happy for her."

"I am, Mother. I'm delighted. It's the poor buggers who do the asking I feel sorry for. She'll throw this one away too."

"You have a cynical streak, darling, did you know that?"

"Along with my jealous streak, wild streak, and funny streak."

"Lexie. Knock it off. By the way, feel free to bring along your roommate. That weird friend of yours or whatever he is. Is he something more?"

"No, mother, he's just my weird friend. Would you like me to make something?"

She waited for it.

"Be a dear and bring something low cal for dessert. None of us needs the extra calories."

"ADRIAN, I FORGOT to tell you. Mom's having a dinner party at some point and you've been invited. Apparently we have to have a boo at Gabby's new man."

Adrian had a dust cloth in his hand. It was his day to do the chores. "Are we happy about this?"

"Well, I have to introduce you to my family at some point. Mom's dying to meet you. She told me to bring my weird friend, so that would be you."

"Your mother has a way with words."

"She was an English teacher."

He gave her a big grin. "Oh God. I ain't goin' then. I got no manners."

He always made her feel better. She loved him. She thought he loved her, in a big sister sort of way.

She hated her life, so she took it out on Donalda, who happened to call with some inane question, just to snoop of course.

"Should I wear blue or red for the last scene?"

"What possible difference does it make? You're rolled up in a rug. You're dead."

"Lexie, you of all people know an actor has to stay in character. But you've been so busy with your precious Adrian you don't pay attention to us anymore."

"He's not 'my' Adrian and I resent that. I do pay attention to you guys."

"You lord it over everyone because Adrian stays with you. You pretend it's something more but everyone knows it's a financial arrangement."

"You know what, Donalda? You'll never know. And I won't tell you because it's none of your bloody business. Come to think of it, you better wear blue. When I stab you in the last scene, I want to see lots of blood."

Lexie hung up.

Susan would call to ask about him, hoping he'd answer the phone.

"Gee, Lex. It seems pretty strange that the only thing he does is walk along the shore. What do you think he's doing?"

Lexie grumped, "Who knows? Beth said the same thing."

Well, she didn't say *exactly* the same thing.

Lexie sat on the toilet seat and bit her nails as Beth scrubbed the tub and delivered her thoughts on the subject.

"For the love of God, Lexie, why doesn't he get off his ass and get a job? He's a freeloader. He'll suck you dry if you're not careful. Don't you read Anne Landers? Columns are full of stupid women who wonder if some guy's taken advantage of them and the answer is always 'duh.'"

"You don't know him. He's very sweet."

"They're always sweet." Beth's rear end moved to the

rhythm of her scrubbing. She finally sat back on her haunches, and wiped the hair out of her face.

"Lexie, listen to me. A stranger walked into your life — what, six weeks ago? He lives in your house with no job, no family, and no friends. You know nothing about him. He doesn't tell you anything. You're not a dumb broad, Lexie, so don't act like one." She turned back to the tub.

"I think he needs help. I think he's in some kind of trouble."

"Wonderful. He's lazy and crazy."

"Beth, don't be mean. I'm serious. I asked him the other day what his favourite memory was and he said the best memories are the ones you can't remember. Isn't that scary?"

Beth threw her sponge. "Yes, that is scary, you blithering idiot. And I'll tell you why. That means he's running from something. And for all you know, it might be the law. And if that's the case then you'll be an accessory after the fact, for keeping him hidden."

"Oh, don't be so dramatic."

Her sister got to her feet. "Fine. When I find you dead in your bed one night, don't say I didn't warn you."

Beth's words stuck in Lexie's craw. She knew Beth was right, but it ticked her off anyway, and her need to defend Adrian was troubling. There was nothing for it. She was going to ask Adrian point blank if he was in trouble.

She didn't have to wait long for an opportunity to do so.

The next day was a Saturday. Lexie was curled up in her chair with a huge mug of coffee, reading a new P. D. James novel, when she heard Adrian come down the stairs.

"I'm off for a walk, Lexie. I'll be back later."

Now the last thing she wanted to do was to haul her bum out of her comfy spot, but this was a chance to tag along.

She threw her book aside and hurried into the hall. "Do you mind if I join you?"

"Not at all. I'll wait."

She dressed quickly and joined him outside. She realized it wasn't the best day to accompany him. The wind, which blew from the northeast and was biting cold, whipped her hair and made her eyes water.

They walked in silence to Dominion Beach. When they reached the sand, Lexie stopped and looked around while Adrian continued down to the shoreline. She saw him pick up a flat rock and fling it sideways into the waves. It skipped twice before it disappeared. He didn't throw any more.

She took a deep breath of clean, fishy air. She could taste the salt on her tongue. The beach was covered with reddish-brown seaweed, thanks to the churning ocean. It was mucky to walk through and her boots sank into the sand as she squelched her way over to Adrian. She stood beside him as he looked out over the water.

"For some reason the ocean always looks more menacing in the winter, more powerful," she mused. "Like it's going to jump right out of the depths and swallow you whole."

He nodded.

"I'm afraid of tidal waves. Which is kind of strange, since I love living beside the ocean. Sort of Freudian."

He nodded again.

She was getting nowhere fast. She cleared her throat.

"Do you like the ocean? You seem to spend a lot of time here."

"I do."

She pointed out over the water. "It's hard to imagine England is on the other side of this great divide."

"I'd visit relatives in Cape Town and walk on the beaches there. It feels funny to be here, on the other side of the Atlantic."

"Imagine that. Maybe you looked over the ocean towards us, and I looked over the water towards you. Maybe the breeze that crossed your beach was the same one I felt at sunrise." She smiled. "How wonderful to imagine it. We think the world is big, but it's not. Not really."

Adrian looked at the sand. "The world isn't big enough. It's difficult to hide in."

"What do you mean?"

"I mean no matter how big the physical world is, your life is still lived inside your head. You take it everywhere. You can never get away."

"What do you want to get away from, Adrian?"

He turned away and said something, but she couldn't hear him.

"Sorry?"

He faced her and shook his head. "Don't listen to me."

He walked away then and she wondered if she should follow. She got the feeling she was interfering somehow, but she started after him. Struggling to catch up, she shouted behind his back. "What's it like? Africa, I mean."

Adrian stopped and looked at the sky. Wispy clouds rushed past them as they headed out beyond the coast.

"The light's different. The sky goes on forever."

"Do you miss it?"

He turned around and grabbed her arm. "Let's go home."

LEXIE CARRIED A laundry basket down the back steps and into the yard behind the house. She crunched through the snow to get to the clothesline. As she picked up her clean sheets she realized she'd forgotten her gloves. Darn. She couldn't be bothered going back for them so she shook her sheets out and hung them up anyway.

Beth always told her she was nuts for hanging out sheets in the middle of winter, but she liked the crisp air to blow through them. The clean smell was wonderful and Lexie considered it a luxury that was free for the taking. It seemed such a shame to ignore nature's small gift.

Before too long, her fingertips were red with cold. She cupped her hands together and blew before she put them under her armpits and jumped around. That's when she noticed Adrian, framed in the kitchen window like a painting. She gave him a wave.

He couldn't have seen her. In spite of the cold, she bent down and made a snowball, intending to throw it at the pane of glass, but when her eyes travelled back to him, the snowball fell from her fingers.

His face was ravished.

She knew in her heart that this was the real Adrian.

THE VERY NEXT day after work, Lexie shouted up the stairs. "Ade, do you have anything you want washed?"

"Yeah, just a minute." He appeared at the top of the stairs with an armful of stuff.

"Here, catch." A whole cascade of dark clothes landed on her head.

"You big jerk. Just for that, you can wash and dry the dishes tonight."

"Oh, no!" He clutched his heart with his fist and staggered back to his room.

She started to sort the wash, going through the pockets of his jeans. There was a small piece of paper, folded in quarters. It was soft, old, worn around the edges. She was about to put it on the counter when she was interrupted.

"WAIT!" Adrian commanded from upstairs. It startled her. She heard him rush down the stairs before he burst into the kitchen. "I left something in my —" He saw her holding it in her hand.

"I didn't open it."

He reached over and took it from her. "That's okay. Thanks."

He kind of backed out of the room.

LEXIE MET SUSAN at the coffee shop on her lunch hour two days later. The minute Susie sat down, Lexie told her what had happened.

"You're kidding?" Susie's mouth was full of ham and Swiss cheese. It was right up her alley, an intrigue she could sink her teeth into. She swallowed and wiped her mouth on her napkin. "Maybe he's an international spy or something?"

"Oh, good God, what in heaven's name would he be doing in Glace Bay if he's an international spy?"

Susie took a gulp of her coffee. "I don't know. Isn't one place as good as another for spying? Is there a directory somewhere that says this city is good for spying and this city isn't?"

"Now you are being stupid. Istanbul and Marrakech and Casablanca are places for spying. They're exotic. No one rushes around and says 'Bond, I need you to go to Glace Bay.'"

Susan made a face and took another huge bite. "You don't know that. Maybe we're the hub of foreign intrigue for the fine people of Marrakech. Are you going to eat that donut?"

That night Lexie got a call from her sister Gabby. It was a relief. First, because it wasn't her mother, and second, because Adrian wasn't home. She knew it was Gabby because she heard her inhale her cigarette first. That girl could inhale a smoke right down to her toes. An ex-boyfriend told Lexie that wasn't all she could do really well.

"Hey Gab."

"Hey yourself. Did Mom get in touch with you?

"Are you kidding? The day Mom doesn't call me is the day I know she's dead."

"Poor Lex," she cooed. "Let me guess. Another diet she wants to shove down your throat or the continuous whine about your single status?"

"Gabby, as you know full well, there are no other topics in the world except my biological clock, Beth's beautiful children, your pending nuptials to an investment banker, and Kate's doctorate." She ran out of breath.

"Tell her to take a hike, that's what I'd do."

"You get away with stuff like that. She's afraid of you."

"Pooh."

"It's true. You look fabulous. You dress like a model. Guys drip all over you. I know for a fact she's jealous. Isn't everyone?"

She inhaled again. "You think so?"

"I know so."

"How do you know?" There was something in Gabby's voice that told her this notion had never occurred to her sister. But Lexie knew. She also knew her mother would never look at her with green eyes. Ever.

"Trust me darling. You have power over her. Something I'll never possess, unless I make a voodoo doll in art class."

"Oh Lex, I love you. I wish I was like you."

"You want to weigh 165 pounds, have frizzy hair and a dead-end job in the same town where you grew up?"

"You know, I could smack you. Why do you put yourself down like that? Is that all you think you are?"

"Well, what else is there?"

"For one thing, people like being around you. You're funny and smart and loyal."

"So what."

"You are an ass, do you know that? I'm trying to tell you being beautiful isn't everything."

Lexie laughed. Was she serious? "Only someone beautiful can say something so stupid."

Gabby hung up on her.

Damn. Now she felt bad.

IT WAS ONE of their typical nights in. Adrian was by the fire. Lexie took a bath earlier in the evening and her hair was in a knot on the top of her head, an old frayed bathrobe wrapped around her. She stood at the sink and washed the dishes. She hollered over her shoulder. "What kind of dessert should I make for the dinner party?"

Adrian entered the kitchen, grabbed a dishtowel and stood beside her to dry the dishes.

"How about triple-fudge chocolate cheesecake?"

Lexie huffed. "Do you want me thrown out on my considerable ass?"

"I refuse to answer that ridiculous question. Now tell me, is there a dress code for this family affair? I don't have anything to wear. I couldn't fit my tux in the carry-all."

"Wear that blue shirt of yours, and those dark pants. I'll iron them. You look great no matter what you wear so I wouldn't worry about it."

She scrubbed the roasting pan with considerable force. "I, on the other hand, will look like something Bastard Jack dragged in."

"Who on earth is Bastard Jack?"

"It's a long story."

"So tell me anyway."

"Bastard Jack belongs to an old bag…"

Adrian's furrowed his brow. "An old bag?"

She shrugged. "That's what she calls herself. I deliver meals to her. Bastard Jack is her rheumy-eyed, arthritic, deaf, flea-bitten chihuahua. I have to have tea with him whenever I go over. He drinks right out of the cup on the kitchen table. It's disgusting, so I don't want to talk about it."

Adrian laughed. "Okay, okay." He dried a few dishes, then crossed his arms and leaned against the counter. "Am I allowed to say something?"

"It's a free country."

"If that little mutt did happen to drag you home, I'd say he has very good taste."

"Oh yes, I'm sure," she grumped. "I wear hand-me-downs from the nearly new store while my sisters look like they stepped out of a band box."

She continued to scour the roaster. Adrian threw the dishtowel on the counter. He grabbed her shoulders and turned her around to face him.

"You my dear, are the sweetest girl I've ever met. Don't change a thing." He put his hands on either side of her face and kissed her forehead softly. "Don't ever forget that."

He looked at her and then took her breath away.

He bent his head and kissed her, gently at first, slowly, and then longer and deeper. He pulled her in, trying to get closer. She reached to put her arms around him, when he suddenly stopped. He moaned a little and hugged her tight.

"Oh, God. I'm so sorry Lexie. Forgive me, I don't want to hurt you."

"You're not hurting me, Adrian. Don't ever think that."

"I'm so sorry." He let her go and left the room. She stood by the sink and stared after him.

He smelled so good. He tasted so good. What was wrong? He looked almost distraught. She didn't dare ask him, because she was afraid he'd leave. Maybe if she just pretended nothing happened, he would stay.

There were times she thought Adrian really liked her. Whenever they walked together, he'd often link his arm through hers and keep her close.

"Are you cold?"

Once she'd said yes, when she wasn't. He put his arm around her shoulders. She'd have happily stayed like that for the rest of her life.

Another time she made an apple pie. He gave her a big hug, saying he loved apple pie. He held her so long she became uncomfortable and made an excuse to walk away. She was afraid she'd jump on him the way Donalda did.

She'd dream of him. Once she thought she heard him cry in the middle of the night. She wondered if he had a nightmare.

Then one night he did.

He screamed and screamed and by the time she got to him, he was sitting up in bed and obviously didn't know where he was. His undershirt was soaked with sweat.

She hurried over to him. "It's all right, Adrian," she whispered. "It's only a dream."

"Sorry."

"Don't be silly."

"Don't leave me, Lexie. Please." He held out his hand and she took it. He wouldn't let it go so she sat on the side of his bed. He finally laid his head on the pillow and closed his eyes. He looked like he wanted to cry.

She began to hum and finally he slept. She brushed his damp hair away from his forehead. "What's wrong Adrian? Why won't you tell me?" She lifted his hand to her cheek and pressed it against her.

"It's okay, Adrian. I'm right here."

Chapter Three

LEXIE'S MOTHER HAD gone all out for the dinner party. The dining room table was a thing of beauty. But then, so was everything in her home. She enjoyed entertaining and did it with style. Some of her acquaintances called her Queenie behind her back, and she knew it, but the joke was on them, as they were the ones who begged for an invitation or were first to arrive at Cynthia's famous brunches and summer teas.

Lexie walked into the kitchen with her meringue and fresh strawberries. "Is this guy royalty?"

"He's Gabby's Prince Charming."

Lexie made a face.

Cynthia spooned chow and pickles into a crystal dish. "Where's your young man?"

"Mother, he's not my young man. He's not young, he's not mine and —"

"Well, I hope he's a man."

"Actually he's not. His nickname is Fruit Loops."

"Really?"

"Mom, why do you think the only guy who'd live with me would be a flaming fruit? Not that I mind fruit. I love fruit. You made sure of that."

"Dearest, why do you make me out to be the bad guy? I suggested no such thing. You could get a man to live with you. But you have to make the effort." Cynthia screwed the lids back on the jars and since Lexie insisted on standing like a statue in front of it, pushed past her daughter to get to the fridge.

"Why don't you ask your sister for fashion advice? I'm sure she'd get you an appointment with her hairdresser."

Lexie crossed her arms. "Which sister are we talking about, Mom? The pretty, the prettier, or the prettiest?"

"Don't start, Lexie."

Adrian poked his head in the kitchen door. "Are we having fun yet?"

Mother and daughter gave him a look. He wilted right before their eyes.

AFTER THAT FIRST awkward moment, Lexie introduced Adrian to her mom, who was as pleasant as could be once she'd gathered her wits. But at the first opportunity, he escaped into the living room. Lexie didn't blame him. The people were easier to deal with in there. Beth's little girls sat on the rug and worked on their puzzle, and he sat on the floor with them. They stared at him with big eyes.

"I'm Adrian. And you are?"

"I'm Michaela," said Beth's oldest. She pointed to her sisters. "Brit, Halley, and Maddie."

Lexie watched Adrian's reaction. He didn't turn a hair. He was more polite than she was. Every time she went to the hospital to be introduced to another niece, she'd pray Beth had come to her senses and given them names that weren't trendy.

Adrian asked to be introduced to the dolls nearby and the girls all babbled at the same time. She knew he'd be occupied for a while, so she went to her father's study. She knocked first.

"Come."

She found her dad at his desk. He'd dozed off with his glasses rested on his forehead. He was the kind of person you'd want in an emergency. His hair was a white shade of grey.

"Hi Daddy."

"Hi Princess." This pet name was a source of irritation to Beth, whom he called Baby.

She sat in the chair opposite him. "Whatcha doin'?"

"Keeping out of your mother's way."

Lexie smiled. "That's all you ever do."

"That's why I've lived to this ripe old age."

They sat in silence. She and her father had always been able to do that — enjoy each other and not say a word. She'd often found refuge in his study when she was growing up. They'd sit and roll their eyes while they listened to the mayhem unfold in the rest of the house. Lexie's mother and sisters were loud. Never once did it occur to them to walk into a room and ask a question. It was hollered down a stairwell or from the front door.

On occasion Lexie would hide in her father's study. A few times she crawled under his desk and sat by his feet. When her mom came looking for her, Dad would say he hadn't seen her. Eventually, they did it a few too many times and Lexie remembered being dragged out from under the desk, her mother clearly annoyed with their ruse.

"I'm surprised at you, William."

Lexie hoped her dad would say something, but he just sheepishly waved her goodbye. Now that she was grown up she knew why. It was too exhausting to argue with her.

"Dad, have you met Gabby's new guy yet?"

He linked his fingers together across his chest. "Hundreds of times."

"What do you mean? He's only been in town about twice."

Dad swivelled. She loved that chair. "Lexie, your sister's brought home the same type of male since she was fourteen years old. I know all about him."

"Why do you think she does that?"

"Because she can."

It was true. Gabby wooed men by looking at them. It was a talent Lexie wished she possessed. Gabby seemed bored by it but Lexie found it fascinating.

She twirled her hair, an unconscious gesture she did to soothe herself. "I wish I was like her."

Her father leaned forward. "You know Lexie, some men only see the package. And some women only have the package to give. Don't change a single hair on that wonderful head of yours. I'd never forgive you."

Her dad. The world's sweetest guy. Adrian was next.

Lexie heard shouts of hello from the front door. Dad said, "More company."

"I'll go." She left the study and rounded the corner just in time to see Kate unwrap a scarf from her neck and unzip her boots. An attractive woman stood behind her, doing the same thing.

This must be her. Kate had told Lexie she had a new girl-friend.

"Lexie." Kate ran and hugged her.

"Hi there, Brat." Lexie kissed her on both cheeks. "You look wonderful."

She did too. She had a pixie cut, her shiny brown hair spiked out every which way. It suited her small face. Kate had huge dimples that made her appear happy all the time. She looked so young. No wonder "Brat" still fit.

Kate turned. "This my friend and colleague, Daphne St. James."

Lexie shook her hand. "It's so nice to meet you Daphne. I've heard a lot about you."

Daphne gave her a relieved smile.

One down, thought Lexie. The whole tribe to go.

When Kate was eleven, Lexie ran into her room for something and caught Kate kissing her best friend. She almost had a heart attack. So did her sister. Kate stammered something, but Lexie didn't stick around to hear it. Instead, she went to her room and shut herself in the closet. She sat and thought about what she'd seen. It never occurred to her that girls could like girls. She felt afraid. It was a big unknown. Her little sister knew something she didn't. She felt stupid and left out and wondered what their mother would say if she found out. From that moment on, she decided to be Kate's champion. Kate was involved in something that would send their mother through the roof and that satisfied Lexie to no end.

She was shallow enough to admit she wanted to see her

mother react to Daphne. Adrian whispered in her ear, "Does your Mom know about her?"

Lexie spied her mother coming from the kitchen. "She does now."

"Katie, darling," her mother sang. She stretched her arms outward and Kate walked into them.

"Hi Mama. You're looking well."

"I should, my sweet. I work hard enough at it." Her eyes fell on Daphne.

"Mom, this is my friend Daphne St. James."

"Welcome Daphne, it's so nice to meet you. We don't see enough of Kate's friends. Please, come in and make yourself at home."

She shook Daphne's hand and steered her towards the living room.

So far, so good. Surely to God, her mother knew what was going on. She was a damn fine actor, if nothing else. Lexie saw her sister relax a little. It was hard on her. Her sisters knew she was gay, but no one said it out loud at home. One of these days, Kate would come out with it and actually tell her mother. But that was Kate's business.

Dad entered the living room and was his usual charming self. She introduced him to Adrian.

"Nice to meet you, Adrian."

Adrian shook his hand. "Sir."

"Lexie tells me you're from Johannesburg?"

"Yes, sir. That's right. Although I haven't lived there in a long time."

"Adrian worked in refugee camps in Tanzania," she said, as if she'd done it herself.

Her father was impressed. She could tell.

"That had to be quite an experience."

Lexie looked back at Adrian and suddenly knew she should have kept her mouth shut. It was none of her business to blab what he did. Maybe he didn't want anyone to know.

"What was your area of expertise?"

"I was hired to help with translations. I know a little Swahili and Kirundi."

"Fascinating. I imagine a person gets burnt out very quickly in a situation like that," Dad said. "It can't be easy trying to help so many people, under such conditions."

Adrian tensed. Lexie could see he didn't want to talk about it any more.

He finally said, "Yes."

"How long were you there?"

"Too long." He turned to her. "I couldn't get another club soda, could I?"

"Of course." She went to get it and heard him say, "Excuse me, sir." He came with her, as if to escape her father's questions. She could have kicked herself. Only a few days before, a television commercial about sponsoring children in Africa had come on. She told Adrian she had a foster child in India. "She sends me drawings, bless her heart." He walked out of the room and went upstairs without a word. She remembered thinking he must have had a terrible time at that camp.

And then she goes and brings it up again. She vowed to keep her mouth shut from now on.

GABBY AND RICHARD were in a rented Lexus. He'd flown in from Chicago and met Gabby at the Halifax airport, and they'd driven up to Cape Breton the night before. Richard insisted he wanted a night with her first, before the family get-together. He managed to keep her in bed for most of the day too and now they were late. She checked her watch every five minutes.

Richard, who was talking into his cellphone, watched her check her watch yet again.

"Why are you so nervous?"

"You don't know my mother. She'll have gone all out for this occasion and I don't want to keep her waiting."

Richard tsked and went back to his conversation. Gabby folded her arms and looked out the car window. When Richard finally said goodbye to his client, he snapped the phone shut and threw it in the glove compartment. His hand lingered on her silk stockings. He stroked her thigh with his finger.

"How long do we have to stay?"

"It's a dinner party."

"I want it to be over soon."

"Richard…"

"I want you back in that hotel room. Wear the red corset and those stilettos. Pretend like you missed me."

Gabby sighed.

IT BECAME A cocktail party. Everyone stood and chatted. Beth and her husband Rory enjoyed Adrian's company. "I might have been mistaken about him," she told Lexie as she passed around the canapés. "The girls love his stories about elephants and tigers."

The doorbell sounded once more. Michaela rushed to the door first. She peeked through the side window. "Mommy! It's Auntie Gabby and Prince Eric!"

Lexie knew right away what she meant. She hadn't watched *The Little Mermaid* with her four thousand times for nothing.

Gabby reached for her godchild the minute she opened the door.

"Come here you little monkey," she laughed. Gabby always laughed. It was the first thing everyone noticed about her. Almost the first thing.

After she covered the poor child with lipstick kisses, she stood and faced them.

"Everyone. This is Richard Becker. Richard, this is my family."

"My God," Beth whispered to her. "He does look like Prince Eric."

Naturally, Lexie never had boyfriends who looked like Ken dolls. She attracted needy types. In university, these pathetic losers hung off her. "Lexie, feed me. Mom didn't send my allowance." Or, "Lexie, if you do a wash, take mine. Our clothes can be dirty together."

They thought they were hilarious. But none of them compared to the jerk who cornered her every Saturday night when he was sloshed.

"You look like you need sex, Lex. How about it? You've got incredible jugs. How about I relieve your suffering? What do you say?"

She put up with these idiots her whole life. They thought she was their mother. They ran to her to complain about their horrible girlfriends. They'd snuggle up and put their heads in her lap.

"You're so great Lex, thanks for listening."

Yeah sure.

One guy was cute. He made her laugh.

"Rub my back Lex." She would. One night he turned over and looked at her.

"You have the most beautiful brown eyes, Lexie."

Her heart skipped a beat. "No, I don't."

"Yes, you do."

He touched her face with the back of his hand. "And the most beautiful skin."

"No, I don't," she whispered.

"Why don't you see it, Sunshine?"

"No one's ever said it before."

"That doesn't make it not true. You need to believe it." He reached for her. That was her first time. He left school shortly after that.

If she was so wonderful, why did he leave? She remembered she cried for a week.

Gabby came over to her and gave her a hug. "So. What do you think?"

"He's definitely hunky."

Gabby smiled at Richard. Lexie loved it when she smiled. Her sister opened her satin clutch and took out her gold lighter and cigarette case. Beth grabbed the baby. "Don't smoke in front of the kids. You know better."

She put them back. "Sorry."

Lexie smirked. She knew Beth wasn't annoyed about the smoke. She was annoyed Gabby looked so damn good. Her hair was like a copper halo. No one in the family knew where she got it.

She wore a stovepipe black skirt, high heels, and a very expensive white silk blouse turned up at the collar. How did she do that? Anyone else would get makeup on it. A pearl necklace was at her throat. She reminded Lexie of a forties film star.

Gabby looked around as their dad poured a drink for Richard. Lexie saw her stop. Gabby's eyes got big and she stayed very still. Lexie couldn't tell what she was looking at.

Gabby said softly, "Aren't you going to introduce me to your friend, Lexie?"

Oh, brother. Here comes the charm. Luckily Adrian will see right through her. She turned to him but something was wrong because he didn't crack wise or pull a face. He just stood there and stared at Gabby. Lexie was fed up. This always happened. She was tired of the little games Gabby played on men. She had no business doing it to Adrian.

She turned back to give Gabby a look that said "knock it off," but she didn't. She didn't recognize the woman who made men dance like puppets on a string. That woman was gone. There was only a girl, and she looked frightened.

"Gabby," Richard said from across the room, "why don't you show your mother the pictures we took in Los Angeles?"

Had he seen it? Had she?

"I'LL GET DESSERT," Lexie said to no one in particular. Not that anyone noticed or heard her. It was like old home week.

Mom's dinner was a roaring success. Kate was content because Mom pretended she didn't know anything about Daphne. Rory and Richard got along like a house on fire and gave Dad advice about the stock market. The girls were as good as gold at their card table, playing with old Barbie dolls her mother was clever enough to have kept. The only ones who didn't talk were Adrian and Gabby. Every time Lexie looked at them, they were not looking at each other.

Beth followed Lexie out into the kitchen with a stack of dishes. She filled the kettle and turned her back against the counter.

"How does she do it, Lex?"

Lexie knew what she meant, but she was cranky so she pretended she didn't.

"How does who do what?"

"I wonder how it feels to have every man in the room want you."

Lexie started to cut the meringue and put it on plates. "Oh shut up. You know how it feels. You're no shrinking violet. That's my department."

Beth reached into her sweater pocket and pulled out a cigarette. She looked at Lexie. "Don't tell. Rory will kill me." She lit it. "I have one a week."

"I'm not telling." Lexie held out her hand and Beth gave it to her. She took a long drag and handed it back.

Their mother flew through the door and clapped her hands. "Chop, chop, girls, let's get dessert on the table." She rushed to grab dessert forks out of the silverware chest that sat on the counter. When they were kids, the girls fought over who would put the cutlery back in the velvet slots.

"Beth, put that horrid thing out. I'm surprised at you. Lexie, your young man doesn't appear to be very talkative. I thought you said he was an actor. Are you sure he's not a mime?" She smiled at her own joke.

"Mother, for the last time, Adrian is not my young man. He's my stupid lodger. He's my miserable, crappy twit of a lodger. He's my rent money. Nothing else."

Lexie looked up. Beth and Mom stared at her. During her outburst, she'd hacked the meringue with a little too much force.

"I don't know what's wrong with you girls. Gabby seems strange as well. Are you all on your periods or something?"

Lexie didn't point out that she was fifteen years away from menopause. Mom liked to pretend her girls were pimply teenagers. That way she was young forever.

Mom reached into the fridge for the cream. "What do you think of Richard?"

"He looks like a Dick to me."

Her mother gave her a look.

"Sorry."

"He seems nice," Beth said. "I wonder how long he'll last?"

Mom filled the sugar bowl and sighed, "I do wish your sister would settle down. She'd make the most beautiful bride."

Beth said ever so casually, "What do you think of Daphne, Mom?"

Their mom kept her head turned away.

"I think she's a lovely woman. I can see why Kate likes her so much."

She carried a tray full of teacups back into the dining room. Beth and Lexie looked at each other.

"She's pretending."

"I'm not so sure," Beth said. "Do you really think she'd be so calm if she knew?"

ADRIAN WAS QUIET on the drive home. It got on her nerves.

Lexie gripped the steering wheel. "So, what did you think of the entire family?"

"Everyone was lovely."

That's all he said. She hated when he was quiet.

"I told you my sisters were good-looking."

She waited for him to say, "not as good-looking as you."

"Yes, they are. They're lovely." He stared out the side window. That was twice he used the word lovely. Lexie kept her mouth shut the rest of the way home.

They walked into the house. Adrian went to bed, after thanking her for a lovely evening.

Gabby called the next day. Twice in the same week was unusual. She sounded chipper.

"Hi Lex."

"Hi."

"What are you doing?"

"Talking to you."

"What's on for tonight? Do you and Adrian have plans?"

Lexie knew the magic name would crop up.

"No."

"Right, right. Tell me. Exactly what is this relationship of yours with Adrian?"

"He's my roommate."

"Is that it?"

"Look, why do you ask me stupid questions? Don't you have anything better to do, like spend time with Dick?"

"His name is Richard."

"Richard then. Isn't he the one you're in love with this week?"

Gabby hung up. That was twice now.

✿

"Hello?"

"Adrian?"

"Yes."

"It's Gabby."

He knew it was as soon as she said hello.

"Gabby. It's lovely to hear your voice."

"Is it?"

There was a long pause.

"Yes."

"Will you meet me?"

"Where?"

She gave him the address.

"I'll be there."

"I'll be waiting."

GABBY OPENED THE door and held her breath. He closed the door and looked at her. He put out his hand. She took it. He put out his other hand. She took that. He pulled her slowly towards him. He pulled her until she stood toe to toe with him, their hands entwined down by their sides.

He touched her cheek with his own, tenderly. He moved his head slightly up and down and then back and forth. Just like that. They stood just like that for an endless moment.

His mouth was open. He brushed his lips on her face with the slightest touch, over and over until he reached her lips. When that happened, they forgot everything.

❧

AT REHEARSAL ADRIAN missed four cues. Donalda was annoyed. "What's going on with him?"

"Take a pill for God's sake. He's fine. Anyone can forget a line."

Donalda put her hands on her hips. "He forgot his character's name."

"It's true, Lexie," Susie nodded. "He seems different. Not his usual happy self."

"Adrian might pretend to be happy in front of you but he's often quiet by himself. He doesn't feel the need to run off at the mouth, like some." Lexie looked at Donalda.

"I'd be in a foul mood too, if I had to live with you."

"Oh shut up, the both of you," Susan pleaded. "You drive me crazy."

Lexie went to her mom's a few days later to copy out her recipe for chocolate cake.

Her mom peeled carrots by the sink. "Lexie, have you spoken to your sister recently?"

She grabbed a carrot and took a bite. "Which one? Why don't you ever say their names? I have three of them. I can't read your mind."

"You got out of the wrong side of the bed this morning. That's not peeled by the way."

She shrugged.

Her mother looked at her. "Are you okay, honey? You seem kind of down."

She pouted. "I don't know."

"Someone needs a hug." Her mom reached over and gave her a big one. It felt good.

"I'm all right. Which sister?"

"Gabby."

Of course. "Yeah. She called the other day and hung up on me."

Mom talked to the carrots. "She hung up on you? Why did she do that? Did you say something to her?"

"Yes, I did. She bugged me about Adrian." She leaned over her mother. "Pass me that glass...stupid carrot."

She did. "Who's Adrian?"

Lexie coughed. "Mother. You only met him the other night."

"Oh, your weird friend. Yes, of course."

She pushed the water button on the fridge and filled her glass. "He's not weird, Mom."

"I'm sure he isn't, dear, but he wasn't very animated."

She drank her water. "No, I guess not. He wasn't his usual self. We probably scared him to death."

"No doubt. Only, I was supposed to pick Gabby up for lunch yesterday. She had three days off, but she wasn't at Karen's. She never called to cancel." Her mother stopped peeling and looked out the window. "I don't know. It isn't like her, not to let me know."

"She isn't like anyone."

Since Gabby worked for an airline, she met most of her high flyers catering to businessmen in first class. She was gone most of the time. The family never knew her schedule. She flew all over the world and could have lived anywhere. She shared an apartment in Toronto with three co-workers because it was convenient for international flights. When she flew into Sydney, she stayed with her parents or Karen, a pal from high school.

Because everyone said Gabby should have gone to Hollywood, Lexie and her sisters basked in second-hand glory. Lexie got a kick out of people when they'd do a double take as she walked by. The woman herself never noticed. But on Lexie's crabbier days, it ticked her off that people held doors open for her sister but not for her.

Their worst moment together was when they walked down the street one day after school. A gang of teenage boys spotted Gabby and started to drool. One of them shouted, "Look, its Beauty and the Beast." Lexie's cheeks went blood red. She was so humiliated. As they walked by, Gabby put her arm around her. She tilted her head and whispered, "I hate it when boys call me the Beast."

LEXIE PRESENTED ADRIAN with a big piece of cake after supper. He looked up and smiled.

"You spoil me."

She sat down with a piece for herself. "That's okay. I like to spoil people." She took a bite. It was good.

"You do too much for everyone. Why don't you save some kindness for yourself?"

"What do you mean?"

"I mean, you never give yourself credit for anything. You give and never take. Most people are selfish, Lexie."

"I like to do things for people I…like."

He stabbed his cake with a fork. "I don't deserve someone like you. I've always been selfish."

"Adrian, you're so kind. Why do you say you're selfish?"

He put his fork down. "I think of myself first."

"There's nothing wrong with that."

"You don't." His hand went through his hair. She loved that. She wanted to reach out and do it too.

"Sure I do. You said you wanted mashed potatoes last night. I was too lazy and threw on french fries."

"Oh, Lexie, that's not what I mean."

"Well, what then?"

"You took in a stranger you didn't know. You treat me better than I deserve and yet you expect nothing in return."

She held up her finger and pointed at the ceiling. "As Mark Twain once said, 'Always do right. This will gratify some people, and astonish the rest.'"

He looked miserable. She lowered her arm and said gently, "You're my friend, Adrian. How else should I treat you?"

"I'm so glad you're my friend, Lexie." He reached across the table and grabbed her hand. "Always remember that. I love you for what you've done for me. You opened your heart and let me in. I never deserved it."

It was hard to focus on anything except the way his skin felt against hers. "Of course you did."

"I'll never forget this. Never. You are the one memory I'll cherish forever."

She cleared her throat and took her hand away. "Adrian, just have your cake. And eat it too."

A WEEK WENT by. Lexie was preoccupied. Everyone said so at the library.

"What's wrong with that one?" she heard Marlene gripe. Marlene was a bigmouth. She cracked gum all day and passed judgement on everyone she came across. Lexie couldn't begin to imagine how she ever got her job. Her vocabulary was atrocious and her people skills were even worse. Lexie's best guess was that she was related to the head librarian. She just never had the guts to ask.

But Lexie sure didn't need her shit today. She ignored Marlene for as long as possible, but she kept it up.

"You've got a face like a poker. What's your problem? Can't get a man?"

"Fuck off."

The two little boys who sat at a table nearby dissolved into snorts. The head librarian resorted to her famous "SHHHH," but it was a lost cause. Lexie had made their day.

Lexie left work early, pleading a migraine. She wanted to make Adrian his favourite supper. He loved beef stew and he needed something to put meat on his bones. She wondered if he was coming down with something. He swore he wasn't, but she knew better. He didn't even tease Sophie, even after she purposely walked on him as he lay on the floor reading.

She stopped by the local corner store on her way home from work. The little bell tinkled when she pushed the door open. There was Lester, behind the counter. He was always behind the counter. He lived there.

He smiled his toothy grin. "Hey girlie, how's my best customer?"

She was his best customer. With the amount of chocolate she'd purchased over the years, he could have retired and moved to Florida years ago. "Hi Lester. Are ya being good?" He loved it when she said that.

His shoulders moved up and down as he laughed without making a sound. She'd never known anyone who could do that. His eyes would crinkle; his face would light up. His head and shoulders would shake frantically, but he never made a peep.

"I'm good girl, good. Are you getting a little somethin' for Sophie?"

Her cat was famous. She nodded.

"I hear tell them fellas over at the pier landed a six-hundred-pound tuna today. Might keep her going for a day or two." His shoulders moved up and down so quickly they were a blur.

"Oh Lester, what would I do without you?"

"Well girlie," he wiped his eyes, "I'm afraid I'm spoken for."

Lester had two widows fighting for his affection. They kept him well supplied with hot tea biscuits, oatcakes, and mincemeat tarts.

Yes, she thought, even dear old Lester has a love life. She picked up her paper, three tins of cat food, a lotto ticket, and her Cadbury bar. She gave Lester his money, and he patted her hand when he passed her the change.

"Cheer up girlie."

Did she look that bad? What was the matter with everyone?

Sophie greeted her at the door. She meowed and meowed. There was something wrong. She looked at Lexie with her sweet furry face.

"What's the matter, my love?" Oh, please don't let anything happen to Sophie. She picked her up and gave her a cuddle, but she kept at it. Gosh, that wasn't like her. Lexie walked down the hall and into the living room.

She stopped dead.

Adrian lay by the fire while Gabby straddled him. Her beautiful body glowed in the fireplace light as they moved as one, her gorgeous copper hair cascading down her back. They had eyes only for each other.

She must have cried out because they turned around, saw her, and immediately scrambled to cover up.

"Oh my God, Lex!" Gabby cried as she reached for her camisole. "I'm so sorry. I didn't mean for this to happen…"

She couldn't think of anything to say, except, "In front of Sophie?"

Adrian jumped into his jeans and started to button them up. "Lexie, wait!"

She walked out of the house with her cat in her arms.

Chapter Four

LEXIE SPENT THE night with Beth. She didn't tell her sister why she needed to sleep on her sofa bed or why she had her cat with her and Beth was too worn out to ask or care. She was busy wading through toys and trying to settle an argument between the girls about who would get to sleep with the giant Pooh Bear their father brought home.

"I'm going to kill you," she muttered to Rory.

Rory shrugged. "Sorry. I didn't think."

Lexie solved the immediate problem by offering to give the girls a bath. She kept them in the tub for about an hour and her nieces couldn't believe their good fortune. Lexie didn't have to talk. She just nodded and smiled every now and again. They were so busy chatting, they didn't notice she never said anything.

She gathered them up in Michaela's bed with Pooh Bear in the thick of things, and read them the longest fairy tale she could find. She didn't know what it was about but it must have made sense because they were content.

When Beth got the baby settled, she came to rescue Lexie. The girls were fast asleep. Lexie waved her away. She wanted to have them entwined in her arms. As a matter of fact, she hugged them for dear life.

Rory took the three oldest with him in the morning. When Lexie asked him where they were going so early, he mumbled something. She realized her sister had arranged for them to go out, on account of her.

Knowing Rory, he'd go to every drive-thru in town to keep them in their car seats. The girls hugged her goodbye. He kissed Beth before he disappeared out the back door. She gave him a gentle push. "See you later."

He shouted over his shoulder, "See ya, Lexie."

"Bye."

Beth poured two cups of coffee. She put them on the table and spooned sugar in both.

"I don't take sugar."

"Today you do." Beth was the bossiest one in the family. It usually annoyed Lexie but not today.

Her sister sat at the table. "Well?" She waited.

Lexie opened her mouth and closed it again. Nothing came out.

"You remind me of the kids. Out with it."

"Adrian and Gabby were making love on my living room rug last night…in front of Sophie."

"Holy Hannah."

"I couldn't believe it," Lexie sobbed as she wiped her watery eyes.

Beth looked at her feet as she digested the news. "What does she see in him?" was her first question. The next thing out of her mouth was "Good lord, I have to mop this floor."

Even though Lexie hated Adrian's guts at that moment, she was really annoyed by the remark.

"What do you mean? He's a nice guy. Or I thought he was."

"If he was such a nice guy, he wouldn't have bonked your sister in front of your furry child."

"That's right," Lexie agreed wholeheartedly before she

snuck her thumbnail in her mouth and filed it down with
her teeth.

Beth suddenly looked at her. "Lexie, I think Gabby's out of
her mind, but aren't you being a little silly to get this upset
about your roommate's love life? He is an adult. He does live
there after all, with your blessing I might add."

Lexie opened her mouth to say something and then closed
it again.

Beth took a big swill of coffee. "You look like a guppy.
Stop that."

My God, she was right. Lexie had told everyone Adrian
wasn't her anything. He was a guy who shared the bathroom. He wasn't her boyfriend. And he'd never given any in-
dication he wanted to be. He'd never tried to kiss her again
after that night by the sink.

Not only was she upset, she felt stupid. She held her head
in her hands. "I'm a moron."

Beth patted her arm. "Ordinarily I'd agree with you, but I
happen to be on your side for once."

Lexie couldn't believe it. "Why?"

"Because that little beast cannot keep her paws off anyone's boyfriend, husband, or roommate."

"God. She hasn't gone after Rory?"

Beth backed up a little. "No. But you know Gabby. All
she has to do is look in their direction and they fall at her
feet. I'm not sure she always does it on purpose." She took
another sip of coffee and banged her mug on the table. "It
ticks me off though. I could never bring a boyfriend home.
Sometimes they'd go out with me just to get invited over. She

even made out with Johnny Ferguson in the broom closet once when he was supposedly dating me." She frowned at the memory. "And why is Gabby with Adrian if she's supposed to be in love with Prince Eric?"

Poor Dick would never be known as anything else.

"She's nuts! Why would she want Adrian when she has a guy who's apparently a millionaire? That's what I'd like to know."

Lexie stayed at Beth's one more night. She couldn't face Adrian yet. She was too embarrassed. Besides, her sister looked tired. No wonder she was cranky. Lexie never knew how much work four small children could be. After the second night, she dragged her rear end around until she finally plunked down on the sofa bed. "How do you do it, Beth?"

Beth yawned as she picked up toys and threw them in the direction of the toy box their dad built for Michaela. "When they're your own, it's not so bad. Besides, I can't send them back."

"I never thought of it before, but how did Mom do it? She not only looked after us but taught as well."

"She's perfect?"

Just then Rory yelled from upstairs. "I need help here! I have one in the tub, one on the john, one missing, and one under the sink."

Beth hollered, "I'm on my way."

"Listen Beth, thanks for everything. You're right. I'm a grown woman and I acted like a kid when I ran out like that. I better go face the music."

Her sister looked back at her and gave her a kind smile. "Good luck, kiddo."

Lexie put Sophie in the van once she wiped the snow off. It was a very stormy winter. As soon as she started the motor she felt better. Good old Betsy, filled with rug-hooking supplies, old library books, theatre props, and clothes Lexie gathered to take to goodwill. That and lots of chocolate bar wrappers.

Her mother always grimaced whenever Lexie took her anywhere in it.

"Really dearest, why don't you trade in this heap of rusty metal?"

"This heap, as you call it, starts in minus 30 degree weather, unlike your precious Seville."

Her mother had no answer to that, but of course always had the last word. "Well, you should shovel it out now and then."

Lexie drove home as slowly as she could. She inevitably arrived but was still hesitant to go in, so she sat behind the wheel and willed her heart to stop racing. She needed to focus on something, so she looked at the house. It had belonged to her Aunt Sally, her father's eccentric older sister, a card-carrying spinster. She and her dad grew up there and when their parents died, Sally insisted on taking care of it herself, despite Dad's numerous offers of help. She was a stubborn old bird.

Of course, now it looked bare and bleak, but in the summer, wild roses bloomed everywhere. And like her parents' home, the sides of this house disappeared under a leafy mass of green when spring arrived. Ivy for an Ivy house.

The backyard was a jumble of wildflowers in summer, thanks to another of Aunt Sally's peculiar ways. She hated grass, refused to have anything to do with it. So she filled her property with lupines, Indian paintbrush, Queen Anne's lace, buttercups, and daisies. Like her aunt, Lexie loved it that way.

She loved everything about her house. The main floor consisted of a hallway, with stairs on the left, and a living room that could be closed with old glass-paned doors. This room took up most of the right side. Despite being small, the shallow fireplace on the far wall threw a great heat. Aunt Sally's favourite white mirror hung above the intricate carved mantle.

The old-fashioned kitchen took up the back of the house, and an ancient harvest table, with a hodgepodge of old chairs around it, took up most of the room. Nothing matched but that was fine.

The shelves underneath had checkered cloth hiding them. There was a pantry, where she baked, as her Aunt Sally did when Lexie was a child. Jars, glass bottles, and preserves took up all the shelves.

Her bedroom upstairs was crowded with old bureaus and Aunt Sally's sleigh bed. The wallpaper was so ancient, its pattern of roses was back in style. Her wooden floors were painted and covered with worn hooked mats that had been there since she could remember.

Adrian's room was across the hall, a smaller version of her own. Beside it was the bathroom, which was large enough for a rocking chair and an old chest of drawers that held towels and books. The best feature was the deep, claw-footed tub, heavenly for soaking in.

Everyone was shocked when Aunt Sally left the house to Lexie. She asked Dad why she would do such a thing. He said his sister recognized a kindred spirit when she saw one.

Running out of rooms to ponder, Lexie shook off her reverie and took a deep breath. She noticed the snow drifted along the front porch stairs. Oh, well done Adrian. He didn't shovel it for her. Here was something else she could brood about. She turned off the engine, grabbed Sophie, and readied herself to face her roommate.

"Adrian!" she shouted as she closed the front door. She waited to hear his feet thump down the stairs.

Nothing.

"Ade!"

The place felt empty. He wasn't home. She went into the kitchen and put the kettle on. She took off her gloves and threw them on the table. That's when she noticed the note propped up against the salt and pepper shakers.

As Sophie rubbed her legs in a figure eight and purred loudly to express her pleasure at being home, Lexie stumbled to the table and picked up the note.

"I'm sorry Lexie," was all it said.

SHE STOOD AND looked at the empty hangers in his closet. The phone rang. She walked downstairs and sat on the chair next to it. She didn't pick up.

"Lexie, it's Mom. Call me please, it's urgent."

She wanted to. She couldn't do it.

The phone rang again.

Mom sounded hysterical. "Lexie. Pick up."

She did. "What's wrong Mom?"

"It's your sister." She heard her mother blow her nose.

"Which one?"

"Gabby."

She got a chill. "What about Gabby?"

"I just received the strangest call from Richard. He's very upset. He called Gabby from Chicago and her roommates were under the impression she was with him. Gabby told them she'd be staying there for a while. She packed her clothes and left. They didn't think any more of it, just assumed she flew to O'Hare yesterday. But she never arrived. He's beside himself. Oh my God, Lexie. You don't think something horrible has happened, do you?"

Lexie took a deep breath. "Gabby's run away with Adrian, Mom."

"Who's Adrian?"

"My weird friend."

"*No.*"

"Yes."

"Is she out of her mind?"

"Is he out of *his* mind?"

There was silence on the end of the phone. "What do you mean?"

"I mean, Mother, she'll break his heart."

Her mother started to cry. "Who cares about his heart? What about mine?"

She didn't say, "What about yours?"

SUSAN LEFT MESSAGES. Lexie didn't call her back. Donalda did too. She ignored them. Finally Susan knocked on her door one night after work. She pushed past her and the frigid air came in with her.

"What's going on?"

"Nothing."

"That's crap. You haven't been to rehearsal. For that matter, neither has Adrian. Did you have a fight?" Sue pushed Sophie over and made herself comfortable on the old sofa facing the fire.

Lexie sat on her floor pillow. "You can't fight with someone who's not here."

Susie's voice rose. "What do you mean he's not here? He's got to be here. He helps me drag Donalda's body off the stage in the final act. You know how my back goes out."

"Looks like you'll be in traction then, doesn't it?"

She crossed her arms. "All right, spill the beans."

"He took off with my sister."

Susie's mouth hung open. "He what?"

Lexie nodded.

She turned as white as a ghost. "*Beth* left Rory and her babies for Adrian?"

"Not Beth, you idiot."

She put her hand over her heart. "Oh thank God." Then she looked puzzled. "I thought Kate was gay?"

"Not Kate, you idiot."

Susie couldn't speak. Then she could.

"No."

"Yes."

Susan put her hand over her mouth then took it away to point her finger in Lexie's face. "Let me get this straight. Your supermodel sister, who's practically engaged to a filthy rich investment banker who lives in a penthouse condo and has a summer home in Florida, left town with a penniless wandering hobo?"

Lexie burst into tears.

Susan got down on the floor and put her arms around her. "I'm so sorry Lexie. I knew you were fond of him but I didn't know you loved him."

"I don't."

❧

LEXIE'S FATHER DROPPED by the library one day and asked to take her to lunch. The older women simpered and giggled.

"Ladies." Dad tipped his hat as he escorted her out.

They settled themselves down at a back table in the restaurant and ordered their usual — spinach salad and club soda. But it was hard to have a conversation. People would come up to the table and talk her dad's ear off. Lexie got impatient, but he took it in stride.

"So, Princess. I hear you've been dealt a tough blow."

She quickly said, "Only because I miss the rent money."

"Are you sure that's all you're upset about?"

"Yes."

"Did you have feelings for this young man?"

"No."

"I see." He buttered his roll. "Well, whatever your

relationship with him, I think he and Gabby behaved badly — to leave town and not tell anyone. Adrian should have given you notice. You were kind to him. And as for your sister's behaviour towards Richard, I find it inexcusable."

She sighed and put down her fork. She didn't feel like eating.

"It's not wrong to admit you like someone, Lexie. Even if they hurt you. It doesn't make you look foolish. You can love someone who doesn't love you back. That's not a sign of weakness. You have a loving heart. It's the most precious thing about you. I hate to see you feel badly about yourself just because you are who you are."

She grabbed a napkin to stop the tears that rolled down her face. She wanted to be in his study, not in a stupid restaurant.

He reached for her hand. "I'm ashamed of the way your sister behaved and I will tell her so, the first chance I get. But I'm very proud of you. Don't ever forget that. You're my Princess. You always will be."

LEXIE'S DAD READ to them at night when she and her sisters were little. He'd gather them on the living room sofa and take out *Little Women* or *Wind in the Willows* and read a chapter at a time. The three younger ones burrowed close to him because they were small. Lexie usually ended up on the floor with her arms around his leg as she leaned on him. She'd close her eyes and listen to his voice.

She'd wait for her father's signal that was meant for her alone. He'd reach out and rub her hair for a moment or two. That was to tell her he loved her, down there on the floor.

She thought her father was most like Matthew Cuthbert of *Anne of Green Gables*. She cried for hours the night they got to the part where Matthew died. She couldn't bear it.

❧

LEXIE WENT TO her cousin Nancy's house, to help with her daughter's birthday party. Nancy said she didn't want to suffer alone. Lexie asked Nancy why she always thought of her when misery was in the offing. Her excuse was that that she loved her.

A gaggle of five-year-olds ran around the house with glee. Lexie brought Beth's girls along so their mother could go to the hairdresser. She didn't often have two hours to herself. Lexie's Auntie Moo was there. It occurred to Lexie she didn't know Moo's real name — but it didn't really matter. She'd never be known as anything else. Auntie Moo kissed her granddaughter, the birthday girl, every time she came within reach. Nancy left the kitchen to try and get the girls to listen while she explained the rules of Twister.

It was soon evident to Lexie that this was Auntie Moo's opportunity to interrogate her. She sort of expected it, seeing as how her extended family was so nosy.

They blew up balloons as they talked.

"Are you all right, sweetheart?"

Lexie blew into stale rubber. "Sure. Why wouldn't I be?"

Auntie Moo blew too. "Don't give me that. I know all about the roommate."

"Who told you?" she puffed.

Her aunt stopped for a breather. "I forget. I'm an old lady."

"You're not old."

"Wanna bet?" She continued. "Well, if you must know, your mother told Beth, who told Rory, who told John, who told Nancy, who told me."

"Great. Did we forget anyone? This is just what I need."

"Your mother's very upset."

"Well, what else is new? She's always upset about something that concerns me. She never leaves me alone."

"Your mother adores you. She always talks about you."

"I know. That's the trouble. I wish she'd talk about someone else."

Auntie Moo gave her a stern look. "The day your mother stops talking, Lexie, will be the loneliest day of your life. I want you to remember that. No one ever talks about you again the way your mother does. And you'll miss that. Believe me. When my mother died, I'd have given anything to hear her voice just once more."

Lexie's eyes filled with tears. "I'm sorry. I know you're right."

Auntie Moo took Kleenex from the sleeve of her sweater and wiped her own eyes. "I know I'm right too."

Nancy yelled from the living room. "Can one of you get in here? I'm so twisted I can't move."

Chapter Five

ALL THAT WINTER, Sophie and Lexie sat by the fire and thought of ways to make the house look better.

"I think we need some new paint for this living room."

Sophie plunked on top of the fliers Lexie had spread out on the floor.

"What colour do you think?"

Sophie gave Lexie her I-could-care-less look and rolled on her back.

"What about little white lights around the room?"

The pussycat ignored her.

Lexie pored over decorating magazines at the library and tried to figure out what style she wanted. She mentioned her plans to Judy, their administrator.

Judy tried to be helpful. "I don't imagine you want contemporary, Lexie. It wouldn't say 'you.'"

Marlene was behind them filing. "Is there a style called 'frump'?"

Judy and Lexie ignored her. They continued their musings at the counter while they flipped through the pages.

"You're the nearest thing to a hippie I've seen," said Judy.

Lexie looked at her. She wasn't sure that was a compliment.

"I mean that as a compliment. You know…you wear flamboyant flowing things, big scarves and skirts you've made yourself."

Marlene cracked her gum. "I can go out and buy a tablecloth too, but you won't see me wearin' it to work."

Lexie didn't rise to the bait. She looked at Judy instead. "I thought I might try two colours for the living room. Eggplant and lime sherbet. Does that sound an odd combination to you?"

Marlene said, "It sounds odd to me. Why don't you throw your dinner plate against the wall and be done with it."

Lexie was about to lose her cool when Judy spun around on her heel and put her nose right in Marlene's face.

"You wouldn't know style if it jumped up and bit your bony little ass!"

Marlene looked stunned. Lexie sure was. Judy was a meek little woman who'd rather die than cause a scene. Her cheeks were flushed and she shook with fury as she grabbed her pen and beetled to the boardroom.

"That one better get herself some hormones," Marlene cracked. "Or a good screw."

Lexie stalked off.

Murder by Mother was destined not to succeed. After seeing Adrian play the hero, it was a comedown to have Todd do it and naturally Donalda nagged Lexie incessantly about such a distressing turn of events.

"How could you have been so stupid, to drive him out of town like that? If he'd stayed with me, we'd still have our leading man. We had such chemistry. He said so. He'd never had a kiss like mine, he said."

"If he stayed with you," Lexie told her, "you'd be dead in the first act. He'd stab you long before I have to. Or he'd have stabbed himself, to prevent you from kissing him like a sex-starved maniac."

Susan tried to referee. "For heaven's sake, will you two pipe down? The audience will hear you."

"Like I care," Lexie growled. "Do you think there's a Hollywood agent sitting out there in the dark? I can tell you for a fact, there's only about fifty family members, and they've been dragged out by force or guilt."

Susan peeked out. "You're right. God. I can't wait for this to be over."

Lexie was horrible through the whole thing. The only time she became enthused was when she stabbed Donalda. Although she was supposed to be dead, Donalda shot filthy looks as Lexie rolled her up in the carpet.

"Not so tight," she grumbled.

Lexie pretended she didn't hear.

Susie and Todd dragged Donalda off the stage as the lights dimmed. By the time they unrolled her, she was as red as a beet. She coughed, "Where is she? I'll kill her."

Lexie had already left the theatre.

Beth gave her a lift home.

"You deserve an Academy Award for knocking off poor Donalda," she said. "The music from *Psycho* played in my head."

❧

LEXIE'S HOT WATER tank leaked one Sunday morning. She was in a dither about what to do, so she called Rory. Poor guy. As the only one in his immediate family who knew a thing about tools, he got stuck with his widowed mother's repairs, his own, and now Lexie's.

Rory was easygoing. How he ever managed to connect with Beth was a mystery.

He carried his toolbox into the house. "What have you done now?"

"God only knows. I hate stupid machine things." Lexie followed him into the cellar. He poked around and did stuff. He told her what was wrong and how to fix it. She tried to pay attention but forgot everything by the time they went back upstairs.

"You deserve a cup of tea and a nice piece of blueberry pie."

He sat at the table.

She put a big slab on his plate, then brought over two mugs of tea and sat with him.

"Oh, boy." He wolfed down a huge bite. "I wish Beth baked like you."

She looked to the heavens. "For pity's sake, don't let her hear you say that."

"Why are you guys always worried about what Beth thinks?"

"You're kidding, right?"

He shovelled more pie in his gob. "No, I mean it. She's an old softie."

"Stop talking with your mouth full."

He grinned and showed her his blue teeth.

Lexie shrugged. "I suppose because she always screamed the loudest."

Rory finished the pie and drained his mug. "That was good." He wiped his mouth on a napkin and sat back in his chair. Lexie loved to look at him. He was a doll. He gave her a little smile. "Can I tell you a secret?"

She was intrigued. She and Rory never got a chance to talk together one on one. "Sure."

"Beth's jealous of you."

Five seconds of silence went by.

"Okay, don't believe me." He folded his arms on the table, quite unconcerned.

"What do you mean?"

"I mean she wishes she could be like you."

"But that's not possible. Why would she be jealous of me?"

"Because you're artistic and you went to university and you're independent."

"She shouldn't feel like that. Look what she does. Raising a large family is a tremendous job."

"I tell her that but she doesn't believe me."

Lexie couldn't get over it. "Gosh. Beth always struck me as having supreme confidence."

"It's an act. You're creative. Gabby's Gabby and Kate's as smart as a whip. She feels like nothing."

"What do you tell her?"

"She's everything to me."

"She's the luckiest girl in the world."

SUSAN CAME OVER to help Lexie paint the living room. She decided on eggplant and lime green, in spite of Marlene.

Susan poured paint into the tray. "I'd never have the nerve to paint a room this colour."

"That's because you've never had a house of your own."

"So nice of you to remind me, Lex."

"Sorry. I didn't mean it like that."

"I know." Susie took the long roller and wrote her name on the wall.

"Stop that. That's all I need — the name 'Susie' emblazoned across the room forever."

"What's wrong with it, may I ask?"

"Not a thing. It's better than Lexie."

"If you could be called anything else, what would it be?"

She didn't have to think too hard. Lexie Davenport.

"GOOD GOD," HER mother said, "It looks like a bordello."

She came over to the house to bring Lexie swatches of material — stuff she'd never use.

"Thanks Mom."

"Oh dear, I didn't mean it like that. Don't be so sensitive. I mean it's colourful!"

"Do you know what a bordello looks like?"

Her mom decided to play along. "As a matter of fact I do. It's how I put myself through teacher's college."

Lexie laughed. They headed for the kitchen to make a cup of tea. Sophie was on the dryer, in the back porch. Her entire mass covered the top of it. She shook to the rhythm of a dark load. Her mother looked at the cat. "I don't know why, but that looks vaguely obscene."

"It's how I get my jollies." She reached for the mugs she made in ceramics class and waited for her mom to tell her not to be vulgar, but there was only silence.

As Lexie busied herself with the tea, she stole a furtive look. Her mother stared out towards the back garden, now covered with snow, her hands clasped in front of her on the table. She looked lonely. She looked different. Lexie felt scared.

Handing her mom a napkin and the tea, she said, "You're far away."

"Yes." Her mother took a sip and looked down at her cup. Lexie got nervous.

"Is something the matter?"

"Yes."

"Oh my God. You're not sick are you?"

Mom shook her head.

Lexie was in a panic. "It's not the babies?"

"No dear, the girls are fine."

She breathed easier, and then came the body blow.

"Your father's having an affair."

HER MOTHER LEFT. Lexie carried her aching body up the stairs and sat in the tub until the water was cold.

Men hurt you. Men betray you. But not Dad. Not her dad. She couldn't picture it. She couldn't make the connection between the sweet man who gave her bear hugs and the man who cheated on his wife.

She tried to remember what Mom said. "Close your mouth, Lexie, you'll catch flies." She sounded like Mom again. Lexie could deal with her better that way. The tea seemed to revive her. Her mother shook her head and smoothed her hair away from her face.

Lexie waited until she couldn't stand it any longer. "*Well?*"

"Well what?"

Lexie crossed her arms across her chest and sat stiff as a board. "Well, I don't know. You tell me."

"What do you want to know?"

"Shit Mother, this isn't twenty questions. You can't drop a bomb like this and make me drag it out of you."

She sighed. "I know. I don't know where to start."

"Before you do, can I ask why you're telling me this? Why I need to know?"

"There's no one else," she pleaded. Her voice got higher and that made Lexie uncomfortable. Her mother was always in control. "Think about it, Lexie. Who do I tell? The gossips at Club? The UCW? My Women's Institute group?"

She got up and paced the kitchen floor, her hands clenched together. "Everyone in this damn town worships your father. Everywhere I go, people tell me how much they adore him. Do you know what it's like to hear women I don't know talk about the time your father brought their children into the world, or saved their child's life?"

She sat again. She sounded bitter. "Would you have me tell Beth? A girl so tired she can't see straight? How about Kate? It takes me forty-five minutes to try and reach her voice mail at that stupid university." She threw her hands in the air. "And I can't tell Gabby because she's disappeared off the face of the earth."

"So I'm the last resort. I'm the loser who doesn't have anything better to do than hear all about it."

Lexie could see the hurt.

Her mother looked down at her lap. "You're the only one I could think of."

Tears fell down Lexie's face. "Mom, do you know how hard this is? I love Daddy. I can't believe he'd do something like this. I can't believe it and I can't bear it." She stopped to grab a tissue out of her pocket and wipe her nose. "A man I cared about walked out on me without a word not long ago. But I always knew there was one man who wouldn't let me down, and that was Dad. And now you tell me he's having an affair? What am I supposed to do about it? How am I supposed to feel?"

Her mother didn't say anything.

Lexie's anger built and she had nowhere to go with it. She grasped at straws. "How do you know this anyway? Maybe some idiot got the wrong idea. You could have it backwards."

"I saw him come out of her house."

"So what? That means nothing. He always wanders in and out of people's houses. He still make a few house calls."

"At four in the morning?"

She couldn't believe this. "You snuck around someone's house at four o'clock in the morning?"

"I'm not proud of it but I had my suspicions and I wanted to know."

"Have you asked him about it?"

"Yes."

"What did he say?"

"He denied it."

"So maybe you're wrong."

The wind out of her sails, she slumped forward, her energy gone. "Oh God, maybe I am."

They were quiet.

Lexie finally asked. "Who is it anyway?"

"Lillian Holmes."

That's when Lexie knew her mother was right.

A FEW YEARS before, Lexie's friend Martha invited her to Halifax for a comedy festival. She was looking forward to it and went over to ask her parents if they'd feed Sophie. They stood around the island in the kitchen and picked at cold cuts and sliced cheese.

Lexie picked up a piece of smoked meat. "This stuff will clog your arteries."

Dad said, "What a way to go."

Her mother laughed. "You better not say that at the conference."

Lexie swallowed. "What conference?"

"A medical conference in Halifax this weekend," Dad informed her.

"You're kidding. I have to go too. Can we drive down together?"

She waited for her dad to say, "Sure Princess…let's ride off into the sunset." But he hesitated. "Actually, I have to take a few colleagues with me. I'm afraid we'd be too crowded."

Mom said, "I didn't know some of the staff were going."

He was vague. "Yeah, it's part of some new orientation."

Mom laughed as she put the leftovers on the same plate. "I'm glad it's you. Imagine having to sit through boring presentations by all those stuffed shirts."

Lexie and Martha spent the day in Halifax window-shopping. They caught up on all their news, and stopped for lunch at a local pub, where they sat at a table out on the terrace. They had a beer and shared a plate of chicken wings under a large umbrella.

That's when Lexie saw her father. He was stopped at the corner across the street waiting for the light to turn green. Lillian Holmes was with him. She was one of the social workers who worked at the hospital. Dad would recommend her to his patients. Lexie liked her: she'd stop Lexie if they ran in to each other to ask how things were. She was interested in hooked rugs, and wondered if Lexie would ever sell her one.

"There's my Dad." Lexie started to wave, but stopped. Lillian looked like a young girl, as she chatted and gestured with her hands. Her face lit up as she threw her head back and laughed. Dad laughed too. He put his arm around her shoulders and pulled her closer. The light turned green and they walked away from Lexie, arm in arm.

"Was that your mom?"

"No, a good friend."

She convinced herself it was too much wine at lunch. After all, this was her father. She enjoyed the comedy festival that night and never thought of it again.

That was around the same time Lexie started to see a psychiatrist after bursting into tears during her yearly check-up with her family doctor.

"Lexie, you're suffering from a little depression."

"Of course I'm not. It's that winter SAD or SAPPY thing I read about in the papers. Not enough sunlight."

Her doctor ignored her. "I'll set up an appointment with Dr. Chow. I'd like his input."

"Dr. Chow? Oh lord, wait till Mom hears this."

"She doesn't have to know."

"You're joking, right? Have you ever known anything to be a secret for more than five minutes in this town?"

"Lexie, you're a grown woman. It matters not a whit whether your mother knows you're seeing a psychiatrist. It's none of her business. It's yours."

After the first awkward sessions, Lexie burst forth like a volcano, but Dr. Chow was calm, the sloth of the medical world. Nothing unnerved him. Which was a good trait to have because when he entered his office, she didn't even let the poor man walk over to his chair before the whole sordid story of the affair came out in a rush. Lexie was furious. At first it was with her dad. By the end of the hour she was livid with her mother.

"Why did she tell me? She knows I adore my father. Why would she hurt me like this?"

"She's hurting too."

"Oh yes, blah, blah, blah," she chimed like a spoiled brat. "If she wasn't so judgmental, he wouldn't be in another woman's arms. She drove him to it."

"Nobody gets driven where they don't want to go. Think about it."

She chewed her nails to the quick thinking about it. It was just crummy having to do it all alone. Her mother dumped this huge burden on her. Why was she was always the packhorse who carried the load?

She wanted to talk to Beth, to see if she knew anything. To sit down at her kitchen table would be deadly. Beth was no dummy. She'd be instantly alert that something was up, and would drag it out of Lexie before her first cup of tea. Lexie didn't know why she was being considerate to this particular sister lately. Normally she and Beth butted heads at every opportunity, but lately she seemed vulnerable. Or maybe it was the talk with Rory.

She offered to go with Beth to buy the girls shoes. This was a monster chore. There's no such thing as one little girl getting new shoes and the others not. She knew that much from past experience.

"Oh God, would you?" Beth sighed. "Rory's hopeless at the mall. He wigs out in the first five minutes. Not that I blame him. I carry the baby. He chases the other three."

"I'll be the chaser." Lexie knew full well her nieces wouldn't run amok. She had candy in her pocket.

They drove the student who worked in the store insane. While she went into the back behind the curtain for the twentieth time, Lexie saw her chance.

"Have you seen Mom lately?" she asked nonchalantly, trying to buckle up three pairs of shoes at the same time.

Beth sighed. "Do you think I have time to run over to Mom's? I can barely get myself dressed in the morning. She never comes over to our house unless it's on the way to her precious club. Just long enough to kiss the girls, but not long enough for them to get their sticky fingers all over her suit."

Beth seemed so fed up Lexie decided it was not the time to ask about Dad. But then Beth roused herself long enough to look at her. "Why do you ask?"

But before she could answer Beth turned her head. "Michaela, get over here now." Michaela slowly dragged herself back from the store entrance. She hated shopping.

Lexie had a brainstorm. "I wondered if she heard from Gabby."

Beth believed her and sat back. "No, I don't think so. She'd obviously tell us. Or tell me anyway. She doesn't want to discuss Adrian with you."

"Why? Because she blames me for bringing him home in the first place? Am I responsible for what happened?"

"Probably."

Lexie couldn't believe she said that.

"I'm only kidding Lex. Of course she doesn't blame you. She worries that you liked him and you'll hate Gabby forever because of what happened."

"Why would I hate her? He meant nothing to me."

Beth looked at her. "I know better."

LEXIE DISMISSED HER sister. Beth knew nothing about what Lexie thought because she didn't know herself. Not really. It was too painful to remember that her heart yearned for Adrian. Their time together seemed very far away.

She spent such a big portion of her life avoiding her own thoughts. She wondered if that's why she kept her hands busy. She poured her emotions into her rugs, knitting, costumes, and paintings. Even the poor walls of her house were coloured with her moods.

She went home that night and opened the trunk at the end of her bed. In it, on top of everything else, was Adrian's sweater. A large cable-knit sweater, the kind fishermen wear to keep from freezing as they haul lobster traps before dawn.

Every vibrant colour she loved was in it. She'd dyed the wool herself, late at night, after he'd gone to bed. The sweater wasn't finished the day he left. She put it in the trunk the night of Mom's phone call and never looked at it again.

Suddenly she knew it didn't matter if she never saw Adrian again. She couldn't leave his sweater hidden away, incomplete and wanting. She needed to finish it, for him. She wanted it near. But she wanted it done.

❧

GABBY LAY ON the bed in the small furnished flat she and Adrian rented in Toronto. She turned over and reached for the alarm clock on the bedside table. It was eleven in the morning. Adrian had been gone for three hours now. She turned the clock around and flipped over on her stomach. She chewed her bottom lip as she hugged her pillow.

It was great in the beginning. They didn't go anywhere because they couldn't stay upright. They spent weeks just being together with no thought of the future. Adrian seemed content with that, so she kept herself busy organizing the finances and making arrangements about her job. She bought Adrian new clothes, since his were almost threadbare.

Whenever she pushed the issue about their inability to galvanize a plan of action, Adrian would suddenly need to go for a walk. Finally, in desperation that morning, she told him the only thing they had to decide was what they'd do with the rest of their lives and where they'd do it.

That's when he disappeared.

She got up from the bed and went to the window. There was no sign of him. She sighed and when she did, she fogged up the pane of glass, so she reached out and traced a heart.

Adrian eventually came home around four o'clock that afternoon. She didn't say anything to him and he didn't offer an explanation. They ordered takeout from a Chinese restaurant down the street and went to bed early. It was only in bed that they seemed to be at ease with each other and during those moments, nothing else in the world mattered. But on this night, Adrian woke up screaming.

Gabby jumped out of deep sleep. Adrian was sitting up in bed, staring at nothing. Sweat poured down his face.

"Darling, are you all right?"

"Lexie. Where's Lexie?"

She tried to comfort him. "She's okay, Adrian. She's fine. Nothing's happened to her."

He was only half awake. "No. I want her. I want her to hold my hand. Please. I need her."

Gabby shuddered.

⁂

LEXIE BARGED THROUGH her mother's back door. "Anyone home?"

She heard the vacuum cleaner as it rhythmically droned above her head. She put her pan of squares on the kitchen table and continued on. She stopped at the bottom of the stairs.

"Mom!" Nothing. "Oh, Mother dear!"

She grabbed the newel post and swung herself back and forth, like she had as a kid. It made her feel better, and it passed the time.

The vacuum cleaner stopped.

"Is that you Lexie?" her mother shouted from what she guessed was the master bedroom.

"Yep. I brought you something."

"Okay, I'll be right down."

Lexie walked back to the kitchen and made a pot of tea. Then she took the low-fat brownies she made that morning and put them on a plate. She set the teapot and cups on the table, and sat and waited for her mother.

They hadn't seen each other for a couple of weeks. Mom must have been embarrassed. She probably got home that night and regretted dropping the mask she so carefully wore. Lexie thought she might be ashamed. But she had no reason to be — she wasn't the one who was cheating. Lexie wanted to tell her that.

Mom walked in the room. Lexie was taken aback. She'd lost weight. She looked older.

"Hi Sweetheart."

"Hi Mom."

"What brings you here today?"

"I was thinking about you. I don't have to be at the library until two. I made brownies this morning. Would you like one?" Lexie poured the hot tea into the china cups.

Her mother looked at the brownies as she sat across from Lexie. "Oh, my. Don't they look decadent? I'm not sure I should. How many calories for one, do you think?"

Lexie's heart sank. With everything else going on in her life, why did she dwell on calories? She wore a size six.

Lexie tried to be patient. "Mom, I think you could probably afford to put on a few pounds. You look a little drawn. Have you lost weight?"

"Oh, who knows. Maybe."

"Mom, you have to look after yourself. You can't fall apart."

Her mother suddenly straightened up in her chair. "What do you mean, fall apart? I don't plan on it. Now or ever."

Lexie reached to cover her mother's hand with her own, but her mother picked up her teacup instead.

"Mom, I know this has been a big shock, so let's figure it out together. We need a plan of action. I'm in your corner, okay?"

"Lexie, what on earth are you talking about?"

She started to lose her patience. "This miserable dilemma you're in. What will you do about it?"

"Do about it? I'm not going to do anything. There's nothing to do."

Lexie thought she'd gone mad. "Did you or did you not tell me about Daddy's affair?"

"Yes. So what."

"*So what?*" She threw her arms in the air and slapped them back down on the table. Her tea spilled over the cup and into the saucer. She was incredulous.

"Yes, Lexie. So what?"

Her mother got up from the table and went to stand by the kitchen sink to look out the large window facing the back of their property, the scene of so many parties and good times. She was still.

Lexie waited.

"Someday you'll know that life is a complicated and difficult journey."

She snorted. "Someday? I know already."

"Yes, of course you do." Mom started again. "I forget you girls are grown. What I mean to say is sometimes we do things that don't make sense to someone else. That's all we can do. We have no choice."

"Mother, you do have a choice. Everyone has a choice. No one gets driven where they don't want to go."

She looked at Lexie and frowned. "What?"

Lexie flicked her wrist in the air. "Oh, nothing. Forget I said that. What exactly are you telling me?"

"I want you to forget what I said the other day."

She groaned, "You've got to be joking."

Her mother didn't answer.

Lexie was suddenly furious. "Now you want me not to know what I know. If you didn't want me to know it, why didn't you go to your minister and spill the beans after choir practice?"

Mom shouted, "I wish to God I had. I'm sorry Lexie. That's why I haven't pestered you on your stupid answering machine for the last two weeks. I feel badly I burdened you with this. I didn't mean it. I had nowhere else to go." She paused. "And I'm not proud of this. I'm not proud at all, but maybe I just wanted you to know your precious father…" She stopped.

"My precious father what?"

She looked at Lexie with tear-filled eyes, but she was angry. "He's a man, an ordinary man. He's not a saint; he's not always the good guy and I'm not always the bad guy. He's your father and I know you adore him. That will never change. He adores you too. He didn't do this to hurt you, he didn't even do it to hurt me. It happened."

She took a deep breath. "But the fact is, I am hurt. I'm ashamed and humiliated. And no doubt everyone in this damn town knows about it. But you know what? I won't give them the satisfaction of knowing how hurt I am. I'm the injured party. I'll hold my head up and let them think I know nothing about it. I refuse to have a screaming match with your father, throw his things on the lawn or run over to Lillian's house and pull her hair."

She stared out the window again. "I'll not leave my wonderful house, my beautiful garden, and the life I've made for myself. If I can't be everything to your father, that's my hurt. But it's a private hurt. It's between a husband and wife."

She gave Lexie a sad smile. "It's not for our children to agonize over. It's not something you should try and fix. It's between two people who loved each other and still do, but not in quite the same way. It's something I have to sort out for myself. It's not meant as fodder for the gossips at the tea and sale."

She suddenly covered her face with her hands.

"Oh Mom." Lexie ran to her and wrapped her arms around her. Her mother pressed her face into her neck. She whispered, "I'm so sorry, Lexie. Please don't tell your sisters."

"I won't."

"What would I do without you? You're my strong one. You're the one I lean on."

"It's okay Mom. I'm right here."

࿐

ADRIAN WALKED IN the rain. He walked so long he had to sit down. While people hurried by with umbrellas and dashed across the street with newspapers held over them, he sat on a wet bench and put his head back. The small droplets seared his flesh. He could hear the hiss as they fell on his skin.

He needed to get to the ocean.

Gabby never asked him where he was going anymore. As the weeks slipped by he realized he'd have to go. He couldn't believe he'd do this to her, but he had no choice.

Gabby thought he was a good man, but he wasn't. He left Binti behind. He had to find her. He had no right to happiness until she was safe.

He had killed her mother after all.

Chapter Six

THE HEAT OF that July was unrelenting. Even the cool Atlantic wind couldn't take the oppression away. There was a haze that lingered over everything. On those endless days of summer, even the water was lazy. It slowly lapped the sand with only enough energy to create a small curl of wave.

It was unseasonably warm even in the early morning, the dew gone before dawn. When Lexie threw open her back screen door and looked out over the cliffs beyond, the water was like glass, a smooth mirror that reflected the new day's sun. In the stillness, she heard the lobster boats as they left the harbour, she listened to the fishermen as they called out to one another. She loved to see them head out for open water, loaded with traps, small against a vast pink horizon.

Lexie would always live by the ocean. How did one breathe otherwise?

LEXIE DRAGGED TO and from work with the enthusiasm of a dishrag.

"I wish it would rain or something," she said to Judy, as they sat in the lunchroom at the back of the library.

Judy nodded but didn't say anything. She picked away at her salad.

Lexie opened her yogurt container. "Even fog would be appreciated. I think I'll go to the beach after work and do my imitation of a beached whale." She thought Judy would laugh but she didn't. Instead, she looked fed up.

"What's wrong?"

Judy said primly, "Since you ask, I'll tell you. You've become almost as annoying as Marlene."

"Marlene?"

"Lexie, I'm old enough to be your mother. I certainly wish I had a daughter like you but I'm tired of hearing you put yourself down all the time. It's as if you want everyone to think you're a big fat failure. Look at me, I've got curly hair, I'm overweight, I don't have a man, oh boo hoo. If you really think that, shut up and deal with it."

Lexie was kicked in the teeth. Mousy Judy just told her off. She was transported back to the principal's office. Not that she'd ever been to the principal's office, but she imagined this was how it felt.

Judy warned, "I'll tell you this once and then never again and I really hope you believe me. Do you know what I see when I look at you?"

Lexie shook her head. She didn't dare say anything.

"I see a beautiful woman, inside and out, who covers herself under big baggy clothes. Who keeps her head down and hides behind her hair. Who has the most beautiful eyes and a complexion to die for, but no one sees that because you won't let them."

She continued to look Lexie straight on.

"So you aren't as small as your sisters. Who cares? You're not even that big. Marilyn Monroe was a size sixteen you know. Just because fashion models look like bony clothes hangers doesn't mean you should. Be proud of yourself. And for heaven's sake, put on a pair of jeans and tuck in your shirt. Marlene was right about one thing. I'm sick to death of those tablecloths you wear."

What could she say?

Judy patted her hand on the way out. Why did everyone do that?

AFTER A FEW weeks of pretending she still liked Judy, it became too much. Lexie knew Judy's heart was in the right place and she was probably right, but the only thing Lexie could remember was that she wore tablecloths to work and was as annoying as Marlene.

Lexie called Kate. Mom was right. It took two days of playing phone tag before she heard her in person.

"Hi Lexie, is anything wrong?"

The heat got to her. "Aren't I allowed to call you just for the sake of calling?"

"Calm down. Of course you can call me. But it's not Sunday. Is everything all right?"

Silence.

"Are you there?"

"I'm sick to death of crying all the time. I'm always crying. I'm boring myself sick with crying. And I don't even know why I'm crying. Because —"

Kate cut her off. "Lexie, why don't you come and stay with me for a while?"

Lexie cried.

SHE TOLD THEM at the library she wanted a leave of absence. It went very smoothly, which surprised her. Then it occurred to her that as administrator, Judy had the final word as to whether she could go or not. That was kind.

Lexie arranged for Sophie to be with her mother while she was away. She fully expected the poor cat to be ten pounds thinner by the time she got back. She wondered if Sophie knew it too, because she clung for dear life when Lexie dropped her off. But even pathetic mews couldn't keep Lexie from going. Kate and Daphne had an old farmhouse off St. Margarets Bay, a prime piece of property on the water that belonged to Daphne's family, and Lexie couldn't wait to see it.

So she closed up her much-loved house. She needed to get away but was wistful as she backed out of her driveway. She'd only be gone for a month or so, but the house looked like it missed her already. It didn't help that it was a drizzly day. It was as if her garden wept, upset that she was leaving.

As she crossed the Seal Island bridge and started up Kellys Mountain, the fog drifted in and circled around the dark evergreen trees like second-hand smoke in a bar. The sky and surrounding lochs became the colour of bleached driftwood and old lobster traps.

When she glanced at the dense cover of fir trees, Lexie thought of "Hansel and Gretel." On dreary, heavy days like this, it seemed well within the realm of possibility that a witch did lurk deep within those woods.

Lexie was always a little lost when she ventured over the Causeway. Her heart stayed behind, but after one long look back, she stepped on the gas and ventured forth.

KATE AND DAPHNE greeted Lexie with open arms when she hopped out of the van. She was sticky from the heat. The temperature rose with each passing mile, and since poor old Betsy didn't have air conditioning, Lexie looked like a boiled lobster.

"Oh, my God," Kate shouted as she hugged her. "You're soaking wet!"

"And look at my hair!" She felt like Bozo the clown.

Daphne laughed. "There's only one remedy. Bomb's away!" The two of them ran around the house so Lexie ran too. They scurried out onto the wooden dock at the back of their property, and did side-by-side cannonballs into the water with their clothes on.

Lexie was a kid again. She tore up the deck and threw herself into the ice-cold water. She created a huge splash. The world disappeared into a million muffled bubbles. She saw the girls' legs as they kicked underwater. It was heavenly. She didn't want to surface. She wanted to stay under water where it was dark and lovely and cold, wanted to leave the bright hot sun and remain hidden.

She held her breath for as long as she could, then popped up and joined the other two. They looked like otters, sleek and round as they bobbed in the water. They laughed as their clothes floated to the surface around them. They gathered the saltwater underneath their T-shirts and made it look like they had big boobs.

At least, they did. Lexie had on her tablecloth and nearly drowned in a sea of cotton. She resolved to take Judy's advice and buy herself a pair of shorts.

They spent the rest of the evening in the bathrobes they threw on after their dip. The deck overlooked the water.

Lexie sat in a comfy Adirondack chair with her feet up and drank cold beer while the steaks grilled. They had a glorious meal outdoors and after a bit, Kate went in the house to retrieve a bottle of ice wine and served it with dessert.

Daphne dug into her raspberries and cream. "So how's the library business?"

"The books are great."

Kate passed Lexie a bowl of raspberries too. "That's it?"

"That's it."

Kate looked at her sideways. "Do you plan on being upset about Gabby and Adrian forever?"

"Maybe."

"Lexie, you have to move on. You can't mope about some guy until you're old and grey. Why don't you try to find someone else?"

Daphne spoke up. "I know. We'll have a party and invite a few friends over. My brother has some nice-looking chaps on his baseball team."

"I hate men."

"We have some nice-looking girls in our bridge club. Will they do?"

"Sounds like a plan."

They stayed out and talked under the stars until late in the evening. Lexie wasn't there to tell Kate about Mom and Dad. She'd keep Mom's secret to the grave. The fact that she knew something that the others didn't made her feel close to her mother. She didn't need to share it anymore.

But Lexie was sad and disillusioned. She felt adrift. She wanted someone to take care of her.

Lexie woke up the next morning and didn't know where she was. Then her head started to pound. She groaned and turned over on her stomach. A hangover. She hadn't had one of those in a very long time, but was worth it. It was just what she needed.

She lay on the narrow, wrought-iron bed for a long time. It was painted white. Everything in the room was in shades of white, sand, or cream. It was beautiful. The wainscoting went up to the bottom of the window and the ledge it created held many treasures, shells and smooth, coloured glass Kate found beachcombing.

A gauze curtain blew in the morning breeze. Lexie had left the window open all night and listened to the crickets as she fell asleep.

She thought of nothing. She wanted to think of nothing. She listened to Kate and Daphne as they woke up and moved around. It was Sunday morning. There was no hurry to leave to this heavenly house and venture into the city.

It was odd to be in a clean, white room, so uncluttered and serene. Kate must be very happy. The room reflected peace. It felt smooth.

Lexie lay there and thought of her bedroom and all the rooms in her house. They were chaotic compared to this, a jumble of colour and lights. Wicker baskets that hung or heaved under the weight of material or wool, paintbrushes and sketchbooks. She had herbs and flowers from the garden drying on every windowsill. And candles. Adrian had been right about that. She didn't know how she hadn't burnt the house down.

She needed to get rid of the clutter, all the unwanted stuff. But it wasn't just her house she wanted to do over. It was her, everything about her.

Judy's message came through loud and clear, and Lexie didn't feel upset with her anymore. She meant no malice, was only trying to help. And Lexie never let anyone help her. It was time she started.

She realized she was more like her mother then she thought. She put up such a wall she was rigid. Lexie wanted to let people in. She wanted to stop being afraid. If no one in her life wanted to love her, she had to accept it. But it didn't mean she couldn't learn to love herself.

After a very hot shower and two painkillers, Lexie moseyed downstairs in her bare feet. The hardwood floors gleamed. There were big white overstuffed sofas everywhere and colourful art on the walls. A huge stone fireplace stood in the middle of the room. It looked like a scene from a magazine.

Something caught her eye.

There on the floor in front of the fire was the hooked rug she had made for Kate last Christmas. It was a primitive piece, a scene with water and birds and wildflowers. It looked so nice against the blond wood, colourful and free.

She'd never thought of her rugs as anything more than doodling with strips of wool. She'd never seen them except amid a hundred other items on her floors at home. It surprised her how beautiful it looked alone on the floor. Lexie was pleased.

She stepped into the kitchen. Daphne sat at the table and read the paper as she drank a cup of coffee. "I didn't know you guys had my rug in your living room."

Kate was by the stove. She raised the coffee pot and lifted her eyebrows as a signal that meant "do you want some coffee?" Lexie nodded her head.

"Oh please," Daphne muttered when she finished chewing a huge bite of blueberry muffin. "Do you know how many times we could have sold that thing?"

"Really?" Her sister handed her a cup of coffee. "Thank you."

Kate agreed. "Oh yeah. I have to beat people away with a stick. I was offered two thousand dollars for it."

Lexie spit out her coffee. "Are you serious?"

"It's true."

She mused into her cup. "Well, well, well. I had no idea."

Daphne put down her paper. "If I were you, I'd get myself a webpage and take orders over the Internet. The whole world would knock at your door in a matter of hours. You'd make a fortune."

Kate laughed. "She'd have to get a computer first."

Daphne gave Lexie a look like she had two heads.

"I'm sorry. I don't have one. They annoy me enough at work. I never had a desire to own one. Not that I could afford it anyway."

"Well darling, whip up a rug while you're here. We'll sell it by Friday and you can buy one when you get back!"

They giggled and stuffed themselves silly on muffins and homemade jam.

Daphne was thoughtful enough to make up the excuse that her mother desperately needed her for the afternoon. She kissed the air and blew it in their direction.

The sisters sat on either side of the fireplace, the magnificent rug between them. The couch swallowed Lexie up in a soft envelope.

"How lucky you are, Kate, to find someone who's so good to you."

"I know. I count my blessings every day."

Lexie gave a big sigh.

Kate put down her coffee cup. "I know you look at me and think I have everything. But my life hasn't been easy. No one's is. Especially when you grow up gay in a small town and you live in fear someone will find out and then the whole town will know. It also wasn't easy being the wonderful doctor's daughter. We all had to deal with that."

She stared at Lexie's rug. "I never wanted to embarrass Daddy or have Mom try and explain my lifestyle to one of her awful women's groups. I was frightened most of the time. I think Daddy knows, but it's not an issue with him. You know Dad. He loves us no matter what."

"What about Mom?"

"My heart tells me she does know. But she's never asked me. It's crazy. But it made my life easier, so I didn't rock the boat. Now that I'm older, I think it makes things worse. I never know where I stand."

She looked at her thumbnail as if she'd never seen it before. "I can't figure out why she's so uninterested in me. She's always after you about diets and exercise. She harangues you endlessly to look better and tries to make you like Gabby and Beth. God, you are so much more than that. " She leaned her head against her knuckles and propped herself up as if she were weary. "I feel guilty when she leaves me alone."

"Why?"

"Because she wears you out. It's not fair."

"I know." Lexie stared at her rug too. "I always feel wrong somehow, like I should just try harder or something. Even when Dad tells me not to change a thing, it makes no difference. Why aren't mothers aware of the power they wield?"

"Well, for what it's worth, if I'd been born first and you'd been born last, I don't think we'd have this conversation."

Lexie grinned. "Is that all it comes down to? You get off scot-free because she's worn out yelling at me? You owe me, baby sister."

"Too bad. Want a swim?"

"Okay."

Kate chuckled as she ran towards the sliding doors. "We have to go in our birthday suits. Mr. Henderson needs his daily eyeful."

Lexie laughed. "Well, he'll get more then he bargained for today." The two of them threw off their robes, and pounded up the dock with their stark white backsides in full view of Mr. Henderson's binoculars. They shouted, "Geronimo," before they took flight for a brief moment and then hit the water with a satisfying smack and a whoosh of white foam.

LEXIE HAD THE happiest weeks of her life. She told the girls at dinner that she needed their help. She wanted to make some changes, a complete makeover. Where should she get her clothes? Where should she have her hair cut? They buzzed with excitement and promised to do their best.

Lexie was on a limited budget. They handed her their gold Visa card and told her to go nuts. She knew she'd never do that, but was touched by the gesture all the same.

On the first day downtown, after they dropped her off on the way to work, Lexie found a stash of bills shoved in her jacket pocket. Never look a gift horse in the mouth. She spent it all.

Over those glorious days, she forgot everything and everyone. She had fun. She'd forgotten how.

Kate met with her between classes to take Lexie to her favourite hair salon. Lexie was nervous. She sat in the chair and looked at Kate in the mirror for moral support. Kate gave her a thumbs up but spent most of her time immersed in a rag that claimed Elvis was seen flying over Texas.

Lexie didn't know what to say when Troy, who had the most perfect eyebrows she'd ever seen, asked her what colour she had in mind. She panicked, so Kate came over and patted his shoulder. "Don't ask her. Give her the works. Money's no object."

"Well then!" he squealed. "Let the games begin."

One of his minions washed her hair and when she returned to the chair, Troy approached her with a critical eye. He lifted the ends of her hair and shook his head. He gave her a small look of disgust.

"Darling. When did you last cut your hair? The seventies?"

"That's about right."

Troy gave his scissors a few practice squeezes. He rolled his neck to get the kinks out.

"Come to Mama."

When he turned her around two hours later, Lexie couldn't speak. Her hair was beautiful. Kate burst into tears.

Troy had taken ten inches off. Suddenly, without all that dead weight, curls fell in soft waves around Lexie's face. It was chin-length and as she pulled her fingers through her scalp, it felt light and bouncy. It shone with highlights or something. She didn't care what it was or how he did it. She gave good old Troy a big tip and smacked him right on the kisser.

Lexie shopped till she dropped. She went into one store where a stylish older woman manned the fort. She swallowed her pride, and asked if she could please tell her how to dress when you're on the plus size side. The woman's eyes lit up.

"Come right this way."

Lexie followed her to the back of the store.

She turned around and held out her hand. "I'm Grace, by the way."

Lexie reached over and shook it. "I sure hope you can help me, Grace. I'm a bit of a greenhorn when it comes to fashion."

"Well, I enjoy breaking in novices. And you'll see. By the time you walk out of here, you'll be slave to fashion."

Lexie set up camp in the dressing room. Grace said the first thing they had to tackle were "foundation garments."

"The fastest way to look like you've lost ten pounds is to buy a very good bra. Don't be afraid of the price. They're worth it." She passed her one.

She gaped at the price tag. "Sixty dollars! Are you crazy?"

Grace put her finger on her nose and tapped it. She mouthed, "Trust me."

Lexie bought three. They lifted and separated exactly as promised. Why wasn't this headline news for women everywhere? Stupid rich women kept it to themselves, that's why.

Lexie loved her new jeans. She loved everything. She was so grateful to this woman and told her she'd never forget her.

"That's sweet of you dear, but I really must go on my break." She reached down and rubbed her calf. "I think my ankles are swollen."

Lexie left the store uplifted, lifted and separated.

Two days later it was off to the makeup counter at a ritzy department store. She never wore makeup. She wasn't sure this stop was for her, but Kate had convinced her.

"Lexie, this is the nineties. They have makeup that makes you look like you're not wearing any."

"Then why would I want it?"

"For the same reason we bought you those silky underthings. You know you're wearing it even if everyone else doesn't. And it's pretty."

So Lexie threw herself at the mercy of the drop-dead-gorgeous young thing behind the counter who commented on Lexie's skin several times. Lexie started to believe maybe her skin was nice.

The clerk sent her home with the whole kit and caboodle. She'd never use it all in a lifetime but it was nice to have.

When she finally had everything, Lexie drove back to Kate's and let herself in. The place was quiet. The girls weren't due home until later that evening, so she went to her bedroom and shut the door. Lexie spread her new things out on the bed and looked at them. She had even bought a few pieces of jewellery. And a large carryall to take everything home in.

She got into the shower, washed her hair, and shook it dry. She put on her new jeans and a crisp white cotton shirt. She did her makeup, sprayed herself with perfume, put on her new amber ring and chunky bracelet, and finally slid her feet into soft leather sandals. She went into her sister's bedroom and looked in the full-length mirror.

Lexie blinked.

She reached out and touched her face in the mirror. "Is that you?"

Chapter Seven

TO SAY SHE caused a sensation was an understatement. She walked into her parents' house to collect Sophie. Beth and Rory's van was outside which meant they were over for Sunday dinner.

"Howdy, I'm home!"

"Hi honey, we're in here," her father shouted. Lexie heard squeals of delight from the girls. They stampeded out to greet her. She heard Rory say, "Girls, girls, let Auntie get in the door."

That didn't stop them. They barrelled around the corner whooping for joy, then bumped into each other as Michaela, who saw Lexie first, stopped dead in her tracks. They stood with their mouths open. Halley looked frightened.

"It's ok, honey, it's me."

Halley looked unsure. They still didn't move.

The silence was deafening.

"What's going on?" Beth shouted. She came in and as soon as she saw Lexie, her hand flew in front of her mouth.

"Oh my god, I don't believe it. Guys, come here quick!" She hopped up and down.

Lexie heard chairs being pushed back from the table in a hurry. Everyone rushed into the doorway.

"Lexie!" her mother cried. Then she hopped up and down.

As if on cue, her nieces jumped all over her.

LEXIE WAS JAZZED by her homecoming. She was inspired with energy. She still had some time before she went back to work so she got busy. She went through the house like a whirling dervish. If it wasn't nailed down, she threw it in a garbage bag, a box for goodwill, or a new storage container.

She threw out the dried flower arrangements and herbs that had hung from the ceiling for years. She washed the walls and considered repainting them, but decided to leave them. But she knew she would do something she should've done years ago. She ripped up the old carpets, revealing beautiful hardwood underneath. It would require an enormous effort to sand them, so she enlisted the help of her fellow actors, promising them a free supply of beer and pizza.

But it bugged her that every time she looked up someone was staring at her.

"*What*?" she yelled at Susan.

"I can't believe what a difference a haircut makes."

"I must have looked like the bride of Frankenstein my whole life."

Donalda said, "You did."

"Thank you Donalda. I love you too."

"Calm down. Even I think there's been an improvement."

"Gee whiz, it's not like I had a facelift. I still can't get this damn weight off. I haven't changed that much."

Susan mulled it over. "I'm not sure what it is. You're brighter I guess. I can see your face."

"You sound like my mother. She walks around like a big

know-it-all. 'I told you so. You should have done it years ago, blah blah.'"

Susan laughed. "Oh, shut up and get over yourself. You're not Julia Roberts or anything."

"You're not even her understudy," Donalda chimed in.

Lexie threw a rag at them.

When the work was done Lexie stood back and looked. Her little house was a thing of beauty. It was still full of old and tattered furniture, and it looked too clean for her liking, but that would be easily remedied. It was the floors she couldn't get over, how her rugs looked on them, and the walls on which she hung her paintings, instead of stacking them in a corner. She still had pillows around — there were Sophie's feelings to consider — but she marvelled at the transformation.

These things were here all along. They'd been hidden under endless junk.

Wow, Lexie, who knew?

She really looked forward to returning to work, and made sure she looked pretty good when she went out the door her first morning back. It was childish, but she wanted to rub Marlene's nose in it.

She sashayed in at ten to nine. She got the reaction she hoped for. Judy beamed at her all morning. Marlene was due at noon. When she walked in, she said, "You look nice," and continued with her work.

That was it. Lexie was so mad. Marlene had done it again. She managed to make her feel like two cents. She had to get over the horrible habit of always wondering what other people thought of her. If the truth were told, she probably never crossed their minds when she wasn't in their line of vision. The only person she lived with was herself. She was the person she had to please, not the Marlenes of the world. She needed to grow up.

BY FALL LEXIE was back in her normal routine. She dated a couple of guys that were all right, but nothing special. She even took one of them home after too much beer one night. It felt like a chore. She said goodbye in the morning and never answered the phone when he called.

They worked on a new play. Lexie said she'd make the costumes. A crowd of them would go out after rehearsal. It was jolly but she went home alone.

Her days and nights were full. But she waited. Something was there and it would come. She felt it in the wind. She didn't know what and she didn't know when, but it haunted her.

❦

WHEN ADRIAN LEFT her, Gabby stayed in bed for a week. She was devastated. She didn't understand what happened. He said he loved her but he had to go. He wasn't good enough for her.

She was desperate. "What do you mean? I don't understand. If you loved me you wouldn't leave me."

Adrian couldn't look at her. "I'm not who you think I am."

She had nothing to lose. "You love Lexie, don't you?"

He didn't say anything.

"That's it, isn't it? Neither one of you told me. You should have told me. I never would have hurt Lexie like that if I'd known. What kind of woman do you think I am?"

"The kind of woman who deserves a man who doesn't leave everyone he loves behind, who is so selfish, he thinks only of his own pleasure. I do love you Gabby, but I can't be here. It's not right. We've hurt too many people. I have to stop hurting people."

Adrian put his face in his hands and cried then.

When she woke in the morning, he was gone.

Then one day she got out of bed, took a shower, and walked into her boss's office and asked for a posting overseas. She needed to be as far away as possible from her big sister.

ONE MONDAY MORNING Beth asked Lexie to come over for lunch. Lexie baked cookies for the kids and brought over the doll clothes she'd made for their Barbies.

The girls greeted her with their usual enthusiasm. It gave Lexie a lift when she hugged their sweet bodies against her. They scurried up the stairs to play with the new clothes. Most of the dolls had their hair hacked off and felt marker scribbled over them, so Lexie didn't hold out much hope their looks would be improved by a new outfit.

Beth unwrapped the tuna sandwiches she'd made earlier. They talked for a while about nothing. Then Lexie got the feeling Beth hadn't invited her over for just this. She reached for another cookie. "Are you all right? You look a little pale."

The dam broke. Beth wept.

She grabbed her hand and shook it to get Beth to look at her. "Honey, what is it?"

"I'm pregnant!"

"Well, that's wonderful."

Beth wiped her eyes. "Lexie, you are so stupid. Do you think I'm happy about it? Do you think I need another little girl running around? I can hardly cope with the ones I've got."

"Maybe it won't be a girl."

"Oh, give it up. Of course it's a girl."

"Well, there's not much you can do about it now."

"No."

Lexie looked at her. "Is there?"

"Of course not. Don't be crazy. I'd never do that. I just don't know if I can go through it again. I have so little energy as it is."

"Yes, there is that," Lexie admitted. "Is Rory happy?"

"Of course he is. He gets the prize. I get to do the work."

"Beth, I hate to be mean, but if you didn't want any more, there are ways to prevent it."

She gave Lexie a look. "Gosh, Lex. Really? I had no idea. Please, fill me in."

"Well, it's true."

Beth folded her arms on the table and put her head down. She was miserable. "He looks at me and I'm pregnant."

Lexie didn't say anything. There wasn't much to say.

Her sister sat up and sighed. "I love him so much."

"He loves you too, you fortunate girl."

NONE OF THEM thought Beth would get married and have a brood of infants. She was too busy being mean to all the boys in town. Tiny and blonde with cornflower blue eyes, she was almost as gorgeous as Gabby, and never lacked for male company. If she liked someone, she let him chase her all over town. The minute he caught her, she dumped him like yesterday's news.

Lexie knew Rory would lasso her. Beth saw him on the soccer field in her final year at school, and that was it. Rory was your typical jock type, tall, dark, and handsome, the sort that never looked at Lexie. His family moved into town and all the girls were in a tizzy. Beth was a cheerleader, of course. She went through her whole bag of tricks to capture his attention. He completely ignored her. That got up her nose.

The more he snubbed her, the more she wanted him. He knew exactly how to play her. Lexie realized it the day she heard Beth casually mention she didn't have a date for the prom. Rory winked at Lexie and never said a word. Beth tried everything. She turned herself inside out. He pretended not to notice. When Beth overheard him say he might take her mortal enemy Jane Townsend to the prom, it was a hellish evening in the Ivy household.

Even Lexie started to feel sorry for her. She decided to tag along with Beth to Rory's soccer games, with the intention of taking him aside and saying enough was enough. But she didn't have to. Before the game started, he jogged over to the bleachers, smiled at Beth, and with everyone listening said, "So will you come with me?"

She crossed her arms and turned away. "I wouldn't go anywhere with you."

He grinned at Lexie. "Well, that's too bad Beth, since I'm the one taking you everywhere from now on."

Beth jumped up and into his arms.

The coach hollered at them and told Rory to stop necking and get his ass on the field.

SUSIE CAME OVER one weekend with four videos. She and Lexie had their own chick flick festival. They watched *Jane Eyre*, *An Affair to Remember*, *Roman Holiday*, and *Romeo and Juliet*.

They sighed at each other when the final credits of the last movie rolled.

Susan said, "We're pathetic."

"That I know."

Susie put her chin in her hand and leaned against the arm of the sofa. "We sit here and watch other people have love affairs. When's it our turn?"

Lexie licked butter off the bottom of the popcorn bowl. "Someone will find you, Susie. You're too nice to be alone for the rest of your life."

"How the heck are they going to find me in that stupid dungeon I work in? Even the mailman can't find our office in that old building. And believe me, young single guys don't usually come waltzing in to have their wills done. If someone doesn't find me soon, I'll be too old to have kids."

"You're not that old."

Susie frowned. "I hate to tell ya, kid, but we're friggin' old."

Lexie put the bowl down and sucked each fingertip clean. "You're a barrel of laughs tonight, aren't you?"

Susie pointed the remote to rewind the tape. "There's nothing else to do."

"Wait. Let's be rebels and not rewind."

"We can't do that. Lester will have to if we don't."

"You know something. We'll never have exciting lives if we can't even leave a video tape unwound."

"God. You're right." Susan stopped.

They looked at the blank television. Neither one of them said anything. Finally Lexie couldn't stand it. She grabbed the remote. "Jesus. Give it to me."

She pressed rewind.

ONE AFTERNOON LEXIE was in the back garden, pulling out the weeds and brambles that choked her flowers. She wanted to establish a little order to the overgrown mess, and come spring, plant a few bushes and shrubs. She loved a wild garden, but it didn't have to look like a jungle.

It was a beautiful day. Warm for October and sunny enough that she wore her old straw hat. She still had baggy smocks for mucking in the dirt.

She looked up. Her father stood by the gate.

"Hi Dad."

She hadn't seen much of her father since she'd come back from Kate's. She told herself it was because she was busy with the house, but she knew in her heart that wasn't it. She didn't know how to act around him, so she stayed away.

"Hi Princess. It's amazing. You look like my mother, kneeling there."

"Really?" This pleased her.

He sat down beside her on one of the old wooden chairs that looked out over the field. He didn't say anything. He listened to the water beyond the cliff, forever moving.

"You were named after her."

Lexie threw her head up. "*What?* I can't believe it. No one told me that."

Now he was surprised. "Oh, I'm sure I did. Or your mother did at some point." He looked puzzled.

"No Dad. Believe me, I'd remember. You always said my mother or your grandmother. I can't believe I never asked what her name was." This revelation shocked her.

"I wish she'd been alive to see you come into the world. She'd be so pleased to know she had a namesake."

"Her name was Lexie?"

"Her name was Alexis, but she was happiest when Dad called her Lexie."

She sat and looked out over the ocean. Her father started to talk.

"My father was a hard man. He had to be. He was a coal miner. That's a job only the strong survive. But it's a life that wears you down."

Dad fingered the brim of his hat. "It took its toll. He liked his drink, and he was difficult to live with when he drank. My mother tried to hide it, but we knew. That's why Sally never married. And why I never wanted to be like my father. I never wanted to hurt my family."

Lexie stayed quiet. He stared ahead as if she wasn't there. "There was one day I remember. He came home and shouted, 'Lexie. Lexie. Come dance with me darling.'" He grabbed her by the apron strings, picked her up, and twirled her in the air. He danced her all around the kitchen. She laughed and laughed."

He stopped talking, as if to keep the memory for as long as he could.

"Was she nice, Dad?"

He looked down at her on the grass. "She was as wonderful as you are."

"Oh, Dad."

She leaned against his knee. He stroked her hair.

🙢

WILLIAM RORY MCPHERSON was born the next spring. No baby was more loved or more welcomed than this little boy. His mother and father adored him. His sisters kissed him over and over. His grandfather William was beside himself, a little boy after four daughters and four granddaughters. They passed him around like a special gift from one pair of loving arms to the next. They were in love with this tiny scrap of humanity who had his mother's blue eyes and his father's nose.

And then he died. At two months of age, in his little crib, in the house with the people who loved him so much.

When Lexie lay awake in the middle of the night, she could still hear Beth screaming.

THEY TRIED TO help but for a long time they were frozen. Stiff. Like someone coming out of a coma, everything was heavy and hard to do.

Mom amazed Lexie. She threw her shoulders back and waded into the job of helping her granddaughters cope with the loss of their baby doll Willie. Kate came home and helped too.

Dad had a hard time in his office with patients who gave

him their condolences one after the other. Lexie found him one day in his study weeping. He looked broken and old. She closed the door quietly and let him be.

Rory coped with the loss of his son the only way he knew how. He kept busy. His colleagues at work knew he didn't do anything, but he needed the routine to keep him sane. They covered for him.

Then he started to split firewood in the backyard. He'd smack the axe as hard as he could and grunt with the effort of it. He tried to kill the heartbreak that tortured him.

Somehow it was left to Lexie to try and help Beth. But there was no consoling her. Beth scared Lexie. She had dead eyes. She looked through people. She answered them sometimes but not often. She cried and cried until she should have had to stop, but she couldn't. She'd go to Willie's room and lean into his crib. She'd rub the sheets, the sheets she wouldn't let them wash because they had his baby smell. She sorted his clothes, folded and refolded small, soft sweaters. She sat in the rocking chair and cradled the stuffed bear Dad gave him.

She wandered as if she had no direction, no compass to guide her. She went to Willie's grave and sat with him hour after hour. Lexie offered to plant flowers. Beth looked at Lexie with her big dead eyes. No, she couldn't do that. She was afraid. Afraid she wouldn't stop and dig him up so she could take him home.

Everyone at the library was nice to Lexie. Even Marlene, who brought her coffee. She saw people as they whispered and nodded in her direction. They felt sorry for her family.

They said so as they checked their books out. She'd thank them and continue pretending to read.

One horrible drizzly day after work, she stopped in at Beth's. The place was quiet. Mom and Kate had taken the girls to McDonalds. Rory wasn't home. His brother invited him to go fishing, an excuse to sit together and share their sorrow.

The house was in darkness. It felt cold and dreary. Empty.

She called to Beth. There was no answer. She wasn't in the kitchen. Lexie walked to the living room and turned on a lamp.

Beth was at the window, her hands and forehead pressed against the glass.

"Beth dear, what are you doing?"

She didn't speak.

"Beth?"

"How can I do this Lexie? How can I stand here and leave my baby in the rain?"

Lexie couldn't breathe. She went over and put her arms around her sister. "Please dear, let me run you a bath. You can put on your nightgown. I'll make you some hot chocolate. I'll sit with you until you fall asleep. Please. Please Beth. Do it for me."

"Okay," she said, like a little child.

Lexie took her sister upstairs by the hand. She sat Beth on the bed while she filled the tub with lavender water. She helped her undress and eased her into it.

"I'll be right back."

She ran downstairs and put the kettle on and then ran back upstairs to make the bed with fresh linen. Lexie needed to run. She didn't want to stop. She tidied the room, and put a new box of Kleenex on the bedside table.

She went back to the kitchen and made a big mug of hot chocolate and cinnamon toast, and carried everything up on a tray to put beside the bed.

She went into the bathroom. Beth was exactly as she left her, so Lexie knelt down and softly wiped her face. She poured water over her hair and washed it as if Beth were a toddler in the tub. She put bath gel on a sponge and rubbed her back. She told her she wouldn't leave her.

"It's okay, Beth. I'm right here."

Lexie got her out and wrapped her in big fluffy towels. She put on her pyjamas and made Beth get into bed, then tucked up the blankets around her.

When Lexie held the mug of chocolate to Beth's lips, Beth drank a little. She even ate a few bites of toast. Lexie dimmed the light and pulled a chair over by the bed so she could sit and hold Beth's hand.

Beth never closed her eyes. She looked far away. If only Lexie could take this from her. If only she could do something.

Tears oozed down Beth's face. "Lexie," she whispered.

"What sweetheart?"

"Why did he die? Why didn't he just live? What difference would it make if he'd just lived? In the whole big scheme of things, why couldn't he stay here with me and his daddy and his sisters? Why did he have to go and not be with us?"

Lexie cried. "I don't know, Beth. I don't know."

"He didn't live long enough to use up a bar of Ivory soap."

Lexie thought she'd crack in two.

TWO MONTHS LATER the girls found a stray kitten in their backyard. They ran in and offered the dear little thing to their Mommy to try and make her happy.

"Can we call him Willie?" Halley asked.

"No dear, we can't call him Willie, but we can pick a nice name."

Elmo became a cherished member of the family. They found out too late he was a she, but Elmo didn't mind. She always purred the loudest while being rocked in Beth's arms.

❧

LEXIE HELPED HER mother put the groceries away. The doorbell rang and Mom went to answer it. She talked to someone, then walked back into the kitchen with the most glorious arrangement of flowers. They must have cost a small fortune.

"Look at these."

"My God, I've never seen anything so beautiful. Who are they from?"

Mom put the flowers down and stared at the card, then put it in her pocket.

"A secret admirer?"

"It's for all of us, actually. From Gabby."

Lexie didn't move.

"When did you get a hold of her?"

Mom averted her eyes. "Only a few days ago. She was in

Japan. That's why we couldn't get in touch with her about Willie."

"This is the nineties, Mother. They invented the cellphone long ago."

"Even in today's world, Lexie, if someone doesn't want to be found, they won't be."

"Well. Isn't she clever? How convenient for her to have the time of her life while we're in a prison of complete and utter horror."

She had to sit. She was weary, with everything and everyone.

"I know this is hard for you dear. It's hard for all of us. Gabby couldn't know this happened. She didn't even know he was born. She didn't do it on purpose."

"She didn't? She gets away with everything. She always runs away. She never has to deal with anything, unless it's something she wants for herself."

Mom spoke up in her best teacher voice. "Listen to me. You have the satisfaction of knowing you helped Beth during the worst moments of her life. Gabby will never have that privilege and she will be the poorer for it."

"Really?"

"Really. You have a heart of gold Lexie. I'm proud of you and Kate for being so kind to your sister. Beth never would have come through this horrible tragedy without our help. If you must know I feel sorry for Gabby."

"Sorry? Isn't she doing exactly what she wants? She and Adrian together in bloody Japan, no doubt drunk on their own pleasure."

Her mother watched her very carefully as she spoke. "Adrian and Gabby are no longer together."

Oh God. The news took a moment to sink in.

"Did you know this all along? Have you been in touch with her since the beginning?"

"No. She told me when I called about the baby. When she finally answered the phone."

Lexie tried to get her head around it. "Then why hasn't she come home?"

"She's afraid of you."

Lexie lit a fire when she got home. She put on some music and opened a big bottle of wine. She and Sophie sat together and sulked. She finished the bottle in no time.

She had to face the nasty realization that Adrian didn't come back because he was in love with Gabby. He just didn't come back because of her. All this time, she thought he was a snake for leaving with her sister, and then it turns out he did the same thing to her. Or maybe she left him. It wouldn't surprise her — she did it all the time.

What a sucker I was. Maybe that was his shtick. That's how he got around. He charmed the birds out of the trees for poor pathetic fat girls and when he got a little bored with that, he charmed the pants off poor pathetic cute ones. That was it. That was really it. She had to stop brooding about a guy she hardly knew. She had to stop pretending that maybe he'd come back, telling everyone she didn't care if he came back, but all the while dreaming maybe he would. She had to get on with her life. She didn't cry. She'd cried enough to last a lifetime. She got mad.

IN LATE SEPTEMBER Susan asked her to go to the Highlands and see the fall colours. A group of friends were headed up for a week's stay at a campsite with cabins. There would be fiddles, Celtic music, food, and lots of liquor.

Lexie wanted to go badly. She needed to get away from the heartache. But she felt guilty. How could she have a good time when she knew Beth was so sad? She told Susan she better not. Susan was disappointed, mostly for her, but she understood. Lexie mentioned the trip to her mother, who told her to go, but she still didn't feel right about it.

The next night, Beth knocked on her door.

"Hey kiddo! Come on in."

It was the first time Beth had been over since the baby died. Lexie took her coat. She sat by the fire while Lexie made the tea. She handed Beth a mug, then took her own and sat in the armchair.

Lexie looked at her. The girl she grew up with was gone. She lived with a sadness that would never leave her. She knew a place Lexie had never been.

Beth got to the point.

"Mom called me. You've been invited to go away for a week."

"That woman! I didn't want her to tell you."

"I'm glad she did."

"Beth, I can't go. I wouldn't have a good time. The girls might need me. You might need me."

"Lexie, I'd never have made it without you. I love you. But I want you to know something."

She nodded.

"When your child dies and you live to tell about it, nothing matters except the important things. The rest is bullshit. Life and death, that's all there is."

Lexie kept quiet.

"I won't waste my time being nice. I've no energy for social graces. It sounds mean but I've had it with people who are sad all the time. Sad people surround me. They think that's what I want. I feel lousy everyone secretly hates to have me show up, because then they have to stop being happy."

Lexie couldn't look at her.

"I know you feel badly for me. But I don't want you to stop living your life. It makes me feel guilty. This is my journey. This is what my life is. It's not yours. You'll never be as sad as I am, because you weren't his mother."

She looked into the fire. "Someone asked me the other day, would I rather he'd never been born, than to suffer through his death like this. You know what I said?"

Lexie shook her head.

"Some people live their whole life and never have love. Willie was adored by all of us. He was loved every second of his life and if ten weeks had to be his lifetime, I'm so glad I was his mother. My girls are the joy of my life Lexie, but my boy was my greatest gift."

Lexie put her hand up to cover her eyes.

"So will you go and have a wonderful time? Please. Please Lexie. Do it for me."

Chapter Eight

LEXIE AND SUSIE threw enough stuff into Betsy that they could have lived in the woods for a year. They had everything. More importantly, they spent a fortune at the liquor commission.

Sue fingered a huge bottle of bubbly wine. "What do you think, Lex?"

"I don't think it's enough. Buy two."

"Okey dokey. How about beer?" They put their wine in the cart and roared over to the beer section.

"How many cases?"

"Two." They dumped those in as well. "What about coolers? We should get some of those. How many packs?

"Two."

"What's my name, Lex?"

"Two."

Lexie dropped Susie off at the grocery store while she went for gas. Susie jumped out of the front seat. "You don't have to tell me." She bought two of everything.

They packed sleeping bags and warm woollies, and off they went. Susie bought a CD with their favourite songs from high school on it. They sang at the top of their lungs as they chugged up Smokey, a mountain almost as menacing as the one Adrian screamed down.

The view was out of this world. The blue ocean twinkled as far as the eye could see. The road was steep and so close to the edge of the cliff that, despite the guardrail, it felt as if there was only empty space beyond the edge. They drove as if on a tightrope. Lexie hugged the centre line around the hairpin turns. Cars driving in the opposite direction did the same. They could read the lips of drivers as they swore at them when they passed in a cloud of black smoke from the burning brake pads.

Susie had a great time. She'd yell out the window, "Same to you buddy!"

For some unknown reason they talked about spitting. Susie told her the different techniques her brothers used. They experimented with disastrous results. They agreed guys were stupid.

Finally they saw the sign that lead into their campsite. They pulled onto a dirt road and came to a clearing. There were ten cars there already.

"Oh my God. Did you know she'd be here?"

Susie groaned. "Of course not. Isn't that typical? She didn't tell us on purpose. What a weirdo."

Donalda waved to them. They could have spit.

Lexie put Betsy in park. "Well, I won't let her ruin my good time." They ran out to greet everyone. They knew most of the crowd, but there were enough new faces to make life interesting.

The cabins were scattered under a canopy of fir trees. Everyone claimed the ones closest to the mess hall. Lexie and Sue were the last to arrive, so they ended up with the cabin nearest the beach, which suited Lexie fine. She was soon sorry it was so far away.

Lexie had a huge load of camping supplies in her arms.

Items dropped left and right with every step. "Help me."

"I can't. I have the beer cooler and, quite frankly, it's more important."

Somehow they hobbled back and forth to Betsy and slowly piled their stuff in the cabin. They looked at each other.

"I don't think this is how it's suppose to look."

A pyramid of gigantic proportions stood in the middle of the cabin floor.

"Shall we sort it?" Susie wondered.

"Nah."

They took off at a run. Then had to come back. They forgot the beer.

The guys had a big barbecue going in no time. Everyone put their contributions on the grill.

Donalda made a huge production about the fact that she was a vegetarian. "I don't eat meat. It's barbaric. I'll have my tofu burger medium rare."

Susie's brother Tom gave her a look. He and his wife, Patty, were there. Then he looked at something else.

"What the hell is that?"

Susie looked where he pointed. "What?"

"Is this supposed to be a *steak*?" He picked up one of their small fast-fry minute steaks. He held it up for all to see and wiggled it back and forth from the end of his barbecue fork. "I can see through this! Christ. I sneeze snot bigger than this."

They gave him a collective, "Yuck!"

Lexie lost her appetite altogether. "God, Susan, how did you ever grow up with brothers?"

"Now you know why I lived at your house."

Tom reached into his cooler. He sounded like Crocodile Dundee. "That's not a steak. This is a steak." He lifted what looked like the right side of a steer and threw it on the grill. Flame leapt into the air. Serious sizzling was heard everywhere.

Lexie left. She couldn't watch it anymore. For the first time in her life, she agreed with Donalda. She needed beer.

Three hours later, she swayed on a bench, as happy as a clam. Susan told someone she hoped Lexie got bombed — it was just what she needed after such a terrible time.

"Yes, Susikins, it's just what I need after such a terrible time." Lexie opened another beer.

Luckily someone started feeding her water after a while, since she didn't know the difference. She talked and laughed and held her hand up for more.

"The bonfire's going!" Everyone teetered off to the beach.

Lexie blissed out at the fire. She sat in the sand with her back pressed against a huge log, wrapped up in a warm blanket. She watched as the orange flames shot sparks up towards the stars. Waves lapped a short distance away and soothed her. This was the life.

Then it happened. Voices came from down the beach, headed towards them. There were great whoops of welcome. Tom greeted his friends from Chéticamp. "Look who's here."

Several figures came out of the dark. Lexie saw only one. A tall man shook hands and slapped the backs of those around him. He wore a big sweater that came up to his chin and a jean jacket over it. She could see his silhouette by firelight. He had a mass of black windswept hair that probably never saw a comb, and dark stubble on his face.

He turned around. She looked at the most beautiful man she'd ever seen.

She watched him the rest of the evening, never saying a word. After he nodded a greeting to them, he went back and chatted with his friends. He stood at the edge of the fire, with a can of beer in his hand.

Susan and Donalda came up from behind the log and sat down beside her.

"Who's that?"

They knew who she meant.

"Oh my God, can you believe how fabulous he is?" Susan gushed. "He's a monster hunk of male meat!"

Donalda squeaked, "He's an Adonis!"

"Shut up the two of you. He'll hear you."

Donalda drooled. "Who cares."

Susie kept right on as if Lexie hadn't spoken. She was as drunk as a skunk. "He's from away but he's here to help some buddies with their boats. Guess what he does?" she burbled.

"Is he a wrestler?

She slurred, "No you big stupid. He's a fisherman who works on those huge trawlers in Alaska. He's one of those guys that roars around and keeps big things from falling off the deck as the ship is being tossed by a raging, howling, icy blizzard!"

"Jesus. How on earth would you know what goes on in a raging Alaskan blizzard?"

"I don't. That's why they call it imagination. And I can imagine all kinds of wonderful things I could do for this big guy."

Lexie nudged her in the ribs. "Susie. Keep your tongue in your head."

"Do I have to?"

Susan finally staggered off to go barf or something. Donalda wasn't far behind. The others started to drift away as well. Some of the logs were nearly empty now. Her big guy and his friends finally sat down. The rowdiness wore off, and someone brought out a guitar and the singing started — Scottish laments, handed down from the old country. It was the best time to listen to them, at the winding down of the evening.

The trouble was they brought back sorrow. Lexie watched the fire. She thought of her family, and how they suffered. Life could be cruel. It was hard to accept. Tears fell from her eyes.

She looked up. Her big guy watched her.

SHE DIDN'T REMEMBER how she got back to the cabin that night. She vaguely felt an elbow or two helping her along. She thought someone pointed her in the direction of her bed, but when she woke the next morning, she was on a sleeping bag in the middle of a mountain of camping supplies.

She lay there for a while. Should she try to get up, or at least move her head? She summoned the courage because she needed to pee. She wasn't as bad as she thought she'd be. It seemed her stupor from the night before was caused more by emotional exhaustion than by beer.

In Susan's case, it was definitely the beer. Lexie heard a groan somewhere in the cabin.

"Susan?"

"Susan's not here," said a quivery little voice, "she's died and gone to hell."

"Are you all right?"

"Never better. I enjoy being hit on the head with a hammer." Susie groaned again.

"I'll get you some aspirin."

"Lexie, I didn't do anything stupid last night, did I?"

"Other than slobber and throw yourself on that big guy?"

"Oh please, tell me I didn't? No, scratch that. Tell me I did."

Lexie gathered her things to brush her teeth and have a very hot shower. Susan rambled in the other room. "I found out his name."

"Oh yeah?"

"It's Joss. Joss MacGregor. Isn't that cool?"

"Very cool. I'll be back."

"That's okay. Leave me here. Just do my a favour and send for a priest on your way out."

After her shower and a big mug of Coke (which was all she could stomach), Lexie delivered painkillers to poor Susie, then made her way down to the nearby cove.

She let the waves and wind keep her company. The sun felt warm on her face. An osprey fluttered in the same spot high above the water as it looked for fish. Its wings kept it still. It spied its prey, and instantly went into a dive bomb and hit the water at lightning speed. It rose out of the waves with a shining, flapping fish in its claws. The osprey rose back into the air, shaking the fish at intervals.

Lexie marvelled at this spectacle, but still felt sorry for the fish.

Eventually she wandered back. She looked at the sand and picked up shells and pieces of driftwood. She found a piece of smooth blue glass, worn down by its endless rolling against the rocks. She saved it for Kate's guest room.

As she neared the campsite, Patty beckoned her to hurry up. When Lexie was close enough she said, "Some of us are going whale watching. Want to come?"

She couldn't think of anything she'd like better.

"Should I wake Susie?" Patty asked.

"Not unless you enjoy nursing the sick."

"Forget it."

Lexie and the others drove to the wharf. She had on a thick sweater she'd made herself years ago. She carried a pair of mitts with her just in case.

She laughed and talked with the girls and didn't notice who helped them onto the boat. She put her hand in the one that was offered and turned to say thank you.

It was him.

He gave her a smile that left her weak. "Welcome aboard."

She couldn't find her voice. She couldn't remember if she smiled at him either.

Donalda had to sit beside her — naturally, just when Lexie wanted to be alone — so she could look at the man who steered them out onto the water.

It was a fabulous day. Windy and cold, but the air so clean she felt as if her lungs would burst. The water was very blue and choppy, whitecaps all around. The fishing boat barrelled through the waves and splashed up salty spray. The sky was full of white fluffy clouds, like fat cotton balls. The hills surrounding them were a huge patchwork quilt of gold, scarlet, and orange. And then, at a distance, they saw the whales. Their grey backs snaked along and curved upwards out of the water. They disappeared, only to break the surface smoothly a few moments later in a leisurely, rhythmic fashion.

When they were close, her man cut the engine. They listened. Soon they heard the puff or snort of air from the blowholes as the whales surfaced. It was a low symphony of sound, one after the other, blowing then leaving, and then blowing again. It sounded as if deep heartbeats came from the ocean floor. And for the first time in a long time, Lexie was happy.

On the way back, she decided it wasn't her imagination. He looked at her. He very definitely turned his head and watched her. She pretended she didn't see it but her whole body screamed with the attention. Maybe she reminded him of someone. It must be a mistake. A man like that doesn't look at a girl like her. And of course, Donalda made her life miserable.

"Oh my God," she whispered. "I can't believe it. Every time I look over there, he looks over here. I'll make my move tonight. Someone said he's coming back again."

She then grabbed one of the other women Lexie didn't know very well. "Joyce, come here."

The woman came over. She and Lexie smiled at each other.

Donalda asked, "Do you know anything about that gorgeous creature steering the boat?"

"He's something, isn't he? I don't know a lot. I know this isn't his boat. He's not from here. I think he's from Alaska. Someone said he's here to visit friends."

"How long will he be here?"

Lexie pretended she wasn't interested, but of course she was all ears.

Joyce shook her head. "I'm not sure. But I did hear that he and a partner started a new business up there, some fish wholesale thing. And you can just bet there's a woman at home."

"Isn't that just too bad," Donalda smirked. "All's fair in love and war."

"That's what I say. Who cares? A guy like that can do what he wants. He must have a girl in every port. At least that's what hubby says." Joyce leaned in closer to Donalda. "And you know what? If I had the chance, I'd forget I was married and be first in line. Wouldn't you?"

They laughed.

It made Lexie sick, the way they talked about him. But she knew she'd give anything to be with him too, damn the consequences.

That night everyone was at it again. It was too foggy and damp for a bonfire, so they took their party indoors to the mess hall. The mist was thick and wet, and there was a fall chill in the air.

Lexie got ready for the evening. She scurried around after her second shower of the day, a toothbrush in her mouth and her hair wrapped up in a towel. It was cold in the cabin, in spite of the space heater, so she jumped around to get warm. She wore an old comfy black turtleneck under her new jean jacket.

She rubbed her hair dry with a towel and put on a little lip gloss.

Susie was in her pyjamas, sulking. "Your skin is disgusting, do you know that?"

"Thanks."

"No problem. Not only do you have an alabaster complexion, you go out and get lots of fresh air without me, hence glowing cheeks. How can you be so selfish?"

Lexie sprayed perfume in front of her and walked through it. "Susie, why don't you get dressed and come over. It won't be the same if you're not there."

"No one will notice."

"Maybe you'll meet someone?"

"Oh, please," she snorted, "As if. We're never that lucky." She looked at Lexie again. "When you look like that, however, anything's possible."

Lexie ran through the path in the woods towards the mess hall. The lights from the windows made it inviting in the dark. She could hear the fiddles and the stomping. The merriment was well under way, and Lexie was happy and excited. It was nice to smile again, to laugh with friends, and tap her foot to music, a luxury she'd not thought possible a week ago. It was good to be alive.

She opened the door and walked into a party. Everyone held a drink. They waved at her. They couldn't talk because the music was too loud. Fiddles and spoons played with abandon. Everyone stomped their feet. Some couples danced and twirled to the sound of the beat.

The set ended. There was a small lull before the music came to life once more. Everyone ran for another drink as they shouted at each other, their ears ringing. Tom hollered to Lexie. Did she want a rum and Coke?

Patty came over and they waxed poetic about their whale adventure. The feeling was still with them, being out on the wild blue ocean, at one with nature on a glorious day. Tom came back with the drinks. They toasted each other.

The music started again. The door opened and Susie came in. She gave Lexie a weak smile. Lexie rushed over to her and yelled in her ear. "Are you all right?"

"No."

"Can I get you something?"

"A head transplant."

Lexie was concerned. Susie laughed. "It's all right, I'm not that bad. Get me a Coke."

Lexie scurried off and Susie sat by her brother. By the time she got back, Donalda was there too. Lexie handed Susie the glass and asked Donalda if she'd like anything.

Before she could answer, Lexie felt a draft of cold air and another swell of noise. More people.

"Oh my God," Donalda freaked. "There he is!"

Lexie turned. Her big guy had arrived.

How was it possible that he got better looking every time she laid eyes on him? He was wonderful. His hair was a shiny mop of dark chestnut — loose curls that hadn't seen scissors in a while. He had stubble on his face, a permanent fixture apparently. But it was his lopsided grin that got to her. He smiled all the time, with those white teeth of his, like he had nothing better to do in the whole world than to be right where he was. His blue eyes snapped with mischief. It was hard to tell what he was thinking, but it looked cheeky. His sweater was the colour of oatmeal. His jeans were faded and old. And Lexie wanted him more than anything.

He set her on fire.

She told her heart to stop, but it thudded in her chest. She tried not to stare at him, but it was a lost cause.

Lexie saw him look at her, but of course Donalda leapt up and ran right over to him. He had no choice but to talk to her.

She turned around and saw Susie eyeball her. She jerked her head to try and get Lexie to go over to him, but she couldn't do it. She had butterflies in her stomach. This was stupid. She had to regroup so she walked into the galley and poured herself a glass of water, just for something to do. She willed her heart to slow down. *Lexie Ivy, stop acting like a teenager.* She drank her water and turned around. He was behind her.

He smiled at her. "Hello."

That guppy thing she was so good at took over.

"Hi," she stammered.

"I'm Joss."

She almost said "I know" but stopped herself in time.

"I'm Lexie." She wasn't aware she said anything.

"Lexie. That's a sweet name."

"Thank you."

"Can I tell you something else, Lexie?"

"Yes."

"You're beautiful." He gave her that grin that turned her insides to mush.

She didn't know what possessed her. "So are you."

He threw his head back and laughed. "I've been called a lot of things, but beautiful isn't one of them. Handsome, maybe, according to my mother."

He was sweet. She forgot everything. She didn't care.

"Don't be so modest. I'm sure you've heard it from a few women, if not a lot of women."

He gave his head a little sideways shake. He didn't say she was wrong.

"Can I get you a drink?" She needed to do something with her hands.

"Sure, I'll have a beer."

She opened one for him. She heard the music in the background but everything else faded away. The only world Lexie knew was the space that existed between them, the circle they made.

"So Lexie. Are you here by yourself?"

She nodded at him.

"Were you waiting for me?"

She smiled and nodded again. He laughed and so did she.

"I've got to tell you, Lexie. I don't stick around. I love them and leave them. But while I'm here, I really love them."

Oh God. "You are the world's best flirt, did you know that?"

"I've had a lot of practice."

She gave him a saucy look of her own. "I bet you have. Do they all fall at your feet so quickly?"

"Usually." He downed the rest of his beer and grabbed another one. "But I'm pretty fussy. I don't seduce every woman I see. Only the ones that look like women." His eyes travelled over her body. "And you look like a woman to me."

He took a step closer and put his arm around her waist. "There. That's better."

She had a hard time trying not to faint from pure delight. "You are so bad."

"No. I'm very good."

He was a brick wall in front of her. She was tiny in his arms. He reached behind and put his beer on the counter. He pressed her against the edge of it, took his hand and lifted her chin. She must be dreaming.

"And I always say, this is the best part." He lowered his head and he kissed her. She'd never been kissed like that before. He made love to her mouth.

She couldn't think. She just was. He lifted his head, put his hand up through her hair and pulled it away from her ear. He whispered against it.

"Come with me."

SUSIE KNOCKED SOFTLY on the cabin door.

"Yesss."

She poked her nose in. Lexie lolled on the couch with a glass of apple juice.

"Is it all right to come in?"

"Sure."

She took one look at her. "You lucky *bitch!* I could kill you."

Lexie grinned.

She jumped on the couch beside her and shoved Lexie's shoulder, almost spilling the juice. "So? Tell me! What was it *like*?"

"Who knew it could be so exhausting."

"I really, really hate you."

Lexie grinned again.

"I want details, Lexie. Put me out of my misery."

"This is all mine. I can't share him with anyone."

"You always were a *stupid cow*!"

They smiled at each other, and Susie got up off the couch, but not before giving Lexie a pat on the knee. "Good for you Lex."

"Thanks, Susie."

"I guess this means I'll have to stay with Tom and Patty for the week."

"Do you mind?"

"Of course, I mind. But if it's not going to be me, it might as well be you. Oh, you mean the cabin? No, I don't mind about the cabin."

They started to giggle.

LEXIE'S DAYS WERE full of hiking in the Highlands, boat tours and beachcombing. But her nights were full of Joss. He came to her every evening, after a day of helping his friends with their boats. He'd shut the cabin door and give her that grin.

"Come here, Lexie."

Lexie got up one morning and tiptoed out of bed. She didn't usually make him breakfast. He wouldn't let her. He'd say there was only one thing he wanted before he left for the day, and it didn't require a toaster. She'd slap his hand and tell him not to be so greedy, but he always got his way.

By the time he woke up, she had orange juice, eggs and bacon, and a mound of whole wheat toast waiting for him. That and a big pot of coffee.

He mumbled from the bedroom. "Lexie?"

"I'm in here. Come and get it."

"You come here first."

"No way. This toast will get cold."

"I don't want toast."

She sat at the table and picked up a piece of bacon. "Never mind then. I'll eat it all myself." She took a bite and poured herself a cup of coffee.

He finally showed up in the curtained doorway with only his jeans on. He leaned against the crossbar with his arms over his head and gave her a smirk. "You sure you don't want to get in here?"

She willed herself to stay seated, even though every nerve ending in her body sparked.

"Joss, believe it or not, I'm sure there's lots of things we could do besides make love."

"Yeah, but nothing's as much fun."

"Fine. Let's just say, you have to keep your energy up."

He laughed and sat at the table. He rubbed his hands together. "This actually looks good."

She dipped a piece of toast in the soft egg yolk on her plate. "Wow. Thanks for the compliment."

He smiled at her, stuffed a piece of toast in his mouth, then washed it down with coffee. "I'm sure you're a wonderful cook. You're pretty good at everything else."

She looked at him under her lashes. "Only pretty good?"

He held his hands up. "I stand corrected. The word I'm looking for is fantastic."

She picked up another piece of bacon, but instead of eating it, she broke it into pieces. "You probably say that to every girl you're with."

He cut his eggs with his fork. "Actually, I don't." He shovelled half a fried egg in his mouth and chewed it.

Lexie kept ripping. "How would I know?"

He glanced at her. "I guess you'll have to trust me."

She sighed and dropped the bacon. "I don't know you well enough to trust you."

He looked exasperated. "You know everything about me. This is it. This is who I am and what I do. It's as uncomplicated as that."

"You're an open book."

"What?"

"Nothing."

He put his fork down and leaned his elbows on the table. "Lexie, what do you want from me?"

"Nothing."

"Again, nothing. Are you sure about that?"

She couldn't look at him. She couldn't tell him she wanted everything.

"Lexie?"

She got up and pushed their breakfast dishes away with one sweep of her arm. He reached out, grabbed her wrist, and pulled her on his lap.

She opened her robe. "I want you."

ONE NIGHT THE full moon shone in the window. Lexie could see the black silhouette of a giant fir tree against its ancient light. There was so much beauty in the world, if one took the time to see it. An owl hooted. The wind was still.

Joss lay beside her, propped up on his elbow, looking at her. The moonlight gave his skin a silver glow. He rubbed his thumb back and forth, gently, over her lips. She took his thumb into her mouth and bit it. When he slid it out, she reached for his hand and pressed her palm against his. She entwined her fingers and made their hands one.

"What are we doing?" she whispered.

"Shh."

She smiled and looked back over his shoulder at the moon. She watched it, as he watched her.

He said, "You're the one I'll never forget."

She pulled him to her and the moon disappeared.

THE MORNING THEY were leaving, Lexie went to the beach by herself. It was foggy and cold. She heard a foghorn in the distance. It moaned its deep sound and warned the fishermen to take care.

She would miss this beach. This was where she met him. They said their goodbyes the night before. She didn't let herself feel anything. It was what it was. He told her that right from the beginning, and she believed him. There was no way to end it, so she had to walk away. She knew what she was doing. She was a big girl. And it was worth every moment.

She stared out at the ocean. Mist lay above the waves and made the line between earth and water vanish. It was grey, all of it. No beginning and no end.

She felt his arms go around her waist. He came up behind her in the damp morning air. Somehow it didn't surprise her, but she stayed focussed. She had to. She didn't turn around.

He held her. She put her arms over his and pressed his hands against her belly. She would be grateful to him for the rest of her life.

JOSS LET HER go and didn't look back as he walked to the truck. He got in and rubbed his eyes with his thumb and forefinger. He sighed, reached into his shirt pocket, and took out a package of smokes. He lit a cigarette and took a couple of drags, but didn't make a move to start the engine.

People were milling around packing up. He saw Donalda out of the corner of his eye. She approached the truck and he pretended not to see her. She came up to the window anyway and knocked on it. He had no choice but to roll it down.

"So you're off?"

"Yes."

"If you're ever in town, give me a call. We could have a good time. I'd make it worth your while."

God. "Take care of Lexie."

Her face darkened. "Don't be stupid. Lexie takes care of Lexie. She'll help herself to someone else's man before the night is over. Don't you worry."

He flicked his butt at her. It didn't miss by much. He turned the key and threw the truck in gear. His wheels churned up the gravel as he left.

Shit.

❧

LEXIE RETURNED TO her little house. Everything was wonderfully the same. She was completely different.

She was alive. She was awake, for the first time in her life. The memory of Joss was something she could play like a record, over and over, as she sat by the fire with Sophie. Her evenings weren't lonely anymore. A real live man had loved her. Not a fantasy. She didn't have to imagine any more what it was like to be taken. She knew.

Everyone was still distracted by Willie's death, but they could see the fresh air and sunshine had done Lexie a lot of good. She should have guessed it would be Marlene who'd sniff out the difference.

She sidled up to her one day at work. "You got some, didn't ya?"

Lexie looked at her. "You bet. And it was fantastic."

Judy was a little more subtle. "You're always smiling these days. Did you have a nice time?"

"The very best of my life."

Judy and Marlene had exactly the same thing to say when she started throwing up every morning in the bathroom at work.

"She is, isn't she?"

"She sure is."

Chapter Nine

LEXIE KNEW BEFORE she looked at the blue stripe in the plastic gizmo. Sophie sat on the windowsill and watched her. Lexie glanced at her pussycat. Sophie gave her small mew, as if to ask, "Well, what's it say?"

She sat in the bathroom for a long time. She tried to keep her heart from bursting. She was overjoyed. She floated in the air. Her very own little baby, Joss's baby. She hugged herself and put her hands on her tummy.

"Oh hello, little darlin'. Mommy loves you so much already."

Then she burst into tears. She didn't know how on earth she would tell Beth.

She swore Susie to secrecy. She had to figure out how to break the news to her family.

"What are you going to do?" Susie wanted to know.

She and Sue walked in the mall, shopping for nothing in particular. It was a good way to pace without having to go back and forth too quickly.

"That's what I want you to tell me. Think of something."

"They'll find out this time tomorrow. You've put on weight already. Your mom will sign you up for a gym membership before the week is out."

"Oh, you're right," she sighed, "This is hopeless."

Susie put her hand on her arm. "If it makes you feel any better, I'm really happy for you. This baby's very lucky to have you for a mom."

"Thanks, Susie. That means a lot."

She told her father first. She knocked on his study door.

"Come."

She stepped inside. "Hi Dad."

"Princess, how lovely to see you. To what do I owe the pleasure?"

She would ease into it slowly. She rehearsed everything. She'd be calm and rational.

She blubbered instead.

"I'm going to have a baby and I don't know how to tell Beth!"

She grabbed the Kleenex box on his desk and pulled out twelve sheets. He patiently waited for her to calm down and stop crying. He seemed weary, but he smiled at her.

"Well, now, this is good news for a change. Is it something you're happy about?"

"Oh Daddy, I'm thrilled. I want this baby. I've wanted a baby of my own for so long. I never, ever thought it would happen to me. When I think of it I want to sing to the heavens and tell the whole world, but I can't."

"Why not?"

"You know why. Because of Willie. It will break Beth's heart if I have a baby now. I can't be around her. I can't tell her how happy I am. She's devastated. I don't know what to do." She hiccuped and blew her nose.

He sat for long time. He didn't say anything. She wondered if he was disappointed.

"I'm very happy for you Lexie. You'll make a wonderful mother." He folded his hands. "Yes, your sister will be upset.

Not because she's not happy for you. She'll have a hard time dealing with a new baby in the family, that's all. And we can't blame her, can we? And you'll want to brag to your sisters. That's only natural. We'll take it one step at a time. Let Beth deal with it however she sees fit. It's difficult, but not impossible."

He always knew what to say. She calmed down. He was right. Beth had every right to be sad. She had every right to be happy.

"What about the father?"

"Oh." Lexie hadn't thought about what she would say about Joss. She'd been too wrapped up about the baby.

She decided to tell her father the truth. "Actually Dad, he was someone I met on my camping trip. I loved him. He was wonderful. I'm very excited he's the baby's father but I'll never see him again."

"Doesn't he have the right to know?"

"I suppose he does. But I don't know where he is."

"I see."

Lexie smiled. "Unless he's roaring around on a ship that's being tossed in a howling, icy Alaskan blizzard."

"Goodness."

Lexie asked her dad not to tell her mom. She wanted to do it herself, so Lexie invited her mother over for lunch. She made a huge leafy salad and a low-cal dessert to make her happy. As she set the table, there was a knock at the door. It opened.

"It's only me."

"Hi Mom. I'm in the kitchen."

Lexie heard her talk to Sophie, who had rapidly gained the weight back after her ordeal with her mother. She came into the kitchen and gave Lexie a quick kiss.

"That cat has put all her weight back on, after I tried so hard to get it off."

"Kids. What can you do?"

"Well, this looks nice."

"Thank you. Sit down."

They enjoyed their lunch. Lexie waited until the tea was poured before she launched into her news. A cup of tea was useful for hashing out life's little dramas. It was something to hang on to.

Mom took her first sip. She smiled. "You look so lovely these days."

"Thanks, Mom."

"I don't know, there's a glow about you."

Lexie beamed.

Her mother realized what she just said. "You're pregnant, aren't you?"

"Yep."

"Oh, Lexie, dear." She stared at her. "Well, well."

"Aren't you happy for me?"

"Well, I don't know the ins and outs or who the father is or how you'll support a child on your own. Or for that matter, how we'll ever tell Beth. But putting all that aside, yes, my love, I'm very happy for you. I can tell you from first-hand experience, there is nothing more wonderful than your first child."

Lexie blubbered again.

LEXIE WAS AT Beth's. She'd made too much spaghetti sauce the night before and brought the rest over for her sister's gang. Of course Beth put her to work making the girls' lunches. Lexie spread peanut butter over eight slices of bread. The big purple pain-in-a-dinosaur-suit sang the same banal verse over and over again from the TV in the family room.

Note to self: Get used to it. It'll be your best friend in two years.

She hollered, "Who wants jelly?"

"I do."

"I do."

"I do."

"Abba Daba do."

That was Maddie. Lexie put some jam on half in case that meant yes or no.

Lexie heard Beth curse at the washing machine. She pounded back upstairs. "Honestly, I swear I go through a box of Tide every three days. I'm broke."

"Why don't you use the cheaper stuff?"

"Because you can't get the stains out if you use the other kind."

Note to self: Use Ivory Snow at first, then Tide.

Beth put the laundry basket on the kitchen table and folded a huge mess of underpants alone. She put them in little piles.

"How do you know whose are who's?"

"I got smart by the time Halley arrived. One colour, one girl."

"Clever."

Note to self: Remember that. Wait. Don't. Not unless I have quadruplets.

She delivered the sandwiches to the girls. They didn't look at her. They put their hands up and stared at that purple bonehead.

"Thank you."

"Thank you."

"Thank you."

"Q."

Lexie walked back to the kitchen and cleared the mess. She licked great quantities of peanut butter off the knife before she threw it in the sink.

Beth laughed. "Stop that or you'll be as big as a house. I swear you've put on weight since that camping trip. I'm surprised Mom hasn't been up your nose about it."

Lexie stood stock-still. She turned around with her hand on her belly. Her face said everything.

Beth understood. She dropped to the kitchen chair and put a pair of Madison's jumpers over her face and cried her eyes out.

Finally Lexie had to go. She hadn't fed Sophie since breakfast. She and Beth hashed it out as well as they could. They tried very hard to be kind to each other.

Lexie turned the doorknob. "See ya, then."

Beth grabbed her in a bear hug. "I'm so happy for you Lexie. No one will make a better mother than you. Please don't be mad at me if I can't hold him. Or her. I will one day. I promise."

Lexie nodded her head furiously and held her back as tight as she could.

She finally felt free. Free to enjoy the next phone call.

"Kate?"

"Hi Lexie! How are you? Daphne and I were just talking about you. Did you make any more of your fabulous rugs?"

"No. Something much better."

"Really?"

"A baby."

She heard Kate let out a whoop. "Daphne, come here. Lexie's having a *baby*!" Then noise and confusion and Kate babbling over the phone.

Her mind went blank. It was the first time anyone said it other than her. It felt incredible. She finally believed it.

Lexie's having a baby.

YOU'D THINK NO one in the world had had one before. Lexie was completely in her own universe. Her little house, her not-so-little cat, her little baby, and her.

She rubbed her rapidly growing tummy while she played classical music. She sang lullabies as a hobby. She ate healthy food, stayed away from alcohol, and ran if a smoker came near her. She took care of her baby girl. And she was a girl. She knew it.

Wasn't it amazing? she told herself. She was a mother now. She just knew these things. She was in the club. She didn't need an ultrasound to tell her anything. And to think, she knew all this before she even felt the baby move. When that moment happened she was in the tub. She browsed through her Dr. Spock manual as she soaked in a hot bubble bath. At first she thought she was hungry. Then something told her to pay attention. There it was, a flutter, as soft as silk. Her daughter let her know she was there. Lexie laid her head on the curve of the tub and knew happiness as a physical thing.

Her life was now lived inside and out. She was as aware of one as she was the other. For her, pregnancy was to float in the ocean and feel the sun beat down on her body but savour the cold wet of her skin underneath. Two worlds lived in tandem, two hearts beating as one.

Her poor family was kind to her. They listened, nodded, and agreed with everything she said. Kate was especially nice. She let Lexie call collect, since she couldn't afford to phone every day. It seemed to evolve that she and Beth stayed away from each other most of the time. Beth was nice when Lexie called, always asked how she was. Lexie said fine and Beth asked no more.

She helped Beth. She and her mom would often take one or two of the girls on the weekends to give Beth a little break. Mom collected the girls at the door. Lexie stayed in the car. Beth waved from the doorway.

One day Lexie had to go inside. They dropped the girls off and her little monkey chose that particular moment to amuse herself with good kick to the bladder. Mom told her not to be so foolish, to go in the house and use the washroom. Beth said the same thing but she busied herself wiping counters.

Lexie went back into the kitchen and sat for a moment to wait for Mom put on her coat. Brit came up to her. "Can I feel your baby, Auntie Lexie?"

What could she say?

"Of course, sweetheart." She did and Brit's eyes got big.

"Mommy, come and feel the baby. It kicked me."

Beth still had her back turned. "That's okay, honey. I'll feel it another time."

Lexie felt awful.

Brittany patted her tummy. "Poor little baby. I hope you don't die too."

Lexie lay awake that night and thought of nothing else. In all her excitement, she just assumed everything would be fine. It had to be. She couldn't live if something happened to her little girl. She'd die.

Surely Sudden Infant Death wouldn't strike twice? Not in the same family? She shuddered. But deep in her heart, Lexie knew it wouldn't happen. She'd be strong, like her daddy. And that's when the baby's name came to her. Jocelyn. Joce for short. Joss.

Lexie and Susie worked on their baby projects in the evening in front of the fire. They knit jumpers and sweaters and hats. Lexie made a quilt for the crib, as well as bumper pads to protect the baby's head and even flannel sheets.

Lexie looked over at Sue one night, working so diligently on her behalf, stitching the seam of a receiving blanket.

"Susie?"

"Yeah?"

"Would you like to be Jocelyn's godmother?"

Susie's head flew up and she held the blanket to her chest. "Really? Me?"

"Of course you."

"But what about your sisters?"

"You're the only one who ever met Joss. It would mean a lot to me."

She couldn't wipe the smile off her face. "I'd love to. More then anything."

"Thank you for sharing this with me."

Susie put the blanket back on her lap. "Hey, I'm the one who should be thanking you. This may be as close as I ever get to having a baby. I'm delighted."

Susie also agreed to be her Lamaze coach. When they walked into their first Lamaze class, most of the other couples gave them wide smiles, to let them know they were truly enlightened and not in the least bit surprised that a gay couple would be there. But Glace Bay is a conservative place. Try as they might, a few of the parents were uncomfortable with the idea and Lexie and Sue knew it. It was mean to pretend they were together, but they couldn't resist. It amused them.

They especially loved to pull the chain of a prim, uptight gal accompanied by her equally prissy husband. The woman faced Lexie as their partners rubbed their lower backs. They were supposed to breathe in and out slowly, not talk. She pointed at Lexie. "How does this work?"

"How does what work?" Lexie asked innocently. Susie gave her a subtle shove with her fist to remind her not to get carried away.

She waggled her finger back and forth between them. "Who's the mommy?"

"I'll be the mommy on Mondays, Wednesdays, and Fridays and Susie will be the mommy Tuesdays, Thursdays, and Saturdays. Sunday's a day of rest."

Mrs. Tight-Ass gave Mr. Tight-Ass a shocked glance. He looked like he had swallowed a lemon.

"Won't that be confusing for the child?"

"We'll wear name tags."

She had heard enough. She heaved her swollen belly away from Lexie and made her husband move her mat to the other side of the room.

"You'll get us in so much trouble," Susie whispered.

"She can bite me."

Lexie spent more and more time at the library in a chair. Her back hurt if she was on her feet for too long. She couldn't bend over to return books on the lower shelves. And she had a hard time typing on the keyboard around her expanding girth.

Marlene walked by and did a double take, as she watched Lexie try and squeeze herself into her seat. "I swear on my aunt Tilly's big toe, you're having triplets. Or twins at least."

"I've asked the doctor. He says no."

She scoffed. "What do doctors know? My aunt Myrna's doctor swore up and down the rash on her backside was nothing to worry about. It killed her dead."

"How can a rash kill you dead?"

"She died of embarrassment showin' it to too many doctors."

"Marlene. Give it up."

MOM AND DAD sat her down one night after Sunday dinner at their house, to go over finances. They helped her with a budget. She didn't make much money so she had to be organized. She'd save money on diapers because she was making her own. She'd breastfeed and she'd already made most of Jocelyn's clothes. Mom pointed out there would be a ton of hand-me-downs from the girls. Lexie realized she had them convinced the baby was a girl. Only Dad asked if it was wise to make so many pink things.

That's when they told Lexie they had a nest egg put aside for her. As a matter of fact, there was one for all of them. They wanted her to know that it was there, if ever she should need it. It was her decision when she wanted to use it.

Lexie was overwhelmed. She felt better now that she knew she had something to fall back on.

"It's important to feel secure," her mother said.

Now that Lexie would soon be a mother, she started to look at her own mother differently. She still drove Lexie up the wall. Her intentions were good, she just went about "helpful" suggestions with a sledgehammer. But Lexie wasn't angry anymore. Life was too short. Being a mother, she was beginning to realize, was difficult.

Chapter Ten

"OH MY GODDDDDDD!"

"Breathe Lexie, nice and slow. Hoo, hoo, hoo. Deep, cleansing breath."

Lexie gritted her teeth. "How about you breathe for me?"

She knew she had Susie's hand in a vice grip, but she didn't give a fig. She was only concerned with the bowling ball of a baby she wanted to bring into the world.

Her labour started on the beach of all places. They were at the cottage. Someone brought a chair down for her. This time she really did look like a beached whale.

Once she got in the chair, she couldn't get out. She sat there for quite a while. She wondered if the pain was the baby or her imagination. She was nine days late. But she waited so long, it seemed it would never happen.

Finally her father came out of the water. As he towelled off, he looked at her. "Are you okay, Princess?"

"I'm not sure. I think I'm in labour. It's not too bad. Maybe these wide hips of mine will finally come in handy."

"PUSH," SAID THE doctor.

"Push," said the nurse.

Push said the lady with the alligator purse.

I'm hallucinating.

Nursery rhymes fired off in her head as she gathered her strength for the finale.

"You're doing fine, Lexie." Her doctor was a colleague of

her dad's. All Lexie could think of was the time she served him potato salad at Mom's annual barbecue. He was certainly seeing her at her best, poor man.

"We have a very big baby here. You need all your strength Lexie. One more big push, okay?"

She could hear Susie somewhere, like a disembodied voice, urging her on. Lexie couldn't believe that between Mom and Beth, they'd done this nine times. They must have been out of their minds.

This was it. She knew it. She pushed with her whole heart and soul. She wanted to see Jocelyn.

"*Wonderful*," her doctor cried. "You have a beautiful baby boy!"

He gave a lusty cry. They put him on her chest and as soon as her arms went around him, he was quiet. He looked right at her. He was as big and beautiful as his daddy.

"WELL," KATE SAID as she held her nephew in her arms. "I don't know about you, but I think even a twelve-pound bruiser like this may have a hard time explaining why his name is Jocelyn."

Everyone laughed. They were all there, all except Beth and Rory, who sent a huge bouquet of flowers. Mom came to her and said Beth didn't trust herself to see the baby with a lot of people around. She wanted this to be Lexie's day and would rather see him in private, later. Lexie understood perfectly.

After everyone had a turn and cooed and fussed all over him, Susie handed him back to his mother.

"His father must have been handsome," Mom gushed.

Susie nodded. "You could say that. But quite frankly I don't have a clue what she saw in him."

Lexie smiled at her.

Dad grinned like a fool "Well, he's not a girl. Shall we send him back?"

Lexie kissed her sweetheart's big chubby fist. "What's a girl?"

She had a dilemma. She honestly hadn't given much thought to a boy's name. It seemed logical to call him after his father. She loved the name Joss, because of the man himself, but worried that it might be too different. Heaven forbid it be trendy.

Everyone was finally ushered out of the room by a nurse who said mother and son needed their rest. They all had to kiss him again before they left. While her boy lay on her chest, snuggled in as if he was a perfect fit, she looked at the baby name book again. If she didn't want Joss, maybe it should start with that letter. She leafed through the J section while she rubbed her baby's soft, round bottom. The search took thirty seconds.

There was the name Joss, a nickname for Joshua. Bingo.

Marlene, Judy, and the library crew came over one day after work to see the baby. They whispered and snickered as they tiptoed in. Lexie had Joshua in his bassinet by her old armchair in the living room. Sophie stood guard, her complete bulk spread under the cradle to cover all bases.

Marlene got there first.

"Holy Mother of God!" she whispered, "Look at the size

of him! If he takes after his old man, it's no wonder you was grinnin' like a Cheshire cat."

Judy hit her on the back. "Shh! You'll wake him up." She turned to Lexie. "He's the most beautiful baby I've ever seen."

"Thanks Judy. He is, isn't he?"

They had all chipped in and gave Lexie a baby carrier. She was touched. She thanked them and gave hugs all around. Even Marlene.

Joshua was a big baby. He rapidly outgrew the pink out-fits Lexie made — thank goodness. Susan set to work and made jumpers that were much bigger and really blue, as if to counteract his initial dealings with clothes.

"It's a good thing he was too young to take anywhere — when he was in that pink stuff," Susan commented loudly as she sewed up a storm in the kitchen.

They kept Josh away from malls and human beings in general those first weeks. Lexie had to. She was handcuffed to the crib. He ate every two hours.

Lexie sat in the armchair and nursed her hungry boy. She stroked his temple with her thumb. He was content. He purred as he ate, a soft hum. His dimpled fist opened and closed against her breast like a kitten.

"I wish his father could see him."

Susan came to the door with the unfinished overalls in her hand. She leaned against it.

"Is it hard, Lex? Do you miss him?"

"At moments like this, yes, I do." She looked at Joshua. "It was my last chance Susie, and I'm not sorry I did it. I just never realized how much I'd love to share him with his father. Joshua is his too. It's hard, Susie, harder than I thought."

One night the doorbell rang. There stood Beth. They looked at each other and never said a word. Lexie took her by the hand and led her over to Josh. He was snuggled up with his knees tucked under him. He had a fist stuffed in his mouth, sucking, even in his sleep. Beth reached down and put her hand on his head.

"He's absolutely exquisite."

It had been a fantasy of hers to have a baby strapped and cuddled under her chin, being stopped by the neighbours to have a peek, as she strolled by. On her first excursion, Lexie tried to stuff him into the contraption Beth lent her, but her girls were teeny tiny things. Her monster just wouldn't fit.

Josh would have none of it. He squirmed and pouted. He looked at her with a big grump on his face. Sophie stared at her as if to say, *I don't blame the kid.*

Lexie put him in his stroller. She wanted him to meet Lester.

"Well, girlie, that's a fine specimen you've got there." Lester grinned from ear to ear. "What's your name, young devil?" He wiggled a finger in Josh's face. Josh tried to grab and eat it.

"His name is Joshua."

"Joshua. That's a fine old-fashioned name. Looks like Joshua's gonna give Sophie a run for her money and that's sayin' somethin.'" Lester shook up and down.

"It runs in the family, Lester. I'll have two Cadburys today. I need all my strength to feed this kid."

❧

JOSS LOOKED OUT the plane window. It was a long flight. Alaska and Cape Breton were on the opposite ends of a very big continent and he wasn't a man who sat still easily. The coquettish woman in the aisle seat added to his discomfort, with her attempts to engage him in conversation. He finally resorted to pretending to be asleep to get her to stop.

He was going home for Christmas — that was the excuse he and his mother cooked up anyway. Helen was worried about her husband. Danny was as stubborn as a mule and wouldn't listen to her when she begged him to retire. She needed Joss's opinion of the situation.

Helen and her youngest boy were close, very close. He was five years younger than the next-in-line brother. Every one of Joss's five brothers was married. Most of them married young. Helen always said if they didn't, the girls on the island would have been up in arms. They were known far and wide as the handsome boys. Joss was the one who wouldn't be caught. Helen knew it would take a special girl to reel him in.

Joss thought of the last time he flew home. It was for Aaron's wedding last September. And that occasion brought back only one memory. Lexie.

He went back to Alaska that fall, determined to put her out of his mind. He could do it. He always did. Why should now be any different?

Mandy distracted him for about a week. She was good at that. But her erotic tricks didn't have the same effect anymore. He thought of Lexie whenever he held Mandy in his arms — about how she looked in the moonlight. He wanted to drink her in that night. She was beautiful, so beautiful. He would never forget her face at that moment.

What a fool he was. So smug in the fact he could walk away. He should've asked her to wait for him. He had to go back to Alaska, he knew that. He and Derek started a little gold mine of a business and he owed it to Derek to help him get it off the ground.

Why didn't he tell her? Why didn't he ask her to wait for him? Was he afraid she'd say no?

He didn't know what to do. But that didn't stop him from doing something: he said goodbye to Mandy. She wasn't happy about it. She raised a big stink and it cost him. He'd only been with her for four months, but she took her chunk of flesh and he was happy to give it. He wanted to be rid of her. Yes, Joss wanted to go home to help his mom. But he also wanted to find Lexie.

❧

LEXIE'S MOM WENT with her for Joshua's six-month needle. He was so big to carry, she needed help with the diaper bag and her purse. But she suspected the real reason her mom wanted to go was to show him off to the other patients in the waiting room.

Lexie was secretly thrilled. Mom didn't mind her son being the biggest one in the room. For the first time in Lexie's life, her mother seemed envious of her. She looked at Joshua as if he was something special she always wanted. It was childish to gloat, but Lexie did anyway.

Everyone did comment on Joshua. People would stop her in the mall. They talked about him in grocery lineups.

She strutted around like a peacock, until Susan reminded Lexie in no uncertain terms that every mother in the world thought that way — it wasn't anything new.

Good old Susan. She knew how to bring Lexie down to earth, before she alienated everyone around her.

They put Joshua on the examining table in the doctor's office. Lexie took off his sweater so the doctor could give him the once-over. He sat like a little Buddha with his numerous rolls. His grandmother twirled her finger at him and poked his belly button. He waved his chunky legs back and forth over the paper liner. He grinned at them with his two bottom teeth and drooled everywhere.

The doctor walked in. He could hardly lift him.

"How on earth do you drag this child around?"

"I'd drag him to the ends of the earth if I had to, Doc."

"He's off the charts as far as percentiles go. I'd have to make a new category. What does he eat?"

"He's still on breast milk with cereal. Should I start him on solid food?"

The doctor looked at her. "If I were you I'd get him a Big Mac on your way home."

When they were done, Lexie and her mom walked along the corridor of the doctor's office. That's when Lexie looked up and saw Lillian Holmes coming towards them. Lillian hadn't seen them. Lexie was about to open her mouth when her mother said, "Walk straight ahead."

Lexie was a mother herself but she immediately turned into a little girl and followed her mother's instructions. She didn't know what else to do.

As they got closer, Lillian lifted her eyes. She gave a start and then glanced around as if to escape but it was too late. Her mother marched forward.

"Lillian. How nice to see you again. I believe you know my daughter, Lexie."

"Yes," Lillian said faintly. "How are you Lexie?"

Lexie nodded her head. She didn't trust herself to speak.

"I don't believe you've met the newest member of our family. This is Lexie's son Joshua. The apple of his grandfather's eye."

"He's lovely."

"William and I have such a wonderful time with him. After the loss of a precious grandson, we're so grateful to have Joshua in our lives. It helps us deal with the pain. Life can be cruel sometimes, can't it?"

"Yes."

"It was nice to see you again. We better get this child home before he gets cranky. Come Lexie."

Mom walked by Lillian with her head held high. Lexie walked behind her.

"Oh Mom, I'm so proud of you," she gushed in the parking lot.

Mom got in the car and promptly burst into tears.

KATE WAS ON the phone.

"Lexie, would you and Joshua like to come with us to Montreal this May?"

"Montreal?"

"Yeah. We're involved in a rather large project. It's too complicated to get into."

"I'm too stupid to understand, right?"

Kate laughed. "Something like that."

"Hag."

Kate ignored her. "Some of the researchers are based at McGill University and a friend on sabbatical offered us his place for the duration of our stay. It's quite big apparently, and smack in the middle of downtown. I thought it might be an opportunity for you to get a breather. You know, from everything?"

Lexie was blessed to have a baby sister like Kate. She always came to her rescue. On the other hand, Lexie was having a hard time with Beth. Sometimes she felt she had to hide away, keep her son under wraps so Beth wouldn't see him.

It was impossible after a while. His grandparents loved to have Joshua over. The girls wanted him. He was the biggest doll they ever played with. They constantly whined for Lexie to visit. Christmas was especially difficult. Mom and Dad wanted pictures of themselves with their grandchildren, their gift to each other. They had a photographer come to the house.

It seemed to Lexie that Beth snubbed Joshua. It should be her son in that picture, not Lexie's. "It should be both of them," Lexie told her.

"I know that," she snapped. "I'm just sick to death of Mom and Dad saying our only grandson. Josh is not their only grandson. Willie was their first grandson."

"They don't mean it like that. It's difficult to explain to people."

Beth whipped around. "Do you know how horrible it is, to say you have four children, when you have five? To tell people their names and leave Willie's out? He hasn't disappeared for me, like he has for everyone else. He's my child. Just because I can't see him anymore doesn't mean he never existed. He's here in this room as surely as the girls are."

Beth's eyes started to water. "You know what really hurts?" She turned to look out the kitchen window. "There are days like today when I can't stand it anymore. The light is the same as the day he died. The wind is the same. Some trigger of that terrible day hits me in the face."

Beth looked back at Lexie.

"Your body remembers, even when you try desperately to distract yourself. Your body remembers and you live it all over again." Beth hugged her arms across her chest to try and hold it in.

Lexie looked down at the floor. It was too hard to see Beth's face.

"Lexie, I know it's difficult for you. But I get frustrated, so angry, when I see the five of them out there. There should be six. Sometimes I do look at Joshua and think, *why's he allowed to stay*? I love Joshua, but why can't Willie be here too? That's all. Why can't he be here with his grandparents too? It's so unfair."

"I know."

"Actually, Lex, you don't."

❧

JOSS DROVE DOWN Smokey on his way to Sydney to buy Christmas gifts for his fifteen nieces and nephews. His mother was delighted to see him. She baked his favourite desserts. His old man was his usual self, obstinate and opinionated. He insisted he was more than capable of handling his lobster boat next season. With the help of Jimmy, a local kid, and Skipper, he'd be fine.

Skipper was a yellow Labrador, a loyal and intelligent dog. No one would believe Joss when he'd tell them his father's dog could steer a lobster boat. Not for hours, mind you, and only in a straight line, but he kept the wheel steady when Danny and Jimmy hauled in the traps. But that didn't afford Helen much comfort. Danny was now in his seventies. He was still a big, strong man, but Helen knew how he suffered with the pain of his arthritic joints from the damp and fog.

His dad didn't look too bad to Joss, who reminded his mother that Danny was the type of man who'd rather die in the boat than on a hospital bed. Most lobster fishermen didn't even know how to swim. They never wanted to get into the water once they docked for the day. If they went over the side, they went over the side.

Helen got cross. "What is it with men? Why do they think it's a good thing if one day they sail away and never come home? Do they ever think of the women they leave behind? The ones who watch from shore?"

Joss had nothing to say to that. His mother wouldn't have heard it anyway. She left her kitchen in a huff.

JOSS LOOKED AT his list when he got to the mall and had armloads of parcels before he knew it. The place was packed. There were a lot of men about, it being only a few days before Christmas, and he ran into a number of people he knew. Everyone from Neils Harbour came down to the city to shop, but of all the people he ran into that day, one of them had to be Donalda. He was actually excited to see her. Joss couldn't remember Tom's last name, so he had planned on phoning some of his mates to get Tom's number once Christmas was over. And Tom, in turn, would surely keep in touch with Lexie.

But here was Donalda, a convenient shortcut to his plan.

"Hi Donalda."

She turned around and looked like she was about to faint.

"How are you?"

"What are you doing here?"

"Shopping. How's Lexie?"

She didn't answer him. Perhaps she couldn't hear him. There was a lot of noise, what with "Jingle Bells" turned up full blast.

"How's Lexie?" he said louder.

"She's married."

He turned around and left.

He was there for Christmas but told his parents he had to leave the next day, that something had come up at work. His mother went into the yard to say goodbye. Aaron was in the truck, ready to take him to the airport.

She gave him a big squeeze. She only came up to his chest.

"Take care, son. I'll miss you. When will you come home again?"

"I don't know, Ma."

He gave her one last kiss.

"Christ Almighty," Aaron yelled. "Enough with the goodbyes. Get in the goddamn truck."

Joss watched as he left the earth. The ground got farther and farther away. He watched until he could make out the shoreline, the coast, then the Highlands in the distance. The hills where he had loved her. He watched until he could watch no more.

₰

HE WATCHED AS he descended to earth. The ground got closer and closer. He watched the city lights spread over the landscape like a grid map, so different from the one he'd left behind many, many hours ago.

Binti clung to him, with her tiny arms around his neck the entire time. The flight attendants had to put his tray on the seat beside him. They fussed over them both. He was grateful to be in first class. There were empty seats around him and it was easier for Binti to settle down in the quiet. She was rattled easily by noise and confusion.

They touched down and stayed put until everyone was off the aircraft. The kind airline crew told him how sweet his little girl was, how good she was. She never cried the whole way, even over the ocean turbulence. He thanked them and walked down the gangway, through the airport and finally to the big sliding doors. They opened and there were his mother and father.

His mother put her fingers to her mouth, so she wouldn't sob out loud. His dad nodded and looked stoic. He walked over and stood in front of them.

Adrian cried.

His mother wrapped her arms around them both.

Chapter Eleven

IT WAS HARD for her parents to say goodbye to Josh. She'd only be gone a month but it seemed like forever to them. As her mother mentioned numerous times, a month away from a child who was almost a year old was an awfully long time.

Lexie was on maternity leave so she didn't have much to arrange, only to convince Sophie it wasn't the end of the world that she had to go back to her grandmother's house. Lexie asked Susan to visit Sophie from time to time, and to sneak her some treats when Mom was out of view. Sue promised to undergo this covert mission with complete discretion.

Betsy was packed to the rafters. Joshua required more equipment than a circus sideshow. The morning she left for Halifax, Lexie drove to her parents' house to say goodbye. Mom ran out the back door. She grabbed Josh before Lexie could protest, insisting that she had to hug him properly. She covered him with kisses.

"You come and live with Grammy. We'll send Sophie off to Montreal with mommy. You can stay here. Won't that be fun? Won't that be fun?"

Joshua put his big hands on both her cheeks and giggled. She grabbed one of his palms and kissed it over and over. She was so upset.

Dad came out and held out his hands for him. Mom reluctantly passed him over. He walked to the big crab apple tree and they stood there for a while. Josh reached out to touch the apple blossoms. Dad talked to him man to man.

Lexie felt terrible, but she looked forward to being with her boy without feeling so guilty.

"Okay, Grampy. We have to go."

Dad came back with his grandson and handed him to Mom so she could put him in his car seat.

"You drive carefully Princess. You have precious cargo."

As she hugged him, he shoved something in her pocket. "Don't say anything. It's a little pin money. Buy our big fella a Montreal Canadiens hockey jersey."

Joshua waved like mad as they drove down the driveway. She saw her parents in the rear-view mirror. Dad held Mom as she cried.

Lexie arrived at Kate's and left Betsy parked in their driveway. She didn't trust the old girl to make it to Montreal. Then she and Kate and Daphne piled all of Lexie's equipment into the small storage rig they had strapped to the roof of their brand new SUV.

Ever the thoughtful one, Kate made sure she had a proper anchor installed in their new vehicle, so it took no time at all to get Josh safely settled in his car seat. Everyone had a last-minute dash to the john and then they piled in and set off.

They had a jolly time as they drove through New Brunswick. Josh's new word was "twee" so he was worn out by the time they hit the Quebec border. Lexie's nerves were shot as they drove between Quebec City and Montreal. The bumper-to-bumper traffic travelled 140 kilometres at least. Giant trucks zoomed past them and blocked out the sun. She threw a sweater over her head and prayed for forgiveness.

How could she have put her child in such danger? Joshua thought it was great. His other new word was "twuck."

She thought it couldn't get worse.

It did.

They went under the Lafontaine Tunnel, a long section of highway that snaked its way below the St. Lawrence River. Lexie swore she could feel the millions of gallons of water over her head. The noise of the vehicles as they zoomed through was eerie. It echoed, like the sound of a holler in a deep well. What if they got stuck? She felt the damp press in on her. She needed to get out of there. Anything was better than this.

Then there was the Montreal traffic. Kate drove while Daphne tried to figure out the lousy map, which neglected to mention that some side streets were one-way.

"Where do I go?" Kate yelled.

"I have no frigging idea," Daphne yelled back.

"What does the frigging map say?"

Daphne flapped the map around. "That frigging street is where we go, but it's the wrong frigging way."

"Will you both frigging shut up!" Lexie yelled.

"Fwig," Joshua echoed.

After a collective nervous breakdown, they found the darn place. It was an older brick duplex, close to McGill, in the middle of an established neighbourhood. Lexie noticed the trees were very tall and whispered in the breeze.

The street was lined with the same style brick home right to the end. The only way to recognize one from the other was by the colourful front doors or the window boxes. The front entrances had wrought-iron gates and railings. She thought what a nice picture this row of houses would make, and resolved to unpack her camera as soon as possible.

The first day they unpacked and sorted themselves out. Daphne and Kate took the master bedroom. Josh and Lexie went in the teenage daughter's room, where there was a double bed but also Marilyn Manson posters, which Lexie gingerly removed and placed in the closet.

"Don't ever like heavy metal, Josh."

He grinned.

She set up Joshua's playpen, but he refused to sleep in it. He was in unfamiliar territory. She was two feet away but it didn't matter — he refused to lie down. He leaned over the side and held out his arms.

"Mama. Mama."

He looked at her with those big brown eyes and his shiny chestnut curls. She couldn't stand it. She was such a pushover. She'd no doubt regret this move when she got home, but she felt homesick too. She needed him as much as he needed her.

Kate and Daphne had to go to school, so Lexie and Josh were left to explore the city. The first morning they headed out, Lexie made her first mistake. She thought cars stopped at pedestrian crossings. She waited to cross the street for ten minutes, incredulous as everyone ignored her and whizzed by. She was so afraid, she ended up walking around the block several times.

Finally, she caught on: she walked when everyone else walked and they walked through red lights. If enough people gathered to make a small crowd, they left the sidewalk together and silently dared cars to hit them. Incredible.

Lexie pushed Josh in his stroller down St. Catherine Street. She gawked at gorgeous and stylish women who walked by her briskly as they spoke their rapid French. They could have stepped out of the pages of *Vogue* magazine. She was a country mouse — a country mouse lost in the big city.

For most of the month Lexie wandered and enjoyed her time alone with Josh. She took him to the park every day. He loved being pushed on the swings. She recognized a few other mothers after a while, and they'd exchange a few words of greeting. They'd point to Josh and hold up two fingers. Lexie shook her head and put up one. The only French she learned while she was there was *mon Dieu*!

They went on the bus. Josh loved to pull the cord to stop it. They liked to go to Old Montreal and take a horse-and-buggy ride through the narrow streets over cobblestones. The hollow *clip-clops* of the horse's huge feet made Josh laugh.

One evening Kate and Daphne mentioned that they'd like to have some of their colleagues over for wine and cheese.

"Oh, that's wonderful," Lexie cried. "A little adult conversation. Yippee."

She spent the next day shopping for their small get-together. She and Josh took their time. They bought red and white wine, different cheeses, and plenty of French bread and water crackers. She stopped at a bakery and went berserk. The choice of small delicate pastries was overwhelming. She thought of Susie when she asked the proprietor for two of everything. The woman insisted that Josh have a lemon tart, as well as a big kiss.

Lexie imagined what it would be like to live in a city and go to small shops for one thing or another. She pretended she belonged. At the end of the day, she'd go home to a small flat and a husband.

The girls got home and between them they assembled the goodies for the party. Then they got dressed up. They'd been in jeans since they arrived. Lexie put Josh to bed early and stayed with him until he fell asleep. She crawled away gingerly and hoped he wouldn't wake. She put pillows on the floor in case he fell off and left the door open. She made sure she had the baby monitor with her.

Finally, the three of them enjoyed a glass of wine together. Then the doorbell rang. Daphne went to answer it. There was a happy commotion as five people arrived at once. Everyone greeted Kate and Daphne with kisses on both cheeks.

Kate introduced Lexie. They shook her hand warmly. Except for one man who took her hand instead, and kissed it gently.

"*Enchanté, mademoiselle.*"

"*Bonjour.*" That was it for her French repertoire.

She spent the evening as the hostess, smiling but not saying much. She tried to understand their conversation, but since it was mostly about their project, it bored her stupid. She poured wine and refilled trays. And proceeded to get a little buzz on. When you don't talk, you drink. She had three glasses of wine before she knew it. The man who kissed her hand came over and sat beside her. She tried to remember his name. She was hopeless at that sort of thing. Then it came to her, Jean-Marc.

"So," he asked with a gorgeous French accent, "how do you enjoy your stay with us?"

"It's been wonderful, now that I know how to walk across the street without being killed."

He laughed. He was easy on the eyes. She looked for a wedding ring but didn't see one.

"Montreal's not known for its patient drivers," he agreed. "I grew up here. I don't notice anymore."

"I assume you work at McGill?"

"*Oui*, in the department of psychology. I am a *professeur*. I try to, eh, what's the word, deliver sense into young students. But they are too busy with thoughts of making love to listen to me."

"Really?" She felt herself blush. She didn't often talk to a nice-looking man about lovemaking.

"I think maybe you are lonely here, all by yourself most of the time. I'd like to take you to dinner one night. I love to escort beautiful women. *S'il vous plaît, oui*?"

He gave her a smile. Lexie's first thought was that she was sure he could talk her into anything or out of anything quite quickly.

"That would be lovely, thank you."

He kissed her hand again.

The party finally broke up. Everyone had to work in the morning. They said their goodnights. Jean-Marc came over and said he'd call her. She nodded and smiled. He kissed both her cheeks and left. *Golly, that was four kisses*, she thought. She felt good.

Kate came over to her as she waved them out the door. "So you little flirt, how did you get our Casanova so interested?"

"As you know darling, I taught Gabby everything she knows."

Lexie did go out with Jean-Marc. He picked her up at the door with a bouquet of flowers. He had all the right moves designed to impress a woman. It was a mild spring night, just perfect for a walk. As they made their way downtown, lights came on all over the city. People were out to enjoy the night air. They talked easily. Lexie was relaxed and happy.

He took her to a bistro on Metcalfe Street. It was dark, intimate, with tables for two covered in red-checked table-cloths. Round glass containers covered with plastic mesh held the candles.

Jean-Marc ordered wine and suggested the specialty, lamb with rosemary. They talked about everything. She told him about her family, the library and, of course, Joshua.

He was a bachelor. His mother despaired that he'd never settle down and produce the grandchildren she desperately wanted.

After dinner, they strolled along the sidewalk and didn't hurry back. He took her hand and she kept it in his. It was comfortable to be with a man. She missed it.

When they returned to the house, she faced him. "What a wonderful evening. Thank you so much. I'll never forget it."

He smiled. "It was my pleasure. May I kiss you goodnight?"

"You may."

He kissed her softly.

"Will I see you again?"

"Yes." He kissed her once more. It felt nice.

"Goodnight."

"*Bonne Nuit.*"

KATE AND DAPHNE were in their pyjamas with big mugs of cocoa cupped in their hands. They sat her down and demanded to know everything. Lexie kicked off her shoes and rubbed her feet. She wasn't used to high heels. "He's just a very nice man. And guess what? He asked me out again. Imagine?"

They threw tiny marshmallows at her head.

A week later Jean-Marc called and asked if she'd be interested in going to a cabaret. She agreed and decided to splurge on a new dress, since she'd only brought the one, and how often did one get the chance to browse in such a fashionable city?

She took the Metro, for a change. She'd never been on it and since it would deliver her to large department stores without having to walk outside, it seemed very convenient.

She soon regretted her decision. There were plenty of steep stairs to get down before arriving at the platform itself. Josh had a great time as he bounced in his stroller. Lexie was worn out.

She finally stood on the platform. There were plenty of characters who stood there with her — university students plugged into their headphones with backpacks that looked like they weighed a ton, old women carting small wire trolleys filled with shopping, and even a few drunks and punks.

She stayed well away from the tracks themselves. She looked around, turning her attention to the crowd on the other side of the tracks. Among those biding their time until the Metro arrived was a tall man with long brown hair. She watched him even though his back was to her, because he felt familiar. He pointed to a poster. A little black girl held his hand. She pointed too. And then they turned around.

It was Adrian.

Someone hit her on the chest with the back of a shovel. She gasped for air. She looked at the child. She was adorable and Lexie knew in an instant that she was African. She didn't know why, she just knew. She stood there and didn't move. The roar of the train approached.

Adrian looked up and didn't see her at first. He slowly turned his head towards her again. He looked shocked, amazed. He threw his hand in the air to greet her, then hesitated, as if he thought better of it.

He disappeared as the blue cars of the Metro rushed between them, with a huge swoosh of air and squealing tires. The doors opened and people poured out as others tried to get on. Lexie didn't know what to do. She panicked and pushed Joshua's stroller into the car. Before she could think of what she'd done, the doors shut behind her and the Metro surged ahead with a jolt.

Lexie hung on to the steel pole in front of her. She put her forehead on its cold metal. She rushed away from Adrian down a long, dark tunnel.

❦

ADRIAN STOOD WITH Binti on the subway platform. Every time a subway car came by, he meant to get on, but he couldn't. He thought if he waited there long enough, she would reappear, somehow miraculously come back to him.

It was her. He was sure of it. And she had a child. She had loved someone. The thought of it made him —

Binti got agitated. "Papa. Papa." She held his trousers in her tiny fist and pushed at his leg.

Adrian looked down and picked her up. "I'm sorry, pet. I'm sorry."

A subway car roared through the station again. This time he and his daughter got on it.

❧

KATE KNEW SOMETHING was wrong as soon as she and Daphne came home at the end of the day. Lexie hadn't started dinner. She sat in the dark, in the living room, with Josh asleep in her arms.

Kate was frightened. "What's wrong?"

"I saw Adrian today."

"Adrian? Where?"

"On the Metro."

"Did you speak to him?"

"No."

"Did he see you?"

"Yes."

"He didn't say anything?"

"No."

"I don't understand. Why wouldn't he speak to you, at least?"

"He doesn't care."

"I'm sure that's not true, Lex."

"I don't want to talk about it."

Kate went back into the kitchen. Daphne looked worried. "What is it?"

"She saw Adrian."

"Really? What did he say?"

"That's the problem. He didn't say anything."

"Oh, gosh. Poor Lex."

LEXIE ASKED KATE to send her regrets to Jean-Marc. She told her to make up some excuse. She didn't want to see him again. Men made your life miserable. She had no energy to put up with them anymore.

Kate did tell him. He called the apartment and left his phone number. He asked her to call him back. She didn't. He eventually got the message.

She stayed indoors that last week. She wanted to go home to her little house, to Mom and Dad, to people who loved her. To Sophie and Susie.

Kate and Daphne couldn't give her much comfort. Lexie knew they felt guilty about not being able to take her home right away, but they had their work to do.

She decided to call Susan. She'd cheer her up, she always did. Susie would be on her side. Lexie dialled the number.

"Hi Susie, it's me!" she yelled into the phone, as if Susie were a thousand miles away, which she was.

"Oh Lexie, do I ever miss you! I can't wait for you to come home. I just can't wait."

"Why can't you wait?"

"I can't wait for you to meet Ernie!"

"Who on earth is Ernie?"

She sounded so excited. "A man I met and it's all because of Sophie!"

"The two of you wandered into a bar and picked up guys?"

"You're so funny."

"But Sue —"

Susie talked right over her. Lexie couldn't get a word in edgewise.

"You know how you told me to make sure Sophie didn't waste away at your mom's? So I go over there and Sophie's in a big snit under the chair in the living room."

She took a breath. "Your mother went to the kitchen to make tea. I knelt down and whispered that the cavalry had arrived. I held out my treats and she just about tore my hand off. She gobbled everything."

She took another breath. "I had to go buy more stuff. I stopped in at the new pet store off Charlotte Street. There was Ernie! He's the owner. He's so nice Lexie. He's so gentle with little animals. He's not much to look at mind you, but then neither am I."

"That's *not* true."

She giggled and continued. "I bought some stuff for Sophie. I went back the next day and said Sophie hated it — a downright lie as you well know. That cat will eat a tin can, if given half a chance."

She inhaled. "He gave me his deluxe brand. The next day I went back and said I'd like a gerbil. He sold me one. His name is Laraby — the gerbil, not the pet store guy. I went back to get more supplies for Laraby and Ernie asked me to go to the movies with him! So we went. The next Friday he called and asked me out again. We went to the show and then to the Dairy Queen for Peanut Butter Parfaits! Oh, Lexie, he's so nice to me. I'm in love!"

There was no way on God's green earth Lexie was going to ruin this girl's day.

"Susie, I'm so happy for you. No one deserves it more than you."

"Thanks, Lexie. I knew you'd be thrilled for me. Donalda's given me the cold shoulder, naturally. By the way, have you had a good time?"

"Yes dear, a great time, but I can't wait to get home."

"Everyone's dying for you to come back. Your parents are out of their minds. All they want is to hold Josh again. Is he bigger? God, what did I just say?! This is Joshua. I can't wait to hold him either, and have Ernie meet him. I've told Ernie all about our big guy!"

Lexie said goodbye to the happiest girl in the world. She put down the phone and wept.

She needed to be home.

Chapter Twelve

IT WAS DÉJÀ vu, only everything was in reverse. As she drove in the driveway Mom ran out the back door and squealed. Dad waved and smiled behind her. Boy, did she need this kind of reception to give her a lift. There's nothing like having your parents glad to see you. Lexie turned off the engine and climbed out to be enfolded in their loving arms.

There was no one there. They were on the other side of the van, clawing at the door, trying to be the first one to reach Joshua. Once they had a hold of him, all hell broke loose. There were tears and kisses and hugs by the bucketful. As an afterthought, they came over and gave Lexie a quick kiss. Then they turned around as a unit and whisked her kid into the house and left her standing in the backyard all by herself.

Well.

Finally Dad stuck his head back out the screen door.

"Get in here, Princess. Give your old Dad a hug."

That's better.

LEXIE INVITED SUSAN and Ernie over for dinner shortly after she got back. She made lasagna and a huge salad, had wine, garlic bread, and strawberry shortcake with whipped cream for dessert. She wanted to impress Ernie, to let him know how special he was, to Susan and her friends.

She'd spoken to Susan on the phone when she got home but hadn't seen her. Lexie had to get her house in order and

Susan finally had a life. She looked forward to seeing her old pal.

The doorbell rang and they came right in.

What is it about the love of a man that makes a woman beautiful? Susan was aglow. She had cut her hair into a short bob that made it look thicker. It bounced around her face. She wore makeup and a nice sweater and skirt.

Lexie knew why she fell for Ernie. He was shy and unassuming. He had kind eyes and a gentle way about him, perfect to reassure small creatures. Lexie loved him.

Sophie loved him too. She came over and rubbed his legs immediately.

"This is a beautiful cat!" Ernie said. Lexie was pleased. So was Sophie.

Susan introduced Ernie to Joshua. Ernie reached down and gave his hand a little shake. Josh gave him his goofy grin.

"Oh Lexie, did I ever miss this little guy," Susan said.

"He's not so little!" Ernie remarked.

"He'll always be our little baby. Right Lexie?"

"Right Susie."

ALL TOO SOON, Lexie had to get back to work. Her maternity leave was up. The thought of it made her sick to her stomach. She and Josh were a team, their own little family. To spend eight hours a day without her other half was going to be as painful as being torn in two.

She fretted about being able to find a daycare centre she could trust. She didn't want the caregivers to treat him like a two-year-old and not understand he was still just a baby himself. There were two thousand reasons why she didn't want him to go.

Then Mom solved everything.

One day, out of the blue, she said, "Would you trust me to look after Joshua when you go back to work?"

Lexie's first reaction was instant joy. Then worry.

"What will Beth say?"

"What's Beth got to do with it?"

"Won't she be put out? You never looked after her girls when they were little."

"Of course, I didn't. She stayed at home with her girls, and had a husband to help her." Mom sounded puzzled. "I did babysit for her. Do you mean to imply I treat Joshua differently than my granddaughters?"

"No."

"What then?"

"She'll think Josh receives special treatment, and she'll hate me."

"Listen dear," Mom said, "you can't walk on eggshells around your sister forever. I have every right to be delighted with my grandson. If Willie was here, and God knows how much I wish he was, I'd behave the same way with him. I don't spend as much time with the girls as I'd like. They're a tribe, all on their own. They overwhelm me at times. Four little screamers…all like their mother."

Lexie smiled.

Mom took her hand. "I'd like to help you Lexie. I see how hard you try to give Joshua all he needs. It can't be easy on your own. You look lonely. I know how much you love him, how you hate to be parted from him. It might make your life easier, if you knew he was with me all day, instead of with strangers."

"I love you so much," was all Lexie could think to say.

"FOR JESUS' SAKE, will ya give it up?" Marlene cried, as Lexie dialled her mother's number yet again. "The poor woman won't be able to take care of the kid if she has to run to the phone every five minutes."

"You're right." She hung up. "I just miss him terribly. I wonder what he's up to, and what he's had for lunch. You know."

"Well, I imagine Bam Bam's pulled your mom on the back of his wagon all morning and just sat down to a plate of ribs."

"Oh, shut up. Why does everyone make fun of how big he is?"

Judy said, "Because everyone's jealous, dear. They all wish they had such a gorgeous child."

Lexie was mollified. "Thank you." She stuck her tongue out at Marlene. Marlene stuck hers right back.

They soon had a nice routine. Lexie got Josh ready in the morning and took him to her mother. She didn't even have to get out and take him inside. More often than not, Mom would wait by the door, run out, and grab him from his car seat. He was always delighted to see her. They'd wave her goodbye.

Mom looked ten years younger with Josh around. Her friends thought she was nuts to run after a baby all day, but she didn't seem to mind.

After three weeks Lexie started to relax and stopped

pestering her mother every hour. That's when there was a phone call for her at the library. No one ever called her at the library. She panicked instantly and ran to the phone.

"Hello!?"

"Lexie, calm down. It's all right. Everything's all right," her mother said.

"Well, if it's all right, why are you calling me?!"

"Everything's fine. Josh is fine. He had a little accident."

"*An accident? What kind of an accident?*"

"Lexie! Get a hold of yourself and calm down. You'll be useless to everyone if you don't stop shouting. These things happen to little kids."

Lexie took a deep breath. "All right, tell me."

"I was over at Beth's and the lid on Joshua's cup came off and he ended up covered in sticky apple juice, that's all. Beth gave him a bath and had Josh by the arm to help him out of the tub, when he slipped. She held on because she didn't want him to fall and hit his head, but I'm afraid his arm came out of its socket."

"*Oh, my God!*"

Judy and Marlene looked frightened.

"*Why aren't you with him?*"

"I had to stay with the girls. Beth had him wrapped up and out the door so fast, I couldn't stop her."

"*Where is he?*"

"At outpatients. Look dear, why don't…"

Lexie threw down the phone and ran for her car keys. Judy ran after Lexie, and Marlene ran after her. "My God, what is it?"

"It's Josh, he's at the hospital and I have to go!" She ran out the door.

Judy hollered after her. "Do you want me to drive you?"

But Lexie and her van had already disappeared.

Passing the poor slobs waiting to see a doctor, Lexie opened the big door that separated the waiting room from the outpatient department itself, and ran down the corridor. She looked into cubicle after cubicle. A nurse yelled at her. She didn't stop.

She found them. Joshua sat on the bed with a tear-stained face while Beth rubbed his arm. A young doctor stood beside them.

"Joshua!"

"Mama!" He held out his arms and she grabbed him. He buried his face in her neck and his legs held her in a death grip.

She gave Beth the dreaded big sister look. "What happened?"

Beth cried, "Oh Lexie, it was all my fault!" She tearfully recounted the story. She said over and over how sorry she was. She never meant to hurt him.

Lexie felt much better with her baby in her arms.

"Of course, it not your fault, Beth. You did the right thing. You got him here quickly and I'm very grateful. Now stop crying."

Beth looked at her and did what she was told.

Lexie turned to the doctor, who they ignored during this exchange. "Is he all right?"

"Sure, he's fine. He can take it. He's a big lad. Once you pop the arm back in place, there's instant relief."

"Well, that's something." She bounced Josh up and down and felt his hot breath on her. He was calmer.

The doctor headed out the door. Lexie was incredulous.

"Well, what do I do? Should I put his arm in a sling for a while?"

"Nope."

"Do I give him Tylenol for the pain?"

"Naw, he's tough. He'd probably beat me at arm wrestling."

She'd had enough. She got in his face. "Listen kid. You think because my son's big, he doesn't have feelings. He doesn't feel pain? If I pulled your arm out of its socket, right about now, you'd bawl like a baby too. So I suggest you brush up on your bedside manner and get out of my way."

She turned to Beth. "Let's go."

Beth followed her like a little lamb, right out the door.

Lexie stayed home for the next few days, more for her sake than Joshua's. She needed to see for herself that his arm was better.

Her mother called. "Dearest, I really don't think it's necessary to hover over him. I'm perfectly capable of taking care of him."

"I know that, Mom. I just need to be here."

"For heaven's sake, stop feeling so guilty, Lexie. You can't be by his side every minute of the day. What are you going to do when he goes to school and starts roughhousing with other little boys?"

"Maybe I'll home-school him."

"You're a lunatic." Her mother hung up on her.

Two days was long enough to convince Lexie that Josh was perfectly fine. Naturally, she fretted all day but there were no phone calls for her at the library. She hurried to her mother's after work. Beth and the girls were over visiting.

Mom was on the phone and she gestured that Josh was upstairs. Lexie nodded and went to get him. She heard Beth's voice. She stopped by the bedroom door and looked in. Beth had Josh on the bed as she changed his diaper. She kissed his tummy and blew on it, making funny noises. Josh laughed his deep rumbly laugh and smiled at her, his hands in her hair.

"Who's Auntie Beth's special boy? Is it Josh? Is it Joshua?" She nibbled his toes. "Yum, Yum, Yum."

Thank you God. Thank you.

☙

LEXIE WAS WASHING the floors one Sunday when the phone rang. It was Susie.

"I'm getting married!"

"Oh my God!"

"Can you believe it?"

"Of course I can believe it. Did he get down on one knee?"

"Oh Lexie, it was romantic. I sat in his living room. He said he had to get something. While I waited, his dog Ian came in. He had a big bow around his neck and a note that said, 'Will you marry me?' *Can you believe it?*"

"What a great guy. You're so lucky Susan. When's the big day?"

"As soon as possible. I mean why should I wait? My mother's driving me crazy, though. She wants a big wedding. Ernie and I want his twin sister to perform the ceremony in his backyard, so his animals can be there. She's a minister."

"I didn't know Ernie had a twin."

"Yeah, Bernadette. Bernie for short." Susie laughed. "Anyway, don't forget Sophie has to come. She's the guest of honour. If it wasn't for her, this never would've happened."

Susan rambled on for twenty minutes and by that time, Josh was soaked and Sophie was ticked because he'd thrown water at her.

Susan's mother Georgie called Lexie the next day. She got right to the point. "Are you having a shower for Susan?"

Lexie was caught off guard. "Ah, I only found out about it last night, but yes, I'd love to give her a shower. I just need to make some plans first."

"Don't worry about plans. I'll tell you everything you need to know."

Lexie rolled her eyes. She knew what Georgie was like. "Mrs. Sheppard, if I have a shower I think I'd just like to have it at my house, with a few of our closest friends. I'll make some canapés and a few veggie trays and we'll have some wine. You don't have to worry."

"Wine? You can't have wine?"

"I can't?"

"No dear. We're all teetotallers. Spirits never pass our lips."

"Oh. You're coming to my shower? I thought…"

"Susan's in a bit of a rush, and we don't have time to have a lot of showers, so I'll help you organize yours. There's a pet. I'll call you in a day or so with the guest list." She hung up.

Lexie looked at the receiver.

Susan called her in a panic the next day. "You're having a shower for me?"

"Well, I…"

"Did my mother call you and invite herself and four hundred friends over to *your* shower?"

"Well…"

"I can't *believe* her nerve! I'm so sorry Lexie. Call her up immediately and tell her to get stuffed."

"As if."

"That woman is so infuriating. I could wring her neck."

"Get used to it. Mothers and daughters come to fisticuffs over wedding plans. Mom and Beth had a hand-slap fight just before we left for the church."

"A what?"

"It's when a frantic mother tries to adjust her daughter's headpiece but the bride wants her to leave it alone."

"I'm so upset…"

"Susie, calm down. I really don't mind. We'll do it her way and the next night, you can come over and we can get sloshed. How's that sound?"

"I love you."

Lexie ran into Beth's the next day. "You have to do me a big favour. Come to Susie's shower."

"Why's that a favour? I'd love to come. I went to a Women and Wealth Management seminar once just to sit in a chair for an hour and not hear the word 'Mommy.'"

Once Lexie told her the guest list, Beth tried to back out but it was too late.

DONALDA CHARGED INTO the library one day and bee-lined over to Lexie.

"What kind of goodies do I make for this shower?"

Lexie had to invite her, unfortunately.

"Why don't you make something sweet?"

"Like what?" Donalda had absolutely no imagination.

"Good golly, there are two million recipes on this island for sugar cookies, alone. Do you really need me to think something up?"

She stood there with her arms folded. "I don't bake."

"Now's your chance."

Fortunately, despite having her shower hijacked by Susie's nearest and dearest, and everyone squeezed like sardines into Lexie's living room, they all had a great time. Susie loved Lexie's hooked trivets and she even loved Donalda's idea of a gift, a huge ceramic pig dressed like a cop that hollered, "Stay away from the cookie jar," when its head was lifted back.

And as planned, she and Susie got sloshed the very next evening.

THE BIG DAY had arrived.

"This is ridiculous," Mom announced as she, Beth, and the girls congregated at Lexie's house to get ready for the wedding. Everyone was in an uproar with last-minute preparations.

Dad said he'd meet them there. Rory managed to get out of it altogether. He pleaded an important golf game with a client. Beth told him he was a coward, but let him off the hook.

Mom struggled with Joshua's outfit.

"What's ridiculous?" Lexie asked. "Here, give him to me."

Her mom passed him over.

"Do I really have to spell it out? A cat as a bridesmaid? Who ever heard of such a thing?"

"Ernie has Ian as a best man," Michaela piped up. She swung her pretty dress back and forth.

"Well, that's sensible. An actual human being."

"Ian's a dog, Grammy."

Mom powdered her nose in the hall mirror. "What! Oh, my God, this is a dignified affair."

"Mom. It's Susan's day. If this is what she wants, this is what she should have."

"All I know is, I'll be as mad as a wet hen if these animals get into a fight and the girls end up with their new dresses dirty," Beth grumped as she did French braids on the three little ones. Michaela absolutely refused, a girl after Lexie's own heart. She liked her hair swinging, along with her dress.

Joshua had on a tartan vest and little bow tie. Sophie wore a bow too but she wasn't happy about it. After the fussing and the fuming, they piled into Betsy.

The wedding was beautiful, with a guest list that included four dogs, six cats, a rabbit, and a snake. Lexie was the maid of honour. She stood with Sophie in her arms. Sophie behaved like the lady she was, and never blinked, even when Ian tried to bite her.

Susan looked lovely. Her dress was simple and elegant. She smiled happily as she crossed the lawn on her father's arm. Georgie, still miffed they weren't in a church, cried through the whole thing.

Ernie looked as if he wanted to pass out, probably because he'd never talked to so many people at once. Bernie announced them husband and wife, and it was done, exactly as they hoped, with their family, friends, and animals under a clear blue sky.

LEXIE WENT INTO a slump. Susan was married. Beth was married. Even Kate was married, after a fashion. Mom and Dad were married. Her grandparents had been married, and their grandparents before them. She was alone.

A few men called her up from time to time to go to the show or a hockey game. She turned them down. She couldn't be bothered. It just seemed like too much hard work.

Donalda called her up to commiserate about being the only two women in the theatre group who weren't married. Lexie told her to go blow.

Beth tried to cheer her up.

"Look at it this way. You don't have to pick up some guy's dirty socks."

"Yes, I do. Joshua's."

"Well, split hairs then."

They sat at Beth's kitchen table. The girls put makeup on their cousin. He sat quietly and let them. Lexie didn't care. She didn't care about much.

"Why don't you get in touch with Joshua's father then, if you won't go out with anyone else. Maybe you're pining away over him?"

Was she? She thought about Joss often, but always had to stop herself. It was too big to think of. It blotted out everything.

"No."

Beth looked exasperated. Lexie needed an explanation.

"Beth, I fell in love with Joss's body, if you must know the truth. The package. I really didn't know him. I mean we were only together for seven days. I'll love him for the rest of my life for giving me Joshua, but it's over."

"I think you hope Adrian will come back."

Lexie didn't say anything.

No one at home knew she'd seen Adrian. She had sworn Kate and Daphne to secrecy. She wasn't sure why, maybe humiliation. Afraid to spoil her happiness, she never even told Susan.

If he'd only shouted her name, she would have stayed glued to that platform, and waited for him to come down to her side. But he didn't. He looked as though he was asking himself why he'd want to get involved with her again.

He knew where she lived. He never sent her a postcard. I mean, how many clues did she need before she got it through her head. He only used her. And her sister.

She went to Mom's to pick Josh up after work and was invited to stay for supper. While Mom put the potatoes on, Josh played on the floor with a strainer and wooden spoon. She sought out her dad.

She knocked on the door of his study.

"Come."

She poked her head around so he could see it was her.

"Hi Princess, come on in."

"Hi Daddy. Whatcha doin'?" Her old question.

"Staying out of your mother's way." They laughed at their old joke.

Lexie thought he looked tired. "How are you?"

"Tired." He put his hand through his hair, and gave the top of his head a little scratch. He smoothed his hair back down again.

"Dad, why don't you retire? You could have done it long ago."

"I suppose so, but I still feel useful. I don't like to throw in the towel and leave these younger men in the lurch. They have young families they don't see enough of as it is."

"But you've certainly done your fair share. You've delivered half the people in this town."

He started to swivel in his chair.

"You know Lex, it's been a rewarding life. Seeing newborns come into the world, so much hope and expectation. And so much heartache when things go wrong. We know that as a family, far too well."

They sat in silence for a while.

"Life never comes out the way you think," she said finally. "I had it in my head I'd be like Beth now, with a husband and a bunch of kids and a normal life. That's all I ever wanted."

"There's no such thing as a normal life, Lexie. Things don't always come out the way we expect, no matter how hard we try."

"Have you tried hard, Dad?"

"What do you mean?"

Lexie chewed her thumbnail. "I don't know. Have things in your life turned out the way you wanted them to?"

His chair stopped. They looked at each other.

"Not exactly. But I don't think anyone lives without regret." He paused. "We've all travelled on roads that may have been better left unexplored. I know I have."

Lexie nodded and continued to bite her nail. She waited, but he said nothing else.

Finally she gave a big sigh. "I feel like the tortoise of the family, while all my sisters are hares."

Dad clasped his hands together, leaned forward and put them on his desk, as if to explain something to one of his worried patients.

"Honey, don't compare yourself to your sisters. It's not fair to you, and it's not fair to them. Everyone has dreams that don't come true. Would you really want Beth's life? Would you want to lose your son? Would you want the struggles Kate has faced in her life?"

Lexie looked at him.

"Yes, I know about Kate, and I admire how she gets on with things in spite of everything. Or, my dear girl, would you really want to be like Gabby, who feels she can't come home because she's so ashamed?"

Lexie got upset. "All I wanted was to love someone, and he went away and never came back. How do I live with that? Or more importantly, how do I forget him?"

She thought of two men when she said that, though Dad thought she meant Adrian.

"Maybe Lexie," Dad said kindly, "it wasn't about you at all. Maybe it was about him, something he wanted to forget, or run away from."

She looked at her father.

"Lexie, I met Adrian once, but once was enough. He was a man in serious trouble. No matter what kind of public face he put on."

Dad paused. "Think about it. He spent his time here wandering the shoreline by himself. A man doesn't walk alone, for months at a time, unless he has a pain so big he has to keep moving, to keep it at arm's length."

She didn't say anything at first.

"How did you get so smart, Dad?"

"If you live long enough Lexie, you learn a thing or two."

Later, as they dried the dishes, she asked Mom a question she hadn't wanted to ask before.

"Mom, did Adrian leave Gabby, or did Gabby leave him?"

"He left her."

"Then I wish she'd come home."

Chapter Thirteen

SHE GOT THE call as she got ready for bed.

"Lexie." Her mother's voice was so faint she could hardly hear her. She knew something was very wrong.

"Mom, what is it?"

"It's your father. Please come."

Her voice trembled. "Where are you?"

"At the hospital."

"Mom, I'll be right there." She hung up and dialled the phone.

"Susan, you need to come and take care of Joshua. It's my dad. I have to go."

SHE RAN INTO outpatients. She could see nurses and doctors. They all looked at her. Crying. No.

She saw Lillian. She sat on a chair, in a corner of the hall, away from everything, her head in her hands. Lexie ran past her. She ran until she saw someone. Her father's old friend, Dr. Smith, waited for her. That's good. Smitty would know what to do.

He grabbed her arm before she could go in the room. Her mother stood by a hospital bed. She could see her father's feet.

"Lexie, please."

Her lower jaw was numb. "He'll be all right, won't he?"

"Lexie, your father died. I'm so sorry. We did everything we could."

Her mother turned around. They reached for each other.

They were drowning in sorrow. From the corridor came the sound of people running. She could hear Beth's voice, then Rory's. They reached for them too.

Beth fainted. Rory and Mom went with the doctor to lay her on a bed, while Lexie stayed by her father's side. She looked at his wonderful face and wondered where he went. How could he just go and not be here? She didn't even kiss him when she said goodbye last night, she was in such a rush to get home. How would they live without him? How did this work? She didn't know what to do. She put her hand out to touch his but she was afraid. It would be cold and her father had never been anything but warm.

She felt an arm go around her shoulder. She turned to see the head nurse beside her. Lexie knew her face, but forgot her name. She steadied her.

"Oh Daddy," Lexie moaned. "You need to come back. I'm never going to see you again."

"Yes you will Lexie."

She didn't understand. She turned towards the nurse.

"Just look in the mirror."

SHE DIDN'T KNOW who drove them home. It was the middle of the night, and the lights were on. Mom's good friends Eleanor and Jeanne waited inside the door. Kind Smitty had called them before they left the hospital. They took hold of her mother and cried in each others' arms before they led her inside and took off her coat. They made her sit with a hot cup of tea laced with brandy. The three of them, friends since they were young, huddled together.

Lexie and Beth sat at the kitchen table and held hands. Rory was on the phone. He called home to tell their next-door neighbour the bad news and to check on the girls.

Lexie had to call her sisters. Mom was in no shape to talk to anyone. How could she tell them? Rory wondered if they should wait until morning to tell Kate, so she wouldn't drive through the night. Lexie said no, she'd want to be with them as soon as she could. She knew Daphne would drive the five hours home.

How do you tell your baby sister her dad is dead? Their father was their rock. He was the one who was steady and sure as the women in his family swirled around him in constant chaos. They could go to him for anything, and nothing they ever did would make him stop loving them. And now there was a big gaping hole.

Lexie told Daphne first because she answered the phone. Daphne would be there to hold Kate. It was her only consolation.

"I'm coming, Lexie. I'm coming," Kate cried. "Oh my God. I'll be there as soon as I can. Tell Mommy I love her. Oh God." The phone went dead. She was coming.

Her mother sobbed from the other room. "Lexie, I want Gabby. I want Gabby home. Tell her to come home."

Lexie went upstairs to find her mother's address book on her bedside table and searched for Gabby's number. There were five different ones, all for her. One was circled with the word "new" beside it.

Gabby picked up on the first ring. Lexie didn't even know what time zone she was in.

"Hello?"

Lexie started to cry. It was so good to hear her voice.

"Gabby, it's Lexie."

"Lexie? Oh my God, what's wrong?"

"It's Daddy."

"Is he sick? What's going on? What's happened?" She was frantic.

"I don't know how to tell you this."

"He's dead, isn't he? Is he dead?"

"I'm so sorry, Gabby. I'm so sorry." She cried so hard she couldn't breathe.

Gabby dropped the phone. She wailed, howled. Lexie couldn't help her. She was too far away.

The wake was delayed a day, to give Gabby a chance to get home from England. She was distraught. A friend, a female voice anyway, called and said she needed a little time to compose herself before she flew over the Atlantic. The friend said not to worry — she would take Gabby to the airport herself.

For two days, it was an endless nightmare. Lexie wasn't sure where she was, or what she was supposed to do. Susan dropped everything and took care of Josh and Sophie. Lexie would go home to get changed and hug Josh. She'd cry with Susan, then head back to the house. Beth and Rory spent more time at home. The girls were very upset, and it made Beth feel better to be home with them.

Kate and Daphne stayed with Mom. Lexie ended up going to the door to thank their neighbours and friends for their gifts of food. They had too much, and still they existed on ice water from the fridge dispenser.

Rory left for the airport to get Gabby, but when Lexie heard the back door open, she thought it was yet another friend with ham or cabbage rolls. She went to meet them.

Gabby stood there with Rory behind her, the suitcases in his hands. She dropped her purse and sagged against the door.

"Lexie, help me."

She caught Gabby in her arms before she fell.

MOM GATHERED THE four of them in her bedroom before the wake.

"Please sit, girls."

They looked at each other and did as she asked. Mom stood by the window in her black suit and held a handkerchief in her hand. She dabbed her eyes before she threw her shoulders back and composed herself.

"We need all our strength, girls, to get through this day and the funeral tomorrow. I want you to make your father proud, by acting like ladies and holding your heads up high. There will be no crying or carrying on. That's behaviour for behind closed doors."

They rushed to tell her she could count on them.

"We have wonderful friends who will help us through this. That's what makes living in a small town so wonderful. But small towns thrive on gossip, especially gossip about those who were well known, like your father."

She took a moment. They waited.

"You might hear rumours that your dad was over at Lillian Holmes's house for something other than hospital business."

Lexie's sisters were indignant that anyone would say such a thing. They all started to speak at once. Mom held up her hand and made them listen.

"I'm the only authority that matters. I want you to know that your dad would never do such a thing. I know…knew him better than anyone else, and so do you. He was, in fact, over at Lillian's because she had a patient in crisis and needed his opinion. The man had a sudden seizure. Lillian dialled 911 immediately, and went to the hospital with him. Smitty was on call and phoned me right away. End of story."

She pointed at them. "So, if any of you hear anything malicious or nasty about your father, you are not to dignify it with an answer. It will be beneath your contempt."

Beth, Gabby, and Kate assured her she would be proud of them. And so her mother provided armour for Lexie's sisters that would keep them from harm. But it was Lexie's hand she looked for as they walked out the door.

Her mother need not have worried. Lexie's dad was loved. As they drove to the funeral home, mourners were lined up all the way down the street. It looked as if the whole town was there. Her mother wept when she saw them.

They got out of the car and walked inside together as a family. Men and women parted to let them pass. Everyone was quiet. They would save their condolences for inside, when they could hold their hands and tell them how much they loved Dr. William Ivy.

A FEW DAYS after the funeral, Lexie took Gabby home to meet Joshua. Gabby had spent every moment with Mom.

There was so much time to be made up for. She and Gabby didn't talk about Adrian. That would come later. They were dealing now with something bigger than that.

Just inside the door they heard Susan and Joshua singing to the radio. Susan danced to Phil Collins, while Josh sat in his high chair, waving his Cheerios around.

"Here he is," Lexie said proudly. "Joshua, this is your Auntie Gabby."

"Tee Abby, Tee Abby!" he grinned and went on with his symphony of cereal.

Gabby smiled for the first time since she arrived. When Lexie saw Joshua, some of the pain she was in floated away. It settled in again, like a blanket of fog, before too long, but for that moment, he helped her. She wanted him to help Gabby too.

THE NEXT DAYS were very hard. Lexie's mother cried over everything. She didn't know whether to keep all Dad's things where they were, or start to sort them out. Lexie and her sisters told her to do whatever felt right. She wanted them each to pick something of Dad's they especially loved. Lexie took his bathrobe, and Kate, his fountain pen. Beth wanted the coffee mug he drank out of every morning and Gabby asked for his university ring.

Lexie sorted through Dad's papers in his desk, to try and help Mom with the estate. It was a dreadful job. She'd pick up an item, a pack of gum he hadn't finished, and hold it to her cheek, as if it could bring him back. She spent more time in his study than her sisters. She felt comfort there, as if he had stepped out and would return any minute.

That's when she found the letters.

Lexie knew what they were instantly. She saw "Darling William" at the top of a page and "I love you, Lillian," at the bottom. They hadn't been mailed — maybe Lillian had left them in his office. Lexie didn't want to know. She gathered them up, slid them into the waistband of her jeans, and covered them with her shirt. Mom walked in a few seconds later.

"Did you find the power of attorney?"

"Not yet."

Her mother sank into the chair Lexie usually sat in when she talked to Dad. She had dark circles under her eyes. She looked old.

"This is so much work," she sighed. "Your father took care of this sort of thing. Why didn't I listen when he told me where things were? I can't remember what he said."

"It'll sort itself out, Mom. I'll help you. We all will."

"What would I ever do without you girls?" Her face crumbled as she reached for her ever-present wad of Kleenex. "I miss him so much, Lexie."

"Of course you do. We all do."

"Even with everything." she said. "I still loved him very much. And he loved me. We kept our friendship. Our love for you girls held us together. We shared our wonderful family, our beautiful grandchildren. She couldn't take that away from me. She never possessed that part of his heart."

Lexie looked at her and wondered how she could be so brave in the face of all that happened. How did she live with the idea her husband loved someone else as well?

"Did he ever admit it, Mom? Did he ever tell you about her?"

"Yes, he told me. Finally. He said he couldn't look me in the eye anymore."

"But I don't understand. How he could do it to you? Why did he do it? You had a good marriage didn't you?"

"Yes, we had a good marriage, but sometimes even a good marriage isn't enough."

"That's silly. It should be enough."

"Lexie, you're young.

"No, I'm not."

"You're still young," her mother continued. "You have yet to learn that everything isn't black or white. Most of us live in shades of grey. There are two sides to everything. I wasn't blameless you know."

"What do you mean? You didn't run out and have an affair."

"Of course not," she smiled. "Most women don't have the time for something like that. We're too busy taking care of our family. I was always busy. I had you girls and my teaching career. I was totally absorbed with your lives, my classroom, the garden and the organizations I belonged too. Sometimes I think your father thought he wasn't important to me. I had no time for him. And he was right. I often didn't. I took him for granted."

"That doesn't justify what he did — to run around behind your back."

"No, but it helps explain it. Your father spent a lot of time at the hospital. It gave her the opportunity to get to know him. She took advantage of it."

"She's a miserable bitch. She took something that wasn't hers to take in the first place."

Her mom gave her a sad look. "Thanks for being on my side. I need it."

"Is it possible to hate someone for something they did, but love them anyway?"

"Yes."

That night, after Josh went to bed, Lexie lit a fire and burned her father's love letters. She didn't look at one of them. That was a part of his life he didn't share with her, or with any of them. She didn't want to embarrass him, even in death.

Chapter Fourteen

DAPHNE HAD GONE back to Halifax shortly after the funeral. The four girls were together with their mother under the same roof for the first time in over ten years. It gave them comfort. Besides helping sort through Dad's possessions, they sat in the kitchen a good deal, talking about old memories. They laughed as often as they cried. But the time came for them to get back into their own routines. Their mother knew that but it was hard for them not to notice the panic in her eyes at the thought of rattling around in a big house by herself. They sat together at the kitchen table and drank their last cup of tea before they started their lives over again, their lives without Dad.

"Mom," Kate asked, "would you like to come and stay with me for a while? Maybe you need to get away for a bit."

Kate's sisters looked at each other. This was the first time Kate had asked Mom to come to her home. It was a big step.

Mom sat at the head of the table. She twirled her wedding ring on her finger. "I don't think so dear. But thank you."

"Why not?"

"I need to be here."

"Are you sure that's the reason?" Kate's voice sounded tight.

Lexie wondered, *why now*? Did she feel safe surrounded by them, or had Dad's death made everything else irrelevant?

Her mother sighed, "I don't want talk about this now, Kate."

She didn't take her eyes off Mom. "Talk about what?"

Gabby spoke up. "Why don't you leave Mom alone? She obviously isn't up to it. She needs to be here. Don't make a federal case out of it."

Kate turned to look at her. "What would you know about what Mom needs to do? You haven't been here, have you? You haven't suffered with the rest of us."

"Girls, don't start."

"No." Kate turned back to Mom. "I don't understand why Gabby gets a say in anything we should or shouldn't do. She comes, she goes. She's a part-time member of the family, so she doesn't get a vote."

Lexie tried to interject. "Kate, calm down. What's wrong?"

Beth leaned towards Lexie and answered for her. "What do you mean 'what's wrong'? She doesn't have to be spoken to like that from someone who doesn't give a damn about the rest of us."

This was bad.

Mom held her two hands in front of her as if to push them away. "Girls, please. We're all overwrought. Just let it go."

"No." Kate jumped up from the table and started to walk around her mother's outstretched hands, as if she were playing musical chairs. She couldn't stay still.

"This is probably the last time the five of us will be alone together, without kids or husbands or lovers hanging around." Kate looked at Gabby as she finished her sentence. She paced up and down, as if gathering strength, before she went back to her own chair, stood behind it, and used it as a shield.

"I'm tired of never saying anything. Ever since Daddy died I've watched all of us. No one ever tells the truth."

She pointed at Mom. "Mom doesn't say anything to Gabby about the endless men she tosses aside. Or why she didn't come home for so long."

She pointed at Beth. "Beth doesn't say anything about how hurt she was when Gabby didn't come home after she heard about Willie."

Lexie was next. "Lexie doesn't say anything about how Gabby broke her heart when she took off with Adrian."

"And Gabby here," she threw her arm out as if to introduce her to an audience, "doesn't say anything about the fact that she broke it."

She paused for a breath and put her hand over her own heart. "And I don't say anything to Mom about Daphne being my lover and Mom doesn't say anything about it either."

She stopped and looked at them. They stared at the table. No one wanted to say anything.

"*Well?*"

There was silence. Kate sighed and sat back down on her chair beside Mom.

"Mom, you know about me and Daphne, don't you?"

She looked straight ahead.

Kate watched her mother with sad eyes. "You know I'm gay, don't you? You know we live together, don't you?"

Mom didn't say anything.

Kate held her hands together on her lap, as if to say grace.

"I don't want to hide this anymore. To wonder if you know, and think maybe you don't, because you never say anything. Do you know how hurtful that is? To have you ignore my entire life?"

Kate finally looked up at Lexie. "You stick your nose in Lexie's business endlessly. You try to make her thinner, or better somehow, as if she needs constant improvement, which is ridiculous since she's the dearest thing that ever walked on two legs."

She turned her big sad eyes back to her mother.

"You leave Beth alone because you know she'll tell you to mind your own business. You tiptoe around Gabby because she looks too damn good. It doesn't matter if she's selfish or shallow."

Kate looked out the window. "Then there's me. You dismiss me. As long as I don't throw it in your face, you can pretend I'm simply a spinster, that I've had bad luck with men, and my girlfriends are just my girl friends."

She put her hand out to hold Mom's arm. "This has got to stop. This has got to end tonight. I am who I am and nothing more. I'd like you to come and stay with my partner and me. We'd love to have you. We'd like to be able to help you. We both love you as it happens. Daphne loves you, Mom. I love you. Daddy's gone. You are my only parent. I need you to *know* me. I need you to *want* to know me. That's all."

Mom sat still, with a wooden look on her face. They watched her. The moment had come. Kate couldn't take anything back. It was out.

Mom stood up and walked over to the window above the sink. The same one she looked out when she made her confession to Lexie, as if she gathered courage from her garden. She could barely see it in the twilight. She spoke as she stared out the window.

"I'm sorry I'm such a disappointment to you girls. I never realized what a miserable parent I've turned out to be."

"Mom, don't be melodramatic. Please." Kate begged. "You're not miserable. I just need things to change between us. I don't want to lie anymore. I love you."

"You could have fooled me."

"Mom, come on," Lexie said, "You know what Kate means."

"It doesn't matter what she means." Gabby could hardly contain her anger. She gave Kate a dirty look. "Her meaning was lost in the spoiled-brat message she just saw fit to deliver, and at the best possible moment too, when all of us are grieving."

Beth turned to Gabby. "Why don't you shut your mouth for five minutes. This isn't your battle, so keep out of it."

Gabby waved her hand at Kate. "It is my battle, when Kate indulges herself with her big coming-out-of-the-closet speech while Mom's in a vulnerable state."

Kate turned around in her seat to face Gabby. "I don't want to hurt her. I only want her to come and visit me, like any mom would. I don't want her to be afraid of me. I miss Daddy so much. If I don't settle this now, Gabby, she'll never come to my house." Kate looked distraught. "She won't come because she'll have to pretend she doesn't know what she knows and I'll have to pretend that she doesn't know either. Do you see what kind of a mess that makes?"

"You need to stop being so defensive when it comes to your lifestyle, as you call it," Gabby said. "Nobody gives a damn who you sleep with. You don't need to rub Mom's nose in it. If she wants to pretend everything's normal, that's the way she chooses to handle it. So grow up."

Beth got up and stood facing Gabby, pointing a finger in her face. "Don't you *ever* talk about lifestyle to us. You don't have the right. You spout off as if you know everything, but lady, you know nothing. You don't hang around long enough to find out what a real relationship is. You spread your legs and move on." Beth was livid. "Kate and Daphne are a couple. They share a home, a life, and a commitment to each other. Rory and I are a couple. We have five children. We nearly lost our minds when our son died, but we hung on to each other and did it. We're still doing it. Lexie struggles to raise a little boy by herself. It's a lonely and difficult thing to do. But she does it."

Beth started to raise her voice. "You, on the other hand, slither around and pick up men to amuse yourself. You make men fall in love with you and dump them. You left Richard reeling. He didn't deserve that. You took Adrian away. You must have known Lexie was fond of him. But still you left. You left Mom and Dad and all of us. You didn't even come back when you knew Willie died. You sent flowers. I had a child who died and you couldn't be bothered to fly home for a day or two and give me a hug."

Tears fell from her eyes. "When were you going to come home, Gabby, if Daddy hadn't died? Never? Were you going to sit on a luxury yacht somewhere and screw all the rich old men on the dock? And you have the nerve to come back here after all this time and tell us that, according to your standards, we're wrong? How dare you."

Gabby stood up and slapped Beth across the face. Then she walked out of the kitchen and went up the stairs. They heard her bedroom door close.

Beth held her hand to her cheek. It was red. She never said a word and she didn't make a sound. Lexie and Mom and Kate were motionless. As they listened to Beth's outburst, all of them had trembled.

Mom was the first to move. "Beth dear, are you all right?"

Beth nodded her head once, took her coat and went home without a word. Her outburst reverberated in their ears. The air was heavy with words, as if they still hung in the air.

Mom sat down quickly and took Lexie and Kate by the hand.

Her voice shook. "We cannot fall apart like this. We've got to stick together. Your father would be horrified if he thought we'd tear ourselves to pieces because of his death." She looked frightened. "I'm not sure what to do."

"There's nothing you can do, Mom," Lexie reassured her. "Beth's been angry since Willie died. She needed to get that out, and Gabby's angry because she feels guilty about not being here when Dad died. Give them some time."

Kate started to cry. "I feel so badly. I never meant to start all this. I was scared you wouldn't come and visit me, Mom. Please come sometimes. Please."

"Kate," Mom said, "I want to apologize. I never realized how I've hurt you. I didn't know how to handle it. I wasn't sure how to act. I assumed if I carried on as if I knew nothing, it would be better all around. I can see I was wrong."

"Oh Mom, I'm sorry I said such awful things. I didn't mean it."

Mom smiled sadly and patted Kate's hand. "If it makes you feel any better, Lexie can tell you that I do a lot of pretending. It's a way of life with me. So don't take it too personally. Right, Lexie?"

"Right, Mom."

Lexie went back to Mom's in the morning to wave Kate goodbye. She didn't get much sleep. She knew no one else did either. They were too battered and bruised to rest easy.

Beth didn't come to say goodbye. She didn't want to see Gabby. Gabby and Mom were in the driveway when Lexie showed up.

Gabby pulled Kate to her. "I'm sorry about last night. I hope you'll forgive me."

Kate hugged her. "It's all right Gabby. We're in a pretty sad way at the moment. It isn't easy. I'm sorry too."

Gabby let her go and walked back into the house.

It was Mom's turn. "Take care of yourself, darling. I promise I'll come and see you and Daphne very soon. I'd love to see your house. Lexie tells me it's beautiful." She started to cry. "I'll miss you so much. It's been wonderful to have you here. Thank you for being with me." She turned around quickly and went into the house as well.

Kate went over to Lexie and put her arms around her. "Lexie, you'll take care of her won't you? She doesn't have anyone now."

"Of course, she does. She has us."

"I mean she doesn't have her mate. It must be awful to be alone."

"Yes."

"Thanks for always being here for me, Lexie. I'm so grateful you stuck up for me. I didn't think I'd do it, but you were there and I felt safe."

"Don't worry about it. I'm always here for you."

She looked at Lexie sadly. "That's the trouble. You're always here for everyone. We depend on you so much. Sometimes I can't bear it. You remind me so much of Dad."

She gave Lexie one more squeeze then hurried into the van and drove away.

On her way back to work, Lexie stopped at Beth's, to make sure she was okay.

"Hello, anyone home?"

"I'm in here." Beth sat in the family room, surrounded by a mountain of toys. Madison was asleep on her shoulder as Beth rocked her.

Lexie waved. "Hi. You all right?"

"I'm fine."

She sat on the coffee table. Beth's cheek was still red. "What did Rory say when you got home last night?"

"God love him," she smiled, "he wanted to go over and knock her block off. I told him I'd done that already."

Lexie smiled at her. "Ya sure did."

Beth shook her head. "I don't know where most of that came from. I know I can be mouthy, but I didn't intend to beat her up like that."

"She'll get over it."

"Maybe. Will you talk to her now? You should, you know. It feels good to fire off a missile every once in a while."

"You know me, Beth. I'm not good with weapons of mass destruction. I'm more your squirt-gun type."

They laughed until they woke Maddie.

Gabby stayed away from Lexie. Every time Lexie went to Mom's, Gabby was out, or occupied with something. Mom was distracted, naturally, and only seemed herself when she was with Josh. Lexie suggested finding a babysitter until things calmed down a bit, but Mom gave her such a look of horror, Lexie immediately retracted the idea. To lose two men in her life was not an option.

Her mother did have help from her friends. Jeanne and Eleanor always had a little too much chicken pie, or macaroni and cheese. They'd pop by and have a cup of tea, coordinating it so that Mom was never alone all day. Lexie wasn't sure Mom noticed, but Lexie did and she called them both to thank them.

"It's no trouble, sweetie," Jeanne said. "You can bet she'd do the same for us if we were in her shoes. God love her, she's been through a lot."

She knows. They all do. Lexie was ashamed, as if she were responsible for her father's behaviour. She wanted to cry on Jeanne's shoulder, but she knew her mother would consider that a betrayal. Jeanne would never betray her. She pretended she didn't know at all.

❧

THAT NOVEMBER WAS dreary. Cold, with a biting wind that flew off the water. Everything was grey and drab — no finery on the trees, no flowers left in their beds, and plenty of colourless stalks that drooped or were trampled down. They waited for winter to come so that they could hide their sad remains beneath the pure white snow.

Lexie and her mother braved the elements to take Joshua for a walk. He needed the fresh air, or so her mother (and the women of her generation) thought. Lucky for her, Josh had a strong constitution.

Along the boardwalk, they braved the wind that gathered its strength offshore. Fog sat snug over the coastline. It too waited for its chance to creep in.

"Your father used to love to walk here," Mom told her. "Whenever he had a bad day, or heaven forbid, lost a patient, he would pace along this shore and let the ocean breeze carry away his woe."

"He never talked about his cases, did he? Not that I remember, anyway."

"Well, he couldn't. Doctor/patient privilege and all that. Thank the lord. Would you want to know who had lice?"

Lexie smiled. They walked along in comfortable silence. She and her mother didn't walk together often. Lexie ran to Dad when she needed someone to talk too. It never occurred to her to wonder if this bothered Mom. Now, Lexie began to notice her for the first time.

She was smaller and seemed to be curved inward, her shoulders slumped forward. She had been tall, and always moved with an easy grace. Now Lexie saw her hunched into the wind, a thin, fragile version of herself. Lexie's throat got tight. She didn't want to lose her mother. What if she wasn't around to drive them crazy or love them dearly? What would happen then? She'd be an orphan.

Mom broke into her frantic thoughts. "Honey, your sister wants to leave soon."

She didn't have to ask which one. "When?"

"In a day or so. I think it's time you two talked. You've avoided each other and that can't go on."

"I haven't avoided her. She's avoided me. Every time I go to your place, she's never there, or she's having a lie-down, or she's in the tub. It's not a coincidence."

"No, that's quite true," Mom said. "She doesn't know how to approach you, so she hasn't. I think you'll have to be the bigger person."

"I am the bigger person," Lexie laughed.

Mom stayed quiet. Then she said, "You haven't seen a lot of your sister because she spends most of her time at your father's grave."

Lexie looked at her. "I didn't know that."

"She goes out there almost every day. She takes a blanket and sits under the birch trees. I'm afraid she'll get sick."

Lexie didn't know what to say.

"She's not strong. I worry about her."

"She must feel awful she didn't see Dad for the last two years of his life."

"Of course," Mom said. "That only stands to reason. But I think it's more than that. And I think it revolves around you, so I wish you'd talk to her before she goes. Who knows when she'll come back to us again."

Lexie called Gabby on the phone that night and asked her to come over after Josh was in bed. Gabby hesitated before she said yes, then sounded resigned. Lexie told her it wasn't her execution, which made Gabby laugh and broke the tension a little. But Lexie was nervous. She cracked open a bottle of wine and drank two big glasses very quickly. She wanted to be on a more equal footing with glamour girl, so she made sure she looked pretty darn good by the time Gabby got there.

Gabby noticed. She sat down on the sofa, took the glass of wine Lexie offered her, and gazed at the fire. Lexie wondered if her sister thought of the night she left with Adrian.

"You look beautiful Lexie. I've meant to tell you since I got home, but the time was never right."

"Thanks."

"I've tried to figure out why it is. At first I thought it was the haircut and makeup. Then I wondered if it was the clothes, but now I think it's because you're a mother. You have a softness about you. It's very alluring."

"Goodness. Am I being seduced?"

She laughed. "That would be Kate's department."

"Gabby, don't talk like that."

"Why not? It's true. She's the one who wants us to know all about it. Never mind, I don't want to get into that anymore. I'm glad she's happy with Daphne. She seems nice."

"Daphne's very nice. And it doesn't hurt her family's quite well off."

"Good for Kate. She's not stupid anyway. You might as well fall for the rich ones. It makes life a lot easier."

"Is that what it's about? Having it easy?"

Gabby looked at her. "Maybe."

"Will you ever settle down, Gabby?"

"Will you?"

"Don't you dare put me in your category. I've had about two boyfriends and you've had ten times that number. You lucky duck."

"Not so lucky. It's an insecure way of living. I'm not sure how it started. Obviously I've quite a reputation. I better not disappoint." She drank from her glass until it was empty, and held it out for another.

Lexie poured her some more. "Beth didn't mean to be so hard on you, Gabby. She told me so. She probably deserved to be slapped for what she said. But her remarks came from a dark place. You have no idea how she's suffered."

"I know. Or I should say, I can only imagine. I've never lost a baby. Or had a baby to lose. What's it like, Lex, to have a baby?"

"I couldn't explain it if I lived to be a thousand." She gave her sister a big smile. "He's the most precious thing in my life. He's the reason I put one foot in front of the other. I can't imagine my life without him. I waited for him to come to me. And he did."

"What was his father like?"

Lexie blushed. "I knew him for seven days. We made love twenty-four hours after we met."

"Good Grief. You guys talk about me!"

"Oh, Gabby, he was gorgeous," she gushed. "He was so big and he made me feel beautiful. It was magic. I never knew it could be like that. Never."

"Well, for heaven's sake, why aren't you with him?"

Lexie looked into her wine glass. "I don't know where he

is. God, I don't know anything about him. We didn't talk about it." She took a sip of her wine. "It seems hard to believe, but it's like we didn't want to know anything else. We had no time to talk."

"Sounds like your bodies did the talking instead."

"That's true."

It was good to be with Gabby. All the pain Lexie agonized over disappeared. The things she wanted to get off her chest seemed to vanish. It really didn't matter anymore. Lexie just wanted her sister back. She needed to be loved by her and she needed to love her sister again. The loss of their father made everything different. Their family was smaller. They had to huddle down and stay safe. It felt right to be together.

They drank two bottles of wine and were on their third. It was midnight and they decided Gabby should stay the night. Then that thing happened that always happens when you've laughed your guts out and yelled about things you remember when you were a kid. You get worn out, tired, then the real stuff comes to the surface.

Lexie poured the last of the third bottle. Thank God Josh slept through the night. She'd pay for this tomorrow.

Gabby took another big sip of wine. "I can't believe Daddy's dead. I pretend he's away, because he's always away from me. Pardon me, I'm always away from him. Same difference I guess." Her head nodded and she drank some more.

"Why did you stay away so long?"

"How could I come back and face you?"

"For God's sake, what did you think I'd do?" Lexie shouted. "Kill you the minute your big toe hit the tarmac?"

Gabby looked at her wine. "I wouldn't blame you."

"Oh, shut up. Blood's thicker than water. I'd have forgiven you long before this."

Gabby stayed quiet. Lexie thought she was sleepy. She wondered if they should go to bed.

Then Gabby said, "I didn't know, Lexie."

"You didn't know what?" Lexie downed her drink.

"That you loved him."

She put her wineglass on the floor. "I didn't know either. Until he left."

"I also didn't know something else."

Lexie gave her a goofy grin like Josh's. "What?"

"He loved you."

There was silence.

"Don't do this to me Gabby."

She looked at Lexie in earnest. "I'm not doing anything."

"You better explain it to me then, because I'd like to know how someone can love you when they make love to your sister in your own house, leave town without a word, and are never heard from again. How's that love, may I ask?"

Gabby warned her. "I won't tell you anything if you talk, if you fight me while I try to get it out. It's too difficult. It's really difficult, all right?"

"Okay."

Gabby looked into the embers of the fire.

"The night I met Adrian I didn't see anyone else that evening. My body was pulled in his direction wherever he happened to be. I've never felt anything like it. You have to believe me, Lexie. I've been with many men. I'm not sure why I never stay with them too long. Perhaps because I've never felt that."

She put her hand through her hair to get it off her face. "Adrian looked at me and I was sure he felt the same way. I didn't want Richard to come near me. I called Adrian the next day when you were at work. He said he would meet me. That was it. He touched me and it was as if I'd never been touched before."

She gave a big sigh. "You finding us *was* an accident. We didn't want to hurt you, ever. When I saw the look on your face, I didn't know what to think. But I knew I didn't want to be around you. I panicked and asked Adrian to leave with me. He didn't want to at first. He said he needed to talk to you."

She looked at Lexie. "I convinced him to go. Finally he said yes, because we didn't know what else to do."

She sounded weary. "It was everything I wanted. It was everything I dreamed of. But then, little by little, he got quiet. Except on the subject of you. He said how beautiful you were and how you felt like home. He felt such guilt over you."

She looked at the fireplace. "I didn't know how to fight that. He wanted me and then he didn't. He was with me, but he wasn't. He'd wander for hours alone. I asked him what was wrong and he said 'nothing.' One night he started to cry. He couldn't explain why. He couldn't get it out. He'd have nightmares."

Gabby rested her forehead against her cold glass. "I tried to help him, but he wouldn't let me. Finally he said he had to go away and figure out why he hurts the people he loves, why he always leaves. He meant you. The only man I've ever loved loves you."

Lexie sat across from her and said nothing.

Gabby looked so sad. "I'm sorry, Lexie. For everything."

"It doesn't matter anymore."

"Yes, it does. I thought he was your roommate. Nothing more. I wouldn't have hurt you like that if I'd known. I want you to believe me."

"I do. I just don't believe the rest of it."

"What?"

"I don't believe he loved me."

"He did. I know he did. You didn't see his face when he talked about you."

"Listen," Lexie said, "a man you say loves me left you a long time ago. Where's he been? He didn't come here, He's never tried to get in touch with me. Does that sound like a man who loves me?"

Gabby didn't say anything at first. Then she agreed. "It doesn't make sense, does it? I can't explain it, but I know what I know. He had something inside that ate him alive. I was helpless to do anything. He wouldn't let me in."

Lexie nodded. "I told Beth I thought he was in trouble. Dad talked about it the night before he died. He said Adrian was lost, that something was wrong."

"This is great, isn't it?" Gabby said. "We both love a man who's disappeared, and we don't know why."

It was the wine that made Lexie talk. "He hasn't complete-ly disappeared."

Gabby gave her a look. "What do you mean?"

"I mean I saw him in May."

She was shocked. "My God. Where?"

"In Montreal."

"Why were you in Montreal?"

"It doesn't matter. The fact is I saw him."

"Did he see you?"

"At first he didn't, but then I think he recognized me." Lexie told her what happened.

Gabby was incredulous. "Why wouldn't he call out to you? I don't understand."

Lexie suddenly knew she wouldn't say anything about the little girl. The only explanation she had come to was that Adrian had a family, and she didn't want Gabby to know. What was the point? She'd been hurt enough.

Gabby was still trying to figure it out. "You should've tried to talk to him. Why did you run?"

"I didn't know what to do. I pushed Josh into the car so fast, I didn't know I was in until we started to move." She was tired and didn't want to talk about it anymore. "Let's go to bed, Gabby. I've had it." She nudged her head towards the staircase.

"You're right, it's been a long night." Gabby got up and followed Lexie upstairs. They looked in on Josh for a minute. Lexie rubbed her hand on his head.

She lent Gabby a nightgown. They washed their faces and brushed their teeth. It felt like they were little girls again. They lay side by side in bed and Lexie reached for her hand.

"Gab?"

"Yeah?"

"Don't ever stay away again."

Gabby left for England two days later. She and her mother had a hard goodbye. Mom held on as long as she could, and Gabby promised she'd come home more often, maybe in the summer. As they got ready to go to the airport, Beth's van roared up the driveway. She jumped out and into Gabby's arms.

"I'm a hag. Forgive me, I shouldn't have said such garbage."

"Only if you forgive me about Willie." Gabby had tears in her eyes. "It was a cowardly thing to do."

"So we're both hags. We're even."

Lexie and Gabby sat in the chairs at the airport and waited for the flight to be called. They held each other's hands. When the intercom announced her flight, Gabby put her arms around Lexie and wouldn't let her go.

"I missed you so much when I left," she said softly. "You're my big sister. You were always the one who made me feel better when anything happened to me and I ruined it. I cut off the one I needed the most."

She let Lexie go to take a tissue out of her pocket. "I'm so glad we've made up. I couldn't bear to live my life if I thought you hated me. I've lost Dad. I can't lose you. You are so like him, Lexie. I feel safe when you're near. I wish I could make it up to you. I'll always love you."

She hugged her again. Lexie hugged her back. "I love you too, Gabby."

They let go. Gabby walked away and put her carryall on the security counter. She turned around before she disappeared.

"Adrian loves you too."

Chapter Fifteen

LIFE CONTINUED WITH a new routine, one without Dad. It was a change they adjusted to reluctantly. Beth's tribe missed their Grampy, and even Josh looked for him in his study.

Lexie was in Lester's one weekend, letting Josh pick out a video at the back of the store. Even at a year and a half, he recognized the purple bonehead when he saw him. While Lexie waited, a local character walked in. She recognized him from around the area, but she stayed away from him. He had a mouth on him and loved to hear himself talk, a joker who knew everything. He had a big booming voice and thought this made him important.

"Lester, me son," he said grandly, "How's life treatin' ya bye?"

"Good, Mick, good," Lester said. Not too many people liked Mick, but Lester wasn't about to lose business over it.

Lexie stayed where she was and hoped he'd leave, so he wouldn't talk to her. Mick asked for his Export A's and a bunch of scratch-and-win tickets. He stood at the counter and chewed on his cud. He took a dime out of his pocket. As he scratched, he gossiped. "I hear them fellas over the road there had a chimney fire last night."

"Yeah, I heard that," Lester said.

"Too much coal, I wager. Some fellas ain't too bright."

"Well now, Mick, it was pretty gosh darn windy last night. Could have been any one of us."

He kept scratching like a chicken. "Did I nearly burn my

place down? No, by Christ, I'm too damn smart."

Lexie had to leave. She came up the aisle but stopped when she heard her father's name.

"I hear they're looking for a new doc in town, ever since that Ivy one died."

Lester gave her an anxious look.

"Well, he better get here soon. I hear that piece of his is pretty anxious for some more bedside manner." He gave a great snort, and shook his head over his tremendous wit.

Before Lester had a chance to say anything, Lexie marched up the aisle and planted herself in front of this piece of dirt.

"Who do you think you are, you pig? Don't ever let me hear you say anything like that again."

She grabbed Josh and started for the door. The pig suddenly realized he was being addressed.

"Suck my you know what."

Before Lexie knew what happened, Lester jumped over the counter, grabbed Mick by the neck, and pushed him out the door.

"Don't you come near this store again, or I'll call the Mounties." He stood in the doorway. Mick cursed at him but left. Lester was stronger then he looked.

He turned around and gave both Lexie and Josh a big hug.

She sniffed into his old checkered flannel shirt. "Thanks Lester."

"There, there, girlie. Don't take no never mind about what that big goof says. He'll get his one day."

"I hope so."

SUSIE LICKED CHINESE food off her fingers. "Did you know that worms grow back the other half if you chop them in two?"

The fact she ate chow mein as she said it turned Lexie's stomach.

"God Susan, give it a rest. I paid a fortune for this. I'd like to eat it."

"Sorry." She continued to shovel it in.

"Who told you that, anyway? Wait, don't tell me. Ernie. Am I right?"

"Of course. Ernie knows everything about animals, reptiles, and creepy crawlies. He loves them all."

Lexie wiped Josh's face with his bib. It was a mess. He held up his plate to his face and licked it off. She was sure if she ordered caviar, he'd polish that off as well. The kid ate everything. He took after Sophie.

They sat at the table and drank their ever-present cup of tea. Josh sat in his high chair with a small bunch of grapes and peeled the skin off each one before he ate it.

"So Susie, how's married life?"

"It's wonderful."

Lexie drew a circle in the fortune cookie crumbs. "What's so wonderful about it?"

"Everything."

"Be more specific."

"Well, let's see. I wake up in the morning, turn over, and Ernie's lying beside me. That's nice. I make supper and he sits beside me. That's nice. I go for groceries and he stands beside me in the checkout line, and —"

"Let me guess…that's nice."

"Very."

"And if you worked in the garden, I imagine he'd kneel beside you. Is that it?"

She hit Lexie's arm. "Stop making fun of me."

"I'm not. I'm envious."

Lexie looked at her crumbs. Susie finally said, "You must find it hard to be alone all the time. Why don't you go out with some guys? I've had two fellows who bowl with us on Friday nights ask about you. They wondered if you were seeing anyone. You'll always be alone if you don't step out the door."

"I can't."

"Why not, for heaven's sake?"

"I don't want to."

"What on earth are you waiting for?"

"Adrian."

Susie looked at her as if she was insane. "The guy who left over two years ago? The guy who took off with your sister? What's wrong with you? He only lived here for two months. He was your lodger. He wasn't your boyfriend. You never even kissed him."

"He kissed me once."

Susie crossed her arms. "Well that's enough of a commitment for most women to throw the rest of their lives away."

Lexie didn't answer.

"Lexie, I love you, but you're nuts. This is a waste. Has he come back to you? Has he written? Has he phoned? I take it he must have broken up with your sister?"

It sounded horrible when she said it out loud.

"Gabby said he loved me."

"Then where is he?"

"She said he had to go away and figure out why he leaves the people he loves."

"I guess he hasn't figured it out yet."

BETH OPENED THE pantry door to get Josh a cookie when she stopped dead. She looked startled.

"Girls, come down here this minute."

Josh looked at Lexie. He recognized the tone, if not the words. Lexie didn't know what she could be mad at.

The girls entered the kitchen reluctantly. They stood as a group, looking guilty. Lexie tried not to grin.

"Who did it?" Beth asked.

"Not me."

"Not me."

"Not me."

"No."

Beth opened the pantry door wider. She gestured for the girls to look inside.

"Well?"

They kept quiet. Lexie had no idea what she was annoyed about. Josh gave her the first clue.

"Elmo!"

She got up from the chair and leaned over the table to take a look. She had to keep her lips glued together so she wouldn't laugh. Beth looked at her and winked.

"Who put Elmo in the cereal box?"

Elmo was fast asleep inside a jumbo box of Alpha-Bits. She wore a baby bonnet and her paws had socks on them. Alpha Bits covered the floor of the pantry.

"Well, if no one will admit it, I guess you'll have to go to your rooms until I tell you to come down." Beth pointed her arm in the direction of the stairs. "Now."

They were a sorry lot as they trooped upstairs. Beth closed the pantry door a little, after she retrieved the cookies and gave Josh two, one for each hand.

"Might as well let the poor thing sleep. Looks like the girls wore her out."

"Oh, my God, they're so cute."

"They are sweet, aren't they? I know how lucky I am."

Lexie thought to herself how Beth had come such a long way, being able to be grateful for what she had, instead of sad for what she'd lost.

"How do you think Mom's doing?"

"She's sad a lot of the time," Lexie said. "Josh takes her mind off it during the day. I think that's why she likes him over. She doesn't have to think."

Beth put her elbows on the table and held her cheeks with palms of her hands. She looked like her girls, just a little kid. "I miss Dad."

Lexie did the same thing. "So do I."

"Lex, can I ask you something?"

"Sure."

"Do you think they had a happy marriage?"

"I guess so."

"Oh."

She was curious. "Why? Don't you think so?"

"I don't know. I suppose. It was something Rory said one day. It just made me wonder."

"What did he say?"

"He wasn't trying to be mean, it was more an observation. That he felt sorry for Dad sometimes, always locked away in his study, like he was shoved aside by all the estrogen whirling about."

"He might be right."

Beth didn't look at her. "Have you heard rumours about Dad?"

Lexie's mouth was dry. "What kind of rumours?"

Beth still didn't look at her. "The kind Mom insinuated the day of the wake."

Lexie was stuck. She was damned if she did and damned if she didn't. She wanted so badly to be able to share this awful thing with her sister. Beth waited for Lexie to tell her how she should feel. Should she believe the rumours or not?

Lexie took a deep breath.

"Beth. Dad may have been lonely from time to time, and maybe it was difficult for them to be together a lot, because of his job and her commitments. But I know one thing for certain. Dad didn't cheat on Mom, if that's the rumour you are referring too. I mean, this is Dad, for heaven's sake."

Beth let out a deep sigh and gave her a big smile. The look of relief was obvious.

"I knew it. God, I feel stupid. Want a cup of tea?"

"ARE YOU ON one of those newfangled diets?" Marlene asked.

Lexie tried to type her orders into the computer but it rejected her. A blue screen screamed at her to say she made a fatal error. She certainly did…horrible hunk of junk. She hit the top of the computer with the side of her fist.

"I can tell you for sure. That doesn't make one bit of difference," Marlene told her.

"I know that."

"You have to hit it on the side and jiggle the bejesus out of the mouse."

Lexie tried it. It worked.

"I told ya." Marlene cracked her gum even faster. She loved being right.

"You're so clever."

"I know."

Lexie looked at the screen to try and find the right link for the department she wanted. "What did you say?"

"I said," Marlene cracked again, "are you on one of them newfangled diets?"

"No. I have a peanut butter and banana sandwich for lunch."

"Oh. Well, it's four o'clock and ya haven't eaten it yet. No wonder ya look thinner."

After Lexie got ready for bed that night, she went in and gave Josh his goodnight kiss. He'd been asleep for hours. She looked in his crib and as always her heart melted when she saw his sweet face. His hair was damp, so she took off his blanket. She rubbed her hand over his head. His hair was long now, and it curled at the bottom.

He looked so much like Joss. *What have I done little boy, to bring you up without your father?* She wanted a child to keep her from being lonely yet she hadn't even thought about what it would be like for him. How would her life be now, if she'd grown up without her dad? She couldn't bear thinking about it.

She went into the bathroom to wash her face and looked at herself in the mirror. She did look a lot thinner, but she wasn't happy about it. She looked worn out.

Lexie went to bed and thought about what she should do. Adrian wasn't coming back. Should she try to find Joss and let him know about his son?

She rolled over and looked out the window. The full moon shone down on her. She rubbed her thumb back and forth gently over her lips, then cried her heart out.

MANY, MANY MILES away, Joss stood by his living room window with a can of beer in his hand. He was there so long, his date came looking for him. She stood in the doorway, wearing his bathrobe.

"Are you all right, Joss?"

He turned. "Sorry?"

She came over and peered out the window. "What are you looking at?"

"There's a full moon tonight."

"That's nice. Are you coming back to bed?"

Joss smiled an empty smile and nodded. She took his hand and led him away from the window.

LEXIE WENT TO ask Dad what she should do. It was a damp, bone-chilling day that matched her mood. She drove out to Black Brook cemetery, whose huge trees were as old as the cemetery itself. White stones spoke of old sorrows. In the summer, the nearby sandbar would be filled with herons and ducks of all kinds. It was a beautiful place and Lexie was glad her father was at rest here.

She drove up the lane and turned the corner. A car was parked near her father's grave. Darn. She'd hoped to be alone. It was awful to be so selfish that you didn't want other people to visit their own loved ones, but she really needed to speak to her dad.

Leaving Betsy parked farther back than she would have liked, Lexie started to walk toward her father's grave. That's when she realized it was Lillian Holmes.

Oh no, you bloody don't.

"Get out of here."

Lillian whipped around.

Lexie started to run towards her. "Leave my father alone. Get away from him. Get away from us and never come back here. Go away. Go away!"

Lillian looked at her as if she was crazy. Maybe she was. Maybe she'd gone mad. She didn't know anything anymore. Lexie tried to shout again but she couldn't. Everything became small, like looking through the wrong end of a telescope.

She stopped and started to sway. "Oh no. Oh no."

All her energy left her. This was too much. She couldn't stand anymore. Lexie fell on her knees and started to sob. She had nothing else she could say. Her heart was broken and she couldn't stand up.

Lillian hurried over to her. "Lexie, let me help you."

"I don't want your help. I don't need your help," Lexie cried. But she couldn't move. Her knees and her hands froze to the cold ground.

"Please, Lexie," she pleaded with her. "You need help. You have to let me help you." Lillian held out her hand.

"No."

But she was so cold. Finally, Lexie didn't care anymore. She didn't care about Lillian Holmes. She didn't care about anything. She just needed to get up. Her stomach heaved and her head ached. Her nose ran as she choked on her tears.

Slowly, Lillian took her elbow and helped her up. It took a long time. Lexie couldn't feel her legs. She grabbed Lillian's coat sleeve since she couldn't walk on her own. What was wrong with her? What happened?

Lexie slumped against her. Lillian took her over to the car and gently put her in the front seat. She closed the door and went around and got in the driver's side. Lexie shivered.

Lexie felt a blanket cover her. Lillian searched in her tote bag, brought out a thermos and poured hot liquid into the plastic cup.

"Drink this. It will warm you up."

Lexie did what she was told because she had no will of her own.

"Lexie, I'm going to take you to the hospital, okay?"

Lexie nodded.

She spoke very calmly and softly, and Lexie liked the sound of her voice.

"You'll be fine. You're exhausted, that's all." She started the engine. "Someone will come back later and get your

car. When we get there, I'll have someone call your mother, and she will come. You'll be all right, dear. Don't worry.
Everything is going to be fine."

Chapter Sixteen

SHE AND DAD walked on a beach. The water got higher. She told Dad to hurry up, but he lagged behind. Pretty soon she couldn't see him anymore. The water kept rising and she couldn't move.

Lexie wanted to wake up. She knew it was a dream, but her eyelids were too heavy. She went back to sleep and this time it was quiet.

There was light in the window. She better get up and wake Josh. She turned her head to get out of bed and saw her mother. Her eyes were closed.

"Mom? Why are you here?"

She opened her eyes and quickly leaned over the bed. "Hi sweetheart."

"What's wrong? Where's Josh? Why aren't you with him?"

"It's all right, dear. Josh is with Beth. He's fine."

Lexie lay her head back down. Where was she?

"Honey, you're in the hospital."

"Why?"

"You were very, very tired, Lexie."

"Yes."

"Do you remember anything?"

She remembered she drank out of a warm cup. It felt good.

"Not really."

"Well, that's all right. Listen, honey, I want you to go to sleep now, okay? Everything is fine. I want you to sleep in and I'll be right here when you wake up." She reached out and stroked her cheek and brow.

Mom is here. That's good. She closed her eyes.

MOM WAS THERE when she opened her eyes, just like she said she'd be. She held her hand. They didn't talk, just sat, like she and Dad used to. It was dusk outside, and the room was dark. Lexie heard people walk up and down the halls. She was content to lie still.

"Mom."

"Yes."

"Did Lillian Holmes bring me here?"

"Yes."

"I thought so."

"Before you say anything, I want you to know that I'll always be grateful to her for helping you. You are more important than anything else."

"Okay."

WHEN LEXIE WOKE up again later, Beth was there. She was so pretty, even with her sad eyes.

"Hi."

Beth smiled. "Wake up sleepyhead. It must be nice for some, to lollygag in bed all day."

"Sorry."

Beth grabbed her hand. She looked frightened. "Don't ever do that again."

"Do what?"

"Don't get sick, Lexie. I couldn't bear it if you got sick."

She looked like she did the day they played hide-and-seek in the woods by the cottage. Beth lost her way for a few minutes, panicked, and called Lexie's name over and over. When Lexie found her, Beth was shaking.

"I'm not sick, Beth."

"What happened then?"

"I'm weary. That's all. Just weary. I haven't slept well since Dad died. And believe it or not, I haven't eaten that well either."

"You've got to take care of yourself, Lex. This whole family would fall apart if you weren't around."

"Oh, pooh." Lexie laughed. "The only medicine I need right now is to see my baby boy."

THE DAY SHE was to go home, Lexie sat on the end of the bed and looked through her get well cards. There was a soft knock on the door. She looked up and there was Lillian.

"May I come in for a moment?"

"Yes."

Lillian walked about halfway into the room and stopped. She looked unsure, but was perfectly composed. She was a striking woman, about five years younger than her mother.

"How are you feeling?"

Lexie was calm. "I'm better."

"That's good."

"Thank you for your help. I don't remember everything, but Mom told me."

"I'm glad I was there to help."

Lexie didn't know what else to say.

"I wanted to let you know, Lexie, that I'm leaving Glace Bay. I found another position in a hospital outside of Ottawa." Lillian hesitated. "I think your life will be much easier when I'm not here. So will your mother's. I deeply regret the hurt I've caused your mother. And you of course. I never wanted that. Your father never had any intention of leaving your mother for me."

Lillian paled and glanced down at the floor. "Your father and I were good friends. He spent a great deal of time talking about his girls. You in particular."

Lexie looked at her but didn't say anything.

She looked up. "He said he loved all his daughters, but he had a special bond with you. He loved the fact that you had his mother's name. But he worried about you, too. He said you were the one who felt the pain, everyone's pain, and you were the one who tried to fix it." She paused. "He loved you very much, Lexie."

"Thank you."

"I said goodbye to him that day in the cemetery. I'd like to think maybe I was there for a reason. He'd be glad I was there when you needed someone."

"Yes. He would."

"Goodbye Lexie."

"Goodbye."

MOM FUSSED. SHE was in Lexie's kitchen trying to find the electric mixer, rooting through the shelves underneath the counter. Lexie watched her and laughed to herself. Josh was on the floor, playing with his trucks.

"These shelves are a mess. How on earth do you find anything around here?"

"It's my mess, so I know exactly where things are. What do you want the mixer for?"

"I want to make lemon pudding. I need to beat the egg whites." She finally spied the missing implement.

"You don't have to do that."

"Yes I do. You need to eat something, get some meat on your bones."

"Someone run for a tape recorder! This is a first: Mom wants me to eat."

She gave Lexie a dirty look, then smirked. "All right, point taken."

Lexie was still on medical leave from work. She'd go back soon. Mom took over, moving into the house, running after Josh, making the meals and doing the wash. She barrelled around as if she had all the energy in the world. Lexie felt guilty until Beth told her to shut up and be grateful. "Mom's in her element. She's taken charge and has a mission."

She did seem brighter, Lexie had to admit, not as unhappy or lonely anymore. It was like Beth said: There's nothing like a child in trouble to galvanize a mother into action.

Dr. Chow didn't like the term "nervous breakdown." He said simply that her glass was full and she spilled over. He called for rest, talk, and an antidepressant to help her recover from the losses in her life. Lexie asked him why Beth hadn't had a breakdown — she had more to grieve than Lexie did. He said everyone was wired differently. And Beth had her husband, who was a tremendous support.

A part of her felt a failure. She couldn't cope with her life, it seemed. She must have done something wrong. Other people didn't agonize over everything. Why couldn't she?

CHRISTMAS CAME, AND with it the snow. Two storms, one after the other, pounded the East Coast. The wind blew the snow into huge drifts, before heading out to sea toward Newfoundland. Glace Bay was a picture postcard, small colourful houses blanketed in clean white cover, occasional black smoke rising from coal stoves, the sounds of civilization muted.

Small chickadees and sparrows flitted among the naked tree branches, waiting for their bird feeders to be swept off and breakfast delivered, while seagulls stood at attention on the eaves of houses to warm their webbed feet. The ducks along Renwick Brook gathered at the edge of the water, hunched over like teenagers sneaking a smoke during lunch hour.

While the main arteries were being cleared, side streets were still blocked and people emerged from their houses one by one dressed in bulky jackets and mitts to start digging themselves out.

Lexie was outside with her shovel. Josh had his shovel too, but it was hard for him to move his arms in his snowsuit. He wandered around the yard, lost in his own world. Sophie was the smart one. She sat in the window and watched from her cosy vantage point by the fire.

Lexie's closest neighbour was Archie Archibald. He was an old character who loved nothing better than to shovel all day, so Lexie made sure she delivered a couple of loaves of homemade bread to him on a regular basis.

Sure enough, she wasn't out for more then twenty minutes before Archie stomped his way through the snow to her driveway, a shovel over his shoulder.

"Right cold today, bye," he said cheerfully.

"Hi Archie. How many driveways have you cleared so far?"

"Started at Myrtle's, but by Christ that one's got a gob on her. Hollerin' from the back step she was, tellin' me how to shovel." He shook his head.

Lexie smiled. "You must be glad you never married, Archie."

"Dodged a bullet there, girl."

The three of them had the driveway done in no time. Lexie tried to convince Archie to come in for a hot chocolate, but he'd have none of it. He was off to the widow Maxwell.

ON CHRISTMAS EVE, Lexie was at her mother's making cranberry punch for Beth, Rory, Kate, and Daphne, when Mom came in the kitchen to put more gingerbread men on a plate. She sighed as she opened the cookie tin.

"I wish Gabby were here."

She no sooner had the words out of her mouth than they heard the back door open.

"Merry Christmas!" Gabby yelled.

Mom ran to the door, with everyone was right behind her. They all tried to hug each other at the same time, while the kids jumped around them like fleas.

"I couldn't spend this Christmas without you guys," Gabby smiled. "A friend filled in for me at the last minute."

Rory looked at his watch. "I hate to break this up but we better get cracking — church is at six."

They laughed and talked as they poured out of the house, joining a hundred other families milling into church at the same time.

The kids were beyond excited, and had a hard time staying in their seats. The minister finally called them up to the altar for the children's talk. Michaela took Josh by the hand and followed her sisters. Reverend Higgins lost control in the first five minutes. His voice couldn't be heard over the din of forty children hopped up on Santa Claus juice. There was a fight over who would hold baby doll Jesus.

Beth hid her eyes, then peeked at Lexie. "I don't want to look. Is it one of mine?"

Lexie nodded her head.

"Maddie?"

"How did you guess?"

CHRISTMAS MORNING, JOSHUA actually slept in. At seven-thirty, Lexie tiptoed out of the spare room and found Mom, Kate, Daphne and Gabby standing in the hall with their slippers and bathrobes on.

"Merry Christmas, you guys."

"Merry Christmas!" they whispered.

"I thought you said Josh was an early riser?" Kate pouted.

"Well, he didn't go to bed until ten o'clock, the poor kid," Lexie pointed out. "I've been lying in there since six, willing him to open his eyes, but he's still snoring."

They stood around like five kids dying for their parents

to wake up. While they waited, Gabby suddenly whispered, "Knock knock."

"Who's there?" everyone whispered back.

"Santa."

"Santa who?" everyone said.

"You don't know who Santa Claus is?"

The five of them broke up and the harder they tried to keep quiet, the louder they got. Poor Josh opened the door with that stunned sleepyhead look, and was so startled, he promptly burst into tears. They all rushed to cuddle him, which only made things worse. Lexie eventually brought him downstairs in her arms, his thumb in his mouth and his head on her shoulder. When he saw the tree, his face lit up.

Mom started getting the turkey ready as soon as they finished breakfast. Kate and Daphne, who went to a creative cooking class every Tuesday night, were trying to convince her to try a new stuffing recipe. "It's wonderful, Mom," Kate enthused. "It's got chestnuts and walnuts and saffron rice and all kinds of goodies. It was a big hit in class, wasn't it Daphne?"

"Oh, gosh, it sure was. There wasn't a smidgen of it left at the end of the lesson." They looked at each other and beamed happily.

Rory, Beth, and the girls arrived later in the afternoon and the family sat down to their Christmas dinner. Mom carried in a fat golden turkey on an heirloom platter and put it on the table. They all said how nice it looked, and that's when the realization hit them that Dad was really gone.

They looked at each other. Mom recovered first. "Rory, dear. Would you do the honours?" She passed him her husband's carving set. Rory looked at Beth and she nodded her head slightly.

Rory stood up. "Of course. Who wants the drumstick?"

Dinner was delicious, except for the dressing. Rory was disappointed. As he helped Lexie clear the table he sidled up to her by the sink.

"Excuse me while I run to my mother's and wolf down some normal stuffing, the kind the whole world's had right about now. Lucky sods."

Lexie put her finger to her lips. "Shh. Kate would be devastated if she knew."

"How can she not know?" Rory whispered. "No one ate it."

"Beth and I grabbed it off everyone's plate every time they weren't looking. The kids helped." She showed him the huge blob of dressing wrapped in some napkins before she threw it in the garbage.

"That's where it belongs." Rory went back to get more dishes.

Gabby came in with another load of plates. Lexie filled the sink with hot soapy water. Gabby grabbed a tea towel out of a drawer and stood beside her. They smiled at each other.

"Are you okay, Gab?"

"Yeah. You?"

"Yeah."

"Still lonely?"

"Yeah."

"Me too."

Once things were cleared away, Rory brought out a gift he'd picked up for Josh: two plastic hockey sticks just his size and a soft puck. They played hockey in the living room. The girls were miffed because they weren't included. Joshua got so excited he took the stick and shot the puck into the top of the Christmas tree. Rory said he would be in the NHL by the time he was seven. Josh gave him his lopsided grin.

Rory took Lexie aside. "You know, if ever Josh wants to play hockey or baseball, I'd love to get him some equipment and take him to his games."

Here was a man. Josh wouldn't grow up without someone. She gave Rory a big squeeze.

Lexie and her mom and sisters went out to the cemetery while Rory and Daphne watched *The Little Mermaid* with the kids.

The snow was undisturbed, except for the small rabbit prints that wound around and through the headstones. The chime they placed on the branch of the birch tree over Dad's grave tinkled in the wind. It was almost twilight. Smooth and glassy ice had formed over the sandbar. They swept snow off the headstone and placed their Christmas arrangement of pine, berries, and holly in front of it.

They knelt down and told him how much they loved him and how much they missed him and to thank him for being the best dad in the whole world. They kissed their fingers and pressed them into the snow so they would melt into the ground above him.

Lexie and her sisters walked away and left Mom to say her private goodbye. She stood in that peaceful place where her husband lay. Lexie glanced back. Her mother looked so alone.

Chapter Seventeen

GABBY SAT AND looked out the window. It rained; a dreary day. She watched people hurry along, big black umbrellas that bobbed like buoys on the water. The rain hit the window and it was a lonely sound. It always had been for Gabby. As a kid, she had hated the sound of rain on the cottage roof.

She had the phone number in her hand. It wasn't hard to find Adrian, once she knew he was in Montreal, but it took a long time to gather up the courage to speak to him. She assumed Adrian hadn't called out to Lexie because he thought she was married, or at least in love with someone. He had seen Joshua, after all. What didn't make sense was that he didn't get in touch with Lexie after he left Toronto. Did he think Lexie would hate him forever for his betrayal? Gabby had no idea. She couldn't think anymore.

She dialled the number. She didn't know what she'd say. She just knew she had to do something. She owed it to Lexie.

A crisp formal voice said, "Davenport Residence. Mrs. Phillips speaking. How may I help you?"

Was she a secretary? Was this his house?

"Yes, hello. May I speak to Adrian, please?"

"Whom shall I say is calling?"

This caught Gabby off guard. "A friend."

"Certainly. One moment please."

She was put on hold. Just a few more moments. She should hang up. She couldn't do —

"Hello?"

Her heart leapt to her throat. His voice was in her ear, so close.

"Adrian?"

"Yes?…Gabby, is that you?"

She didn't speak. She didn't dare.

"Gabby."

"Yes." It was a whisper.

"Oh, my God. Where are you?"

"It doesn't matter." She talked as if reading from a script for the first time.

"Gabby. I'm so sorry for everything. Please believe me."

"I wanted to call you and tell you Lexie isn't married."

There was a pause. "Lexie? This is about Lexie?"

"Yes."

"I saw her in Montreal. She had a baby with her. It was such a —"

"She still loves you." Gabby had her hand in a tight fist as she tried to remember what she was supposed to say. "There's no need for you to stay away from her now."

"Gabby, you have to listen to me. I know I hurt you and Lexie very badly. I need to explain. I was in a bad way then. But I've sorted things out —"

"Look, I can't talk to you Adrian. We're in the past. I've sorted things out too. I've moved on with my life. I'm in love with someone else." She had to swallow. "I'm glad things are better for you. I just wanted you to know about Lexie, because I know you love her and I want to make up for the hurt I caused you both."

"Gabby —"

"Call her. Goodbye Adrian."

She hung up the phone and let go of it as if it were too hot to hold. She stared at nothing. She felt nothing, until she tried to open her fist. It was stuck together with blood from her fingernails pressing into her flesh.

❧

ADRIAN LAY ON his bed. It was the middle of the night, pitch black except for the nightlight outside Binti's room. He couldn't sleep, so he heard her the minute it started.

Her screams were bad this time. He leapt up and raced into her room. She sat up and stared at the wall in front of her.

"It's okay, baby. Papa's here." He reached for her and she put her arms around his neck. He sat on the bed and snuggled her close. The screams stopped but her cries kept her hot and agitated. Adrian took the small face cloth he kept by her bed, dipped it in a basin, and wiped her face.

"Shh. You're all right. Papa won't leave you."

The girl's breathing slowed as her tiny shoulders shuttered with the last of her sobs. She stayed glued to his chest. Adrian rocked her.

The day he finally found her was both the happiest and saddest day of his life. He entered the orphanage and was greeted by one of the sisters who pointed to a file on the desk. She had a thick stack. There were so many orphans. But only one "file" was called Binti.

He found her all alone in a small crib at the back of a room crowded with cribs. Flies landed on her head. It was hot. She wore a diaper, that was all. She looked just like her mother. She watched him with her big, sad brown eyes, and he thought his heart would stop.

"It's all right Binti. I've come for you."

The sister said not to pick her up right away, she'd be frightened, but when Adrian held out his arms to her, she held out hers, too. He picked her up and she put her head against his shoulder with a small sigh, as if to say, "what took you so long?"

It took him forever to get official permission to adopt her and take her out of Tanzania. For the first time in his life, he used his father's connections — and was grateful for them.

To bring Binti home to his mother was the best medicine for them both. She helped him. His father did too. They had no grandchildren, so they were more than ready to welcome a child into their lives. And more than ready to help Adrian heal his broken heart.

Adrian's mother appeared in the doorway, wearing her bathrobe.

"Is she all right?"

"Yes, she's fine, Mother. Don't worry. I'll stay with her, you go back to bed."

She whispered, "I'm awake now." She came in and sat on the rocking chair by Binti's bed. "It's almost four. That's very good. Soon she'll be sleeping through the night."

Adrian nodded. They sat quietly for the next few minutes, as Binti's eyes slowly closed, despite her attempts to keep them open.

"Adrian?"

"Yes?"

"Is anything the matter?"

"No. Other than this upset every night."

"May I speak frankly?"

"Of course."

"I know the past few years have been difficult, more difficult than you probably let on. And you've done such a marvellous job with Binti, but there's something else."

He waited.

"It's very evident to me that you're pining away. For something or someone."

Adrian looked away.

"Someone other then Binti's mother. Am I right?"

"I can't talk about it, Mother."

"It's this girl from Cape Breton, isn't it? Lexie. The one who was so kind to you."

He chewed his bottom lip and looked at the floor.

"You said she understood your having to go back to Africa and find Binti. Now that things are settling down a bit, why don't you give her a call? I'm sure she'd love to hear from you. I'm surprised you never contacted her when you got home, but then again, you've been so wrapped up with our precious girl."

"As you say, I've had other things on my mind."

"You're still a young man. You should be living a young man's life. The worst is over for Binti. She's progressing, and your need to hover over her is lessening. Do yourself a favour, dear, and start being happy. For her sake, as well as your own."

His mother rose from the rocking chair and caressed his cheek for a moment, then leaned over and kissed the top of Binti's head. She left the room quietly.

Adrian sat and rocked his child, tears falling from his eyes. What a mess he'd made of his life. Hearing Gabby's voice on the phone was an utter shock. She was a secret he shared with no one. Lying to his mother about Lexie, listening to her try and fathom his misery without knowing the truth, made him sick.

He wasn't sorry he left Gabby to get Binti, but he was sorry about the way he left. He should have trusted her — she might have understood. But Adrian couldn't think clearly back then. He was so racked with guilt that coloured everything. He handled it all the wrong way and that was his biggest regret. Now he was desolate. Gabby was in love with someone else, and it was his own fault.

And so, night after night, as he came in to rock Binti to sleep, he thought about her. And night after night, another thought made its way in. So slowly at first he didn't recognize it, but it soon took over the memories of Gabby.

Lexie.

Lexie and that island and that house. The place where he was finally able to rest. The place where he stopped running for a while.

Gabby said Lexie loved him still. He didn't know she loved him, not for sure. The thought of her waiting for him filled him with longing. He loved Lexie first. Who wouldn't love her? He wondered if she'd take him back. Maybe he could start over in that wonderful little house by the ocean.

Lexie. I want to come home.

❦

"LEXIE, YOU LOOK so much better," Susie said, as she and Lexie washed dishes after dinner while Ernie showed Josh the new critters.

Lexie dried the forks. "I feel really good, which is something I didn't think I'd say too long ago."

She put them in the cutlery drawer and grabbed a plate. "And get this — I may even go out on a date. It's time I got back in the saddle, don't you think?"

"Well dear, they'll ride you off into the sunset before too long. You are lookin' pretty fine, as they say."

"I am, aren't I? I may give Gabby a run for her money."

LEXIE SPENT THE next morning at the library, looking after the "orphans"— books abandoned on any old shelf. Despite pleas to leave them alone and let the librarians put them back correctly, people insisted on shoving them in any available space they could find. It drove Lexie nuts. As she muttered under her breath, she heard Marlene and Judy talking in the next aisle.

Marlene cracked her gum mile a minute. "Lexie will be an old maid if she's not careful. She must think she's the queen of Sheba or something."

"Hardly," Judy replied. "She is pretty fussy though. Remember that poor fellow who only used the hurricane stuff as an excuse to talk to her? He was pretty cute."

"It don't seem to matter if they're good, bad, or ugly. She snubs them all."

Judy corrected her grammar. "Doesn't."

"Does too."

Lexie called Susie the next weekend. She asked her if she'd set her up with one of those bowling ball buddies of hers.

"I'm glad to hear it!"

"We could go out on a double date. That way it won't seem so awkward."

"Sure, anything you want. I'll call and make the arrangements and let you know where and when. Good for you kid, it's about time you came out of your shell."

"Yes. I think it's time."

Lexie ran into Donalda at the grocery store one day. She hadn't seen much of Donalda lately, preferring to be home with Josh in the evening. Donalda looked her up and down. "So. They told me you lost weight. What plan were you on?"

"The nervous breakdown diet." She didn't know why she was always so mean to Donalda. The woman just rubbed her the wrong way.

Donalda nodded. "Right. I know that one. You get on the scale and collapse with fright."

Lexie smiled. "So, what's new with you?" She might as well talk. There were five people in front of her.

"Oh, this and that. I'm at the theatre pretty much every night. There's nothing else to do. You'd know about that. At least I'm not the only one on the shelf."

This broad's an idiot. "Well, as a matter of fact, I have a date on Saturday night with someone called…um…?"

"Who?"

"I don't know. Just some guy."

"Where are you going?"

"I don't know, somewhere."

"You sound like you're looking forward to it. Don't over-whelm him with your enthusiasm."

LEXIE PUT ON her lipstick in front of the bathroom mir-ror as she tried to remember why she thought a blind date was a good idea. She grabbed her purse and went downstairs to sit with her mother.

Mom smiled at her. "You look like you're about to be tarred and feathered."

"I do? I'm just tired, that's all."

"Maybe. Maybe not."

"What do you mean?"

"I mean, my dear, your body language tells me every-thing I need to know about how you feel about this even-ing."

"It does not! I don't enjoy blind dates, that's all."

"Then why in heaven's name did you ask Susie to set you up?"

"I have no clue."

"Lexie, dear. You need to figure out if this is how you want to live your life."

Lexie put her head back on the edge of the chair and looked at the ceiling. "You're right."

"Why do you wait for a man who in all probability won't come back to you?"

"I don't know," she sighed. "I don't think anyone will ever love me."

"Where did you ever get the idea you're not worthy of someone's love?"

She stopped looking at the ceiling and looked at her mother instead. "I wonder."

"Lexie. I know I made mistakes when it came to your weight. I've apologized for that. I can't go back and erase it. But you can't use that as an excuse for everything."

Lexie picked at an edge of her fingernail.

"I used to get after your sisters too. Maybe you didn't notice, you were so busy being offended. Beth can tell you. I always told her she had a big mouth and a temper. I lived in fear Gabby would come home pregnant. And well, you know what I did to Kate. She says I ignored her whole life."

Mom slapped her magazine shut. "Being a mother is bloody difficult. You want your kids to be perfect. You want them to be better — better than you."

She shook her head as if she couldn't believe what she'd done. "What an incredible waste of time and energy. Unfortunately, you don't learn that until you're old and grey."

Lexie said, "It's just as well you did harangue me. I can't seem to make a decision about anything. I'm a classic ditherer."

She smiled at her. "You were quite fearless at one point in your life."

"I was?"

"Yes."

"When?"

"When you decided you wanted a baby. You weren't

married, you knew the father had no intention of staying with you, you didn't make a lot of money, but you did it anyway. That's brave. You jumped off a cliff that night." She leaned towards her. "And are you sorry? I don't think so. You have the sweetest child who ever drew breath. You can't imagine your life without him."

She leaned back, satisfied she'd made her point. "That's what happens when you take a chance. You need to stay brave."

Lexie started to smile. "I never thought of it that way. You're right Mom. I'm not a complete failure."

"Who called you a failure?"

"I did."

"Well, give yourself a big slap for being so stupid and move on."

"Okay. Thanks."

"You're very welcome. Now you better go and get this evening over with."

"Oh God, that's right. I have to bowl! What was I thinking?"

Mom flipped her magazine open again. "You haven't done a lot of thinking for quite some time now. Ta Ta. Have a great time."

She started to read, so Lexie had no choice. She dragged herself outside and drove off.

She saw them as soon as she arrived. Susie waved and beckoned her over. Lexie looked at her date. He was a man. That was about all that registered. She hung up her coat and walked over.

"Lexie, I'm so glad you're here," Susie smiled. "I want you to meet our friend. This is Ronald. Ronald MacDonald. Ronnie, this is Lexie."

Ronald MacDonald stood and shook her hand. Lexie tried to keep a straight face. She hated that idiotic clown of fast food fame almost as much as she hated the purple thing.

"It's so nice to meet you, Lexie." He seemed pleasant. She greeted Ernie and they sat down to their meal.

Lexie asked Ernie about his animals. Susie asked her about Joshua. Lexie asked Ronnie what he did for a living. He said he sold life insurance.

Susie said quickly, "Let's look at the menu, shall we?"

After a while, Lexie tried to follow the conversation and smile every so often, but her mind wandered back to the conversation with Mom. Lexie needed to be brave, she said. Brave how? Wasn't it brave not to settle for less, not to settle at all? Wasn't it brave to go it alone if she had too? She had her home, her son, and her job. Why did she need a man, any man, to complete the package? Who was she fooling? She didn't want to be here.

"Lexie?" Susan looked at her questioningly.

"Yes. Sorry. You were saying?"

Her date smiled at her. "I said, it must be quite interesting to work in a library."

"Actually, it's a downright bore most of the time."

"Why did you get into it then?"

She noticed he had a piece of goop at the corner of his mouth. She tried not to look at it as she answered him. "Well, I always loved that pencil with the little stamp fastened to the top that showed the date. It was my ambition in life to use one."

Ronnie looked like he needed a drink. "How fascinating."

Susie gave her the hairy eyeball. Lexie shrugged.

"I must go powder my nose. Lex?"

Lexie sorted the olives to one side of her Greek salad.

"*Lexie.*"

She startled her. "What?"

Susie smiled benevolently. "Do you have to powder your nose?"

"No. Yes." Lexie followed her into the bathroom.

Susie slammed her purse on the counter. "What in God's name is wrong with you?"

"What do you mean?"

"I mean, you're clearly somewhere else this evening."

"No, I'm not."

"Well, you're as high as a kite, then."

"Don't be stupid."

Susie seemed exasperated. "That's the only explanation I can think of. I mean, for God's sake, you went to university so you could use a pencil with a whatsit on it? Ronnie will think you're a nut."

"What do I care what he thinks?"

"I thought the whole idea of this date was for you to meet men, and actually try to impress them. To get them to ask you out again some time in the near future," she hollered. "At this rate, Ronnie will hightail it out of here like a scalded cat."

"Why? Because I told him about a pencil? It happens to be the God's honest truth. That *is* why I wanted to become a librarian. What's wrong with that? Why do I have to change what I think for someone else's gratification? If he doesn't like my answer, he can go blow."

Susie looked at her with resignation. "You don't want to be on this date, do you? Your heart isn't in it."

Lexie's eyes watered. "Well, do you blame me? Good grief, his name is Ronald MacDonald! I keep picturing him with big floppy feet. And now I have to go bowling on top of it."

She pulled off a piece of paper towelling and tried to blow her nose, but it was too stiff. She reached for toilet paper instead.

"What am I going to do with you?"

Lexie sniffed. "Tell him I had the flying axe handles and had to go home."

"The what?"

"The runs...the trots...oh forget it." She dismissed Susie with a wave of her wrist. "Let's just go and get this stupid evening over with."

Susie grabbed her purse. "That's the attitude."

They went bowling and it was everything Lexie imagined. They knew how to bowl. She didn't. She didn't understand how the scoring went. She didn't understand how to position her feet. She worried about having to disinfect her hands and feet when she got home. She could see Ronnie look at his watch.

Just when Lexie thought she'd scream, Susie let out an exaggerated yawn and said she hated to be a party pooper, but she had an early day tomorrow. Ronnie asked if Lexie needed a drive home. She thanked him but declined. He looked relieved.

Lexie kissed Ernie goodbye and then grabbed Susie in a bear hug and whispered, "Thank you."

Susie whispered back, "I figured you suffered enough for one night."

Mom was in the same spot when Lexie got back.

"How did it go?"

Lexie threw herself in her old armchair and hung her arms out at her sides. "He was a clown, there were too many olives in my salad, and I hate bowling."

"That good?"

"I don't want to talk about it."

"Fine," Mom said. "I'd better go."

"I think Susie's fed up with me."

"Do you blame her?"

"No," Lexie sighed. "I drive her crazy."

"You're good at that."

"At least I'm good at something."

❦

JOSS LAUGHED INTO the phone. One of his clients had just told him a dirty joke. The guy never ran out of them. Joss laughed at that as much as the joke itself.

The girl who answered their phones put her head in his office doorway. She didn't bother him often, so he looked up right away.

"I'm sorry, Mr. MacGregor. Your mother's on line two and she says it's important."

"Gotta run, Harvey." Joss hung up and pressed a button. "Ma?"

"Joss dear?"

"What's wrong?"

"It's your Da."

"What happened?" This was serious. She never called him at the office.

She sounded like she was crying. "Da broke his hip. He fell on the boat. I knew this would happen."

"It's all right. I'll be on the first plane home."

"No dear, don't do that. Your brothers will take care of things. I just wanted you to know."

"Ma, listen to me. They have their own boats to take care of. Da can't lose his license. I won't allow it. I'll be home as soon as I wrap up things here."

The sound of relief in her voice was obvious. "Thank you Joss. What would we ever do without you?"

❧

LEXIE TOOK JOSH out of his car seat. Mom said he didn't have a nap, so she was assured of a good night's sleep. At least she hoped so. Josh ran ahead and scampered up the porch steps.

"Sope. Sope!"

Sophie was mewing inside. Josh hit the front door with his fist as Lexie looked for her keys. She finally unlocked it and he rushed in.

"Just a minute, big guy," she laughed. "Let Mommy take off your jacket."

He jumped up and down, in a hurry to give Sophie her supper. Lexie got him unzipped and he took off, pulling his jacket sleeves inside out in his rush to get to the kitchen.

She hollered down the hall. "Don't give her too much, sweetie."

The phone rang. She grabbed the mail on her way in and shuffled through it as she headed for the phone. Opened the Visa bill. Yuck.

"Hello?"

"Lexie?"

"Yes?"

"Hi."

"Hi." Lexie wasn't really listening. She had her ear on the noise in the kitchen. It sounded like Josh was pouring out a whole box of cat chow.

"Sorry, who's this?"

"Adrian."

She hung up and sat down quickly. The phone rang again and this time the answering machine did the talking.

Beep. "I'm sorry Lexie, I don't want to frighten you. Please let me talk. I know I have no right to call you out of the blue, but I didn't want to just show up at your door. Maybe I should've written, but I was afraid you'd tear it up. This is my only way to reach you. Please Lexie, I need so badly to —" *Beep.* Message cut off.

It rang again. She waited. *Beep.* "Please take my phone number." He gave it to her. "I'll wait for your call. I need to speak with you. That day in Montreal, I thought you were a dream, and then you were gone. I want to explain —" *Beep.* He didn't call back.

Lexie stared at the ashes in the fireplace.

"Mama!"

She went into the kitchen, cleaned up the cat chow, and washed Joshua's hands. Then she put him in his high chair and sliced half a banana into a plastic Bunnykins bowl, to tide him over until she got his supper ready. After all his chicken, fresh peas, and sweet potato was gone, up they went for his bath.

When Lexie got him into his pyjamas she cuddled him in the rocking chair by his crib, and picked up the first book she could reach off the floor.

"Let's see, what have we got tonight." She showed Josh the cover. "*Sleeping Dragons All Around*. This is a really good book, isn't it? You like dragons."

He nodded and stuck his thumb in his mouth.

She turned the pages. "We'll start with Glump, since he's your favourite."

Josh nodded again.

"Glump is simply a dimplish, blimpish balloon belly, a slumpish lump, a WIMP of a dragon, with his tail zigzaggin around the room, his chin draggin along the floor, with HICCUPS like no one's heard before. The whole floor shakes but Glump NEVER wakes, so I must tiptoe, tiptoe softly as I pass…"

Halfway through the book, Josh was asleep. Lexie tucked him in, kissed his cheek, and closed his door partway. Then she took off her clothes and got in the shower, scrubbing her skin until it hurt. Lexie washed her hair, got out of the tub, and put on her red flannel pyjamas with the tiny white hearts. After brushing her teeth, she put down fresh water for Sophie, made sure the doors were locked, the coffee ready to go for the morning, and the lights were turned off.

But instead of going to bed, she grabbed her duvet, wrapped herself up in it, sat in the old armchair, and dialled Adrian's number.

He picked it up on the first ring.

"Lexie?"

"Yes."

"Thank you. If only you knew how much this means to me."

"What do you want, Adrian?"

"Can I come and see you?"

"When?"

"Now."

"Where are you?"

"A half an hour away."

She hung up the phone.

MARLENE TAPPED LEXIE on the shoulder. She nearly jumped out of her skin.

"Good gravy, girl! What's the matter with you? You're like a cat on a hot griddle."

"Marlene, don't sneak up on me. You'll give me a heart attack."

"Looks like you're about to have one now. You're as flushed as a toilet."

Even in Lexie's hyper state, she had to respond. "Where do you come up with these revolting sayings of yours?"

"I make them up. It gives me something to do while I put these damn cards back in alphabetical order."

"Marlene?"

"Yeah?"

"You kill me."

"I try."

After dropping Josh off at Mom's, Lexie picked up two bottles of wine and cleaned her house. She had no idea why. She had a bubble bath and took a long time to get ready. She decided she would stay casual. She didn't want him to think it took her all evening to get ready, even if it did.

Lexie didn't know what would happen, or what she'd say, but she needed to have everything in order. She needed to be prepared, unlike the last time they laid eyes on each other.

She dialled the phone.

One ring.

"Lexie?"

"I'm here."

He hung up.

SHE WATCHED THE taxi pull into the driveway. He got out and came up the steps. Her heart pounded as she opened the door.

He looked wonderful. His hair was shorter, but still gorgeous, and he'd filled out a little. He seemed more at ease, more sure of himself. He looked so good, and smelled even better. He wore jeans and a white shirt underneath his brown suede jacket. She wanted to hold him so badly she didn't dare move.

He stopped and caught his breath. "Oh, Lexie. How beautiful you look. It's so good to see you again." He gave her that familiar smile, the one she dreamed of night after night. "If only you knew how much I wanted this moment to happen."

She couldn't speak at first. She finally whispered, "Come in."

He took off his jacket and draped it over the chair in the hall. She walked ahead of him into the living room, as she had so long ago. She stood by the fire. He looked around.

"I don't recognize anything, except the furniture. Look how wonderful the floors are. And your rugs! They're works of art."

It pleased her to hear him say so.

He turned. "And dear old Sophie."

Sophie opened her eyes and gave him a look. She yawned and went back to sleep.

"Good old Soph. Nothing ever rattles that creature. I see she's as fat as ever."

"She's not fat, she's fluffy."

He gave her a big smile.

"Would you like some wine?"

"Yes, thank you."

She went into the kitchen and poured two glasses of red wine. She took them back into the living room and asked him to sit down.

They looked at one another.

This was the night that would change everything.

ADRIAN FIDDLED WITH his wineglass before he put it on the table beside him. "I'm not sure where to begin."

"I won't make this easy for you, Adrian. I'm not a hostess tonight."

"Of course, of course."

She took a sip of wine. Her throat was dry. "You asked to see me, because you want me to hear you out."

"Yes. I have so much to explain." He looked towards the fireplace. "I'm just not sure where to start."

"I'm not the same woman you left behind."

He looked back at her. "No, I can see that."

"It's nothing you can see on the outside. It comes from living."

He looked at her intently. "You never knew me when I lived here, Lexie." He looked back down at his hands. "I want you to know me."

"Why should I?"

"Because you were my friend when I needed one, and I disrespected that friendship. I'd like the chance to apologize for my behaviour. I've missed you very much."

She took another big gulp of wine. "You have a very funny way of showing it."

"I know it seems ridiculous. To leave and never get in touch. There are reasons for it."

She was uncomfortable. "So now I get to hear your excuses. I'm not sure I want to."

"I understand that."

"No, I don't think you do." This was a mistake. Part of her wanted to go over there and kiss his perfect mouth until morning. The other part wanted to slap his face, over and over again.

She got up. "Maybe you should go."

Adrian got up too. He came over and took her by the hands.

"Sit, Lexie. I need to tell you about someone. A girl I loved, in Africa."

Gabby had it wrong. This wasn't about Lexie. He wanted to ease his conscience. He was sorry he hurt her as a friend. That's what he called her, a friend. Now he wanted to tell her about the girl he left behind. The one he loved.

She shut down. *Pretend you're in a play, Lexie, then you don't have to be you.*

She sat only because she didn't have the strength to stand anymore. He took that to mean that she was ready to listen, and began.

"I worked in a refugee camp in Tanzania. You knew that. I was there for almost two years when a girl arrived with her baby. She was with a group of displaced people who arrived from the West, from Burundi. They were forced to leave their homes, because of tribal warfare between Hutu and Tutsi tribes. They were in pretty rough shape when they arrived."

He took a drink of his wine. "It was my job to try and get some information from them. Most of them spoke Swahili. When it came time to take her name, she didn't speak. Refused. One of the women told me she never spoke, so I asked them to give me the information I needed. They said they didn't know her. She'd joined them on the road one day and followed them."

Adrian took a breather, as if to gather his thoughts. He was agitated.

"Here I was, a master of language, and I couldn't communicate with her." He clasped his hands together and held them tightly. "It was frustrating. I needed some information, to try and help her. I wanted her to get back to her family. I wanted to do something. She was so small and helpless. She had beautiful big brown eyes that looked like they'd seen the end of the world."

Adrian looked at her. "She was so alone, Lexie. The people from the same villages gather in their separate groups most of the time. It's so frightening to have your world taken away from you. They stay near each other for comfort. But this girl had no one. She hovered close to the group she came in with, but stayed apart."

Adrian's demeanour had changed. He was no longer the confident man who walked in. She felt more familiar with this man. Her heart thawed a little, and she forgot about herself. There was only the story to listen to.

"One day, a long line formed outside the doctor's tent, where they gave vaccines to the children, to prevent measles. It's a deadly disease in these places. It kills so many. There aren't enough health facilities in the country. It was hot and windy. The kind of day you want to scream because there's no escape from the sand or the dust. I happened to walk by with forms for the office, when I felt a small tug on my sleeve. I turned around and there she was. She looked frantic. She held up her baby girl. I knew there was something wrong. The baby was limp, unconscious. They'd stood at the end of the line in that hot sun."

Adrian wrung his hands. "I grabbed the baby and she ran after me. I went into the medical hut, and asked someone to help me. They took the baby and put her on a table. Two nurses started to undress her. They did what needed to be done. Her mother stood by the bed, so I left."

Adrian had to stop and swallow.

"At dinner that night, one of the nurses came up and told me it was a good thing I brought the baby when I did. She was dehydrated and suffering from sunstroke. So many things can happen to these children, who are vulnerable already. It's heartbreaking. It makes me so angry.

"I went back to the medical tent the next day. There she was. She sat by her baby in a makeshift cot in a corner of the room. She turned around and smiled the sweetest smile. She came over and took me by the hand, back to the cot."

"The baby was awake and looked much better. I touched her cheek. I pointed to the baby and said 'Binti,' the word for 'daughter' in Swahili. She nodded her head but said nothing else. Since I had no other name, that's what I called her."

He stopped for a moment and looked down. "I felt protective of her and the baby. I soon realized she was very attached to me."

Lexie finally spoke. "You saved her child."

"Yes. Soon I found excuses to see her, or to be near her. She didn't speak, but I knew how she felt about me. One of my friends noticed it and told me to back off, because it wouldn't do to have the staff give more attention to one than the others. I thought he was being overly dramatic. I wanted her close to me. She was alone. I hated to see her without a friend."

Adrian got up from the chair and paced, as if to stay ahead of the facts he brought to light. Lexie got edgy. This didn't feel good.

"One day she came over and handed me a small piece of paper. I felt uneasy as I took it, because sometimes people watched us, but it seemed a harmless enough thing to do."

He stopped and looked down at his hand as if he held the paper. "It was a small drawing of the view just outside the camp, a lone tree against the flat plateau that made up our landscape. I pointed to it and then to her and I. She nodded her head."

He closed his fist and suddenly dropped in his chair. He didn't look at her. His eyes focussed inwards.

"We arranged a signal to meet, because to go near her all the time looked suspicious. Three small stones in the hollow by the office. If I put them there, we'd meet at the tree after sunset."

Adrian did look up now, as if to make her understand. "I should never have done that, lure her out of the camp after dark. I didn't think because I was selfish. I wanted to make love to her."

Adrian grabbed his wine and gulped it down. "Everything was fine for a while. We'd meet and we needed no words. I thought about how I might get her out of that camp, her and Binti."

Adrian didn't speak for a long time. Lexie watched him. His face looked haunted as he stared in the fire.

"Adrian, you don't have to talk. I don't need to know anymore. I don't want you to be upset."

He looked over at her, but it was as if she hadn't spoken. "One day I couldn't find her. I went to her tent. I'd never done that before. I asked an old woman if she'd seen her. She didn't say anything, just lifted the covering on a little bundle by her side. It was Binti. I knew something was wrong. She'd never leave her child unless it was to come to me. I looked everywhere for her. The sun was going down and I ran out of places to look. Then I thought of the hollow. There were three stones…I hadn't put them there."

Adrian found it hard to keep his voice steady. Lexie didn't want to hear it.

"I started to run. She might have gone to the well. I had to believe that. I started to panic because I had a feeling I couldn't get rid of. Something was wrong. I shouted 'Binti' over and over. I had no other name. I looked and looked and had to keep going. I was responsible for her, Lexie. She had no one else."

Adrian looked at her, bewilderment in his eyes. "What had she gone through to make her never want to speak again? Where were her husband, her mother, and her family? Why was she so alone?"

Before Lexie knew what happened, Adrian got on the floor and grabbed the old pillow he used to love to sit on. He held it close to his chest, and rocked back and forth. She wanted him to stop.

"Adrian, please stop. Please. It's all right. I don't want to know."

He was past hearing her. He wasn't in the room anymore. He ran on an African plateau, under a moonlit sky, out of breath and searching.

"That's when I found her."

He started to sob. He wouldn't stop. Lexie got on her knees

and tried to hold him but he just rocked and rocked. She couldn't believe this was happening. He was in desperate pain.

He put his hands over his face, as if he didn't want to see. "Oh Lexie."

She tried to hush him like a baby. "Don't Adrian. Don't."

He cried into his hands. "The things they did to her, Lexie. The things they did to her."

Oh my God. This has to stop.

"Adrian. She's not in pain anymore. She's not there." She was frantic to try and help him in some way. "It's over dearest. It's all over. She's safe now. She's not there. She's at peace now."

He didn't talk. That part was over. But he cried. He cried his heart out. She sat on the floor beside him, her arm across his back. She gave him Kleenex. Sophie came over and rubbed against him. He picked her up and held her close, stroking her fur over and over. He stopped rocking so hard. The three of them swayed together until the embers died away.

LEXIE TOLD HIM she'd get him a taxi. He was calm now, but he didn't say very much. She said he should try to get some sleep. He turned before he left.

"I didn't mean for it to be like that. I only wanted to explain."

"It's okay Adrian. You need to rest now." And she opened the front door for him. "Goodbye."

"Thank you." He took her hand for a moment and gave it a squeeze. Then he turned around and left. She watched the red tail lights fade into the night.

She took her clothes off and crawled into bed. It was near daybreak. She fell into a dead sleep.

Chapter Eighteen

JOSS SOLD MOST of his possessions and paid up the lease on his apartment. He wouldn't be back. He was going home to Cape Breton to stay.

His father was pretty low when he arrived. He shouted and grumbled about everything. Stuck up in his bedroom like an old woman, he refused to read or watch television. His mother was ready to wring his neck. But Joss knew the temper was really fright. To Danny, not being on the water meant he was dead.

Joss sat with his dad on his first evening back. His mother brought up their tea on a tray with a plate of ginger cookies. Joss waited until their tea was almost gone.

"Da. You have to retire."

His father shoved his mug onto the side table. "Who says so? You?"

"Yeah, me." Joss took a deep breath. This wouldn't be easy. "Da, lobster fishing is for men my age. You've had your run. It's time to let go."

"Christ Almighty," Danny yelled. "You want me to give up my licence? I'd rather be put down."

"I don't want you to sell it to a stranger. I want you to sell it to me."

His father looked at him. "You live half way around the world. I thought you wanted to get away from here. You made that pretty damn clear when you left."

Joss tried to be patient. "Da, I was twenty then, of course I wanted to leave. That was ten years ago, but I'm a grown man now and I want to come home. I'd like to buy you out and take over the boat. You know I'm good at it."

His father didn't say anything. He grabbed his tea again and took a mouthful. Joss waited.

"Well, I don't know."

"I won't put you out to pasture. I expect you to come and work for me. I'll need a hand. Someone has to drive the boat."

His father looked out the window that faced him, the one that looked out over the harbour. "I expect a good price."

"Of course, Da."

He cleared his throat. "Well, son. I guess we have a deal." He held out his hand and Joss shook it. His father hung on to it, tight. That's how his mom found them.

❧

LEXIE KNEW THERE was unfinished business, but she didn't want to deal with it. She opened her heart again, just a little, and it slammed shut before she had a chance to let it out.

Lexie finally understood Adrian's pain. It explained a lot. But she knew all she wanted to know.

He didn't call the next day or the next. She wasn't sorry. She had to deal with her own heartache. She had to steel herself, not get involved with someone else's sorrow. She didn't want to walk around like an open wound anymore.

When Lexie got home from work on Monday, there were six messages, all from him. She didn't call him back.

On Tuesday, she was at work, when Marlene hurried over.

"There's this guy out at the desk who wants to know if you're here. Looks like a dish," she winked and cracked.

"Tell him I'm not."

"Frig off! A guy like that comes calling and you brush him off? You need someone to adjust your antennas."

"Marlene, it's none of your business. Please tell him I'm not here. Please."

"Well, you're a brick short of a load, if you ask me," she said as she walked away.

When the day was over, Lexie said, "Goodnight girls," and pulled her car keys out of her purse. She pushed the library door open with her hip, the usual load of books and papers with her. And there was Adrian, waiting by Betsy.

Her heart did that usual cartwheel when she laid eyes on him, but her brain told her to keep him at a distance. She was tired of being upset. She needed normal. She just wanted to find some schmo who worked nine to five, had a beer on the weekend, and watched the hockey game, end of story. Maybe Ernie had a brother.

"Lex, don't run away from me."

"I won't run. I'll drive."

"I haven't finished what I wanted to tell you."

"You mean there's more horror in store for me? I can't bloody wait to hear it."

She opened the car door and threw her stuff in the back. Adrian put his hand on her coat sleeve.

"Don't touch me, Adrian."

He let go.

"I don't intend to have a scene here in the parking lot. Not with Judy and Marlene in the window behind me."

He looked over her shoulder. "You're right."

"I know I'm right. As a matter of fact, forget this. Get in the damn car."

She got behind the wheel and roared the engine to life. Before Adrian had his door closed she took off. She had no idea what she'd do, but it felt good to be in charge. She tore up the street and dared other cars to hit her. She squealed her tires and hit the brakes as hard as she could at every stop sign. Adrian knew better than to say a word.

Lexie drove home. She hadn't intended to take him there but it was too cold to stand around outside and have an argument. She took her keys and jumped out. She ran to the front door, had it open in a second and stormed inside. She threw off her coat. She didn't know if he was behind her or not. She ran upstairs, tore into her room and lifted the trunk at the end of her bed. She grabbed Adrian's finished sweater.

She ran back down the stairs. He stood in the porch. She threw the sweater at him.

"Take this and get out of my life."

Lexie turned on her heel and went into the living room. Sophie sat at attention, aware that something was wrong. Lexie turned towards the fire and stared at it while she waited to hear a door slam.

Nothing.

She turned around and he was there.

She pointed at the door. "Didn't you hear me? I want you

to leave me alone. I want you to go away and never come back."

He held up his hands. "Wait. Just wait."

"Wait for *what*? For you to tell me another horrible story of man's inhumanity? Why did I need to know that story, Adrian? Couldn't you just go to a therapist and spill your guts? Instead you come here and spill them all over me and my stupid rugs."

What the hell was she saying? She walked back and forth. She didn't know what to do.

He pleaded with her. "I came back to explain. I wanted you to know why I couldn't seem to focus. I tried to fit in but it was an act. I was dead inside."

She watched her feet as she moved around the room. "You want me to know something that happened a long time ago. Something that has nothing to do with me. Why? You only lived with me for two months because I felt sorry for you. You didn't have to come back here and reveal this sensational reason as to why you walked along the shore constantly. I was quite happy with the assumption you were crazy."

She looked up at him. "Why are you here, for God's sake? You wanted to tell me what? That you loved someone else and she died a horrible death?"

She threw her hands in the air. "Fine. I'm glad you got it off your chest. Good old Lexie is a shoulder to cry on. She has no feelings of her own to worry about. You can vomit your grief all over the room, because I'm a big girl and I can take it."

Adrian looked very upset. She didn't care.

"But guess what? I'm not that pushover you left behind. I'm not the girl who squealed with fright at the sight of you and Gabby. What a pathetic moron I was. What a loser, to hope that you liked me…to think that maybe you felt something for me. To pine away because of your disloyalty."

She walked closer to him. "I'm not that big girl you walked out on. She doesn't live here anymore."

She left the room and went into the kitchen. She needed a drink of water. Her throat was parched from shouting. She sat at the table.

Adrian followed her with his sweater in his hand. "I did not come here to vomit my story and leave. To tell you about another woman. That's only part of the picture."

"Can you not understand? I'm no longer interested in what you have to say. It doesn't matter. You don't figure in my life any more."

He looked at her. "Please Lex, I came back to explain that day in the subway. I couldn't believe it was you. I couldn't believe my eyes and then just as suddenly you were gone. I thought you were a dream."

He held the sweater in a tight grip. "I saw you push that stroller. I saw the baby and I couldn't think. I wasn't sure what to do. The only explanation I came up with was that you were married. I knew I had no right to interfere with your life, to mess anything up for you, so I didn't call out." He sat down on the kitchen chair beside her. "I wanted to shout across that track that I missed you. That I loved you all along."

Her mind went blank for a minute.

"You loved me all along? If you loved me all along, Adrian,

you wouldn't have been with my sister in front of the fireplace. That was loving all right, but it wasn't me."

She ticked off another reason with her finger. "Or, you would've come back as soon as you left her, to beg my forgiveness. All this time without so much as a phone call or a letter. And I'm supposed to swallow that you love me? You must think I'm a fool." She turned away from him.

"That's the other part of the story, Lexie."

She stared out the window. She saw a crow on the power line, hunched against the freezing wind. She knew how it felt. "I don't want to know. I couldn't care less."

"You do care," he yelled at her. "You do want to know. Otherwise you wouldn't be so angry. If I meant nothing to you, you wouldn't be so furious with me."

"You think you know everything. Don't you dare presume to know my feelings."

He threw the sweater on the back of the chair next to him, put his elbows on the table and leaned towards her. "I loved you for being there when I needed somewhere to hide, someone to take care of me. I wandered for so long. I was tired. I had to stop moving."

He shook his head. "But I was frozen. I was afraid to love anyone. I caused a woman's death, because I dared to love her. It was my fault she died. My friend tried to tell me that, but I didn't listen. How arrogant and pompous to presume I knew everything. I killed her."

"That's ridiculous."

"It's not ridiculous, Lexie. I took her out of the confines of that camp. I called attention to her. Maybe the people who killed her family were looking for her. They wouldn't have found her if I hadn't made her such a walking target. All because I couldn't keep my hands to myself."

"Adrian, you don't know that. You don't know who killed her."

"Well, whether it was deliberate or just a random act, it doesn't matter, does it? Dead is dead. And if it wasn't for me she'd still be here — with Binti."

Lexie pictured the little girl at the Metro station.

Adrian closed his eyes. "What madness had she been brave enough to escape from? To save her child's life…only to have me throw it away when she was finally safe."

Lexie didn't know what to say.

He opened his eyes and straightened his back. "And then guess what I did? Just guess?

She shook her head.

"I ran. A selfish coward who thought only of his own pain. I ran until I met you. By the time I did, I was numb with shame."

She said nothing.

"I left a little baby girl all alone."

There was nothing to say to that, so they sat for a long moment.

"I loved you Lexie, but I didn't know how to bridge the wall I created around me. You were the same way."

"What do you mean?"

"You had your own wall."

"No, I didn't."

"Yes, you did." He shook his head. "You always put yourself down and kept people at arm's length. I didn't have the energy to know what to do about that. I was in a dark place."

"Not so dark that you didn't see Gabby." Let him explain that.

"Gabby was a moment in time. You're forever."

Lexie stayed quiet.

"I had to do the right thing. I couldn't live with myself anymore. I had to go back for Binti."

"Adrian, you've been gone a long time. You could have called me at some point."

"Think about it. The last time I saw your face it was stricken. I begged you to let me talk and you ran out. I didn't know how to say I was sorry."

"You say, 'I'm sorry.'"

"I *am* sorry. I only thought of myself and the baby. I left her there, with no family, with no one who cared about her. I had to go back, Lex."

"So what happened?"

He heaved a big sigh. "It took me a very long time. When I went back to the camp, she wasn't there. I went through all the paperwork I could find. Some of the refugees were sent to another camp. After that they were separated again. Some were able to go back to their homes while others stayed. I travelled everywhere, through a whole network of camps, before I realized I should search the orphanages too. That took months. I was almost ready to give up, when I found her."

He smiled at Lexie sadly. "She was all by herself in a crib. I'd know her anywhere. I picked her up and she never opened her mouth. She held onto my shirt and wouldn't let me go."

"Oh God, Adrian. How awful."

"I finally got her home to Montreal. But it's been a struggle. She was so traumatized, she'd scream if I left her. She's very small and suffers from health problems. Mother and I were worried she might have developmental problems as well, but she seems to be improving."

They looked at each other.

"Now I feel terrible."

"Don't be silly," Adrian said.

Her anger disappeared. She rubbed her temples because her head throbbed. "I must be the most self-absorbed person in the universe, to never imagine that someone else might have their own battles to fight. I'm sorry."

"I want you to forgive me. I should have tried to get in touch with you. That was selfish of me."

"Fine." She was worn out. She leaned her head against her hand. "Look, I have to go and get my son. My mother will wonder where I am."

"What's his name?"

"Joshua."

"Are you still with his father?"

"No."

He looked at her intently. "Then I have a chance?"

She looked right in his eyes, reached over and took his hand. "I'll be the strong one now. You don't love me Adrian. You only think you love me. You were lost and I gave you refuge. That's all. We don't really know each other. It's too complicated. We both have so many challenges ahead of us. I have my son, you have your daughter. We live in different worlds. It wouldn't work."

She gave his hand a pat, and then let it go. He looked forlorn.

"Take that sweater. I did make it with a lot of love. I hope it keeps you warm. I'll always remember you. And for what it's worth, Adrian, you are a good man. You didn't cause that girl's death. You saved her. You saved her child, and so you saved her. That's all a mother would want, for her child to live and be safe."

He put his head down on his arms for a moment. Then he looked at her with his big blue eyes.

"Lexie. I love you. I don't think I love you. I know I do. I've hurt you badly and I don't blame you for being careful. Please believe me. I need you to believe me."

She needed to be in control. "I'm sorry. This is for your own good. You need to make a future, not dwell in the past. That's what I need to do, too."

She tried to explain. "I've struggled but I feel stronger now. I want to make it on my own. Do you see? I'll always love you as a friend Adrian, and I'm glad you came back to explain what I couldn't understand. My father was right. It was about you, and not about me. That makes me so relieved. I thought you left because I meant nothing. But I know that's not true, because I am something, and someone. I'm Lexie Ivy and I'm Joshua's mommy. That's enough for me."

She got up and went to get her coat. She didn't leave him any choice. She opened the front door and stood beside it. When Adrian walked by her with his head down, Lexie locked the door behind him and together they went down the steps and over to Betsy.

"Would you like a lift somewhere?"

He looked at her. "No, thank you. I think I'll walk."

She couldn't do it. She couldn't risk it. She reached up and kissed his cheek.

"Goodbye Adrian."

He nodded and walked away. She started the van and drove down the street in the other direction, but she watched him in the rear-view mirror. Finally, she tore her eyes away.

WHEN LEXIE CRAWLED into bed that night, she stared at the ceiling. She rubbed the sheet on the empty side of her bed. Why had she sent him away? He was someone she had cared for from the first moment she laid eyes on him. He told her he loved her.

Every man she ever loved left her. It was too hard. She didn't want to chance the pain of rejection again. She had a son to consider. She couldn't bring herself to imagine that it would work. So she refused to imagine at all. Adrian was a dream. Life was real.

Chapter Nineteen

LEXIE NEEDED A distraction. She arrived at Beth's to find Michaela on a stool, Beth with a pair of scissors in her hand. The girls were very excited. Lexie was horrified.

"Do you want me to do Joshua's when I'm finished?"

Not on your life. "That's okay, Beth. I like his hair long." She looked at Josh who sat on her lap. He turned around and grinned at her. He was his father through and through.

"You'll have to cut it at some point," Beth pointed out. "He's so gorgeous. He'd look like a girl if he didn't have the body of a weightlifter."

"Did you hear your silly Auntie Beth?" Lexie bounced him on her knee. "Golly, Josh's getting so heavy, I worry about Mom being able to carry him around."

"I think he's the combined weight of all the girls," Beth laughed. "Okay Michaela, are you ready?"

"Don't cut a lot Mommy."

"Don't worry, honey. I'll just trim it."

And she did. She barely took anything off, she was so cautious. Michaela was content. The other three girls couldn't wait their turn.

By the time she got to the baby, Beth was in her glory. She had it down pat. Lexie didn't dare open her mouth, because she knew Beth would bite her head off if she dared to criticize her. But it was difficult not to look amazed.

Brittany's hair was shorter than Michaela's. Halley's was

shorter that Brittany's and poor little Madison looked like a Benedictine monk.

When Madison got off the stool and walked away, Beth looked a bit worried. "Do you think I cut it a little short?"

Lexie was no fool. "It's fine."

She heard Mom come in the door, followed by a terrible screech. "Beth, come here quick, the girls must have got hold of the scissors!"

She tore into the kitchen. Beth held the scissors in her hand.

Mom held her heart. "Oh, thank God. You have to be careful, Beth. Don't leave sharp things around where they can reach them."

Beth looked dismayed. That's when their mother looked at the huge pile of blond hair all over the kitchen floor.

"My God, Beth. What have you done?"

She looked like she wanted to cry. Lexie couldn't hold it in anymore. "Yes, Beth, what have you done?"

Beth got red in the face. Then she held her nose and covered her mouth. The three of them started to laugh. They laughed so hard, tears streamed down their faces. Just when they had settled down, dear little Madison walked back into the kitchen and they started all over again.

Poor Rory screeched louder than their mother when he came through the door. He shook his head and told Beth it would cost more money to fix the problem than it would have cost to take them to the hairdresser's in the first place. Rory took her in his arms and said not to worry. He'd keep her.

After supper, Mom, Beth, and Lexie sat in the family room and nursed their tea. Rory was on the computer and the girls took Josh downstairs with them to watch videos.

Lexie asked Mom, "How's Kate?"

"Oh, she and Daphne are enrolled in a scuba diving course." She rolled her eyes. "They have every night of the week booked with one thing and another."

"I hope they learn to dive better than they cook," Beth smirked. "Rory still whines about that horrible dressing. I had to buy a big chicken two days later and stuff it, just to get him to shut up."

"Your man is set in his ways," Lexie smiled. "You spoil him rotten."

"Well, that's what I'm here for."

"You're such a Susie Homemaker," Lexie said.

"Nonsense, it's not about being a Susie Homemaker. I treat him nicely because he treats me nicely. I know what's important in my life. Willie taught me that."

They sat and thought about it.

Mom said, "Always let your husband know you love him, girls. It's the little things in life that add up to the big things, the everyday gestures. Don't ever take them for granted, because one day, they aren't there anymore and you'll wish you had one more chance." She looked at Lexie, and smiled sadly.

"Is it bad, Mom? Living without Daddy?" Beth asked.

"I'm extremely sorry to say that most of the time it doesn't feel any different. Your father wasn't home that often anyway, or I was out, or he was in his study."

She clasped her hands. "But I miss him dreadfully when

I lie in an empty bed. He used to sing in the shower and I miss that. And when I hear a creak at night, I still go to give him a shove and send him downstairs to take care of it." She sighed. "And I sure miss him on holidays, or when the children visit, to chuckle over the milestones — like missing teeth — you know, silly things like that."

Mom turned to Lexie. "You must get lonely, all by yourself in that house."

Lexie took a gulp of tea. "It's become a way of life, I'm afraid. I've become so set in my ways, no one would have me anyway."

"I can't believe that," Mom scoffed. "There's lots of men who'd want you, if you gave them half a chance."

"She wants Adrian," Beth said.

Mom looked fed up. "He left you in the lurch and then he left Gabby. Isn't that enough of a clue to tell you he's not dependable?"

"He is dependable. He was sick when he was here. He's not like that anymore."

"And how in the world would you know that?" Beth asked.

Lexie scratched the side of her teacup. Then took a sip.

"How do you know?" Beth persisted.

"He told me."

Mom and Beth looked at each other, and then back at her. "*When*?" Mom shouted

"The other day."

"Have you gone crazy?" Beth yelled.

"He came to see me."

"Just out of the blue? With no warning or anything?"

"No. He called first."

Beth threw a teddy bear at her. "You rat. You never told me!"

Lexie shrugged.

"I tell you everything. Just why in the world would you keep this a secret?"

Lexie put down her cup. She grabbed the bear and hugged it.

"Because I didn't know what to say. I didn't know what I felt myself, so I could hardly explain it to someone else."

"Why on earth would he come back like this?" said her mother. "After being away so long. I don't understand." She shook her head, and then looked as if she remembered something. "Is that the night you asked me to babysit Josh, the night you wanted to go for a drink with friends? I knew you acted a little funny."

Lexie nodded.

"So?" Beth asked. "Why the hell did he come back now?"

"To tell me he loved me."

They looked at her and couldn't speak.

"Can I have some more tea?"

Beth looked at Mom. Mom looked at Lexie.

Beth crossed her arms. "No! You can't have any tea. Not until you spill your guts."

"Fine. I'll get it myself." Lexie got up and walked into the kitchen. She heard Beth behind her. "Rory?!"

"What?"

"If the kids want anything, will you get it for them because I can't be interrupted."

There was a pause. "What are you three up to? Having a séance?"

"Yes."

"Okay then. While you're at it, find out who wins the football game next Saturday."

"Oh, shut up." Beth was in her chair by the time Lexie came back with her tea.

It was a long and painful process. When she told them about Binti and her mother and Adrian's terrible journey, they were incredulous at one moment and in tears the next. It really did sound like a soap opera after a while, except the people were real and it was too tragic, even for daytime television.

"Oh, that precious child," her mother cried, as she wiped her eyes on her napkin, or what was left of it. "Thank God he went back for her. I'm sorry I said he wasn't dependable. He's not weird at all."

Beth also cried into her napkin. "That poor girl. My God, there is so much horror in the world. We don't know anything that goes on."

Lexie listened to the two of them prattle on about Adrian's story. When she said it out loud, it felt different, so hurtful and sad. Poor Adrian.

They were finally quiet for a while. Then Beth said, "Lexie. There's something I don't understand. I know Adrian had to go back for the baby. But how did he explain Gabby? If he loved you, why did he go with her?"

"I asked him that. He said Gabby was a moment, but I was forever."

Mom and Beth looked at each other. It was Beth who spoke first. "Who on earth talks like that? God. How romantic."

"What did you say when he told you he loved you?" Mom asked her.

"That he didn't really love me."

Beth's hand had reached up to blow her poor red nose again, so her arm hung in mid-air. Her mother had wiped her eyes at that moment, so she played hide-and-seek. After those few frozen seconds, they lowered their arms and waited.

"I told him he only thought he loved me — that I was a safe place when he needed one. I told him our lives were different and I had learned to stand on my own two feet. So basically I said thanks, but no thanks."

Beth and Mom looked down at their hands and didn't say anything. They sneaked peeks at one another. They stayed like that for so long Lexie got annoyed.

"It's my decision you know, and I think I made the right one." She wanted them to understand. "He upsets my life. I need a smooth ride from now on. I've suffered from way too much drama, up and down like a stupid yo-yo. I'm finished with that. Adrian's the past. I need a future."

"I'm sure you're right," Mom said, rather sadly.

"You know best." Her sister sounded sad too.

"Look. Think about it. How can I be happy with someone Gabby still loves?"

It was Beth who opened her mouth first. "Look, it might sound cruel to say all's fair in love and war, but in this case it's true. Adrian didn't come back for Gabby. He came back for you."

Lexie gave them a worried look. "You think I'm wrong?"

"Lex," Beth said softly, "You've waited for him for so long. And then you send him packing? Does that sound sensible? I don't understand."

"Mom?"

"Dearest, the choice is yours. Only you can decide what to do. But I know you. Sometimes you're afraid to jump, that's all."

LEXIE CALLED KATE and told her the story.

"Lex, Adrian was gone a long time. He's lived a life we can't imagine. He's travelled in a world we can't know. He had no reason to come back to you, except one."

She sat with her dad in comfortable silence and touched the headstone when she left.

Lexie lay in bed that night and thought it over. She opened her window and listened to the tide. She heard the water moving, always moving. One day she'd be gone, but the water would remain. It called to her.

Jump, Lexie, Jump.

She told Josh. He grinned.

She told Susan. Susan punched her arm for not telling her sooner. She said whatever made Lexie happy, made her happy.

She didn't call Gabby.

She told Beth. "Well, it's about fucking time."

She told Mom. "You deserve every happiness, darling."

She held her breath and called Adrian. She didn't know if he'd still be there, wherever there was.

He picked it up right away.

"Lexie?"

"Come home Adrian."

She heard the phone go dead.

Chapter Twenty

JOSS WENT INTO Sydney for supplies, whistling as he drove, something he did a lot of these days. Why hadn't he come back years ago? It was good to be around his brothers and their families. He and Aaron especially chummed around like they did when they were younger. His parents were happier than he had seen them in years. His dad was pretty agile with his cane. He'd sit in the garage and watch Joss repair his nets. There were always a group of fellas that hung around out back all day, his father's cronies and his own.

Joss thought he'd buy the small house just down the road. Old Mrs. Morrison finally went into a home, and her place was for sale. He knew his mother was delighted with the prospect of him being so close.

He ran around Sydney, picking up this and that for the boat. It was close to supper hour. He figured he'd have a beer and a steak at the tavern before he headed out for the long drive home. When he opened the door, a thick fog of smoke hung in the air. The hockey game blared from TVs all over the room and guys were hunkered around tables drinking draft.

Joss sat down with someone he knew from school. That's when Tom came up behind him, three sheets to the wind, and slapped him on his back. "Holy shit, look who's here."

Joss turned around.

"Christ," Tom bellowed. "I haven't seen you in a dog's age. I thought you were still up north."

"I came home to help my old man with the boat."

Tom smirked, "Ya sure? Didn't cross your mind to come back and give some more to Lexie?"

Josh stood up. "Don't talk about her that way."

Tom picked up on the tone. "Sorry, sorry, no offence meant. Just thought you might want to pick up where you left off."

"Why would I? She's married."

Tom screwed up his face. "Married? Shit, Lexie's not married. Who told you that load of crap?"

Joss threw a twenty-dollar-bill on the table and walked out the door.

❧

SHE WAS ALONE, waiting on the porch. She didn't think of anything or see anything. The ocean kept her company.

Car lights turned onto the street and the taxi pulled up. He got out, ran up the steps, and stopped. He looked at her. He wore her sweater.

"Lexie —"

"Don't talk — hold me."

IT WAS MORNING. Sunlight poured in the window. She had to get up and call Mom to tell her what time she'd pick up Joshua. She threw off the duvet. Adrian grabbed her arm and pulled her back to him. "Come here. Where are you going?"

She snuggled up close again. "I thought you were asleep."

He rubbed her arm. "I can't sleep. I'm afraid you won't be here when I wake up. Just stay with me. I need you."

Adrian was a gentle lover. It felt wonderful to have someone hold her. She'd been so lonely. He kissed her over and over, softly. This is what she needed, someone to love her. She wanted him to take care of her.

"Thank you Lexie," he'd murmur against her mouth between kisses.

"I love you Adrian."

As he ate his breakfast, she went to get Josh. Mom met her at the door with a wide smile on her face.

"How are you darling?"

"Wonderful."

"Bring him over for supper why don't you?"

Lexie gave her a look. "Mom. I don't want to drag him all over town right away. We need some time together."

"Of course," Mom nodded. "You're right, but if I can help in any way, you know, take Josh in the evening if you want to go out, you only have to say."

She leaned over and kissed her. "Thanks, Mom."

She carried Josh down the steps. She looked over her shoulder. "By the way, tell Beth not to call me. I don't have time for twenty questions."

"I'll tell her you said that." Mom blew her a kiss.

"THIS IS JOSHUA. Say hi to Adrian, honey."

Adrian reached out to shake his hand. "Hello Joshua."

Joshua hid behind her leg and wouldn't look at him.

"Sorry about that," she laughed. "He's not used to a lot of men I'm afraid, only his Uncle Rory. We're a family of women."

"I remember."

"Do you want to watch *The Little Mermaid*, sweetie?" Josh nodded against the back of her knee.

"I'll just get him organized and be right back."

"I'll pour you a cup of coffee and start these dishes," he smiled.

Oh, this was so much fun, the three of them playing house.

Josh and Sophie settled in on the big sofa with a juice cup and crackers and laughed at Sebastian, the hermit crab. Adrian and Lexie sat across the table from each other in the kitchen and held hands.

"Can you believe this?" she grinned. "It's us. Together. Do you know how often I wanted this to happen?"

Adrian smiled at her. "Really?"

She drank him in. "Yes. And I always wanted to do this." She reached over and put her hand through his hair to brush it off his face.

He kissed her hand. "We belong together. I always want to be with you."

"Even when I have to go to work?"

"Even then."

They laughed. "Marlene will be happy."

That night in bed, as Adrian held her, he asked about Joshua's father.

"Was he someone you were with for a long time?"

"No."

"Why did you break up?"

"He left."

Adrian looked down at her with a worried frown. "Were you upset? That must have been awful, to leave you when you were pregnant. How could he do such a thing?"

She didn't know what to say. She didn't want to talk about

it. She hugged him tighter. "It doesn't matter now. I have Josh, and now I have you. What more do I need?"

They went for a walk on the beach the next morning. Josh chased around after seagulls and tried to make them come to him, but they were too high. They talked about how this would work — where they'd live and how they'd manage their children.

"I have to go back soon and tell Mom what's happened," Adrian said. "I told her I'd be away until I knew where I stood with you."

They walked arm in arm, over the hard sand. "So she knows about me?"

"Yes." He smiled at her. "I told her all about you. She wants to give you a big kiss, for being so sweet to me."

She looked up at him. "It was my pleasure."

He kissed her quickly, then stopped and did it properly. "No. It's all mine."

They walked back to the house. A car drove by and suddenly screeched its brakes, which startled them. Lexie glanced over and there was Donalda, sitting behind the wheel, looking as if she'd seen a ghost.

She rolled down the window.

"*Adrian*?"

"Hi."

Lexie pointed at him. "Remember that guy I had a date with?"

Donalda rolled up her window and laid rubber, as if to get as far away from her as fast as possible. Poor Donalda.

LEXIE TOOK JOSH over to her mother's house. "Thanks for this, Mom."

"No problem. You two need some alone time."

"I know, we have to make some plans. Why don't you bring him over about four, and we'll have supper together."

"Sounds good. Can't wait."

Lexie ran down her mother's back steps just as Beth's van pulled up in the driveway. All the girls were asleep in their car seats.

Beth smiled at her. "Hi, I was just passing and I saw Betsy. So, tell me — how's it going with lover boy?"

"He's wonderful. He's so considerate of my feelings. It's like he doesn't want to break me or something."

"God. What a drag!"

Lexie hit her on the arm. "Get lost. We aren't all in heat."

"I know. Poor you." She glanced in the rear-view mirror. "Oh, hell, they're about to wake up. Have to dash." She blew her a kiss and zoomed out of the driveway in a hurry.

Lexie muttered, "Huh. I'll show you passion." She drove home and ran into the doorway of the living room out of breath. She started to unbuttoned her shirt.

"Hurry up and take off your clothes."

Adrian threw his magazine in the air and chased her up to the stairs.

"I HAVE TO go and put the oven on," she laughed, as Adrian tried to keep her in the bed.

"I want to snuggle. Please."

"Two more minutes."

She held him close and listened to his heartbeat. This was so nice, so peaceful. She needed this. But she still had to put the oven on if they were going to have pot roast for supper.

"All right. I'll give you two minutes. Then you have to get back up here and give me a hug." He looked at his watch and put his hands behind his head. "Starting now."

She giggled, grabbed her robe, and threw it around her. She ran downstairs and turned on the oven.

The doorbell rang.

God, Mom's early.

She ran to the door and opened it. "It's not four yet," she laughed.

Joss was standing there.

Chapter Twenty-one

HER MOUTH DROPPED open. She grabbed the front of her robe and held it in front of her, as if to protect herself.

"Joss. My God." Her heart pounded. It was so painful, she wanted it to stop.

He gave her that gorgeous lopsided grin and looked her over from top to bottom. "Hi, Lexie." He put his hands in his jeans pockets. "I'm glad to see I have the right house."

She practically screamed at him. "Why are you here?"

"I wanted to see you."

Her pulse banged in her ears. "What for? Are you crazy?"

He didn't say anything.

So she did scream at him. "You can't just show up now. What are you doing to me?"

He took his hands out of his pockets and rubbed his hands together. "Look, Lexie. I didn't want to scare the life out of you. I just wanted to talk."

Her tears scalded her eyes. "About what!?"

"Lexie, whoa. Maybe I should go."

It was the first time she ever saw him look unhappy. She couldn't just yell at him by the door. She didn't know what to do. Then she heard Adrian call out, "Time's up."

She looked over her shoulder and yelled back up the stairs. "I'm coming."

"Hey. Three's a crowd. I'll go." He turned around.

She reached out to grab his sleeve. "No! Wait. I'm sorry. You just gave me such a surprise. I didn't mean to yell at you."

"Look, Lexie, if you have someone else, all you have to do is tell me. Are you married?"

"No. No. It's not that." She tried to think. And then she didn't think. "Could you wait in the kitchen till I get dressed?"

"I don't want to make trouble."

She pulled him in the door. "It's no trouble. Just go to the kitchen and stay there. I'll be right down."

He shrugged. "Okay, then." She pointed the way and he walked down the hall.

Lexie's mind was a blank. She ran upstairs, went into the bathroom and threw cold water on her face.

She heard Adrian say, "You're a minute late."

She ran into the bedroom and sat on the bed.

"Adrian, I know this sounds weird, but someone has shown up and I have to talk to them in private. I didn't know they'd be here, so it's a big surprise. But I really need to talk to this person, and if I don't do it now, it may be my only chance."

He looked confused, but said, "Well, sure, don't worry about it." He got out of bed. "I'll get dressed and go for a walk. How long do you want me gone?"

"A couple of hours, maybe."

"All right." He looked so sweet as he gathered up his things. He was always so considerate. She went right up to him and kissed him hard.

"I love you Adrian. Don't ever doubt that."

He held her for a minute. "Are you in trouble, Lexie? Is there anything I can do?"

She kissed him again, as if to give herself courage. "I'm not in any trouble."

He put on his jeans, threw his sweater over his head, shoved his feet in his loafers, and grabbed his jacket.

"Could you go out the front door?"

He nodded. She hugged him. "I love you."

"I love you too."

He left.

She washed her face again. She splashed the water over and over as if to clear her head. She grabbed her jeans and the first T-shirt she saw, stopping at the top of the stairs to take several deep breaths. This couldn't be happening.

When she went into the kitchen Joss stood by the sink, looking out at the view through the window.

She looked at him. God, she didn't want him here. He frightened her. He set her on fire and she didn't want to burn.

He turned and smiled. "Did your friend leave?"

She nodded.

"Is this your house?"

"Yes."

"It's nice."

"Thanks."

He kept his eyes on her. Stop it. Stop it.

"What do you want, Joss?"

He put those hands back in his pockets. "I told you. I wanted to see you."

"Why now?"

"Can I sit down?"

She realized she was as rigid as plank. She needed to relax. She also had to calm down and stop being so rude. She blew out a big breath of air. "I'm sorry. Of course, you can sit down. Would you like something to drink?"

"No thanks."

He walked across the kitchen and they sat. Her heart raced. She tried to inhale slowly. "What did you want to see me about?"

"I wanted to see if you were going out with anyone."

"You stroll in *now,* to ask me for a date?"

He gave a little laugh. "Yeah. Basically."

She stared at him.

"Look, Lexie, I'm not good at explanations. I'm a pretty simple guy. I just wanted to see if you remembered me."

To borrow a line from Susie, as if she could forget.

"Yes, of course I remember you. But the last time I saw you, you were on your way to Alaska, to rock the world of about a hundred other women. That's what you do best isn't it? That's what you made clear from the start."

He looked down at the floor. "I suppose you're right. That is the way I've lived my life. But a man can change."

She watched him. "How did you find me, Joss?"

"It wasn't hard."

She floundered, "But, why are you back here? I was under the impression you were a mystery man and no one could contact you."

"Well, I was under contract in Alaska — but it wasn't a permanent job. I always knew I'd come home."

She couldn't believe it. This was too much. "Was I supposed to know that? Where's home?"

"Neils Harbour."

Maybe three hours away.

She folded her arms on the table in front of her and laid her head on them. She didn't know what to think. She was in a deep well of sorrow.

She finally lifted her head to look straight at him. "Why didn't you tell me?"

"We didn't talk a lot, as I remember."

He'd betrayed her. "I thought you were from far away."

"If I was from that far away, why would I be helping a bunch of friends in Chéticamp?" He said it as if it was easy to understand. "I was home that fall for my brother's wedding."

He stopped for a minute and leaned towards her. "Look, Lexie, all this is irrelevant. I came back here to see you. It's as simple as that."

Her energy seeped away. "Why? Oh God, Joss. Why have you come?"

He gave her that look that turned her insides to mush. "I want you."

She couldn't say anything.

"Lexie, you were special. I knew that from the very beginning. But I assumed when I left that the usual thing would happen. I'd eventually forget about you and move on to the next girl." He rubbed his hands over the tops of his legs, as if they bothered him. "That's how it's always been. But every time I was with someone, it was your face I saw. That's never happened to me. I couldn't get you off my mind. Gradually, I realized maybe it was the real thing. It took me a while to figure out."

"Why did you stay away so long then?"

He smiled. "I was stupid. I'd started a new business and bank managers don't care about your love life."

She put her hands over her face. He talked, but she didn't want to see him anymore. It was too hard to look at him.

He sounded confused. "I don't know what's wrong, Lexie. I didn't mean to come here and hurt you. I only wanted to tell you, I think I love you. In fact, I know I do."

She still wouldn't look at him.

"I came for you once. Someone told me you were married. So I left."

She took her hands away. "What?"

He didn't answer her question. "I look at you and I want you so bad it hurts. I thought maybe you felt something for me too. But if you have someone else in your life, I'll go away and never come back. It would be my own fault, for not getting here sooner. If you want me to go, I'll go."

Big tears rolled down her face.

"Hey now, hey now, don't do that, Lexie. I'm sorry. I don't want you to cry."

He reached out to take her hand. He stood and pulled her to him, to comfort her. He held her and cradled her head. "Don't, baby girl. It's okay, Lexie. I'm right here."

She put her hands up to reach around him and he picked her up in his big arms.

She buried her face against his neck. "You have to go Joss. You have to go."

He held her tighter.

"But before you go, take me upstairs and love me."

He didn't need to be asked twice.

WHAT WAS SHE doing? What was she going to do? "Joss, you have to go."

She tried to leave. She tried. He held her back.

"You love me, Lexie."

He was behind her. He put his hand up through her hair.

"No."

"You love me, Lexie." He kissed the nape of her neck.

"No."

"I know you do. You can't make me believe you don't." He pushed her down, leaned over and held her head between his hands. He rubbed his thumb slowly over her lips. Oh no. She took it inside her mouth and bit it. He slowly slid it out and kissed her. She disappeared inside that kiss.

It took every ounce of energy she had to tear herself away. "Joss. Let me up."

Her voice was cross. He got up immediately.

She got up off the bed and put on her clothes. He stared at her as if he couldn't believe it.

"Joss, I don't have a lot of time. I know you won't understand this. I don't understand it myself. But you have to go."

"Why?"

"Because the man I love will be home in fifteen minutes."

"What did you just say?"

"You heard me." She rushed around and straightened things up.

He jumped off the bed and started to put on his own clothes. "The man you love is in this room."

"I'm so sorry. I don't mean to hurt you." She brushed her hair and passed Joss his shirt and shoes.

He looked angry. "And how long have you known this man if you can get into bed with me, ten minutes after I show up at your door?"

She ran into the bathroom to throw more water on her face.

"I've loved him for years."

Joss waited for her to pass through the bathroom door. He grabbed her arm in his big hand and made her look at him. "Years? Is that what you just said?"

"Yes."

He came very close to her. "Tell me Lexie. Did you love him when you made wild love to me in that cabin for a week? Was he the love of your life then?"

She pulled her arm away. "I don't have to tell you anything. You just have to get out of here."

"Fine." He threw on his shirt, grabbed his jean jacket, and started down the stairs. She was right behind him. She didn't have a thought in her head. It happened too fast.

She heard the front door open. She thought she'd faint. Oh, my God. Adrian.

"Yoo hoo," sang Mom, "it's only us."

And she and Joshua walked in the door.

The four of them stood there and didn't move. Mom was startled. Joshua stared at Joss. Lexie was behind Joss so she didn't see his face, but his body went rigid. Lexie put her hands over her mouth. She didn't want to scream.

Joshua started to look frightened. "Mama, Mama." She ran down the stairs past Joss and picked up her baby, more to comfort herself than anything.

Some of the shock started to wear off Mom. She looked at her. "Do you need me, Lexie?"

Lexie shook her head no.

"Then I'll be in the kitchen." She looked at Joss. "Excuse me." She went down the hall.

Lexie watched her go, because she didn't want to see Joss's face. Finally she had to look. Joshua pointed at him.

"Who dat?"

She didn't say anything. Joss looked at her. The hurt in his eyes was more than she could stand.

"I'm your father."

And before she could say a word, he ran down the stairs and out the door.

Lexie held onto Josh for as long as she could, but he wanted to get down. He wiggled out of her arms and ran to the kitchen. He wanted Sophie.

She put her hands up and pulled her fingers through her hair and kept them there. She had no idea what she should do. She was numb. To stay in one spot seemed sensible, because if she moved she'd become undone.

Her mother stood in the kitchen doorway. "Lexie?"

She broke the trance. Lexie ran to her and sobbed. Her mother held her as she wept.

"What is it sweetheart?" She rubbed her back. "Honey, was that Joshua's father?"

Lexie simply nodded against her sweater.

"Come and sit down." Mom pulled her along and sat her down. She went to the fridge and poured cold water into a glass and brought it over to her. She also brought a box of tissue. Then she turned and grabbed a clean tea towel. She put it under the faucet to get it wet, then wrung it out and came over to Lexie. She wiped her daughter's face, as if she were a little girl, then put the cold cloth on the back of her neck. Lexie breathed a little slower. She drank some water and blew her nose. Her eyes were swollen.

Her mother sat down beside her. "Where's Adrian?"

"He'll be back soon."

"Does he know that…" She paused. "That your friend was here?"

Lexie shook her head no. "He knows someone was here, but not who. I asked him to go for a walk and come back in two hours. God. Poor Adrian. What have I done?"

"Darling. What's this all about?"

She gave a deep sigh. "Mom, I don't know. I can't think."

"Well, did — for God sake, what's his name?"

"Joss."

"Well, did this Joss just suddenly show up? I don't imagine you knew he'd be here."

"Of course I didn't know," she cried. "He just turned up out of nowhere. I can't believe this. Why? All I want is a nice little life and the minute I think I have it all figured out, some catastrophe happens."

Lexie pulled her hair back again. She wanted it off her face, as if she needed to see more clearly. "I thought I'd never see him again. That stupid idiot let me believe he was from far away. I honestly never —"

"So why has he suddenly come back? Why now?"

She was furious. "Oh that *stupid* man. He comes back to tell me he loves me. Loves me! He said he came back once and someone told him I was married. That's crazy. Who'd do that? If he really loved me he'd never have left me. He should never have let me go."

Lexie jumped up and started to pace around the kitchen. "Then the fool tells me he's from Neil's Harbour! Can you believe it? He's from Cape Breton, the *stupid, stupid* man."

"All right, Lexie," her mother said impatiently, "we've established he's stupid. Now tell me something. Why did he come down the stairs looking as if he'd just thrown his clothes on?"

Lexie sat down on the chair beside her again. "Oh my God, Mom. I went to bed with him two minutes after Adrian left. What am I doing?"

"I have no idea what you're doing," she frowned. "And I take it by his reaction to Joshua, you didn't tell him he had a son before he whisked you upstairs?"

Lexie shook her head and stuffed her fist in her mouth to keep from screaming.

"Okay, calm down." She pulled Lexie's fist away. "Let's think rationally. Don't get too frantic. If you see him again, you'll explain that you didn't know where he was, but he's more than welcome to visit Joshua from now on."

Lexie's eyes widened.

"He's the boy's father," Mom said firmly. "If he wants to see his son, you have no right to keep him away, no matter who you're involved with. You'll work it out. You don't have to figure it out today."

"Next." It was as if she counted off a list. It gave Lexie a little focus. "If you jumped into bed with him, that must mean you still have feelings for him."

"I don't!" she hollered. "It was just lust, or something. It was stupid. I love Adrian! He needs me. I love Adrian. I've loved him for so long, and now he comes back and he's so sweet to me. How could I have betrayed him like that? I'm so ashamed of myself."

She wiped her eyes. It seemed all she ever did was cry about something. It frightened her. She didn't want to lose herself, didn't want to kneel on the frozen ground again. Her baby needed her.

Mom stated it as if it were simple. "All right, Lexie. Then you have it figured out. You love Adrian. You want him in your life. You don't owe Adrian any explanation. He was gone for a long time too. You were allowed to have other men. He left you. And you're certainly allowed to have Joshua's father in your life."

That made sense.

"I know men," Mom said before pausing. "I thought I did. I don't have a great track record, though do I?"

Lexie gave her a weak smile.

"But I do know one thing. Don't you dare tell Adrian what you just did. A man's ego is pretty fragile, and I don't think he'd understand, you being with him and then with someone else twenty-four hours later."

Lexie made a face. "How about twenty-four minutes later?"

"God! What am I going to do with you? You told me you and Adrian wanted some time to talk over your future."

She gave her mother a sheepish look.

Mom glanced around. "Not to mention the fact you're supposed to be cooking dinner. I can't smell anything." She looked at Lexie. "You were cooking all right, but it wasn't my pot roast."

Lexie cheered up a little. Her mother patted her hand.

"Look, why don't you go lie down for a few minutes. Then have a shower and put your face on. I'll keep Adrian entertained down here for a while and we'll make something else for supper."

"What will you tell Adrian?"

"That you had a visit from your son's father and it upset you to see him out of the blue like that. I'll tell him the truth — just not the whole truth."

Lexie reached over and took her hands. "Thank God you're here. I'm so glad you're my mother."

Mom smiled at her. "Go."

She lay on her bed and put the covers over her. She smelled Joss's aftershave on the sheets. When she rolled over she smelled Adrian's on his pillow. If it weren't so pathetic she'd laugh.

Her whole life she spent alone, waiting to meet someone, waiting for someone to love her. Now she had two men who said they did. The thing that bothered her the most was the look on Joss's face when he saw his baby. But he had no right to be upset. He left her. He didn't try and find her, or call her. How was she supposed to let him know? If she were really desperate, she probably could have tracked him down, but he told her he was as free as a bird. She didn't want to be the one to drag him back to earth.

She heard Adrian return and her mother give him a friendly greeting before they went back into the kitchen. Pots and pans banged around, so her speech must have worked.

Lexie stripped the bed and remade it with fresh sheets. She took a hot shower and did what Mom told her to do. By the time she got downstairs, she looked almost normal.

They had a nice dinner together, the four of them. She looked at Adrian and her heart melted. He was her love. She needed him. He needed her.

Mom kissed her goodnight. She patted her face as she left, as if to let her know she'd done a good job. Lexie got Josh ready for bed.

Adrian came and sat in the bathroom rocking chair, while Lexie knelt on the floor and gave Josh his bath. He had too many bath toys in with him.

Adrian watched her. "Your mother said Josh's father came today. Are you all right?"

"Yes."

"Do you still care about him, Lexie?"

She turned and looked at that sweet face, so full of love and concern. "No. I don't. You have to believe me."

He smiled at her. "I do believe you. Why wouldn't I?"

She shrugged. She pulled the plug and Adrian handed her a towel. She wrapped Josh up, lifted him out of the tub, and dried him off. He hated that. He always tried to escape. He finally wiggled free and ran away, his little bum disappearing into his room.

Josh finally went to sleep. She left his room and closed the door a little. Downstairs, she curled up with Adrian on the sofa in front of the fire. They stayed like that for a long time.

It must have been midnight when she said, "Take me upstairs Adrian, and love me."

LEXIE HAD TO go to work the next day. Adrian said he'd spend the day on the phone and start working out some of the details for the changes they planned to make.

"I have to go home soon," he said, as he was about to scramble her some eggs. "I see you with Josh, and I miss Binti so much. She'll wonder where I am. If I had to stay in that stupid hotel room one more night, I'd have gone out of my mind."

"You poor love. I've been so mean to you." She hugged him around his waist and pressed her cheek into the space between his shoulder blades.

"I can't scramble eggs, if you won't let me go." He tried to look around at her.

She kept hold of him. "That's too bad, you'll have to do it anyway."

"Okay. You asked for it."

He poured the eggs into the frying pan and stirred them like mad, deliberately shaking while he did it. Josh chuckled in his high chair and started to twist and shake too. She held on against Adrian's back and felt her tears sink into his robe.

Lexie kissed Adrian goodbye four times. He waved to them from the front door as she drove Josh out of the yard. How often had she dreamt of that? Being together as a family.

Mom waited in the back porch. Lexie got Josh out of the car and he ran to his grandmother, who bent down to kiss him.

"Hi sweetie pie," she laughed. "What should you and Grammy do today? Shall we bake some cookies?"

Josh nodded, grinned and barrelled inside.

Lexie staggered up the steps and Mom held out her arms to her.

"Mommy." She choked back tears. She couldn't fall apart. "I'm lost."

Mom kept a firm grip on her. "No you're not, sweetheart. It's just been too much, too much emotion. Anyone would be dazed and confused." She rubbed her back. "Gosh, you have two handsome men saying they love you. That doesn't happen every day."

Lexie sighed and let her go. She reached for her ever-present Kleenex. "There was a time when I'd have been delighted with such a scenario. It just goes to show that movies and real life are vastly different."

"Gammy!" Josh was impatient for her to come inside. He rushed out and pulled the hem of her sweater, grunting as he tried to move her.

"Listen, monkey, I'll be right there."

"Josh, come give Mommy a kiss." He ran over and gave her a smack, then grabbed his grandmother's hand.

Chapter Twenty-two

LEXIE WAS SUPPOSED to go straight to the library. Instead she drove up Susan's street. Her car was still in the yard, and Ernie's was gone, thank goodness. Lexie pulled in, got out, and knocked on the back door. The radio blared inside. Susie would never hear her knock, so she tried the door and it was unlocked. She entered the kitchen, patted Ian and other assorted animals that hurried over, and went over to the radio and shut it off.

"Susie!"

"Is that you Lexie?"

"Yeah."

"Why are you here? Just a sec, I'll be right down."

Lexie heard her walk around upstairs, open drawers, and turn off the water. Finally her footsteps descended. She walked into the kitchen and stopped.

"What's wrong?"

Lexie put both her hands over her mouth. "Susie, help me."

She reached for her. "Lexie, it's all right. Come here." She took her by the shoulders and led her out into the den and sat her on the big sofa there.

"Tell me what's wrong."

Tears poured down her cheeks. She couldn't make them stop. She had trouble swallowing.

"I love Adrian, Susie."

"I know that, you told me. He hasn't done anything to hurt you?"

Lexie howled. "No! He's the sweetest man alive. I'm the stupid one who's hurt him."

"Don't be silly. You've never hurt anyone."

She jumped up and screamed. It made Susie jump.

"I'm so *stupid*. I can't believe how *stupid* I am."

"Lexie, for heaven's sake, shut up and tell me what's wrong."

She sat down and felt like a huge weight was on her. "Susie…I can't believe this."

"For the love of Mike, will you spit it out."

Lexie held her head in her hands. "It's Joss. He's come back."

"Are you kidding!?"

She threw her head up. "Do I look like I'm kidding?"

"How did he find you? I mean, what did he want? I mean, where's he been?"

Lexie jumped up again, her hands clenched into fists. She punched down the air. "He loves me! That stupid man says he loves me."

Susie didn't say anything, so she looked over at her. She looked excited, not horrified.

"After all this time he came back from Alaska to find you and tell you he loves you?" She ended on a high note. "Oh my God, how romantic!"

"Will you shut up. I need your help."

Susie was still distracted. "Well, what did you do, when he knocked on your door? I assume he didn't call first."

"UGGG," Lexie screeched. "I kicked Adrian out of bed and told him to go for a walk and I went downstairs and told Joss to make love to me."

Susie put her fingers over her mouth and squealed. "That's

so…Hollywood! Who does that? Who ever gets that lucky?"

Lexie went over and sat in a chair. She tore at her hair. "You think this is *lucky*? You think I wanted this to happen? He's ruined my life."

Susie gave her one determined look. "Listen lady, if you've come here to ask my advice, I'll give it to you. I want you to answer me one question. If Joss showed up at your door before you knew Adrian wanted to come back, what would've happened?"

Lexie opened her mouth but Susan held up her hand. "This is me, Lex. You owe it to yourself to answer the question. And remember, I know when you're lying."

Lexie wouldn't answer her. She looked at Susie's carpet.

Susie waited.

Lexie's tears started again.

"There's your answer. You'd have done exactly what you did. You'd have had him up those stairs so fast his head would spin."

"But Adrian." Lexie sobbed.

"I'm sure you think you love Adrian," Susie said kindly. "You loved having him in your life. Who wouldn't? He's a sweetie. Look what he does. He rescues children, for heaven's sake. *I* love him."

"What have I done? I sent Joss away. I told him I didn't love him. I told him I loved someone else. And then Mom came in the door with Joshua, and oh, Susie. He looked at his child and he knew right away. The look he gave me broke my heart. He hates me now. I've lost him forever."

If it was possible to cry any more, she did. Susie came

over, knelt down beside her, and put her hand on Lexie's knee. Lexie kept her face hidden.

"Listen to me. I was the only one who knew Joss. I was there the night you met. I saw him look at you across that dance floor. Five minutes after you went into the galley, he had you by the hand and pulled you out the door. I saw it."

Susie took her hands away from her face and made Lexie look at her.

"That man loves you. He says he couldn't get to you sooner. But he's here. He came right up to your door as bold as brass and told you he loved you. I don't think he's the sort of man who would do that if he didn't mean it."

"Susie. He's from Neils Harbour."

Susie shook her head. "Can you believe it? The boy next door."

LEXIE AND JOSH got home at suppertime. The lights were on in the house as they drove up. Adrian was in the kitchen. He'd made spaghetti sauce and it smelled great. Sophie watched every move, in the hopes he'd drop a piece of ground beef.

Adrian kissed her and patted Josh on the head. "How was your day?"

"I was a little tired," she admitted. She took off Josh's jacket and he roared down the hall. "Sope. Sope."

"Come and sit down. I'll get you a club soda. I see you still drink the stuff." He went ahead of her into the kitchen, and she followed. Her feet felt like blocks of cement.

Lexie sat at the table, which was already set. Adrian went

to the fridge, took out the bottle of club soda, and poured Lexie a glass. He added some ice cubes and put it in front of her.

"Thanks Adrian," she smiled. "You're so nice to me."

"Now Josh, what would you like?"

"Apa ju."

"I'm good at this dad stuff." Adrian laughed. "I know that means apple juice."

She watched him take the bottle out for Josh and put the juice in a sippy cup. He passed it to him.

"Here you go, young man."

"Q."

"And that means thank you, right?" Adrian laughed again. Lexie gave him a smile. At that moment she couldn't have laughed to save her own life.

After dinner, Lexie ran a bubble bath for herself. She lay there and listened to Adrian putter around in the kitchen and talk to Sophie.

Dear Adrian. She smiled in spite of herself. She'd dreamed of this moment for years. Adrian here, with her. She took slow, deep breaths and made herself calm down and think.

She was a grown woman. Everyone thought they knew what she wanted. Everyone had advice. But it wasn't their life, was it? To see Joss out of the blue like that unnerved her, that's all — befuddled her brain to the point where she couldn't think. Her knee-jerk reaction to Joss was a one-off. He was a gorgeous man. They never talked, so they did what they did best. That's all. She'd only known him for seven days. He told her he would leave and he did.

Adrian travelled the world to find his child and then came back for her. For her. He said she was forever. Her loyalty was to him. Susan thought she was right but she wasn't. She didn't know Adrian. Only Lexie knew Adrian. She was the only one.

He knocked on the bathroom door softly, and opened it. She looked at him. "I love you Adrian."

He came over and knelt beside her. He traced her face with his finger, and then put his hand at the back of her neck and pulled her towards him so he could kiss her. It took a while. He finally let her go. "And you, my love, are the sweetest girl in the world." She reached up. He didn't mind getting wet.

THE FULL MOON shone in the bedroom window. Adrian lay with his head on her breast. She thought he was asleep.

"Lexie?"

"Mmm?" She rubbed his temple with her thumb.

"I didn't get a hold of my Mum today. They weren't home. I'll try tomorrow."

"Okay."

"I was thinking."

"What about?"

"Maybe I should go home to talk to her face to face about all this. I think it will be a big adjustment for her. And for Binti." He sounded worried.

"I'm sure it will be."

"I didn't want to say anything before, but my feeling is… she assumed you and Josh would come to live in Montreal. I planned to move into an apartment close to them."

She stayed still. "Is that what you want?"

He didn't say anything for a few moments. "I'd be happy to stay here. I'm a little concerned about Binti. To leave some of the programs she's involved with. She's had to fight so hard to recover her health."

"That's true."

"But it would have to be something we could both agree on." He rubbed her arm. "I know this is your home. I'd never take you away if you didn't want to go."

Lexie didn't say anything.

"All I know," he whispered, "is that wherever you are is home to me."

She rubbed his temple again. "Why don't you go to sleep, love, and we'll worry about it in the morning."

"Okay." He sounded drowsy. "I love you."

"I love you too."

Lexie looked out the window. The moon filled the room with a ghostly light. She desperately wanted some sleep, but it wouldn't come. She tried to relax, tried to think of nothing, but there was a feeling she couldn't get rid of. It tugged at her. It was something Beth said once. That her body remembered, even when her mind could not.

She stared at the moon. There was something. There was something she'd forgotten. Her room faded away. It was dark and hot. She felt like she was suffocating. She strained to see something. That's when it hit her. It was a big shock.

SHE CALLED IN sick the next morning. She told Adrian they needed to talk, that she had the day off and she'd be right back after she dropped Josh off. He said he'd have French toast for her when she got back.

Lexie gave Josh to her mother. "I need you to keep him until I call you."

"What's wrong?"

"I may be making the biggest mistake of my life, but it's something I have to do."

Mom didn't say anything. She nodded. Lexie grabbed her hand, gave it a squeeze and was gone.

She thought perhaps she should go to Beth and talk to her, but changed her mind. This was not something anyone else could help her with. This was her journey. This was what her life was.

She did stop at the beach, however, got out of Betsy and leaned against the hood. She didn't go down on the sand. She filled her lungs with great gulps of cold air to give herself courage. She watched the water she loved so much, coming in and going out, never staying still. Her life had been like that, always at the mercy of tides and wind. Today, for the first time in her life, she was going to set a course. Lexie would cut the rope. She'd let Adrian go. She'd release the anchor she'd been clinging to. She had to. He didn't belong to her.

WHEN LEXIE CAME in, she took off her coat and put her keys and purse on the table. Adrian was reading the paper. She looked at him. He had the most perfect face. She loved that face. She'd loved it from the first moment she ever laid eyes on it. It killed her to do this.

He gave her a big smile and got up. "The French toast is in the oven and I put on a fresh pot of coffee."

"Thanks."

"Let me get you a mug." As she sat, he poured her a cup and put cream in it.

"I'll have it black."

"No large double double?"

This is so hard. This is too hard.

"No. Thanks." She cleared her throat. "Adrian, we need to talk."

He gave her the coffee and took his seat. "I know. I should tell you about the information I found out yesterday. You wouldn't believe how expensive it is to move."

"I'm not moving."

He looked up quickly, surprised. "Oh. All right. I thought we said we'd talk about it first?"

"You're not moving either."

He didn't say a word. He didn't move a muscle. He waited for her to say something.

Lexie pushed her hair back out of her face and took a deep breath.

"We love each other Adrian. I don't doubt that for a minute. From the first moment we met, we needed each other. You wanted a home. I wanted someone to take care of."

She gave a big sigh. "But — as much as we mean to each other, as much as you say you love me — you're not in love with me. "

His face was a mask.

She kept on, before she lost her courage. "We lived

together for two months. In all that time, in spite of our caring deeply for one another, you kissed me once. I want to ask you something. If Gabby were here, instead of me, do you think that would've happened?"

He bent his head and looked down at his lap.

"I was there the night you and Gabby met." She kept her eyes on him. "I saw it. I saw it right away."

Adrian held his forehead in his hand, as if he didn't want to look at her.

"And then Adrian," she leaned towards him, "I saw the two of you together in front of the fire."

He gave a big sob. He couldn't keep it in.

She rushed around the table and knelt beside him. She tried to look at his face, but he wouldn't let her see his tears. She cried too. "Adrian. I've only ever seen a man look at a woman like that once before. When Joshua's father looks at me."

Adrian finally laid his head in his arms and wept openly. Lexie held on to his knees and leaned her cheek on his thigh. After a while he put his hand on her head, as if to tell her he loved her down there on the floor.

He pulled her off her knees and sat her in his lap. She snuggled against him. When he was calm enough, he spoke. "The night you took me home, I laid on my bed and wept with happiness. I'd been so alone, so heartbroken. I'd wandered for so long."

He hugged her tighter. "You were beautiful. You fed me and washed my clothes and made me laugh and made me feel as if I was wanted, as if I was worth wanting, and worthy of being loved. I didn't deserve to be loved."

He stayed quiet for a while. She was content to stay in his arms. "I loved you. You were my best friend. I could hide from the world when I was with you."

He tucked her in even closer. She was against his neck, so she couldn't see his face.

"The night I met your sister, I fell in love with her the minute she walked through the door. It wasn't something I could control. We had to be together. We lived in the moment and didn't think about who we'd hurt in the end. That is until you found us. That's when reality hit us in the face. We were upset and confused and ashamed. It seemed easier all around just to leave."

"What happened when you did leave?"

"It was wonderful for a while. Except for the terrible guilt I felt about you, and of course the guilt I carried everywhere, about Binti and her mother. I needed redemption."

He sighed, "And how did I do it? I hurt your sister. I left her too. I felt if I didn't start to make up for the mistakes in my life, I'd drown, and I didn't want Gabby with me when I did. I tried to explain it to her, but I wasn't very forthcoming. I was so mixed up then. I didn't think. I handled it all the wrong way. I made her believe she was a mistake." He stopped for a moment, as if to gather his thoughts.

"I have to tell you the truth, Lexie. I owe you that much."

"Okay." She waited.

"Gabby called me."

"My God. When?"

He cleared his throat. "Not that long ago. When I heard her voice my heart nearly stopped. I was so happy. I tried to apologize. She was very cold and distant. She said she wanted to right a wrong and she called to tell me you were unattached. She thought the reason I stayed away from you was that I saw Josh in Montreal. She said she'd moved on, that she was in love with another man. Then she hung up." Adrian faltered. "I thought she hated me."

"Never."

"That's how it felt. And the idea of you here, not married as it turned out, excited me. It brought all the wonderful memories back. You and I together, safe in our little house, the house I loved so much. You and Cape Breton Island and the house all became one in my mind. I loved it. I loved you. I needed you to comfort me again. I was lonely, Lexie. I needed a woman to love. I thought Gabby was lost to me."

"She loves you, Adrian," Lexie whispered against his skin. "She adores you. She'll love you until the day she dies. She told me that."

"Oh God." He sounded tortured. "What have I done to you both? Why am I so cruel to every woman I love?"

Lexie sat up and held his face so he would look at her.

"Don't you ever say that again. Every woman you've ever loved loves you. Binti's mother loved you. You saved her baby when you ran for help. Binti loves you. You saved her. I love you because you saved me from loneliness and Gabby's so in love with you she hasn't been with a man since you left."

He closed his eyes. Lexie kissed him softly. "We are all the luckiest women in the world, to have been loved by you."

They spent the rest of that day holding each other in front of the fire. And they spent the night together in each other's arms, even though they knew it was over. It was something they would always share and never forget. A memory worth keeping.

Lexie finally knew the truth. A woman can love more than one man. But only one is the love of her life. Adrian was a moment in time. Joss was forever.

Chapter Twenty-three

IN THE MORNING, Lexie helped Adrian pack. His plane left around noon, so they had time for a leisurely breakfast, except neither one of them wanted to eat. But they did share a cup of coffee at the kitchen table. They held hands while they waited for the taxi by the front door. Lexie reached into her pocket and gave him a folded piece of paper.

"Gabby's number in England."

Adrian hugged her. They stayed that way until the taxi arrived. They didn't say goodbye — he only held her face in his hands and kissed her forehead.

And then he was gone.

She called her mother. "Could you take Josh for a couple of days? I'm sorry. I need to be by myself for a bit."

"Whatever you want, honey. Lexie, are you sure you want to be alone?"

"Yes."

"You call me if you need me and I'll be right there."

"I know Mom. I love you."

She hung up and called work. She told Judy she still felt rotten and she would be off work for a few more days. Judy told her to drink lots of liquids and go to bed.

She did go to bed. She lay there and let the silence comfort her. She couldn't cry anymore.

She slept for a very long time.

The phone rang the next day. She sat in her armchair

with Sophie in her lap. She let the machine get it. It was Beth. "Lex, Mom's told me and we think we know what happened, but it doesn't matter. I'm here if you need me. I just wanted you to know, I love you." She hung up.

THE PHONE RANG again. This time it was Susie. She picked it up.

"Susie."

"Are you okay? I stopped by the library today and they told me you were sick."

"Sick at heart."

"What did you do?"

"I told him to go."

"What did he do?"

"He went."

"Oh God. Does he hate you?"

"No. He loves me. I love him," she whispered. "But I told him he belongs to Gabby. And he didn't disagree."

There was a long silence.

"What will you do now, Lex?"

"When I can put one foot in front of the other, I'll try and find Joss."

⁂

GABBY LAY IN bed and listened to her roommate Poppy talking on the phone with her fiancé. She put her head under the pillow and stayed like that until Poppy hollered that she was off the phone.

Gabby finally got out of bed and ran herself a bath. She lay there for over an hour. Poppy knocked on the door.

"You okay in there?"

"Yeah."

"Are you going to that swanky club tonight? Pam's going."

"No. I don't think so."

"Why don't you go, Gabby? It'll do you good."

"Maybe. We'll see."

"Listen, my flight's at six. I'll need to get in there soon."

"Sorry, I forgot. I'll be right out." Gabby pulled the plug and got out of the bath, wrapping herself in a towel. She wiped the steam off in the mirror and peered into it. She looked closer and put her fingertips up to the corner of her right eye. There were fine wrinkles she'd never seen before.

Gabby sighed.

That's when the phone rang.

❧

LEXIE WENT TO bed that night and slept again, almost twelve hours straight. She got up and had her usual tonic, a hot shower, and then a bubble bath too, so she could float and not think. She went downstairs and fed Sophie while the kettle boiled for her tea, then sat at the table and ate a bowl of Cheerios. She went into the living room with her mug and bundled herself up in her fleece throw, took two lovely mouthfuls of tea, and called Gabby's number.

It rang three times. Finally a voice answered. Whoever it was sounded rushed.

"Hello?"

"Hi. May I speak to Gabby, please?"

"Sorry duck, she's not here. You just missed her."

It occurred to Lexie that she loved a British accent. It reminded her of Adrian.

"Oh. This is her sister Lexie and I wondered where I might reach her."

"Hi Lexie," said the voice. "This is her roommate, Pam. Golly, you guys sound alike on the phone."

"I know. Everyone says that."

"Just a minute, Lexie, I just got in the door. I'll ask Poppy if she knows."

"Thank you."

She must have held the phone to her chest, because Lexie could hear voices, but they were muffled. Finally, she came back on.

"Sorry. Poppy says Gabby got a call from some guy and she threw her things in her bag and ran out the door."

Lexie's stomach fluttered.

"Do you know where she went?"

"Poppy says she's off to Dorval."

"Dorval?" Lexie couldn't think for a minute.

"Dorval Airport in Montreal."

"Thanks a lot, Pam."

"I'll tell Gabby you called."

"Thanks. Bye."

"Cheerio."

"Cheerios." Lexie laughed. She hung up and put her head on her arm. And smiled. The world was unfolding as it should. She needed to go and bring her baby boy home. He'd miss his Mommy by now.

✤

GABBY DIDN'T SIT still the entire flight. She managed to get on the first plane out of Heathrow, after begging a friend to let her take the next jump seat, instead of the one on the next flight. As soon as the plane landed, she was out of her seat in a flash. The pilots gave her a hard time. "Hey, he must be pretty special. You never run like that for us."

Gabby tore up the gangway, ahead of all the passengers. Her co-workers were surprised. Gabby was always so put together, always as cool as a cucumber. Her hair fell out of its bobby pins as she ran.

She went through the last sliding doors and there he was. He looked as fabulous as she remembered. He held a huge bouquet of white lilies. But he had to drop them. She ran up to him and jumped in his arms and held him so close.

"I love you, Adrian. I adore you. Don't ever leave me again."

"I'll never leave you, my love. Never."

She pulled away and touched his face, to see if he was really there. He grabbed her hands and kissed her fingers.

"Take me home, Adrian."

WHEN LEXIE GOT in the door with Josh that night, her answering machine was flashing. She pushed the playback button.

Gabby was crying. "Lexie, I want you to know that this little sister loves her big sister very much."

LEXIE NEEDED TIME to pull herself together. She spent her days after work playing with Joshua and her nieces.

She'd have dinner with Mom or Beth on occasion. No one brought up the subject of her future, for which she was very grateful. She'd go over to Susie's, but even they avoided the topic. It was too raw.

And then one Saturday morning, about two weeks after Adrian left, she woke up and knew she was ready. She lay in bed and thought about what she'd say to Joss, but almost instantly the words jumbled together into a big ball. Maybe she wasn't ready. She sat up and chewed her nails. That didn't help, so she reached for a favourite book on the bedside table, *Bartlett's Familiar Quotations*.

Words, words. She needed words for courage. She flipped through the pages.

I can't go on/I really can't go on/I swear I can't go on/so/I guess I'll get up and go on.

Lexie nodded. "Dory Previn, whoever you are…you're pretty darn close."

The bedroom door suddenly swung open and Josh stood there in his pyjamas with feet. He grinned at her. She had all the words she needed.

ONCE LEXIE DELIVERED Joshua to his grandmother, she stopped at Susie's to get Joss's address. Susie was in the yard with her bathrobe wrapped around her. It was a chilly spring morning, but the winter's back had been broken. She leaned her arms on the window edge. "I wish I was going with you, Lex."

Lexie patted her arm. "God. I wish you were too. What if he doesn't want me, Susie?"

"Get lost. Of course he'll want you. Just bat those big brown eyes and he'll beg for mercy."

"I'm so scared."

"As a famous shoe once said, just do it."

Lexie kissed her. "I love you."

"Right back at ya."

As Lexie drove, she tried not to think. She counted potholes instead. Frost coming out of the ground made for a bumpy ride. She was glad it wasn't tourist season. As dirty patches of snow disappeared, they revealed a winter's worth of litter along the highways. The ground was mucky and the grass yellow and matted. It didn't lift her spirits.

But once she drove onto the Englishtown ferry, she perked up. She got out of the car and for the few minutes it took to cross the water to a narrow spit of land on the other side, she revelled in the sea air. The wind whipped up the spray from the ferry and hit her face with tiny needles of salt water as she leaned over the rail. She watched, mesmerised by the strength of the tide as it buffeted the small vessel. If she fell in, she'd be gone in a flash.

Time to get back in the car.

She headed for Smokey Mountain, ahead of a line of cars from the ferry. The cars spread out eventually, most of them passing her. She was happy to let them go. The realization of what she was doing started to weigh on her and she fought the urge to turn around and go home.

Now it was nothing but trees and the coastline. Imagine getting lost in the woods out here. You could walk for days and even then never be found. She felt beads of sweat above her upper lip. What if she had a flat tire? This place was too empty.

Finally a sign for Neils Harbour. What a relief. A few vinyl-sided houses scattered here and there heralded the edge of town, then suddenly it came into view. After miles of dark green forest and the occasional glimpse of blue ocean through the trees, Neils Harbour was a welcome sight.

As with most of the more rustic villages in Cape Breton, this one was built around its natural harbour. A red and white lighthouse off the point, a welcome beacon for small boats in stormy weather, faced the ocean. Shingled houses painted white with the occasional blue or red house thrown in seemed to grow from the large outcropping of rocks that made up the landscape. Boulders covered with lichen and moss were scattered among the houses, sheds and run-down garages, and every second building faced in a different direction.

The wharf along the edge of the harbour and the outbuildings needed for the business of fish and lobster made up the rest of the scenery. Colourful lobster boats both in and out of the water looked as if they were placed there for photographers only. This was the stuff of postcards.

Lexie drove through the village slowly, craning her neck to read the numbers on the houses she passed. She pulled over to let a couple of cars go by. They were obviously locals who needed to get where they were going. She almost despaired of ever finding it, when suddenly, there it was.

The house was a tall box, its shingles painted bright red, like the shed "out back" and the garage where fishing gear and nets were being sorted. Lobster traps were piled on top of one another along the side of the coal house, old ones and obviously new ones, each with its own colourful buoy painted orange and green.

Lexie drove into the fairly steep dirt driveway and stopped the car. Her mouth was dry and her hands shook. When she got out, a stiff breeze blew her hair around and the car door almost slammed shut on her fingers. As she rounded the front bumper, Lexie heard the snap of sheets and towels on a clothesline, colourful flags heralding her arrival.

A dog barked, but it wasn't angry, more of a *who's there* kind of bark. Then an old and very fat yellow lab came out to greet her and didn't let her by until she patted his head thoroughly.

By the time Lexie got past him, a large woman stood on her back porch, wiping her hands on a tea towel, an apron around her flowery dress. Her greying hair was swept into a twisted bun and her face was full of wrinkles, but she still had the look of a handsome woman.

"Hello, my dear," she greeted Lexie. "Now what can I be doin' you for today. You're not collecting for the cancer, are you? I'll just go get my purse."

Lexie smiled at her. "No. I'm looking for Joss actually. Is he around?"

She laughed. "That boy's always around. He eats everything I bake before I get it on the table."

Lexie laughed. Joss's mother made her feel better.

"Why don't you come in for a cuppa? He should be back soon."

"That would be lovely."

The kitchen was a blast furnace. There was a big coal stove in the far corner, just like her grandmother used to have. Mrs. MacGregor's baking was lined up on both counters.

"Mercy, it is warm in here. Sit dear, and I'll get you a good brew." She turned to the large kettle on the stove and started to make the tea.

Lexie loved Joshua's grandmother already.

She placed a cup and saucer in front of Lexie along with a big plate of goodies from the morning's baking. She poured their tea and sat down on the other side of the table. "There now, nothing like a good cuppa. So my dear," she said, after a big gulp from her teacup, "who might you be?"

"I'm Lexie Ivy, I'm a friend of Joss's."

She laughed. "Lord love a duck, that boy has more girls than hens in a henhouse. Well, it's very nice to meet you Lexie. You're just about the sweetest thing I've seen in a long time. God Almighty, I wish I had a daughter."

She leaned close to Lexie. "I had six sons. One bigger than the other. It's a wonder I lived to tell about it." She slapped her hand on the table and grinned with that wonderful grin Lexie loved so much, the one Joshua gave her every morning in his crib. Lexie just beamed at her because she couldn't do anything else.

She held out her hand. "Well, my dear, I should introduce myself. I'm Helen."

Lexie shook her warm, floury hand. "It's nice to meet you Mrs. MacGregor."

"Oh, heavens, don't call me Mrs. MacGregor. That was my mother-in-law's name. It makes me feel old."

"Gosh, you're not old. You look wonderful."

"Wonderful, you say?" she smiled. "Yes, indeed, I should've had daughters. My boys wouldn't notice if I grew a turnip on my head."

They both started to laugh. Lexie wanted to stay in this kitchen forever.

"Instead," she confided, "all my boys have wives who drive me foolish. Those girls pester me day and night for my recipes, because my spoiled brats won't eat anything that doesn't taste like Ma's."

"So Joss is the only one not married?"

"Well, it's not for lack of trying on the part of every woman from here to Yarmouth. But that baby boy of mine is a hard one to catch."

"He's the youngest?"

"That's right. He was supposed to be my girl, and he was the biggest of the lot."

Lexie looked around the room and thought it must have been a wonderful kitchen to grow up in. How lucky Joss and his brothers were.

Helen watched her. "You wouldn't have anything to do with why my Joss has been moonin' around here for the last while?"

Lexie kept her head down. "Has he?"

She put her hands together in front of her. "Yes, indeed he has. Are you the reason?"

"Yes. We had a fight."

"And you're here to kiss and make up?"

"I'd like that very much," Lexie said softly.

"Well, it's none of my business of course. But the sooner you two make up the better. He's had a face like a dog's dinner for quite a while now." Helen looked at the clock. "It doesn't look like he's coming back any time soon, so best you go down to the wharf."

Lexie looked at Joss's mother. "I'm so glad I met you. I hope I see you again."

"Well, I sure hope so too. Usually I never get to meet the girls Joss goes out with, so this was a real treat. It was very nice having you here."

They both rose from the table. Helen walked her to the door. They stood together on the porch and Helen pointed to the wharf, a little farther down the road.

"Goodbye dear. Good luck," Helen smiled.

"Thank you. And thank you for the tea."

The fat dog accompanied Lexie to the van. She made sure she gave him a fond farewell. Mrs. MacGregor watched her go and waved as Lexie went down the driveway.

Lexie pulled up to the wharf and sat behind the wheel for a few minutes. She had to gather her wits. She thought Joss would be at the house. That's how she'd rehearsed the scenario in her head. The dock was the last place she wanted to be. It was smelly and slippery, full of bait containers and old dirty buckets. Not to mention the rough and tough fishermen. She stuck out like a sore thumb.

But there was nothing for it. She hadn't come all this way to back out now.

Lexie got out of the van and looked first one way, then the other. She'd have to walk around an old wooden storage shed to get to the wharf. As she passed the dark cavernous opening, she saw two men inside. They were looking at some equipment and having a conversation, so she decided against interrupting them.

She walked further and soon came to the wharf itself. There were four boats tied to their moorings. A man came out of his wheelhouse and gave her a wolf whistle. "Hello, darlin'. Looking for me?"

As if.

She kept going. As she approached the last boat, she saw him. He saw her at the same time. He was coiling rope. He had on a thick red flannel jacket and big billy boots, so he could slosh around in the cold dirty water that gathered by the bilge pumps on the boat. He dropped the rope, jumped up from the boat and onto the wharf. She waited for him to come to her. He went the other way.

"Joss! Wait!" He didn't stop. She ran after him. She thought maybe he hadn't heard her.

"Joss, please wait."

He turned around and stood still until she was closer.

"What do you want?"

"I wanted to find you," she shouted against the wind, "to tell you I do love you."

"You love someone else, remember? You told me that quite clearly." He walked away again.

"Joss, listen to me," she begged, "There's a reason for all that. Something happened to me, and I was in the middle of this huge mess but I couldn't tell you about it. Not then. Please let me explain."

He turned back and pointed his finger at her. "You and I talked in that kitchen and I told you I loved you. You took me upstairs and you sure as hell loved me back and not once, *not once*, did you mention the fact that you were the mother of my child."

He turned away and kept going.

"I know, Joss." She ran after him. "That was unfair. I should've told you right away, but you frightened me. I was so shocked to see you after so long."

"I don't care anymore," he shouted.

She stopped. She was out of breath. Damn it.

"Fine," she yelled, "Fine! Whatever. Just walk away from me like you walked away before, you *stupid* man." She picked up a piece of gravel and threw it.

She was so mad she was stamped her foot. "What gives you the right to come back and get mad at me? You left me, you idiot! Was I supposed to fall at your feet when I saw you? Did you think you were so wonderful, I'd do it again?"

He looked over his shoulder. "That's just what you did. Or do you do that for everyone?"

She threw another rock at him and this time it winged his shoulder.

"You are the biggest jerk alive! I *hate* you. I hate you so much that you better not ever come near me again."

She started to run back to Betsy.

"Fine, lady!" he hollered back. "I have my pick. You're one in a long line of women I can choose from. *I don't need you.*"

She turned her head, "*And I don't need you either!*"

She ran all the way to Betsy and yanked open the door. She jumped in and started her up.

Lexie roared down the highway and drove away as fast as she could. She saw him in the mirror. He stopped and watched her go.

"I hate you!" she yelled and then started to cry. "I love you, you big jerk."

Naturally, when she got home she went to bed and cried her eyes out. She had put more clean sheets on her bed in the last week than she had in her entire life.

Lexie didn't tell Mom she was home. It was nighttime. She'd tell them about her hideous disaster tomorrow, when she didn't spit every time she mentioned his name.

After she emptied virtually every drop of liquid in her body, she got in the shower and stayed there until the hot water tank emptied. Over the course of the last few years, it seemed as though she had cried enough tears to fill the ocean. She went to bed and resolved that no man would ever hurt her again. She'd focus on the real love of her life — her son.

HELEN WASHED THE dishes. She watched Joss out in the garage, through the kitchen window. He sat and pretended to mend his net. It was near twilight and it would soon be dark. He hadn't come in for his supper. Even his father wondered what was up. Helen told Danny he was fine, to leave him be.

She finally put on her sweater and went out the back door. Skipper came towards her, wagging his tail, looking for a treat. She reached into her pocket, gave him a dog biscuit, and patted his head before crunching over the gravel to the open garage door. Joss didn't look up.

"Are you all right, Joss?"

"Yep."

"Did that girl, Lexie, come to see you down on the wharf?"

"You sent her there, did you?"

"Well, she wanted to see you, so yes I did. Was that a mistake?"

Joss didn't say anything.

"Joss. You know me. I stay out of my sons' love lives. Thank God, or I'd never sleep a wink. I've never ever given you any advice. True?"

He nodded his head, but still looked at the net in his lap.

"That girl loves you."

He said nothing.

She watched him. "Your dinner's in the oven."

She walked back to the house with Skipper.

IN THE MORNING, Lexie called Susie and told her the whole mess.

"It's all my fault," Susie snivelled. "If I hadn't said anything, you'd still be with Adrian. I'm so sorry Lexie."

"Even if I'm a very old maid, I'm still glad I let Adrian go. You should've heard Gabby's voice on the phone. I did the right thing."

Her friend wept. "You're too generous for your own good. Everyone takes advantage of you. You have to stick up for yourself."

"Believe me. I sure did when I pelted rocks at him."

"You threw rocks?"

"You're darn right I did. I hit him once too."

"Good!" She heard Susie blow her nose. "Because if I ever see that poop again, I'll hit him with a rock too."

It was time to get Josh. She went to Mom's and he ran to her. "Mama, Mama." He put his arms around her neck and hugged her until she could hardly breathe.

"Oh boy, did Mommy ever miss you." She held him in her arms for a long time. He was content to let her.

"So?" Mom said.

Lexie didn't get the chance to tell her anything before Beth's van pulled up and her gang descended on the peaceful house. The girls gave her hugs. Josh wanted to get down to be with his cousins, and the five of them ran into the sunroom to play. Lexie and her mom and sister sat at the table and Lexie told them what happened, from the very beginning.

"I'll be fine," she smiled. "I have my son, my health, and my home. I'm a lucky woman. I had Adrian's love, when I needed it. Gabby has the man she waited for her entire life. It does my heart good to know they are together."

"I'm sure Joss will come back for you," Beth said.

"Whether he does or doesn't, I'm still glad I went. And I got to meet his mother. Joshua has two wonderful grandmothers." She turned to her mom. "But no one will ever be able to replace you, you dear old thing."

"Who are you calling old?"

IT WAS A long weekend, so the next day she and Josh played together. They built cities out of blocks and Lexie read him stories as he sat in her lap in their big comfy chair. "You're going to love this one, Josh. It's the story of a little bat who gets lost and his mommy has to find him."

Josh looked at her with big eyes. "Po bat."

"Don't worry, sweetie. His mommy finds him in the end." Josh nodded and put his thumb in his mouth.

Mom came over in the afternoon and Lexie invited her for dinner. She had a new recipe she wanted to try.

"As long as it doesn't have walnuts and saffron rice in it, I'll be happy," Mom informed her.

Joshua sat looking out the window. Lexie went over and picked him up. "Wanna go for a walk, mister man?"

"Wak."

Lexie put on his jacket. "I'm going to take Josh for a walk, Mom. Want to come?"

"Not today, dear. I think I'm getting a sniffle. You two go and I'll watch the casserole."

So Lexie took Josh to the beach. The sky was cloudless. There wasn't any wind, which made it very pleasant. They roamed the shore. Josh ran after tiny sandpipers.

The water was a deep blue. It twinkled with sunlight and the waves came to talk to her. She loved her island, this piece of rock surrounded by water. Water protected her from the outside world. She would never leave this place.

Josh ran ahead of her. She saw him stop and point.

She looked. There was Joss. He stood at the edge of the bank.

Suddenly the only world she knew was the space that existed between them, the circle they made. She broke into a run. Joss slid down the bank as he tried to get to her. She laughed and cried at the same time. She picked up Joshua and kept going.

"Who dat, Mama?"

"That's your Daddy, sweetheart. That's Daddy."

Joss ran to her, picked them up in his big arms and twirled them around. He let her go, reached for his baby, and held him up in the air. Josh gave him a grin. His Daddy gave him one back.

"I love you little boy. And I love your Mommy."

He put Josh down, took a step closer, and put his arm around her waist. She had a hard time trying not to faint from pure delight.

"There, that's better," he smiled.

She gazed at his beautiful face.

"So Lexie, are you here by yourself?"

She nodded.

"Were you waiting for me?"

She nodded again, as tears ran down her cheeks. He remembered.

He took his hand and lifted her chin.

"I always say, this is the best part."

And then he lowered his head and he kissed her. She knew that kiss. It was hers alone. She couldn't think. She just was. He lifted his head and put his hand up through her hair pulling it away from her ear. He whispered against it.

"Marry me."

LESLEY CREWE IS the bestselling author of several novels, including Chloe Sparrow, Kin, and Her Mother's Daughter. Lesley lives in Homeville, Nova Scotia. lesleycrewe.com

A Note on the Type

MINION IS AN Adobe Original typeface designed by Robert Slimbach. The first version of Minion was released in 1990. Minion is inspired by classical, old style typefaces of the late Renaissance, a period of elegant, beautiful, and highly readable type designs.

FF META WAS designed in 1991–93 by Eric Spiekermann based on the typeface created by the German Post Office (Bundespost) in 1984 as an exclusive corporate font.